Lou Giroux: NOPD Detective

J.E. Jack

Edited by Marcel Jack.

Book cover design by ebooklaunch.com

I dedicate this book to my family who are still on this earth, to include family members of a furry disposition, and those who unfortunately went to the great beyond during the writing of this story.

Special Thanks

I just wanted to give special thanks to those that have read my book in advance and provided valuable feedback.

Gunter Barber, Jarrod Jack, Marcel Jack, Vicky Landry, and C.C. Prescott.

Without you, these stories wouldn't be near as good as they are. And to the rest of my readers who support me. Thank you all very much!

Contents

Chapter One

My name is Lou...Lou Giroux, to be exact, but that's not my real name. My real name is...or was...Denny Depré but I haven't gone by that name for a long time. But, that's a story for another time. Every couple of decades, I change names. I'm not immortal but I grow older every year at a fraction of what other people are used to. I look to be mid-30s but in reality, I'm well over 100. Wild, huh? I guess I better explain that...and the last name I chose for myself kind of explains it...in a way. Loup Garou...or around here, they say Rou Garou. At any rate, when I last changed my name, I was in a dark humor and just said "screw it, Lou Giroux it is...it fits." Why? Well, I'm a werewolf...sorry to let the cat out of the bag, or rather, the wolf...but it's true. For the most part, it's pretty damn cool, except that it's excruciating to change forms, which, contrary to popular belief, I can do at will. There's only one time of the month that I have no control and yep, you guessed it—it's during the full moon. I don't know why it happens that way. I just go into a rage and can hardly think straight. However, over the years, there have been some medicines and other things that help keep it in check. Thankfully, it's been a long while since I've lost control, thanks to modern medicine. Hey, even us supernatural freaks need science, too.

So, I'm a werewolf. Eat your heart out...no seriously, I could eat your heart out, but I'm a reformed werewolf and I will actually go out of my way to stop others from eating your heart, or any other body part. I work for the New Orleans Police Department. I've been here a few years and worked my way up to detective. Beats being a rookie. I've done lots of jobs over the years and I've gone all over the world, but I have to say, being back home—yeah, this is home—and doing the Lord's work is truly a blessing. I enjoy helping people. Hey...don't give me that look. Monsters can have hearts too, even ones they haven't eaten. But seriously, in this world, monsters come in many forms—some supernatural, others natural. The things I've seen, it doesn't take supernatural abilities for someone or something to be a monster. That's where I come in. I try to keep the peace in the natural...and the supernatural world. I also try to keep the two worlds from colliding. All sorts of nasty things happen to people on both sides of the line when that happens, so we...ahem..."monsters" do our very best to keep the veil between the two realms very distinct.

Why am I telling you all this? Well, I enjoy telling stories and I feel the need to share. I mean, you aren't going to tell anyone, are you? Even if you did, no one would believe you. Sure, that's how stories and lore and all these wild "first hand" accounts get started, but no one really believes any of it.

So now that we got all that out of the way, let's get into the meat and potatoes. It was late October when I got the call. It was from my partner, Dick. He's a vampire. Usually, vamps and wolves don't get along. Everyone likes to stick to their own kind but sometimes, you have folks like Dick and myself who see the bigger picture and can set aside our differences to work together. That comes at a price, though. If you don't hang out with your own kind, then they won't hang with you. It's a bit of an "us versus them" mentality, but that's okay. I really didn't want to hang out with them anyway, but we'll get into that later.

"Hey man, there's been a murder and I really need you to get down here," he said.

I had just woken up from a bender drinking all night and was a little groggy, not to mention I had a tremendous headache. I took the phone away from my ear and squinted at the clock. It was early morning...like 4:00, on a Saturday.

"Christ, Dick, what are you doing calling so early?" I asked.

"I was called specifically to come look into this," he said.

"Oh," I said, thinking that this might have an... "our kind" of thing involved in it. Usually, we are called in to investigate crimes that involve something otherworldly. There's not a lot of "us" in the department, but there are some. There's not nearly enough, though, to go around in investigating normal crimes, let alone supernatural ones. It's not unusual to work several cases at the same time. I always laugh at the TV investigators that seem to never have more than one case to work and they always wrap it up in about 45 minutes' time. But in the real—ha—world, it's never like that.

"Where you at?" I asked.

"I'm in the 8th precinct at the Port of New Orleans, underneath the Crescent City Connection. Don't worry, you'll see all the flashing lights when you get here," he said.

We disconnected the call, and I got up off my couch. I had to get there quickly, but I didn't want to get there reeking of booze, so I took a quick shower and gargled some mouthwash. Thankfully, because of my natural healing abilities, the hangovers never stick around long and with the shower, I was wide awake. I live in Algiers Point, near the west bank of the Mississippi River. Those that live there would colloquially say the "best bank." The port of New Orleans was just a few minutes' drive from my house, on the other side of the Mississippi.

Dick was right. It was like a regular Mardi Gras parade with all the police and emergency service vehicles, all of them with their emergency lights flashing in the parking lot of the port. I rolled up and got out of my car, an old beat-up black Crown Victoria with tinted windows that every police officer I know calls "Crown Vic" for short. It was a mess, but it was my mess. It had rust spots in certain areas and yeah, I could have upgraded, but I honestly liked the car. It was like me—old and beat up but it was faithful, and although at one time it had the "that's a police car look," it was so beat up now that no one took a second glance at it.

I walked up to Dick, who was standing over the body. A sheet covered it, and I didn't see it at first. The body is usually covered out of respect and to keep the prying eyes of the public from taking pictures. With the advent of cameras on phones and every other device imaginable, it was just one extra thing to think about, but with it being so early, I doubted anyone was on the perimeter just waiting to take a photo.

"Glad you could make it, Lou," Dick said. Dick was definitely the professional here. Where I am rough around the edges, Dick was the consummate professional of this partnership. For the record, Dick isn't his real name either. He's like me—changing identities or names every few years. Trust me, it's annoying and sucks at times because you can really make some good friends in the...uh...real world, but it's better than having people question why we don't get older and cause problems. Anyway, his real name at one time was Richard, and every alias since that time has been some sort of related name, like Rick or Rich...but it's

Dick these days and, to be honest, sometimes he can live up that name quite well. Dick continued, "We have a young woman, no ID. One of the dock workers noticed her body caught on one of the pier pilings and she was bobbing in the water."

I bent down and lifted the sheet. The woman looked to be mid-20s with dark hair. She was attractive, her body was athletic, and she was still wearing the clothes she evidently lost her life in, which consisted of jeans and a pullover sweater. She didn't look like a "working girl," and she hadn't been in the water very long, otherwise she would have been bloated like a fish. Have you ever seen a person who's been in the water for a while? Well, it's disgusting...but then again, most dead things, no matter the location, become disgusting after a while. Looking over her face, head, and neck, I noticed there were no apparent injuries. I sniffed...hey, don't look at me like that. I can smell and hear things that most people can't. It really does help out at times. I smelled a hint of perfume, lotion, and...cinnamon? Well, I wasn't sure where the cinnamon came from. Perhaps it was part of the perfume, but it was weird to me because it didn't work well together. So far, there was no supernatural spin to this, just some poor girl that was dead. Sad...but it happens far too often, especially in this city. I looked up at Dick and asked, "Did you find anything?"

"No, they pulled her from the water over there, and I haven't picked up on anything," he said, pointing at the area where they found the victim.

I pulled the sheet back over the body and stood up. I walked over to where Dick had indicated and over to the edge of the dock to look down into the water. Nothing special there. It was dark out but...oh yeah, along with the smell and hearing, I can see pretty good in the dark, too. Nearby, there was a ladder that went down into the water. Dick followed me and I asked, "Who found her?"

Dick looked down at his notebook. "That would be Mark Landry, age 41, employed here at the port for the last 10 years. When he noticed the victim, he grabbed a couple other guys and went down that ladder there to...well, to help her initially, but once he realized she was dead, they lowered some rope to lift her up and laid her where you saw her."

"Well, that was above and beyond," I said, thinking that most people would have just left the body in the water and be okay with calling the police with the mindset that "it's not my problem; it's their problem now."

"Yeah," Dick agreed.

"Did you talk to him yet?" I asked.

"I did, but I didn't get anything more out of him...and besides being a little cold, he responded normally," he said.

That spoke volumes to me. The guy was telling the truth. He really did just find the body and had nothing else to do with it. Dick…well, being a vampire, he has this ability to feel the blood flow in things around him. I'm not a vampire, so I don't know how it works. He tried explaining to me in the past and now I just take it for granted. If someone is lying, their heart beats faster and adrenaline kicks in. My partner Dick notices that.

"Well, that doesn't leave much, does it?" I said, more of a statement than a question.

"I agree. There's nothing here that leaves us much to go on," he said, then continued, "Once we get her prints and her identity, we should have a little more to work with."

"Who called you to look into this?" I asked. It was our "weekend" off. I say that tongue-in-cheek because when you're a detective, you're always on call, especially when you investigate normal, as well as abnormal situations. I really miss the days before cell phones. You could really disappear for a day or two, but with technology came instant communication and now…well…you're ALWAYS on call.

"Captain Benoit," he said.

"Ah…" I said thoughtfully. Dick and I have two "bosses." One is Lieutenant Martine, who was one of the "normies." That's what I liked to call beings that didn't have any extra abilities or afflictions. You know—just a regular person, like you are. She's a good lieutenant, though. Captain Benoit is our other "boss" and even though he wasn't over the homicide unit, he was one of the few that knew what was behind the proverbial curtain and the only one that would call us to investigate situations that would require our...um...special abilities. Lieutenant Martine didn't enjoy sharing us as a resource. She didn't understand why the captain, who wasn't in her direct chain of command, had access to part of her team but she knew enough about office politics to realize that sometimes, things make little sense and it's just better to keep your mouth shut than to cause a commotion. This was especially true for decisions made above your pay grade.

"Strange, though," I said. "There's nothing here that would suggest..."

I trailed off, but Dick knew what I meant. We've worked together long enough to know each other. Heck, we can even finish each other's sentences at times.

"Yeah, I'm not sure why we were called on this one," he said.

"Well, I'm sure we'll know more shortly," I said.

I know I complained about technology, but it isn't always a bad thing. The fingerprints, if we have hers on file, should come back within the day, depending on the diligence and the workload of the latent print examiner. Before...well, it could take weeks.

"I'll go in and talk to the captain; you can go on home. I got this," I said. I knew that the sun would be up before long, and my partner had an aversion to working during the day. Amazingly, and also contrary to popular belief, vampires can actually go out in the light of day...well, now they can, again thanks to modern medicine and magic. They are, however, severely weakened and would rather not do it if they can help it.

"Thanks," he said.

The coroner had been standing by, waiting for us to finish. When we were done, they moved the body to the back of the van and left, but not before the crime scene tech took fingerprints of the victim. I got back into my Crown Vic and headed over to the office. The sun was peaking over the horizon when I pulled into the parking garage.

Once parked, I decided to get a quick nap. I knew nothing was going to happen for the next few hours anyway, so I turned off the car, cracked the window to let fresh air in, and went to sleep.

Chapter Two

I woke up to a knock on the window, which caused me to wake with a start and momentarily forget where I was...but I smelled the perfume of Lieutenant Martine before I looked out the window to see her looking back at me. She had short, medium brown hair which matched her complexion. She was constantly in the gym, either doing things like Cross-Fit or practicing martial arts like Krav Maga or whatever the latest fad was. Maybe it was Brazilian jiu-jitsu...I don't know...but she could take care of herself and looked it. She was like a bronze goddess—petite yet toned. Though she didn't necessarily need to rely on those skills. I've seen her shoot, and I wouldn't want to be on the receiving end, even with my quick-healing ability. I looked out my driver's side window into her hazel-colored eyes.

"Hey Lieutenant, what are you doing here on a Saturday?" I asked and got out of the car. She didn't answer my question.

"You were called in last night?" she asked.

"Uh, yes ma'am...well it was more like very early morning," I said.

"I don't like that I don't know what you guys are up to or when you're called out for other stuff. I seriously don't like not being notified first," she said. "I can never be sure what y'all are up to. How can I take care of you both if I don't know what's going on?"

I imagine she said this mostly for herself, but I answered, just to make sure. "I don't know, boss. I guess the higher-ups like the way Dick and I do things."

"I guess but I'm not sure why they have such a hard-on for you guys," she continued. "I seriously don't understand it. We're the homicide unit and I'm supposed to oversee it but then there are some homicides that don't end up in my reports; they're routed differently. It doesn't make sense." She stopped short and looked at me like she realized she'd said too much. The visible change was apparent as her face became a wall devoid of emotion.

"Well, anyway, I just don't like my people getting taking advantage of or being kept in the dark," she said.

We've worked together a long time and even though I did have an idea of what was going on, sometimes it was just best for everyone involved to play dumb. People that end up finding out that the world doesn't work like they're led to believe have drastic reactions at times. I've seen it before and it's not a pretty thing.

"Sure, boss, I'm sure they have their reasons…" I mumbled.

She nodded, then said, "Well, don't stay out here all day. We've got other cases to solve."

She slapped the roof of the car, indicating the conversation was over, and headed toward the elevator. I took a deep breath, watching her go, and waited 'til she was in the elevator and out of sight. I waited to save us both from uncomfortable silence. Sitting there for a moment longer had me thinking about the case. So strange…there was really nothing "abnormal" about it so far. Hopefully, the forensics would come back with something.

I got out of the car and headed inside, taking the same route that the lieutenant did. I could have taken the stairs, but trust me, I'm not worried about my health. Besides, I didn't want to end up huffing and puffing. You know how that story goes.

I entered the Detective Bureau's office and looked around. Nothing fancy here. The bullpen or open room was full of cubicles where every detective had their own desk with a laptop in a light grey cubicle to call their home. Mine…well, besides the files piled up on the desk, there was nothing to give it away as mine. I kept it pretty clean of personal information because, to be honest, the more stuff you have, the more people have to ask questions about and I like to keep my life private…well, as private as I can without being rude. Dick's desk was across the aisle from mine. I think he followed the same rule I had. A new detective that didn't know any better would have thought our cubicles were open for the taking if it wasn't for those files piled up.

I wasn't alone this morning, as there were a couple of other detectives working on whatever they were working on. One thing about being a detective—although the work schedule was normally Monday through Friday 0800 to 1700, the reality was that your hours were all over the place and you came and went as you pleased, as long as you did your solid eight hours a day. Truthfully, just doing eight hours was rare, as there was always overtime...sometimes paid, but most times not. I mean, New Orleans always seems to have budget problems, but then again, I'm not here working for the pay, that's for sure...but I do enjoy the work.

Detective Green (Rhonda to her friends, which sometimes I was and sometimes I wasn't) and her partner, Detective Jimmy Allain, were at the other end of the row. They looked tired—like they had been up half the night...kind of like the night I just had. It looked like the $5 coffee shop cappuccino they were holding in hand wasn't helping either.

"What are you two doing here? You guys look exhausted," I said.

Rhonda sat down in her chair. She looked to be a little out of shape, but she was smart and didn't take crap from anyone. She was a good detective and had recently joined the department. She had been a detective over in the panhandle of Florida for years before coming here to New Orleans. Her husband transferred out here for a job, so she transferred too, and fit right in.

Jimmy, Rhonda's partner, was a skinny fellow. Nice guy, though—very socially adept. He made talking to witnesses and eliciting information look easy because of his demeanor. Those two being paired together made a good team.

"Oh, hey Lou, I didn't see you over there," Jimmy said.

"Yeah, just came in. Got called in for a case under the bridge," I said.

"Oh, I haven't heard about that one yet," he replied.

The homicide unit here in New Orleans is kind of small. Sure, we have more than our fair share of homicides, but news travels faster than a juicy high school story. We all kind of hear about one another's cases and current goings-on in the city.

"Yeah," I said, "Waiting to hear from the crime lab. Have a Jane Doe. Don't know who she is, so kind of stuck at the moment."

"That always sucks," Jimmy said. "Well, hopefully, they'll have something."

"So...you guys look beat," I said, bringing the subject back up and asked again, "What did y'all get into?"

"Strangest thing...we got called in to investigate a dead body in City Park," Jimmy said. He trailed off as if lost in thought, thinking about the event.

"What's strange about it?" I asked. "The only crimes taking place there that I've heard about were bums that drank themselves to death—well, that and maybe one or two sexual assaults."

Rhonda piped up from her cubicle. "It was one of the worst things I've ever seen."

That piqued my interest. She'd seen a lot and to hear that coming from her, it must have been bad. I also found that the location they were talking about was a bit problematic, too. City Park was huge—1300 acres— but it was also a neutral ground of sorts for all the "special" people in the vicinity. It was the only place nearby that was considered a sort of hallowed ground, meaning that if you had beef with someone, you couldn't hash it out there. If you did, the High Council of the city (the unknown council that handled "our" types) would put out a warrant for your death. The reason it was neutral ground was that every sect, race, species or whatever has ties to the natural world. Whether you were a druid, a witch, a sprite, or any other persuasion, sometimes you needed to perform rituals in a wooded area, so it became a written rule that it was sacred ground and no violence was to take place...at least no violence from our kind of folks to each other or to "normies." One street over, though, or even across the street from the park, it was a different matter altogether.

"Oh, yeah?" I asked, trying not to sound too interested. "What did you find?"

"I found out that I never want to go to that spot in the park again…not that I had a habit of going there, but what I saw, I'll never forget," Jimmy said.

"And?" I asked. It was like pulling teeth here. I tell you, some people get wrapped up in a story and totally miss what others in the conversation really want to know.

Jimmy saw the look on my face and got back on topic. "It was on the north side of the park. You know that hill that's supposedly the highest point in New Orleans?"

Of course I knew the hill, but I acted dumb in order for him to continue talking. They called that hill LaBorde Mountain, ironically enough since New Orleans was pretty darned flat. It was 42 feet above sea level, which made it the highest natural elevation in the city.

"The body was at the top," Jimmy continued, "And it was in pieces. Scattered all over the etched stone map of New Orleans."

This tidbit of news concerned me as chills ran down my spine. That place in the park was particularly special to some of "our kind" in the area. Some magic or other types of rituals conducted needed to be executed at the highest natural point in the area and that was a popular location to conduct some of those ceremonies.

"How many pieces were there?" I said with a little too much interest because Jimmy looked at me funny, so I quickly added as I shrugged my shoulders, "Call me morbid, but I'm curious. I don't know."

"Five? Maybe six? I don't know, but there was enough to go around," Jimmy said slowly.

"How were they arranged?" I asked.

"Why the interest, Lou? You look a little pale. You know something?" Jimmy asked.

"No, not at all. I've been reading books on the occult, and this sounds like that," I said, hoping I sounded convincing. When you've lived as long as I have, I've learned to be quick with my wit, but I still had trouble controlling how I looked. The chills that had run down my spine had settled in my stomach, and I was beginning to feel queasy.

"Well, if you must know," Jimmy began, "they were placed in different locations on the map...but the strangest thing was that someone had drawn one of those circles with a star. You know—a pentagram—over the entire map. They placed a body part in each section of the star with the torso being almost on top of the section in the middle."

In the back of my mind, as soon as he mentioned the place, I knew that the case should have been mine and Dick's. So why wasn't it? Was there a mix-up of some sort? Was it supposed to be our case and the unknown lady under the bridge was theirs? I didn't know, but to hear what

Jimmy was telling me was pretty upsetting. Somebody was trying to create a rift in the city, and they did it in such a way that they were rocking the boat pretty hard. I just hoped whoever the message was intended for didn't rock back, but I wasn't holding my breath.

I needed to talk to Dick, but knowing him, he was probably sleeping...you know, being a vampire and the fact it was pretty bright out from what I could tell from the sunlight coming through the shades on the window. I must have been deep in thought, thinking about everything when I came to because Jimmy, as well as Rhonda who had joined the conversation, were both looking—no, they were staring—at me with concern. "Jesus, Lou, you don't look good. You okay?" Rhonda asked.

"Yeah, yeah...I just ate something that didn't agree with me this morning, I guess," I said. Trying to make an exit from the conversation, I added, "I think I'll make a pit stop by the bathroom."

"Are you sure? I have some Rolaids," she said, trying to be helpful.

I got up and shook my head as I passed her, heading to the bathroom. My mind was racing a mile a minute, trying to keep up with itself, and I needed to throw water on my face. Walking into the bathroom, I headed straight for the sink and looked at myself in the mirror. Yep, I looked pale, all right. I washed my face and looked at myself again. The water seemed to help as my body calmed down. Just a haggard, rough-around-the-edges face looking back at me. I also noticed that I had gotten water all over my suit jacket…not that it mattered much. I tended to go through my suits rather quickly since when I do…uh…change, the suit doesn't survive my…gift. So, I tend to shop at Goodwill or other secondhand stores for my clothes. A good throw in the wash or quick trip to the dry cleaner and they're as good as new…and cheap!

When the shock of what I heard had passed, I decided I needed to get a look at those crime scene photos. Since it happened this morning, I doubted the photos would be ready today. I made a mental note to check them later. Until then, if I could keep my mind focused, I had to write the report of what Dick and I did today. Yeah, it's funny—even when we're called out on "special" cases, we still have to fill out the paperwork. You'd think that they wouldn't want a paper trail, but I guess they have some way of keeping it secret. I don't know. I just peck away on the computer and see that it gets done. After I'm finished with what I've got to do, it becomes someone else's problem.

I went back to the detective area and, thankfully, Rhonda and Jimmy were too busy to notice me. I sat down at my desk and my stomach started rumbling. Okay…one thing you need to know about my condition—since I heal fast, I also burn calories fast. My metabolism is through the roof, so I get hungry quite a bit. I now understand why my wolfie ancestors tore into people. They were insatiably hungry and as you know, hunger can make people "hangry" enough to turn into monsters!

I checked my top drawer for my emergency rations, which was comprised of a honey bun which, who knew how long it had been there. Thankfully, the preservatives would probably keep it edible for eternity. Since I don't really gain or lose weight, I wolfed it down. Sorry, no pun intended...okay, maybe a little. After that, I turned back to my computer and pecked away. After I wrote what had happened, questions began to form. What was Jane Doe doing before she was dropped in the water? Why did she not have anything on her? What or who killed her? What was that cinnamon smell? I really needed to find her identity; it would really help with pointing in a direction to follow. My mind also started wondering about Jimmy and Rhonda's case.

I thought maybe I should go talk to Captain Benoit about the possible mix-up with getting the cases switched, so I headed toward his office. As I turned the corner, I remembered that it was Saturday and he probably wouldn't be in. Surprisingly, the door was open and the captain was busy looking at his computer, so he didn't notice me. I rapped my knuckles on the door to announce myself. The captain looked up. "Ah, Giroux, come on in. What do you need? Got anything on that case I called you and your partner in on this morning?"

"Ah...no, not really, sir, but I do have a question," I said as I came into the room and sat down in one of the two chairs that were opposite from him.

"Ah, one sec," Captain Benoit said, as he raised one finger to hold a minute while he finished something up on his computer.

I took that moment to glance around the room and look at the decorations. As far as offices go, his was nice. It was larger than most of the offices in the precinct; had an ornate, solid wood desk; nice, cushiony chairs; and pictures, accolades, diplomas, and certificates that adorned the walls. Whoever organized it had done an excellent job, as it wasn't too imposing or cluttered considering the number of things to look at. The moment didn't last long because whatever he was working on, he finished and looked back at me.

"What question do you have?" he asked.

"Well, sir, usually you have us look into...certain cases, but I think there might have been a mix-up," I began.

"What makes you think that, Giroux?" he asked.

I told him about the case Jimmy and Rhonda were working on with the death in City Park, which I learned about from talking to them. I then went on to explain that because of the nature of that death, it probably should have been one of those "certain" cases that we were called to investigate.

"Hmm...yeah, I can see how you could think that, but I wouldn't worry about it. Just stick to the case you're working," he said after thinking a moment.

"But sir, I..." I began to say before being interrupted by the captain.

"No, I get it Giroux. I really do. The cases that you get from me come down from above and they don't make mistakes. It does sound strange so I will inquire, but continue on with the case you're working and leave that other case to the other detectives for now," he said, then added, looking for confirmation, "Okay?"

The whole thing felt off, but Captain Benoit had never led us wrong before, so I nodded and said, "Sure."

"Oh, and one more thing, sir."

"Yeah?

"The lieutenant," I said.

"What about her?" he asked.

"I think she's getting a little irritated about having her folks tasked with things without her knowing," I said.

"Are you getting tired of being tasked out, Giroux?" he asked.

"No sir, not at all. I feel like that's my job. I was just telling you because I think it's important for everyone to be on the same page...well, as close to the same page as possible without breaking those "rules.""

"Well, don't you worry about it. I'll handle the lieutenant," Captain Benoit replied.

Chapter Three

I still didn't feel quite right when I left the captain's office. Something about it all really bugged me. I looked down at my watch. The place I had in mind to visit next had just opened, so I followed up on my hunch there.

15 minutes later found me on Decatur Street in the world-renowned French Quarter and I stopped off at one of my favorite haunts. It was a bookstore called the Bookshop that had been around for…well…as long as I can remember, and was usually the first place I'd go to find more information, either in the books or from the proprietor. It was the kind of place that made one reminisce about a library, complete with a sort of reverence where those searching for books spoke in hushed tones. I walked through the aged and heavy wooden door and heard the bell tinkle overhead, which announced my arrival. This early in the day, especially on a Saturday, there weren't many customers, nor were there many people milling around in this part of the French Quarter. Most were

probably still dealing with the hangovers they got from Bourbon Street the night before.

"Hey Harry," I said to the old man behind the glass counter.

The man didn't say a word; he just looked up and nodded with a grunt. He was an older gentleman, and most would have thought he was the proprietor of the store, but he wasn't, so I walked further into the store to find them.

"She's up on the third floor," the old man said as I passed the counter.

There were few places in New Orleans and surrounding areas that had a neutrality clause that was respected by all the kin. This place was another one. However, saying that just because it was respected didn't mean that rules weren't broken from time to time, as with the potential case in City Park.

I walked past rows of dusty shelves that were filled top to bottom with a copious number of books, toward the back of the store and then up the flight of stairs to the second floor, which presented more bookshelves. I continued on up the stairs to the third and final floor. When I arrived, it was dark. The overhead lights were off, but the windows that overlooked the street below brought in enough daylight to see clearly. The cave-like room had several tables with boxes full of vinyl records...and that was another reason I loved this place. They had such a great selection of vinyl, ranging anywhere from Big Band, to Motown, to the 80s. Classic.

I felt the floor shift slightly beneath my weight and looked down. I could see through the wood slats to the second floor. It always creeped me out, but the floor bore the weight. Harry said she was up here, but I didn't see her. Then my nose twitched as her scent gave her away before she spoke, and she obviously smelled me, as well.

"Ah, I thought I smelled a wet dog in here," the voice said.

"I'm not wet, though I did take a shower this morning," I replied.

There was movement at the far end of a table near the wall and a small shadow jumped up onto the table to gaze clearly at me. It was a cat with a swirled chocolate brown and heather grey coat, whose brilliant green and gold eyes had years of wisdom peering out. I stepped closer.

"Don't you dare try to pet me. You know I can't stand that," the cat said.

"I'm sorry, Hannah," I said. "I wasn't going to. Just wanted to get closer to discuss something that I didn't want to travel."

Hey now, don't act surprised. Of course she's a cat...well, I think she's a cat. Obviously, I know she's more than your normal, run-of-the-mill, house cat. Most cats don't like me too well, with my condition, but Hannah had always appeared to me as a cat, and I've never asked any questions. She could be a witch; she could be something else entirely. There are some things in this world you just don't ask about unless they tell you first. Anyway, this cat, or rather Hannah, had owned the bookstore ever since the beginning. She had a good grasp of the city and knew the gossip and murmurings.

She hopped to the table closest to me and sauntered over as if she didn't have a care in the world. She stopped short and looked up at me. "What is it you would like to discuss?"

"Have you heard of anything going on in City Park?" I asked.

She cocked her head to the side. I wasn't sure if that was a habit of being a cat or because she was thinking about something. She didn't immediately reply, so I figured the latter.

"Should I know of something in City Park?" she asked slowly, but her voice almost sounded apprehensive. Or, maybe it was eagerness to learn something new happening in the city.

"I guess not," I replied. "If you don't know anything, then perhaps it was nothing, or it was just a coincidence."

"Nothing that happens in this city is a coincidence," Hannah replied.

I looked down at her and she stared back. She had quite the poker face; she rarely showed emotion but even if she did...I mean, I don't read cat.

"I thought it was worth a try to at least ask you," I said and turned to go.

She said nothing until I reached the top of the stairs, then she spoke up. "Be careful. I'm not saying I know or don't know anything, but I'd be careful with anything that involves City Park."

That stopped me cold, and I turned around to face her, but she had already hopped off the table and back to where she had been sleeping before I came into the room. All I saw was a disappearing tail. She was like that. I wouldn't call her a friend, but we worked together from time to time. She certainly had her own concerns, but if her concerns fell in the same direction my concerns traveled, then she was more forthcoming with information. I wasn't her only customer, however. There were plenty of people, monsters, and other beings who used her as a resource, so you could trust her...but only to a point. She never betrayed anyone, at least as far as I've known, but she held her cards close. I certainly couldn't blame her for that if she wanted her shop to remain neutral ground.

"Should I bring some catnip next time?" I asked.

All I heard was a disgusted hiss and some choice words that I could only pick up with my acute hearing. I must have struck a nerve.

"I'm sorry. It was a late night last night," I said.

It doesn't pay to upset people (or cats, as is the case here), especially those that you may need as an ally in the future. In a town where I don't have a lot of friends, I try to treat the ones I do have (though they may not be on my Christmas list) with at least care and courtesy so they don't completely write me off.

My apology must have worked because I heard her whisper and yawn from her dark corner, "Whatever. See you next time."

I headed back downstairs and when I reached the ground floor, Harry was still at his post behind the counter. He hadn't moved one inch from the spot he was in when I entered the store.

"She still asleep up there?" he asked.

"Yeah, I only bothered her momentarily. She went back to napping," I replied. Harry then nodded as if he expected that reply.

As I passed him and headed toward the door, the unusually quiet Harry spoke up again. "Stay safe out there. Strange things are going on in New Orleans."

I stopped and looked at him midway through the door. He stared back at me, blank-faced. I nodded and walked out. I could hear the bell over the door ring as the door closed. I would have asked him what he meant, but that wouldn't have gone far. From my past dealings with him, the fact that he spoke this much of a warning sent off alarms, and I was grateful that he spoke at all. It was enough to let me know that something was indeed going on and I had better be on my "A" game.

So now, I was back on the street and had no idea where to go next. My stomach rumbled and since I wasn't very far from Café Du Monde, I walked over. It was a nice day and getting a hot beignet, which was kind of like the French's version of a hot doughnut that's been dusted with powdered sugar, sounded appealing. I couldn't resist. I also didn't mind the chicory coffee. One thing you have to understand—most people who live in the surrounding areas of New Orleans don't hang out in the French Quarter. The majority of the people that you see milling around either work there, are tourists, or they're college kids from the local universities.

As usual, the café was packed, but I had nothing else to do so I waited in line, which was shorter than normal. I soon got my glorious goodness delivered to me in a small paper bag. If you can come away from eating a beignet without looking like a major coke addict due to the powdered sugar, you'll have to share that tidbit with me. I can never seem to escape unscathed.

Now that I was momentarily sated—and believe me, it's always momentarily—I decided to return to my house. I had already seen the captain, which was per usual, and there was nothing else to be done. I had to wait for the crime scene techs to be done with their analysis before I could do anything else.

I was back home by noon. So far, it had been a productive day, albeit not a progressive one. I did a lot of stuff but nothing to really show for it, except I had more questions that I needed to find the answer to.

When I walked in, I was greeted by...oh, yeah...I haven't told you about her yet. I got sidetracked earlier because I wanted to hop right into the story. My freeloading roommate, Morgane, greeted me. Well, she isn't really my roommate, nor is she my pet, but she's a rather larger-than-normal crow that had taken up residence with me years before. Again, I know she isn't a crow, and she had let things slip over the years, but again, I respect privacy, so I don't ask who or what she really is or was. Kind of like with Hannah the cat—there are some things that are just considered rude to ask or even say. It's kind of like asking a lady her age, but 10 times worse...almost along the lines of a racial slur. It's just not something one does, or at least not someone that has class would do.

Why do I keep her? Hmm. I have to think about that one. Maybe it's because she keeps me company and doesn't bother me. For someone that lives a long time and doesn't maintain healthy friendships with "people" of his kind, companionship, regardless of the form, becomes important. We respected each other's privacy and the best thing is, as long as I don't block the window she uses as an entrance and she can come or go as she pleases, there's really no problem...Most times.

"Where have you been? I didn't see you when I woke this morning?" came the squawking voice.

"You know—duty calls," I said.

Seeing that she had just flown through the window from outside, I asked, "Where were you?"

"You know—nature calls," she replied. She hopped closer and cocked her head to one side, taking one good look at me with her left eye.

"You're dealing with something that you aren't sure about," she said.

For a crow, even a shapeshifter of who knows what, she was very perceptive.

"Yeah, a couple of murders took place last night and I'm not sure whether they were or weren't connected," I replied.

I walked into the kitchen and made myself lunch.

"Any leads?" Morgane asked.

"Nope, just dead bodies and a bunch of questions," I said.

She hopped up and down out of frustration. "Well, that doesn't help, does it?"

"Nope."

"Well, I'm sure you'll figure it out," she said as she hopped and then jumped up into the air to fly over to her perch, which sat in the living room. The small shotgun house wasn't that big, so it didn't take long to move anywhere within it.

I followed and slumped on the couch with the sandwich I made and proceeded to get a Guinness record in how quickly I finished eating it.

The crow was content to sit there for a while and I thought I might fall asleep for a bit when she cawed loudly, which startled me awake.

"What's up?" I asked.

"Do you want help? I could ask around," she replied.

"Nah, I don't know exactly what's going on, and I don't want you to get involved. There's no telling who or what is behind this and I'm not sure how bad it might become," I replied.

"You mean that the big bad wolf is worried about me? Squawk!" she said.

"It's been a long time since I was the big bad wolf, but no...not exactly...but just the same. Stay out of it for my sake for now," I requested.

The bird let out a whistle and flew out of the room to another part of the house. I wasn't sure, but I think I may have insulted her...but who really knows? Again, I am a werewolf, and I can barely talk to others of my kind, much less others. It's a strange existence, but it's funny what a person, or being, can get used to.

I wondered about my partner, Dick. I would have to meet up with him later tonight to see what his thoughts were. He lived in the Garden District, a pretty posh part of town. He always hated having to come over the Crescent City Connection to the west bank. I'm not sure why, but perhaps it was bad memories or something…I don't know. The more I thought about it, there were quite a few things I didn't know about those I kept around me. Dick, Hannah from the bookstore, even my own "roommate." Sure we all got along, but we all had secrets, and some of the relationships begged the question, "Were they friends or just professional contacts?"

The last time I had friends, you ask? Oh, so now you're getting interested in my story. At first, it didn't seem like you wanted to give me the time of day, but since you asked. Hmm…you know, I really can't say. The last time I had "real" friends was when I was in the military and before I turned into this hidden beast in front of you. Sure, I've gotten by since, but the last true friends that are more like family? Yeah…it was way back, but that's another story for another time.

Saturday came and went after I got home and slept the rest of the day. I was going to call Dick but then thought better of it. I might as well wait until we get more evidence back from the lab technicians, which wouldn't be until Monday at the earliest, since they didn't work weekends. I decided just to stick around the house.

The next day, I didn't have plans for the afternoon, and I lived walking distance to a little bar named the Crown and Anchor that had a pizza joint around the corner. Not a bad way to waste some time—eating and throwing back a few rounds. I stopped off at the pizza joint first and ate a large pizza. After that, I walked around the block to the bar. There was a famous British TV show that used a blue police phone booth to travel through time. I hadn't followed the series myself; I mean, come on, when I live in the world of the weird, I needed nothing else to add to it. I'm not saying it was bad, it was just something I hadn't followed up on. Anyway, this bar had a replica of that phone booth as the entrance, which added to the character of the place. The folks behind the bar knew me by first name and every once in a while, there'd be live music and, on some weekends, they'd watch that show I was talking about. And you better believe there'd be hell to pay if you talked too loud during an episode. What can I say? Some folks take that stuff seriously.

"Hey Lou!" I heard the familiar voice call my name when I went in. I looked behind the bar to see a petite, cute blonde named Samantha...Sam for short. She reminded me of family long past and I treated her like a little sister.

"Hey Sam, how's the day treating you?" I asked.

"About the same as usual. You?" she replied and without waiting for a reply, "You want the usual?"

I nodded, and a moment later, I had a beer in hand. I'm honestly not picky when it comes to beer, but there was one that I really liked and they stocked it. I looked around the bar and it was empty, save for me.

"I guess I saved you from being bored," I said.

She looked around the room and said, "Sure...I mean, I could always be doing something but since you're here, I guess I'll wait on you and shoot the bull."

Another thing I liked about this bar was that they let dogs in. Hey! Don't look at me like that! I didn't mean me. I meant they let patrons who have dogs...well, never mind. I like them, and most like me, except those that have been touched in some way by off spirits. But off spirits can mess with anyone and not just dogs.

Off spirits? Oh, they're of the world and not of the world. They aren't ghosts, but they aren't the fairy folk either. They're something else and thankfully, I don't know much, nor do I want to know much about them. All I know for sure is, if an off spirit is involved, it can make everything a bit more complicated.

The afternoon passed and after a few more pints, more people arrived...drunks...just kidding. I saw familiar faces, and some I knew from experience were no more human than I was, but through magic, hid their true forms. Elves, dwarves, witches, you name it...there're all kinds. Most are okay, but as with normal folks, there's always going to be some bad seeds. If you've read about it or heard of it...well again, there's a reason why. It's because they exist.

I saw one face I recognized enter the pub—one who had recently retired from the Marine Corps and worked at the local military base. We'd be become friendly over the past couple of months. I always had a soft spot for those who served. There had been times in my life where I engaged in conflict, myself, so though I held people at arm's length, but there was no harm in being friendly and having acquaintances.

"What's going on, Larry?" I asked.

The man still maintained his military haircut, which, of course left little hair behind. What was left was dark, which went well with his dark eyes. Upon hearing his name, he looked out into the darkness across the room. Coming in from outside where it had been bright, his eyes had to adjust to the dark, but when he saw me, his face broke into a grin.

"Ah Lou, keeping the world and New Orleans safe?" he asked.

"As much as I can...but you know, I am a government worker, so I can only do so much. It's in the manual," I replied as I snickered.

"Ha, me too," he said as he came over and patted my back with his left hand.

"What are you having?" he asked.

"No, I think you got it last time. What are you having?" I replied.

"Well, if that's the case and since we're both poor government workers, I'll let you...let's see, I'll have a whiskey sour," he said.

I looked at Sam, who had heard the conversation, and nodded, then looked back at Larry. "Hitting it hard early, huh?"

"Nah, I'm gonna be nursing that drink all evening. It is a school night after all," he replied.

"Uh huh," I grunted back.

And that's how it was. It's amazing how friendly people can be in passing. It also goes to show how easy it is to make "friends" when you have similar jobs—military, law enforcement, first responder types. They all know the game and speak the same language.

Later that evening, I looked at my watch and decided that it would probably be best to stumble back to my place. Larry had long since left and Sam was replaced by another bartender named Boz, a six-foot fellow that looked more comfortable being a bouncer than a bartender. He never said much, only enough to get your order. I had my suspicions that he had something "extra" in his bloodline, maybe back a few generations...this was the case with many people. But again, who really knew?

I left out the same way I came in—through the blue phone booth. The weather was comfortable, and the moon rose on the horizon. It wasn't quite a full moon, but I could feel it pulling at me, anyway. Thankfully, like I alluded to earlier, I had medicine and magical charms that helped to keep me in check. Of course, had it been a full moon, it would've taken everything I had and even then, it's sometimes difficult to avoid succumbing to the wild energy and...well...my instincts.

I heard the ferry toot its horn nearby, signaling that it was about to leave the shore. The ferry connected pedestrian traffic from Algiers Point to downtown New Orleans and the French Quarter. For a buck or two, one could catch a ride from Algiers and not have to pay parking fees because, let's face it, parking could be a real hassle in the city.

I was halfway back to my place a few blocks away when a faint smell drifted across my nose. It was pungent and now that I focused, I also caught a small noise that probably only I could hear. I wasn't sure what it was, but I immediately sobered up. So much for all the beer, but honestly, I couldn't complain. The fast metabolism and healing had saved me more than a couple of times.

I followed the scent to an abandoned house. It was set back off the roadway and looked to be in disrepair, which seemed odd but not totally out of place. People were always buying houses in this area to fix up and either move in or flip them. The odor was stronger now and the sounds louder; it seemed like voices, but I couldn't quite make out what was going on.

I hopped over the waist-high fence that lined the street and went deeper into the yard toward the house. Unlike the other houses on the street that were well lit, this one was dark and didn't look like it had any power connected to it. But darkness was a friend of mine. It hid me well from most people and things, but in the dark, my eyesight was still pretty good. Granted, if it were pitch black, I'd be like anyone else and would have to rely on my hearing, but tonight, I was okay.

Whatever I smelled or heard was coming from the house, so I bypassed the front steps and porch and went to the side. Most houses in the area didn't have room for large yards or driveways for that matter. Most residents and visitors parked on the street, which sometimes created its own problem when driving through the neighborhood. But I digress...I went around the side slowly. Whatever was ahead, I didn't want to alert it. When I got to the back of the house, I peered into the back yard. Nothing.

Chapter Four

Well, between you and me, that was odd. I knew something was there or had just been there. And since I was pretty sure it didn't pass by me, I looked up and that's when I first caught a glimpse. A large, dark figure was crouched at the edge of the roof, looking down at me. It scared the bejesus out of me. Here I thought I was going to get the drop on whatever was going on, and whatever this thing was, it knew I was there. I should have just gone home.

"Werewolf...what do you want?" the creature said.

The voice was deep. Being that it was dark outside and the creature was dark, I couldn't see clearly enough to identify it. With the height that it sat and the wind drifting the other direction, I couldn't identify by smell either.

"Well, since you asked politely," I replied, "I am a police officer...well, a detective...and trying to keep the peace."

"A werewolf detective?" the creature said.

"Yeah, I know. What's the world coming to?" I replied. "Mind telling me what's going on and why you're on this abandoned property?"

"I could, but then, what would I get out of it?" the thing asked.

One had to be careful when dealing with things that were not of the normal world...well, the world as you know it. When it came to bargains and favors, things on my side of the world took things pretty seriously. I didn't say anything; I just waited.

The thing stood up, and it looked to be humanoid. Then it stepped off the roof and floated down toward me. When it came closer, I got a whiff, and that's when I knew what it was, though it had been a while since I had come across one. It was a vampire, but not the normal kind. There were undead and then there were really undead. This kind of vampire was alive, but only barely. It smelled of rot because half of it was rotting. Due to their ghastliness, these kinds of vampires didn't usually hang out with other kinds, or even their own, really. They were generally outcasts of the world.

"What? Don't like what you see, werewolf?" the creature asked.

I say creature because, seriously, they were barely sentient. Sure, they could talk, but really, what did they have to say? Better yet, who would listen?

"No, not really," I replied.

Its face smirked. "At least you are honest, but why are you bothering me? I've not broken any accords...yet."

This concerned me and kind of goes back to my job of keeping the peace. People kept an uneasy peace through these written and unwritten accords.

"Were you planning to?" I asked.

"Maybe I have already. Maybe I haven't. Maybe I will break some tonight. Perhaps even right now."

"That would be a mistake," I replied.

I couldn't help but feel my body tense up. I mean, you know how it is. When you feel like you're about to get into a fight, your body reacts. Mine is no different. Sometimes it really does have a mind of its own...for real.

Vampires, no matter what kind, were dangerous. They were inhumanly fast. Some could fly, some could shape-shift. I learned quite a bit from Dick, my partner, but he wasn't there that evening, though I wished he was.

I looked at the creature; it bared its fangs at me.

"Listen, that might work on some, but it won't work on me," I replied and then continued, "If you want to break accords and attack a keeper of the peace, go ahead, but don't say I didn't warn you if you happen to survive."

"I think I will take my chances," it said.

The attack happened so quickly. Even with my speed and extra ability, it was extraordinarily fast. I felt him slam into me and I was flying through the air before my mind even registered what had happened. Well, so much for being cordial, I thought to myself.

When I landed, I hit the ground on my back. I used the momentum to throw my legs up and roll into a fighting stance.

"That wasn't a good idea," I said.

I could feel the rage within wanting to be released. It was so easy to lose your thoughts to such rage and it was a struggle to remain in control, even with magic and medicine.

The creature lunged at me again, but this time I was ready and rolled to the side. Unfortunately, I was still too slow, and it grabbed my leg and threw me across the yard, where I landed against a wood fence. I would have gone through the fence if the trajectory of the throw had been straight, but it was an arc, and so it was more of a glancing blow as I fell to the ground.

"I thought this was going to be tougher," the creature said.

"It's about to be," I replied.

Again, it quickly closed the distance and repeatedly kicked me in the side, hard. It hurt. I think it might have broken my rib. This was not a good spot to be in.

The next thing I knew, the kicking stopped, but then I was flying through the air again. This ugly vampire was strong. I fell in a heap on the other side of the back yard. The silvery moon glowed through the trees overhead and onto where I landed. It wasn't a full moon, but it was bright. I looked up and I could feel myself give way to the "change." Well, that's what I call it. I'm not sure what other people with my affliction call it. The vampire wasted no time and was on me again, kicking away. The proverbial "kicking a dead horse" would soon become "kicking a dead werewolf" if something, namely myself, didn't change soon.

Contrary to popular belief—I know the stories—they think that werewolves just turn into large, cutesy wolves or into a dog-like form. I don't do that but there is a more terrifying form, even for me, and that's the beast that is within. The in-between. The half man-half hulking beast on two legs. Within moments, the nasty creature kicking me witnessed just that.

I told you before that it's a painful process. Bones snap into place, skin stretches, muscles morph and enlarge. I try to avoid it, but since I was already deep in pain all over my body, not to mention a possible broken rib, I might as well let 'er rip.

Strange what you think about in high stress moments. As I lay there on the ground welcoming the change, I looked down at my shirt and had a moment of regret. I really liked that shirt. It was going to be ruined and funny enough, that made me even more enraged, which kind of helped the change progress. I felt my hands and shoulders grow first. Then my face felt extremely hot. You know why werewolves howl? It's because it is effing painful.

Effing? What? I don't really like to cuss. What's wrong with you? Anyway, getting back to the story...It was painful, and I screamed or howled. The kicking stopped and I stood up, towering over the vampire. Yeah, I know you see me. I'm not that tall—maybe five-nine—but when I change, I'm almost six-eight.

The ugly vampire didn't even flinch. He knew I was going to change. After the momentary pause as I stood up, he launched another attack using the ends of his fingers as miniature spears. They were razor-sharp and ripped into me. I grabbed his shoulders and tossed him into the air, but he merely floated a few feet away into the air. It didn't faze him. I launched myself and tackled him into a roll and came up on top of him. I clasped my hands together and lifted them over my head. With a meaty hammer, I came down with all my might and hit the figure below me. I felt him squirm...then I heard laughter. It was strange, creepy, and considering the source, it threw me off. I stopped and looked down at the vampire I had pinned underneath.

I was clearly winning here, or so I thought, but what was so funny to this thing that I had dead to rights? I honestly would have left him alone had he not instigated conflict. Like I said, I just keep the peace and as long as sentient beings keep the peace, I couldn't care less what they do, but this one decided to follow through and attack me. Had I not heard the noise in the first place, I would have never bothered and that's when it hit me...figuratively and literally. I had smelled something and heard talking. Shoot...he hadn't been alone. With that thought, the literal hit took place. As soon as I realized my mistake, a figure flew out of the darkness with breakneck speed and barrelled into me. The force of the blow took us at least 20 feet before we came to a stop. The next thing I knew, the creature—another vampire—grabbed a hold of me and lifted off into the air.

This wasn't good. I couldn't fly, and I had to do something quick before the ground became too far. Vampires are strong, but a werewolf geeked up on adrenaline might be a little stronger. I grabbed its hands and pried them from my shoulders. In wolf form, I'm pretty heavy, so the vampire was unable to get very far at that point, so when I forced it to let go, I dropped maybe 30 feet to the ground. For most humans, that could probably kill them. For me, it was jarring but not particularly life threating. I quickly recovered and bolted to my feet, only to find that the threat was gone. I looked up at the night sky. No sign of the flying vampire. I looked back at the ground to search for the one I had been pummeling, and it, too, was gone. Very peculiar.

It was peculiar because one, they had the advantage and they left before the fight was over. And two, it was peculiar because these guys were usually loners; I had never heard of these kinds of ugly, rotting vampires working together before. In all my years, I had never seen such a thing, which is what initially lulled me into thinking the first one I encountered was alone.

Since the fight was over and the threat was gone, my anger no longer pumped through my veins, so I shifted from my wolfman form back to my happy-go-lucky self. It's kind of like an adrenaline dump on steroids. I needed to get home to rest and recover. The change doesn't take very long. I went from wolfman to battered and bruised Lou in less than a minute. When I had completed the transformation, I stumbled back into the street where I about knocked Larry, my retired Marine friend, over. That shouldn't have happened, but I was hurt and wasn't paying attention to smells or sounds, for that matter.

"Jesus Lou, are you okay? What happened? Where's your shirt?" he said.

"Yeah, I'm fine," I replied.

I mean, I was fine, but I was sure I looked like hell to him and I had to think fast.

"I was mugged," I couldn't think that quickly at the moment and that's the first plausible thing that came to mind.

"Seriously?" he said.

He glanced around to see if could see any danger or find the culprits, but I knew he wouldn't see anything; they were long gone by now.

"We should call the police," he said.

Immediately, I began to think a little more clearly. That was the last thing I needed. Granted, it would be handled behind the scenes, but honestly, I didn't want some poor rookie wrapped up for hours doing the paperwork on something that would never see the light of day. It would disappear into the ether and would beg more questions if the rookie ever followed up on it, which I doubt they would, but you'd be surprised at what people will and won't do.

"No man, it's okay. I am the police, and I'll report it, but right now, the danger is over. I just want to go home and call it a day," I said.

Larry looked at me with concern. "Are you sure? You look pretty beat up."

"Yeah, I'll be fine."

"All right, well, I'll walk with you a bit. Crazy, getting mugged around here. I thought it was one of the better areas," he said.

Obviously, New Orleans isn't known for its safety. I mean, come on...people who didn't live here knew the city for two things: Bourbon Street and Voodoo...and maybe crime. But to those that lived in the area, we knew the good areas, as well as those to avoid if you could help it. However, just because it was considered a "safe" area surely didn't mean that there wasn't any danger at all. Again, kind of what I said earlier in regard to the rookie—you just never knew people and or what they may or may not do. That being said, I didn't want Larry to worry.

"I think it still is. You know how things are. I wasn't paying attention, and you know that most muggings happen because of that," I said.

"Yeah, well still...we live right down the street," he said.

"It'll be okay," I assured him.

And believe me, if I ever caught up to the dastardly duo, it would be okay. They wouldn't get the drop on me again. Larry helped me to my house and went on his way after he saw me open the door and go inside.

"CAW! What happened to you?" Morgane said as soon as I closed the door.

"Long story..."

Chapter Five

The next day being Monday, I headed into the station at the normal time. Before work, I'd had a large breakfast comprised of a four-egg omelet with ham and cheese. It was fantastic. "It should hold me over 'til noon," I thought, which was really ambitious because it never did.

Anyway, I headed in like I said and saw Dick was already at his desk. Yes, he likes to work nights, but unfortunately, being a detective doesn't preclude him from working during the day. He looked the same as any other day. If I had to guess, I thought he might wear the same suit all the time. That, or he had a few that looked so similar that I couldn't tell the difference. Either way, I have to say, he looked sharp. I glanced down at my own $10 special and it looked like I had just pulled it out of the dryer. Oh well.

Detectives Greene and Allain were at their desks, busily working away on whatever they were working on.

Of course, by this time, my healing ability had completely done its job, so no one would have known anything about what happened the night before, except, of course, for Dick. This was fine with me. I had to tell him because that encounter was a strange one, but I couldn't do it in the open. The area is small enough as it is, and I didn't need one of the other detectives to hear about it.

Dick looked at me. I don't know how he did it, but he always seemed to know when something was on my mind. I know I take things for granted, but to see him out during the day always surprised me. It wasn't until just recently—40 or so years ago—that the medicine, along with the magic, advanced to the point where vampires could go out during the day. What a strange world we live in...as if it weren't strange enough. Anyway, I stood up when he saw me and, without missing a beat, he followed me as I walked out into the hallway.

"What's up?" he asked nonchalantly.

"How do you do that?" I asked. "You always seem to know."

He shrugged and, after a moment of thought, replied, "How do you change? You don't know; you just do."

I shouldn't have asked such a dumb question, but the dumbest question is the question you don't ask, right? No, it was still a dumb question. I decided not to dwell on it and opened my mouth to tell him about the night before, but then clamped my mouth shut as I caught a whiff of perfume.

Lieutenant Martine came around the corner. She had just finished working out at the gym and she was ready for business. She was freshly showered and in her detective attire. A business skirt looked howling good on her. Listen, I don't urinate where I swim and I learned long ago that relationships only bring heartbreak eventually, but I can still appreciate someone's form and hard work. Like, even though I'm rough around the edges, I can still stop and appreciate the beauty of things around me.

"Hey detectives, how was the weekend for you two?" she asked.

Dick shrugged. Again, he was a man of few words.

"Always a day too short. I blink and it's gone," I said.

"It does seem that way," she said.

She didn't know the half of it. The more time a person has lived, the quicker it seems to go. Eventually she would, as all of us come to understand.

"Did you get any more information on the case you were working Saturday morning?" she asked.

"No, not yet, Lieutenant. I haven't even checked my email yet. I'm hoping that something will come through," I replied.

"Okay, if you need anything, I'm available."

Both Dick and I nodded until she passed and continued to her office.

When the hallway was clear, I nodded for him to follow me into the men's bathroom. Obviously, I did a quick sweep visually to see if anyone else was there. I didn't really need to, as I couldn't smell anyone else, but it's always best to check. When you became complacent, even with your own abilities, accidents happened.

Once I was sure, I turned to Dick and told him what had happened the night before. He listened and for a long moment, he didn't say anything. He took it all in and just when I thought he would have something profound to say in response, all he said was, "Weird." Not very profound in my book, but I had to agree.

"Right?" I said. "I've never heard of them associating with others. I thought they were strictly solitary."

"They are, or at least they used to be," Dick replied coolly, then continued, "Something must be out of the order of things."

"I'm not sure, but I think it's something we should keep an eye out for," I said.

"Agreed," Dick replied. "By the way, got a hit on the body we found in the river."

"Oh really? Do we know who she is?" I asked.

"Yeah, she was a...hmm...dancer, and worked at one of the clubs on Bourbon Street," he replied.

Bourbon Street, like I said before, is a place that everyone knows New Orleans for. It was lined up and down with bars and clubs of the adult variety. And it wasn't very far from the Mississippi river—only a few blocks.

"Hmm, indeed," I replied. "Did she have a name?"

"Yes, her name is Violet Vicente. Apparently, she didn't live here. Only came in for the weekends to work and do shows. However, we have her fingerprints on file since all dancers have to be vetted to work at those clubs," he replied.

"Strange. Why were we called to check this one out? Did you hear about the City Park murder that Green and Allain are working?" I asked.

"Yes, they filled me in right before you came in. You think somehow the lines were crossed, and we ended up on the wrong case?" he asked.

"That's what I thought, and I brought it up to Captain Benoit, but he said it happened as it was supposed to and we were on the right one. Said he'd check and make sure, though," I replied.

"Something about this doesn't bode well, Lou."

"Yeah, it doesn't smell right. Anyway, we should head over to the place where Ms. Vicente worked. Maybe they could give us times she was last seen," I said.

"Good place as any to start," he replied.

And that's how we ended up at the Top Level Adult Entertainment Club about 30 minutes later. We used Dick's vehicle to get there, which was a black SUV. It screamed "cop" like my own beat-up Crown Vic, but Dick was all about style and whenever we went somewhere, he insisted on taking his vehicle. Once we parked, we headed through the front door of Top Level. It wasn't the best club, but it certainly wasn't the worst, though it had been many years since I had stepped foot in that kind of establishment. I know people have to work and for some, it's all they got, but I always found it depressing, so stopped going. But who am I to judge? I'm just a man (okay, not really just a man) with a huge secret to almost everyone I know.

Since it was early, there wasn't much activity. The club was open, but not ready for business. We walked in and immediately I knew the manager was a pig. No, seriously, he was a werepig. I know it sounds crazy, but he was. He was a big fellow with little eyes, and he didn't sweat, but he had an aroma that reeked of it.

Seeing that we weren't the usual crowd and I guess our professional demeanor gave way to him making his way over to us. "Can I help you?" he asked.

"I don't know. Who are you?" I asked.

"I'm the manager, Mr. Sus" he replied with a slight squeal in response.

"We're with NOPD and would like to ask you some questions," I said.

"Oh, come on, we run a legit business here. How many times are you gonna come in here to harass us?" he said.

"How many times has NOPD come in here to harass you?" I asked.

"Uh…" he began.

"So, not lately then?" I finished for him.

He shrugged sheepishly, but the girth of his neck made it look like he didn't shrug at all.

"Right. Do you know a Vivian Vicente?" I asked.

"Viv?" he replied. "Yeah, what did she do?"

"Well, she was murdered Saturday morning," I replied.

I could see Dick shift his head to listen closely.

"What?! She was just here Friday night and missed her shift last night. Oh man, that is horrible. She was a beautiful girl."

"What time did she leave?" I asked.

"She left her normal time, just after midnight Friday night," the manager replied.

"How long had she worked here...and did she have any enemies?"

"I don't know—not quite a year. We have quite a turnover. People come and people go. As for enemies, I don't know. I run a tight ship here and don't get personal with the employees. I mean, don't get me wrong, I care for each and every one of them, but I keep it professional. I make sure the bouncers don't mess with the dancers and the dancers don't mess with the chemicals, at least not on the premises...you know what I'm saying?" he said.

"I get you. You want nothing to happen here that would ruin business or have NOPD show up to shut you down."

"Right, but damn, I've never had a girl in my employ die before."

"Do you know who saw her last?" I asked.

"Maybe Brian."

"Who?"

"Oh, Brian Stearns. He's one of the bouncers, and was working that evening. As a matter of fact, he worked Saturday and Sunday night, as well."

"Is he here today?" I asked.

"No, but he'll be here tonight."

"Give me his address and we'll go pay him a visit," I replied.

"Sure," he said and disappeared down a hallway to the side of the open room.

I turned to Dick. "What do you think?" I asked, "Get anything?"

"Nope, I think he reacted normally."

"I think so, too. I didn't smell anything," I said.

Most people reek of fear when they're lying, especially when it comes to murder. The mind and body will give most people, even those with special abilities, away because they have no control over how they respond unless they're a sociopath or using strong magic. Sweating profusely, adrenaline dump, hands shaking, etc. I didn't get that feeling here. He reacted genuinely.

The manager gave us the address, and it was near Tulane University, along one of the side streets. It was a popular area with large houses that had rooms or apartments for rent, most of which were occupied by university students. The problem was the lack of actual parking spaces and narrow streets, but that's part of the charm, I guess. Anyway, we headed over there and it was, like I thought, a house with multiple apartments. We knocked on the door of unit one, which was on the first floor. No one answered. I knocked louder—just short of beating the door down—but still no one answered.

"Hey!" I heard a voice call out from above, so I looked up. There was a young lady in a robe on the balcony. Apparently, my unrestrained knocking on the door interrupted her morning.

"Can I help you?" she asked.

"Yes, we're with the Police Department. Have you seen Mr. Stearns?" I asked.

"No, I haven't. Haven't seen him all weekend," she replied. "Do you want me to leave him a message?"

"No, that's fine. I'm sorry to have bothered you," I said.

She made no reply other than a wave of her hand to ward off anything else and disappeared back into her apartment. I turned my attention to Dick. "You get anything?" I asked.

Dick shrugged, and then his face went blank with a concentrated look. Lips pursed with focus and eyes closed. Then, as quick as he started, he snapped out of it. "No one's inside here, but there are two people on the second floor, including the one you just spoke to. I believe they were...umm...busy when we arrived."

I raised my hand to ward off any more explanation. "Okay, we're good here. No need to continue."

Dick smirked and asked if I was sure, which I ignored.

Like I said, Dick had the ability to listen to blood. He could feel it, and this was one of his many talents, identifying how many might be out of vision. I left my business card in the door with a note asking Mr. Stearns to call me.

A couple minutes later, back in Dick's ride, I turned to him and asked, "I wonder where he could be."

"No telling," Dick replied.

"You think we can stop by City Diner? I could go for one of those pancakes," I asked.

Dick shook his head and then stepped on the gas. City Diner was a greasy spoon with pancakes bigger than your head and for someone like me, that meant I would stop by to fill up from time to time. Unfortunately, we didn't have time for a sit-down meal, so we decided to forgo City Diner and instead stopped at a fast-food drive-through. In the end, it didn't really matter to me—just something I needed to momentarily stop this constant hunger I have.

Dick and I walked through the door and back to our cubicles. Detective row felt different from what it had this morning. Like a nervous energy had stolen into the area and loitered, slowly building in excitement. Lieutenant Martine's face was expressionless with intent as she spoke to detectives Green and Allain. I spoke under my breath, but I knew Dick could hear me. "I think they got a lead in their case."

Dick nodded his agreement and never broke stride. We arrived mid-conversation.

"... and that's all you have?" Lieutenant Martine asked.

"Yes, we have an address already and we'll head that way shortly, Lieutenant," Allain replied.

I looked over to Green, who was still very much a part of the conversation, but she gathered her purse and keys, which only confirmed what we heard. With the conversation between the lieutenant and Allain winding down, I interjected out of curiosity.

"Where's the hot date?" I asked.

"Good news," Allain replied. "We got a hit on the body we found at City Park. We're heading over there now to see if anyone else lives at the address."

My ears perked up. "Oh yeah? What's the name?"

"Oh...uh...his name," Allain replied as he lifted the paperwork in his hand to confirm, "is a Mr. Brian Stearns, apparently he is...or was...a bouncer at a local strip joint."

Chapter Six

A llain saw me stiffen at the mention of the name. The case Dick and I were working just became more complicated.

"You, okay?" he asked.

"Well, I don't think you need to head over to where he lives," I replied. My mind was going a mile a minute, trying to figure out just how deep this rabbit hole went. At the same time, but on another track, my mind was racing, trying to figure out how to move forward since now that our cases were obviously connected, we would be working together to solve them. Since they were "normies," it would require a delicate touch and I'm not always known for that. Lieutenant Martine's face was tense. She was processing the information, too.

"Why not?" Allain asked.

"Dick and I were just there, following up on the case we're working. I guess your victim and mine worked at the same place," I replied.

"Woah...are you serious?" Allain asked.

Green, who was standing nearby, heard what I said and interjected almost at the same time that Allain spoke. "Wait, you think our cases are related?"

"I don't want to jump to conclusions, but I wouldn't be surprised. When does coincidence ever come into play with cases like this?" I asked.

"Almost never," Dick said coolly.

"Agreed," I said.

"I agree," Lieutenant Martine said. "I want you all to work these cases together and keep me up to up to date about it. I'll have to brief the higher-ups. We may have a serial killer on our hands."

We all agreed, and Lieutenant Martine left to go to her office. Dick and I took a few minutes to brief Green and Allain on what we had so far. Truth be told, it wasn't much other than a name and a body in the morgue...which wasn't much different from what they had so far with their case.

I had wanted to see the photos from their crime scene, and I guess the only good thing about all of this was now I could access those, and it wouldn't be out of the ordinary, nor would it raise questions. I asked for them and after Green forwarded the case number to my email, and I logged into the case management system to review the file. Attached were jpeg photos, and I clicked on them to bring them into full view. To say it was gruesome was an understatement, even for me, and now I understood why they were shaken up when I had seen them the morning following the incident. The pictures showed the concrete map of New Orleans that had only been there for a couple of years and on the map, the body torn asunder and strategically placed.

I clicked the plus sign with my mouse and the picture grew larger on my computer screen as I zoomed to look more closely. It didn't really help. The photographers did a good job, but the body parts were too large to see exactly what areas of the map they laid over. I guessed I would have to go out there myself and look at it firsthand. I printed out one photo to take with me so I could see how things were laid out when I arrived. However, I would have to wait 'til after work. This was something I wanted to follow up on alone. I didn't want to lead us somewhere that I would wind up regretting for the sake of Allain and Green.

"The manager of the club we went to—he said that victim worked all weekend, but that couldn't have been the case if he was murdered Friday night," Dick said.

"Yeah, I think we'll have to follow up on that," I replied.

"We can take it," Green said. "I was all prepared to leave anyway and it'll give me a chance to stretch my legs. Besides, the victim was our case to begin with and we can at least go question the manager."

I was wary at this prospect. On one hand, it was just another normal police/witness interaction. I was sure both Green and Allain had talked to special people before, unbeknownst to them. However, with the way things seemed lately, I didn't feel quite right letting them go talk to the werepig manager, but I still had to act normal, so I let it go.

"Have me on speed dial if anything pops up," I said.

"Okay, Dad," Green said as her lips turned up in a grin, "but don't worry, I will."

I turned to Dick once they left. "We need to go talk to Captain Benoit."

"You really think that's a good idea?" he replied. "Usually, he only likes us to brief him when we have all the evidence."

"I know, but something about the way this is unfolding, I feel like we should let him know just in case it spirals wider than it should."

Dick shrugged his shoulders in response and followed me when I left the room, being careful to slip by Lieutenant Martine's office so she wouldn't see us. The last thing we needed was her asking why we were going to go talk to the captain. If I told her we had to brief him, she would get upset because part of her job as a lieutenant in the department was doing just what we were going to do—brief the higher-ups.

We walked to Captain Benoit's office and thankfully, he was there.

"Captain? A moment?" I asked at the doorway.

The captain sat behind his heavy desk, reading a report in a manila folder. He didn't see us until he looked up when I spoke. He raised his hand and motioned us to enter and have a seat, then looked back down at the report in his hand to finish reading.

After a few seconds, he closed the folder and put it on his desk, and gave us his undivided attention.

"What can I do for you two?" he asked.

I relayed all the stuff that had happened so far, and he listened impassively while I spoke. When I finished, he raised his hand to his chin and rubbed it, while deep in thought. After a moment, he spoke. "This sounds like it's becoming more complicated."

"I agree, sir," I replied.

"Well, do what you can, and keep me up to date. Also, watch out for Green and Allain. We don't want to ruin them," he said.

"Already on it, sir," I replied.

What he meant by "ruin" was that some people didn't adjust well when they found out that the world they knew wasn't what they had thought. Some minds can no longer hold it together and unfortunately, some of the folks you see that are out of their minds were once "normies" who saw too much one day and were never the same since. I mean, even those of us who were "normies" at one time and became something different (like I did), there was a period of adjustment and that's not always easy. In fact, it's quite traumatic and some don't make it. But I suppose that's true of most people that face trauma of some sort—some make it through, and some don't.

I waited until after work and headed over to City Park. The sun was still high in the sky and the listed park hours let me know it was open for another couple of hours. Not that it mattered. It was a large park, and I'm sure there had been many times and many types of people who accessed the area after hours.

I parked in the designated parking area, which consisted of gravel, then went down the path that took me across a footbridge spanning a waterway. I looked down as I passed and saw nothing out of the ordinary in the water. After the bridge, the pathway headed deeper into the woods. And although the sun was still up, it was at a point that it cast shadows, which only deepened by the minute. You never know what you might come across out here, so I remained on guard. Other cars in the parking lot let me know that it was more than likely there were other people enjoying the park. I saw a couple walking hand in hand. I saw another group of people, who wore workout clothes and were breathing heavily from walking the path quickly. When they saw me, they shied away and didn't make eye contact. I can't blame them as when I looked down at my own thrift store suit, I knew I looked out of place here in the woods.

Soon, I was alone on the path that criss-crossed other paths, but I found my way just fine. I finally came to the spot in the trail that I remembered from my previous times out this way; it sloped upwards and had logs placed every so often in the ground to assist with walking up the trail. At the end, I found the "mountain" top. I know, like I said, it's not a mountain at all—just a large hill and not very large, at that. Maybe if there weren't so many trees around, it would look different, but honestly, if you didn't know that it was the highest point in the area, you wouldn't have guessed it.

It was quiet now; not even birds were chirping. I felt a chill run through me, and I wasn't sure if it was the weather or something else. Either way, it just felt weird to me. When I made it to the top, I looked down where I stood, and just like in the picture I had with me, there was the map of the city of New Orleans etched into the concrete slab. The slab was clean. I was impressed. Whoever cleaned it did a good job. I couldn't even tell that just a couple of days ago, there were blood and literal guts all over that slab. Absolutely no inkling of what had taken place. Had the walkers I came across just a few minutes prior only known, I'm pretty sure this place would have been empty for weeks.

I looked at the photo and made comparisons. One arm lay roughly where the French Quarter was located...or maybe it was the Port of New Orleans. The other arm rested in the township of Metairie, while the legs were positioned over in the west bank, with one over a town named Gretna and the other in a town called Westwego. While the body was obviously decapitated, the head was placed at what appeared to be where I was currently standing, in City Park. The torso lay directly under the head, partially in the center of the star. All this led me to believe that if I was seeing this right, there were probably going to be a few more bodies and some other gruesome sights. I had a hunch the placement of the bodies on the map was a good indication as to where they would be found.

The problem now would be jurisdiction. Some of those areas are covered by different law enforcement agencies and if I went sticking my nose in a different area without letting them know—well, let's just say, that creates bad blood. However, I didn't want to go bringing in others quite yet because then it would lead to briefings and egos. I'm pretty sure every police department or sheriff's office has someone like me—the one who investigates the "special" situations, but some of the smaller agencies don't, so with them, you have to tread extra lightly. Thankfully, I had good relations with the Jefferson Parish Sheriff's Office and the Gretna Police Department, so I didn't think there would be an issue there.

I stayed around and took photos with my cell phone, so I could have a quick reference. I then decided to walk the trails surrounding LaBorde Mountain, to see if my nose could pick up the scent of either another body or cinnamon. Nothing stood out to me. I must have lost track of time because I then noticed that the sun had sunk below the horizon and the shadows lengthened into plain darkness. Thankfully, because of my natural abilities, I could see quite well in the dark, but I didn't see, hear or smell any civilians. I still couldn't shake the feeling that I was being watched. I don't have what you call a true sixth sense but sometimes out of the blue, I just get a weird feeling...and I've learned to trust that over time.

I had my sidearm in its holster underneath my jacket and lowered my hand to rest on the butt of the pistol. I needed to leave before they locked the gate and my ride got stuck where I couldn't drive out, so I made my way back toward the parking area. I was careful not to rush too much and create noise or prevent me from hearing anything out of the ordinary in the environment.

I know I mentioned this park is used for a lot of different reasons, from general enjoyment of the local population to religious and ceremonial needs. I neglected to mention that some creatures and things of a supernatural bent chose to live here. Mostly because it was considered hallowed ground and was, as a rule, safe.

I hadn't gone 20 feet down the trail when suddenly, I knew I wasn't alone. Nothing in particular gave it away. I mean, I still couldn't see or smell anything, but regardless, I knew I wasn't alone. Don't ask me how—I just did.

I cautiously moved to the center of the path and lowered my center of gravity a bit, so if something jumped out at me, I'd be able to use my weight to throw or move out of the way. Most "surprises" can be avoided if you're aware of your surroundings.

It grew dark, and the sound of rustling leaves grew in my ears. I looked around and saw shapes in the woods, or rather, I saw trees...but these trees moved.

Chapter Seven

I felt like calling out, "Halt, who goes there?!" but I felt silly, so I bladed myself by positioning my body 45 degrees toward the threat, keeping my strong hand and my pistol to the side farthest away. I wanted all the advantages I could get and by doing that, I could draw with my right hand and use it, even if whatever was in the trees was fast enough to grab my left arm. One shape became two and two became four. Before I knew it, there was a small crowd of shapes in my view. I heard a voice call out from the dark shadows in front of me. It sounded hollow, like wind going through an opening in a dead tree.

"Relax. We follow the accords here, werewolf. There is no need to be afraid, unless you come to bring harm to us," it said.

My brain ran through all the options of what this could mean, and when one of the shapes stepped out onto the pathway, my assumption was confirmed. Dryad.

What's a dryad, you ask? Well, they're wood spirits and look like trees. Their skin is made of bark, and they can transform into trees. No one would be wiser to walk past one on a sunny day, which I suspected happened quite frequently in this part of the park. However weird it may sound, I never heard of them being predatory. They could be dangerous, no doubt, but the only cases I ever heard of them causing harm were in self-defense. Though they did like to play jokes on the unsuspecting, which is why when you walk through the woods at night and hear things, it's usually these dryads trying to scare you or just having a good time.

"No, I'm not here to bring harm," I replied. I stood upright and took my hand away from the firearm to prove it. Besides, if they all attacked me, I really didn't have a fighting chance, anyway.

The dryad that came to the path cocked its head to the side and looked at me. Its eyes—well, I couldn't tell if they focused on me or not—appeared to be looking right through me. But after a short moment, it shifted its gaze from my face and looked around me as if looking at my aura (if I had one), then it sniffed.

"What you say is true, but these are strained times," it said.

"When are they not?" I asked nonchalantly, to lighten the mood. It didn't appear to affect its mood at all. The figure stood still, as if I had said nothing at all. "Right..." I said slowly. "Why are times strained now?"

Again, it stood still. In the darkness, I wasn't sure if it was the female or male variant. They looked very similar, and they were still half tree, so some of their mannerisms and attributes were alike, as in movement, thought, and their slow, deliberate speech.

"What brings you to our woods, werewolf?" it asked, ignoring my question.

"There was a murder here and the accords of safe haven weren't followed," I said.

After a short thought, it replied, "Ah...you must be the one that works for the law keepers."

I get this from time to time. People that weren't normies, like me, rarely work in positions where you're surrounded by them day in and day out. I know I mentioned it before, but it's an anomaly, so if anyone ever mentioned a werewolf and NOPD, it's me. If they had mentioned vampire, it would have been Dick.

"Yes, the one and the same," I replied. "Do you or any of your group know or see what happened here the other night?"

"Unfortunately not. Someone used great magic to blanket the area in darkness. We did not see a thing, nor did we hear anything," it said.

"That stinks. I was hoping for something," I said.

No reply came, and I felt I had hit a dead end when it suddenly spoke. "We did smell cinnamon in the air that evening."

That jogged my memory from my own crime scene involving the dead dancer, Ms. Vincente. "Cinnamon?" I answered. "Do you know why?"

"No."

"Besides me and the officers that were here the other night, have you seen anything out of the ordinary or anyone from the other side of the veil that came through?" I asked.

"People, creatures, and all things come through here from time to time. We don't get involved."

"Why did you stop me now?" I asked.

"Just because we don't get involved doesn't mean that we don't hold the standards and want to keep things balanced. What happened here is in the middle of what we call home and to upset the balance here requires a reckoning," it replied. "Also, we haven't seen werewolves out this way in a very long time, so we wanted to know your intentions."

"I see. Well, as I told you, I'm trying to find whoever did this," I said as I shrugged my shoulders. I was at my wit's end so far; just a bunch of questions and no answers. "Well, if you need anything or find out anything, you can…" I was about to leave my card, but realized they probably didn't use cell phones. "Well, you can contact me."

"We will send a messenger if that indeed comes to fruition," it said.

The encounter was apparently over because the figure stepped back to the tree line, along with the other shadowed dryads, then they sort of melded back into the darkness. I was alone again on the path. By this time, it was full-blown night.

The parking lot was empty. All the day trippers had gone home, leaving only me. I walked up to my car and found that my left driver's side tire was flat. I bent down to take a closer look; a knife or something sharp had punctured it. I glanced around to check if anyone was watching nearby or was about to attack, as someone could have done this to delay me and divert my attention from my surroundings. I didn't see, hear, or smell anyone or anything. Whoever did it was long gone, which in all honesty, I would have rather they'd stuck around. I know what you're thinking and you'd be wrong. I wasn't looking for a fight or payback, but I did want to identify who did it.

This small act concerned me. It was a subtle way of telling me to back off without being overt enough to show who was behind it. This told me two things—one, they knew I'm looking into this and two, I should keep my eyes open. You never knew when a mild threat could turn into a real and immediate more serious one.

I changed the tire and went home. As I drove, I didn't go the most direct route. I took different roads and even doubled back on myself a couple of times to see if anyone was following me. Of course, in this day and age, it was probably a moot point with all the available technology. Hell, they probably already knew where I lived or had a tracking device on my car that I was unaware of, but old habits die hard, so it took me twice as long to get home.

Morgane squawked as I entered.

"And a good evening to you," I said.

She didn't reply, but hopped on the counter and cocked her head to the side, looking me over. At this point of the day, I was tired of getting sized up; it seemed like it was a common theme lately.

"Long day?" she said.

"You could say that," I replied, then changed the subject because I didn't want to talk about it. "Morgane, in all the years I've known you, you never hang out with other crows."

She bobbed her head up and down before screeching, "They like me not...but I like them not either."

She then flew and landed on my shoulder. Before I could do anything, she pecked at my ear. "That's for trying to change the subject. What's going on? Squawk!"

I took my hand and placed it on my shoulder; when she stepped on it, I lowered her back down to the counter. I then went to the fridge, grabbed a cold one, and sat down.

"Have you seen anyone hanging out around the house lately?" I asked.

"No," she screeched, "Should I?"

"I don't know, but I think someone is telling me to leave the case I'm working on alone."

"Really?"

I told her what happened at the park, and she hopped from leg to leg while I did. I know, it's a weird relationship having a conversation with my bird friend, but it's strange what you get used to. When I finished retelling my tale, she cawed loudly and flew to the top of the cabinets and looked down, agitated. She beat her wings, then folded them and settled down, apparently deep in thought, and didn't make a sound.

"Morgane?" I asked, "Are you okay?"

"Of course I'm okay. Squawk!" she replied, "I am concerned, however."

"Why?" I asked.

"Because your description of events has me thinking about things best not spoke of," she replied.

This also happened from time to time. Even though I didn't know her background completely, I realized she knew quite a bit. Don't let the little feathered body fool you. There was a brain there and one that doesn't forget. On more than a few occasions, something she thought about either solved a case or led me down the right path, so I was all ears when she spoke.

"Those deaths are special; it all means something," Morgane squeaked out but as she continued, her voice dropped into a low, conspiratorial tone. "The balance is being shifted, though who is involved, I know not...but this reeks of dark magic."

"What makes you say that?" I replied. "I agree that something is being pushed to rock the boat, but why dark magic?"

"The smell of cinnamon you mentioned. You will find more bodies in those locations and when you do, you will smell cinnamon, but it's not cinnamon—it's calycanthus floridus," she replied.

"What?" I asked. "I've never heard of that."

"It's commonly called Carolina allspice and you can find the plant most everywhere here in the southeast. It's not used very much in ritual, but I know it can be used in this instance to bind things together to make a spell more powerful."

"What kind of spell?" I asked. I've never studied the occult, Voodoo, or the dark arts of wizards and witches, but I have come across them from time to time.

"That I know not. But someone is making sure that these events are bound together," she said.

My mind raced, thinking of people I could reach out to follow up with. I should petition the regional high council located here in New Orleans. No, you wouldn't know anything about it, but every region in the world has a regional high council that covers an area. Like I've mentioned before, these councils are to keep the peace and resolve conflict between the different types of non-normies.

I decided to wait on that, though, as I needed to find the other bodies for evidence. It was necessary to get as much information as possible before I presented it to the captain and the higher-ups. There was a clause in my…uh…"special" employment that I could jump rank if the need ever arose, but thankfully, it hadn't yet and I didn't want to start now. The less people know about me, the better. There was one time in my life where I went out of my way to make contacts to try to make the world a better place, but that backfired so badly. Well, I learned my lesson, but that's a story for another time. If you're lucky, I'll tell you about it sometime later.

The next morning, I called Dick and told him I would be in the office later than normal and that I was heading over to Lafreniere Park in Metairie. The park is the largest one in Metairie, and according to the photos of the map with the various bodies positioned, it looked like one of them may very well be where the park was located. I wasn't absolutely sure, but since the head was placed over City Park in New Orleans, I figured it couldn't hurt to start there.

The park is very picturesque, if you haven't seen it. It's home to a lake, a few playground areas, soccer fields, and a bird sanctuary. Around the perimeter and through the park is a jogging trail, as well as quite a few walking paths. I arrived at about 7 AM and there were a few cars there already, with people enjoying the bright and sunny morning as they jogged or enjoyed the scenery. In the lake, there was an island that was accessible by one bridge and that bridge was behind a locked gate. This was to keep the birds safe from park visitors, and in some way, probably keep the people safe from the birds. The geese that lived there could be highly territorial.

I parked my car and meandered for a bit, taking my time, and breathing in, smelling, hoping that I would pick up on a scent. I looked out of place, as there was a stark contrast from my cheap suit and the bag of donuts I bought on the way to the park as opposed to the other folks that were there in fitness attire. I just nodded with my wolfish grin and acted like I was supposed to be there, which didn't really matter because it was a public place and most people were too caught up in themselves to notice others.

As I walked to the east and approached the island, I caught a very faint whiff of decay. I kept hoping to be wrong because for something as heinous as murder to be committed in such a pleasant place seemed a travesty...polar opposites...a dichotomy, if you will. The further I went, the more I knew that I'd be disappointed and sure enough, when I got to the bridge and its locked gate, I knew the smell came from the other side. No one would have noticed the smell unless they had some serious olfactory talents or were special like me. Dogs would pick up on it, but since the ones brought here were on leashes, their owners wouldn't have thought anything of it if one stopped and took interest.

I decided I should probably call one of my contacts with Jefferson Parish to come over to look. Since this was out of my jurisdiction, it was the polite and right thing to do. I took out my phone and called the only contact I knew who worked these kinds of cases.

"Hello, this is Cormac McDougall," the voice on the line said.

"Hey man, this is Lou Giroux, NOPD," I said quickly.

"...I can't come to the phone right now but if you leave your name, number and a brief message, I will be sure to get back to you," the voice continued.

Oh, for the love of all things holy and not, this was the last thing I needed. "Cormac, this is Lou from NOPD. I'm looking into something at Lafrienere Park. Call me back," I said. I hung up and returned the phone to my pocket, but before I removed my hand, I felt the phone vibrate, indicating a call. I took it out and saw that it was Cormac.

"Hello?" I asked.

Without so much as a greeting, he began, "What are you doing in my area, Lou? Is this sanctioned?"

That was a good question. Sometimes when we were working the special cases, "sanctioned" meant we could go anywhere and do pretty much anything to resolve a case. Since there were so many moving parts to what I was working on, I didn't it run it up the chain of command.

"Uh...No Cormac, that's why I wanted to talk to you before I did anything," I replied.

"Where are you?" he asked.

"I'm at Lafrienere Park," I replied.

"Okay," he said and disconnected, which left me uncertain. He had never been that short with me before. It had always been professional, but something didn't feel right this time. Of course, it could have been one of those days. Lord knows that I've had them, too.

I didn't wait but a few minutes before I saw him coming up the sidewalk. He stood about six feet and towered over me in human form. He had short, brilliant white hair; a goatee that matched; and eyes the color of blue frost that would make lesser men melt if he ever focused on them in anger. He wore a long coat and even though we were heading into winter in a couple months, it was still warm—too warm for a jacket like that and although it made him stick out, he had been wearing it every time I saw him.

"This is a very large park, Cormac. How did you get here and find me so fast?" I asked.

He looked at me and gave me a sly grin. He raised his right hand and made a swirling motion. Oh, I forgot to mention...Cormac is a wizard.

Chapter Eight

"Right," I said.

"Yeah, just did a location spell and then walked through the portal," he said.

"That sure comes in handy. I bet you save a ton on gas," I replied.

"Yeah, but you know as well as I do, I have to keep up appearances. If you hadn't sounded so urgent, I would have driven," he said.

"How could you know it was urgent?" I asked.

"I didn't. I just needed an excuse to magic myself here," he replied.

Wizards and witches could practice, but they couldn't practice openly unless it was sanctioned or within the properly designated areas. And as a wizard, he certainly could have been downright wealthy with his considerable talents. Lord knew he didn't work at the Sheriff's office for the money, but he, like I, felt a certain need to make things right.

"How do you do that with no one seeing you?" I asked, with what I'm sure was a look of curiosity.

"Easy. I make myself invisible, open a gateway, and step through. Once I see what's going on, and when no one is watching, I pop back...okay, so are we done with 20 questions? What are you doing here?" he asked.

This was completely different from how he sounded on the phone.

"Are you okay?" I asked, "On the phone, you seemed..."

"Right...my boss was standing there, and I had to make it seem important," he said.

"Well, I think it's going to be pretty important here shortly, but we need to keep it quiet. I feel that this will disrupt...both worlds," I said.

"Hmm...that doesn't sound good. What do you got?" he replied.

"I'm working a case and I believe it's a multiple murder and uh...I think," I said as I nodded my head toward the island, "That there's something waiting for us over there. I can smell it."

Cormac's eyebrows raised a little when I said that, which all but confirmed that there was something over there. He knew what I was. Heck, all of us in southeast Louisiana that worked special activities knew each other. That didn't make us close friends or anything, but we did have a mutual respect for each other's abilities and talents. For instance, if I had to take Cormac down for whatever reason, I knew he could probably beat me if I wasn't quick. Although I am magic resistant doesn't mean I'm immune and the things that I knew he could do...well, let's just say, we all respected each other and didn't want to test the waters.

"I see," he finally said, then added, "Well, let's go check it out."

He stepped up to the gate and took the lock in one hand, closed his eyes in concentration, and waved his other hand over it. I didn't hear what he said, but he muttered something, and a slight glow appeared around the lock. I glanced around to see if anyone near saw us, but no one was paying attention to our actions. I looked back. The lock was open, and Cormac swung the gate open.

"If anyone outside those in the know asks," he said, "We received a call about a murder and the gate was open when we got here, all right?"

I shrugged, nodded my agreement, and followed him across the bridge. As we did so, we disturbed the seagulls who took refuge on the railing of the concrete bridge. They laughed and cawed while looking at us accusingly as they flew away, since we had disturbed them.

My nose was working overtime. I could smell all different kinds of birds on the island. To be honest, I was getting hungry, but don't worry—I wasn't about to start chowing down. I like my food cooked these days. When we stepped on the island, I smelled a new, yet familiar, smell. It was a hint of cinnamon. I followed it until the smell of rot overpowered it, which brought us to the very center of the island where a corpse greeted us. I've seen my share of dead bodies and the state of this one wasn't bad considering the location—out in the open, surrounded by water and carrion birds. It looked to be a female with short, brown hair, fully clothed in jeans and a nondescript top that might have been black but now appeared brown with mud.

I looked around and from this vantage point, trees secluded the area from prying eyes. Even the folks that walked on the nearby wood bridge that skirted the sanctuary island couldn't see us.

"Well, it's confirmed. You were right. Not that I had any doubts," he said.

Looking at the body at our feet, I leaned in closer to see if I could identify anything strange about it, but there was nothing out of the ordinary for a body at that stage of decomposition. I stood and looked at him. "I got nothing," I said.

He looked down at the deceased and reached into his coat to pull something from an inner pocket. He then stretched his hand out over the body and murmured a few words as he waved his hand in the air, letting dust or dirt or some sort of spell component fall.

I waited a few moments for him to finish, which he did abruptly. He snapped his hand back quickly and then turned to look at me with a gleam in his eye. Apparently, whatever spell he cast didn't come back the way he wanted it to.

"What are you investigating? And just what have you gotten me into?" he asked.

I cocked my head to the side and looked at him carefully, then asked, "What did you find?"

"Absolutely nothing, which tells me there is high sorcery here. The spell I cast always brings me back something...an image, a smell...could be small, sometimes large...but it always brings me something. But not this time. When that happens, I know there's something serious going on, so spill the beans. What have you got?" he asked.

"I'm still not sure. I'm still trying to figure it out, but there are other locations in the area where I think we're going to find more bodies...at least three other locations," I said.

"Jesus, Joseph and Mary, Lou, are you kidding me? This isn't some quick wrongling deed done here. You're talking about some major wrongling, like human sacrifice and dark magic," he replied.

"Voodoo?" I asked.

"No, what are you thinking? Seriously? I mean, I know there's dark Voodoo, but this isn't it," he replied.

I really didn't know. When it came to the mystical arts, I purposely avoided them unless it was mystical arts in the kitchen. Now that I could totally get behind and have on several occasions. On a side note—did you know that's why New Orleans has some of the best restaurants in the world? It's not just the cooking, but also the magic that goes into it. You'd be surprised.

"Something big is coming," Cormac said.

"What do you mean?" I asked.

"I don't know, but considering what you told me, I smell cinnamon, which indicates a binding spell. Something that has that many deaths and locations involved…well, I'd venture to guess it was a summoning spell and not your run of the mill, 'let's summon a demon or imp'," he said. "We really need to alert the council."

"Man, I really don't want to deal with them until I have all my ducks in a row and find all the locations. Once word gets out, I'm afraid whoever did this will simply disappear or worse—attack—because they know how close we are. In fact, I think they already know," I said as I thought about the flat tire I had the night before.

"Things are going to get weird, then," he said. "You said there were others?"

"Yeah, over in Gretna, and another in Westwego," I said.

Those two places were small towns on the west bank of the Mississippi River, but as the crow flies, it was south of New Orleans. That was how New Orleans got the nickname "Crescent City." If you looked at it on a map, the Mississippi River wrapped around the city in the shape of a "U", or…ta da!…a crescent.

"That's my jurisdiction, as well. Well, they have their own police departments, but those agencies are so small, they uh...don't have people like us, so I better tag along," he said.

"Fine with me," I said.

I know a lot of my kind think I'm a lone wolf and, for the most part, I am. I told you before about the troubles of hanging out with non-law-enforcement kin, but it didn't mean that I didn't like hanging out with people. And besides, when facing danger, having an extra person around is always helpful.

My phone buzzed loudly in my pocket. When I pulled it out, Dick's number was displayed. I clicked to answer and said, "What do you need, Dick?"

"I think you need to head back to the office. Lieutenant Martine is upset," he said.

"Do you know what about?" I asked.

"No, I don't know what's going on, but I think something's up. She said that she wanted you to come back right away, and you know how she gets," he said.

Unfortunately, I did. She had a way about her that when she was angry about something...well, for being a "normie," she was still a force to be reckoned with.

"All right, I'll be right there...maybe 20 to 30 minutes," I said and disconnected the call.

"Everything all right?" Cormac asked.

"Yeah, my lieutenant wants to see me," I replied.

"Oh...well, good luck," he said, and smiled as if he could tell by my facial expression that I wasn't looking forward to it.

"Yeah, yeah," I replied and continued while nodding toward the body, "Do you mind taking care of this? And letting me know the identity as soon as you know?"

"What?! That's just like you. Get me involved and then take off, leaving me to deal with the mess," he said.

"But it's your jurisdiction. Trust me, if this was in New Orleans, I'd be dealing with it," I said.

"Right. You'd probably hand it off to a uniform," he said.

"Maybe, but I would get it handled," I said, a smirk forming on my lips.

"Oh, get out of here, and I'll let you know. But all joking aside, Lou, if you go to the west bank looking for other bodies, let me know. I may have some spells that will help locate those victims," he said.

I arrived at the station and headed up to our little piece of paradise on the third floor. When I entered our office, I could feel something ominous, almost like an extra presence had entered. I smelled nothing nor did I hear anything out of the ordinary, but something was different and something within me pinged my conscious to warn me. I stopped and looked into Dick's cubicle; he wasn't there. For that matter, neither were Greene nor Allain. The rest of the detectives were steadily working, either on the phone or typing out case notes.

I walked through the rest of the office, nodding to friendly faces as I went. However, my mind raced. Just what was going on here that needed me?

When I arrived at the lieutenant's office, I heard her shout from behind me, "We're in the conference room."

If we weren't meeting in her office, then that meant we had visitors, and when I whirled around, my suspicions were confirmed. It was a full house: Greene; Allain; Dick; Lieutenant Martine; Martine's boss, Captain Thibodeaux; Captain Benoit; Thibodeaux and Benoit's boss, Deputy Superintendent Savoie; and two other people I didn't recognize.

"Good, I'm glad you could join us, Detective Giroux. Now we can start," Lieutenant Martine said.

She called me by my title and last name. This didn't look good. It was like when your mom called you by your first, middle and last name when you were in trouble, and I had no idea what for. I looked at Dick when I entered the room; he looked back and shrugged lightly. Okay, he didn't know what this was about either. Greene and Allain looked about as confused as the rest of us were.

I took my seat at the conference table and looked at the two newcomers. They were well-dressed, but immediately, something was off about them. Again, for all my powers and super senses, they don't always come into play when figuring out a problem and these two...something about them spoke of problems. One looked to be an older middle-aged man with dark hair that had gone white over the years and eyes that looked out from tortoiseshell eyeglasses. His suit was designer-made and probably cost 10 times more than my thrift store special. The lady with him fit well. She was young and beautiful, with a smile that said she always got what she wanted. It was also the kind of smile that hid shark teeth if she didn't get it. I couldn't help it, but I immediately didn't like these two newcomers.

"Good morning, everyone. I know some of us made introductions but since we are starting the meeting, let's go around the room and introduce ourselves, so everyone is aware of who is who," Lt Martine said, then she started with her own introduction.

I now realized what was going on and understood why Lieutenant Martine was upset. This was a leadership briefing, probably on the two murders (and likely more) we were working, but this one was different than usual. Usually, cases like ours didn't warrant such high official visits so early. In the grand scheme of things, the case was just starting, so this was extremely irregular.

With where I sat and after I saw how the introductions were making their way, I realized I was going to be last. I knew everyone else, so I paid little attention to what they said, but when one of the officials—the lady—began to speak, my ears perked up and I nonchalantly paid more attention.

"I am Celeste Dufrene. I'm from the mayor's office and there is some interest over at City Hall about what happened at City Park," she said and then sat down. Short, sweet and to the point. Next came her counterpart, the older man.

"Hi everyone. I am Robert Arnaud, and I'm also from the mayor's office, like Ms. Dufrene," he began and said a few more words, but at that point I turned my attention to the lady that was with him. She sat at the far end of the opposite side of the table from me. She looked around the room like she owned the place. It seemed odd to me, so I leaned in and sniffed. She wore a subtle perfume and although no one would have smelled it at the table, I could, but only because I directed my focus on it. The perfume smelled of cinnamon, but there was also a scent of plum that overpowered the cinnamon. I was going for another sniff when I heard Lieutenant Martine speak. "Detective Giroux?"

Apparently, I had become so focused that I hadn't noticed that it was my turn to introduce myself and when I realized it, all eyes were on me. Mixtures of curiosity to concern to anger from the police leadership for wasting time.

"Oh...my turn?" I said, knowing very well it was, and continued like nothing happened, "Lou Giroux, NOPD detective..."

Chapter Nine

Now that we were all introduced, I expected we were all to play nicely and share what we knew about the case. But with everything going on, I felt it would be a better idea to hold the cards close to my chest on this one until I figured out more about it. I looked over at Dick and he returned a look that gave me the impression that he felt the same.

To Greene and Allain, however, this was just another run-of-the-mill murder case. Who cared about who knew what? I almost felt jealous of them for not having to think about all the possible ramifications of this crime. To them, this was just an ill-fated occurrence in the city of New Orleans, which unfortunately happens from time to time. But for Dick and me? Well, we had other things to worry about. Power play? Politics? Dark arts gone bad? There were so many ways this could play out and none of them were good. And why was Captain Benoit so cool about all of this? He didn't so much as blink an eye at Dick or me.

I decided to keep cool and learn as much as I could from the two officials. Detective Green started off with what we had so far, which, truth be told, wasn't much. She mentioned they talked to the manager of the club, Mr. Sus, but said he told them that when Dick and I had interviewed him, he had gotten Brian Stearns mixed up with someone else and that he wasn't there over the weekend, after all. She mentioned the only connection between our victims being the club, and that was pretty much it. There wasn't much fluff as it was straightforward and professional.

The city officials took everything in, and Mr. Arnaud asked Green if there were any other murders associated to which she responded that, as far as she knew, there hadn't been. Of course, I knew there were more, but I was holding back on disclosing that tidbit of information until I knew exactly what we were dealing with.

"Thank you, Detective Greene," Lt. Martine said. "Do you have anything to add, Detective Giroux?"

All eyes focused on me again. I felt like a fox in a henhouse that had been caught. But I remained cool, cleared my throat, and replied, "No, ma'am, I have nothing to add. Sounds like Detective Green pretty much covered everything we know so far."

Dick must have heard my heart beating because he cocked his head to listen and turned to look at me. I could feel him weighing me and was obviously curious about what I knew because he knew I just lied...ahem...it wasn't an actual lie, but I did skirt the truth. Yes, I knew more, but I honestly had nothing to add to the briefing because nothing was concrete. The fact that I found a body at Lafreneire Park...I mean, come on, that could have been a total coincidence. And that's how I rationalize things to make them feel acceptable in my mind. Hey, don't look at me like that. Anyway, the lady's eyes lingered on me as everyone else went forward with the meeting. I could feel her bore into me. There was something about her. I knew she knew more than she was letting on. This was merely nothing more than a probe to see how much we really did know. Perhaps the mayor's office was in on it. It wouldn't have surprised me one bit if that, in fact, turned out to be the case.

I felt a pressure in my head and it surprised me. I don't usually get headaches. My natural healing ability (or unnatural, depending on how you look at it) didn't allow me to have many ailments unless it was an immediate or direct result of a fight. But a pressure-building headache? I couldn't remember the last time I had one of those.

"What do you know?" I heard a voice in my mind, and I knew at once it was Celeste Dufrene in my head. I almost jumped like I had been shot, but I caught control of myself before I panicked. It's not every day you have two voices in your own head. I now knew two things: one, that Ms. Dufrene definitely wasn't a normie, and two, she was in my head. I have had dealings with this kind of intrusion before, which meant she was either part demon or siren, or maybe she worked with magic. Either way, I didn't have time to dwell on that now, as I had more pressing matters to attend to...like how to get this intruder out of my head. I immediately focused my mind and conjured a wall around my conscious thought, while thinking and replying to the voice in my head, "Get out!"

Ms. Dufrene and I locked eyes. I could see that this intrusion wasn't easy for her either, but she maintained a level of detachment and coolness that one would chalk up to snobbery, which, in her case, probably happened quite a bit.

The pressure didn't subside, and I could feel little rivulets of sweat bead up on my forehead. It's strange what you notice in a fight, whether it be physical or mental.

"Detective Giroux?" Lt. Martine asked. "Are you okay?"

The amount of concentration it took to keep my mind shrouded was extremely taxing, but I managed to respond. "Yeah, I'm okay. Feeling a little off at the moment. Must have been something I ate."

Or maybe it was the fact I was trying to throw this she-witch out of my mind. She was still there. "Oh, come on, let me in," the voice said, then taunted playfully, "I promise to be gentle."

"Get out!" my mind screamed.

I saw the shark smile appear on Ms. Dufrene's face. She seemed to enjoy this. Probably because she had not faced many obstacles before when she used this particular skill.

"I know what you are, werewolf, and I know your partner is a vampire. I've read your files."

"Get out!" I maintained my protest.

I heard Lt. Martine's voice, though it was faint because even though I was fighting in my mind, the meeting and the focus was still on me from her question to see if I was okay.

"If you need to take a moment, I think we can continue this meeting without you," I heard Lt. Martine say.

"Good," I thought to myself.

"Good?" the voice said. "You haven't gotten away from me, Detective Giroux. I will find out the secrets you keep."

"Good luck...dang it...get out!" I almost cracked. When you're throwing an entity out of your mind, it's best to maintain focus on one thing, the goal in this case being to get it out as quickly as possible. To engage in conversation can lead to loss of focus, then the defenses begin to crumble.

"Yes, Lieutenant, I think that would be a good idea. Thank you," I said.

Abruptly, I felt the pressure subside, and she was gone, just like that. It was like coming up for a breath of fresh air after holding your breath underwater for an uncomfortable duration. I could feel the freedom of being alone with my thoughts again.

All eyes in the conference room were still on me. Dick looked at me with mild interest, as did Captain Benoit. Everyone else turned their attention back to the meeting. Mr. Arnaud dismissed me without saying a word. And Ms. Dufrene? She looked me straight in the eye and gave me a huge smile—a knowing smile. And to be honest with you, it scared the bejesus out of me. I needed to figure out exactly who she was and just what the hell was going on here.

I quickly left the room and went straight to the bathroom to wash my face. I wiped my face with a wet paper towel and looked at myself in the mirror. Yep, still me. I felt violated and only through sheer willpower and focus was I able to keep her from the rest of my thoughts and mind.

I wasn't sure what to do next. I needed some help with this, so I left the precinct straight away and headed toward the old bookstore. I had to go speak to Hannah and figure out if she knew who Ms. Dufrene was.

The bookstore was busy and so was Harry, who looked to be dealing with a young, pimply-faced man with thick eyeglasses about some old, out-of-print book. Harry said nothing to me directly but looked at me and nodded upwards to let me know Hannah was in her usual place. So off I went again, to the back and up the stairs. When I reached the third floor, I stepped out onto the creaking floor and looked around. It was quiet and cool, but I wasn't alone. There were two people in the room looking at the old vinyl records, exclaiming to one another how they hadn't seen some of the band names in years and showing each other ones they liked. Tourists of some sort, as they had camera gear with them, and they were obviously a couple. There's no way that Hannah would come and talk to me until these two left.

"Oh look, they have the Bee Gees," the woman said.

"And Waylon Jennings over here," the man replied.

The conversation went back and forth. I walked to the middle of the room and thumbed through the boxes myself. They really did have a good selection here. The couple stopped talking out loud to one another and I had to chuckle a little. They felt totally comfortable until someone showed up and now, they didn't say anything. I was kind of banking on this, though. I moved closer but didn't look at them. I even started to mumble the band names, and I kept edging closer to them. I could tell they were getting a little concerned by my presence. I could see them from the corner of my eye glance my way as they moved farther away, but I kept edging closer, not in a dangerous way, but in a way that made it uncomfortable.

They left shortly without saying another word. I couldn't help but feel a little bad and hated that I ran them off, but I really needed to talk to Hannah.

"Why did you go and do that?" I heard the voice before I saw her.

I turned to respond, "Do what?"

"Don't act like the dumb dog you are," Hannah replied. "You know what you did, running those people off."

"They weren't going to buy anything. They were just browsing," I said.

"So, you can't just run our customers out. You know how many impulse buys we get that help keep the lights on?" she asked demurely.

I honestly had no idea about their sales but she was right—this was a business first and foremost, and a supernatural hangout and refuge second.

"Your silence speaks volumes. At least you're thinking about it," Hannah continued.

"Hannah, do you know who works over at the mayor's office?" I asked, because on the one hand, I really needed to know and on the other, it provided me with an escape to change the subject.

The cat just cocked her head to the side and looked at me quizzically. "Do you think you can change the subject that quickly?"Busted. "I was sort of hoping so, Hannah. Come on, this is important," I said.

"Everyone says that, Lou, and seems to me you say that more than most when you're in here asking questions," Hannah replied.

That might be a tad true, since I relied on her quite a bit for information and goings-on in the city. In fact, at that moment, I realized that I probably needed to start working on other points of contact for information and not rely so heavily on Hannah. It always put her in a spot and, to be honest, I was never really sure if the information she provided actually helped other than a nudge. But she was someone I knew and was friendly with…even if we mostly bantered back and forth. Sometimes, that's all you need.

"Okay, let me start again. Do you know any half-demons, demigods, sirens, mind-reading enti-ties—anything of that nature—that work for the mayor's office?" I asked.

She let out a surprised meow. "Oh, that is serious. Why do you think there is one?"

I told her about my encounter with Ms. Dufrene back at the police station. Her tail flicked back and forth in agitation as she mulled over what I had said.

"I don't know of anything like that who works for the mayor. The only person I know over there that keeps an eye on things for the high council is Smidge," she said.

"Smidge?" I asked.

"Yeah, you know him, or rather…know of him," Han-nah said. "He is a statue over at City Hall."

"The golem?" I asked. I hadn't thought of that thing in a long time. Golems were stone creatures that could take on different stone forms. I remember a time in Europe that

I found out that not all stone gargoyles were lifeless, but some were golems who took that shape.

I vaguely remembered that there had been a golem placed in City Hall. Usually, they were dispatched to different areas by regional high councils around important, high-profile places and important "normie" people in case something otherworldly took place and those individuals needed help that only "we" could provide.

Golems weren't dumb. In fact, they were quite smart, but they didn't talk very much because they didn't need to. Their main purpose was to remain out of sight in plain view.

"Yes, the golem," Hannah confirmed, "And he's always there, unless I'm mistaken, or he was moved somewhere else."

"No, I think you might be right. I'll go follow up and see. I really appreciate it," I said.

"You can appreciate it all you want, but you going to buy a record?" the cat purred. "It's only fair since you ran off the other potential buyers."

I did owe her one. I probably owed her quite a few.

"Uh...sure, I'll take this one," I said as I reached down and grabbed the closest record because it didn't really matter to me.

I said my goodbyes and got halfway down the stairs before I looked down and saw what I'd picked up. Dr. Demento's Greatest Hits, a record full of novelty songs. The way this whole case was going, the song entitled "They're Coming to Take Me Away, Ha-Haaa" seemed very befitting.

I stopped at the counter and handed the record over to Harry, who looked at it, then raised an eyebrow at me. It wasn't something I usually picked up here. (Let's face it, I rarely purchased anything here.) I shrugged back innocently, and he shook his head and continued to ring me up.

I paid for it and left. Next stop would be City Hall and a certain stone figure I hoped could help me.

Chapter Ten

The main part of City Hall that housed the mayor's office was in the Central Business District (CBD as the locals call it), surrounded by tall buildings that towered over it. It was a stone's throw from the Superdome, where bands and other shows took place, as well as where a pretty popular football team played. The City Hall building looked out of place with a design that came from the mid-1950s, but for that time period, it looked very nice. I even remember when it first opened, but time hadn't been kind and what passed for cutting edge in the 1950s looked quite antiquated by today's standards.

I stopped by the guard table and flashed my badge. The guard behind the desk didn't even bat an eye. Saw my badge and nodded me on through. I took the main stairway to the second floor and made my way quickly to where I knew the mayor's suite was located. I was careful to be cognizant of my surroundings, though. The last thing I wanted was to run into Ms. Dufrene here, of all places. I didn't see any statues, so the golem had to be somewhere else on the premises.

Where would a statue be placed? I didn't see any in the foyer or the hallway here. I parked in the parking garage off Poydras Street and came in from that direction. I thought maybe there was a courtyard I missed. So, I headed back downstairs and out the door facing Duncan Plaza, a park the size of a city block across the street from City Hall. I was in the right spot because leading up to the doors of City Hall were several statues that lined the walkway leading to the door I had just exited. The statues were of prominent figures who called New Orleans home. One I immediately knew as Louis Armstrong, the world-renowned jazz singer and trumpet player. The others I wasn't sure about, but they had plaques with background information on each one. I also noticed one sign that indicated the statues were on loan from some prestigious art museum.

I looked around. There were plenty of people out walking around. This also presented a problem for me. I didn't know which one was Smidge. Yes, golems were made of stone, but they could change shapes.

I suddenly felt very awkward and exposed as I walked close to old Louis and said Smidge's name out loud. In retrospect, I should have waited until the evening, but too late. I was in it now.

Louis didn't respond, so I guessed the golem wasn't impersonating him. I went to the next statue and said his name. As I did so, I noticed two people walking past that likely heard me, so I quickly cleared my throat and brought out my phone, pretending to search for a contact. I stared at the screen and mumbled Smidge's name as I went down the list that wasn't there. When the coast was clear, I continued to the next statue and then on to all the others. About 10 minutes later, I was back to ol' Louis.

"Too bad you aren't here anymore, Satchmo. I'm sure you could have helped me out...at the very least, played some music," I said as I stepped back to look around the area, my mind contemplating what I was going to do next.

I looked up and almost urinated on myself with surprise. Louis was staring right back at me. The concrete eyes were still concrete, but they now appeared to be a highly polished form of concrete that regarded me like I was a bug. I immediately thought that this might come to blows if I didn't say something quickly. After all, the golem was here to guard and protect.

"Smidge?" I finally croaked out.

"I see you, werewolf. Are you going to mark your territory on me?" it said.

The response took me off guard at first. My mind was behind the power curve due to the surprise. Did...did this piece of rock just insult me?

We both looked around quickly to make sure the coast was still clear and, except for a couple of city folks walking down the street, it was. We then looked back at each other.

"Uh, no. I hadn't planned to," I said. "Listen, I know we don't have much time, but do you know a Ms. Dufrene who works here?"

The golem didn't reply right away. It took its time and when it did, it didn't answer my question, responding "I have all the time in the world."

This was going to be a long and tedious conversation which, along with trying to make it look like I wasn't having a conversation with a statue (which I totally was) just made the situation even more absurd. Moments passed before I tried again. "Listen, I work for NOPD. I am investigating a murder and I need to know who Ms. Dufrene is. I think she may be key in understanding what's going on."

A few more moments went by before the response came slowly and deliberately in a low, rumbling reply. "I do not know a Ms. Dufrene."

"Blonde hair, expensive tastes, can hop into other people's minds? Ring a bell?" I asked.

"Everyone in this building has expensive tastes, werewolf, but hopping into minds? That's not good," Smidge said.

I wanted to scream out, "Thanks, Captain Obvious," but I didn't want to attract attention, so I screamed silently to myself out of frustration. "Right...it's not...so she works in the mayor's office. Maybe an assistant or something? Works with another guy, Mr. Arnaud."

"Yes, I do think I know the one called Mr. Arnaud and there has been one of that description that I have seen with him, though I didn't know there was anything about her that made her special," Smidge replied. "She came here about a month or two ago. Still new to the building. Mr. Arnaud, though...he has been here for years."

"Do you know what they do here?" I asked.

"No, not really. I suppose they look into city interests on behalf of the mayor," Smidge replied.

I was nowhere closer to finding out the mystery behind Ms. Dufrene, and that worried me. I don't like it when too many unexplainable things hit me at once. And although I knew a little bit more, I didn't know much more, and I wondered if this whole trip had been a waste of time. The only new information I had was that she had only been here a short time and that could possibly mean something. Sometimes when it came to investigations, facts that seem of little significance and of no consequence alone can lead to big revelations when pieced together with other facts picked up from different events and sources.

It had been one long day so far, running around the sprawl of metro New Orleans, and I was getting tired and hungry. I felt my cell phone buzz and looked to see that Dick was calling. I said a quick goodbye to Louis...I mean Smidge, who surprisingly gave me the slightest of goodbye nods. I know they have their job to do, but I'm glad I'm not made of stone. That had to be one boring existence. My phone buzzed again, and that brought me out of my meandering thoughts of being a golem.

"Dick, what's going on?" I asked.

"Lt. Martine was looking for you. She thought you would be at your desk following the meeting," he said.

"Geeze, how long did the meeting go after I left?" I asked.

"About another hour," he said.

I looked down at my watch and realized I had left about an hour and a half ago.

"Really?" I asked, surprised. "What on earth could they have talked about for another hour?"

"To be honest, I zoned out because after our detective briefs, it switched to a brass meeting between our department heads and the mayor representatives and we were stuck for the ride. It devolved into the representatives from the mayor's office throwing around accusations about how we aren't doing our job...blah, blah, blah...you know the drill," he said.

"Ugh," I sighed, "I hate those kinds of meetings that change to something that doesn't even concern you. Then you get stuck because they forgot about you and no one gets dismissed."

"Tell me about it," Dick said. "I just experienced it. Anyway, the Lieutenant was worried about you and wanted to see how you were."

"I'm fine, but Dick, did you feel anything during the meeting? Like a probing...in your mind?" I asked.

The voice on the other end remained quiet for a few moments. "No," he said slowly. "Why? Did you?"

"Why did she single me out?" I thought to myself and then I said to Dick, "Hmm...maybe it was nothing or my imagination, but there's something different about Ms. Dufrene."

"Now, that I did pick up on, though I'm not sure what she is. But something was definitely off about her," he agreed.

"Well, I will let the Lieutenant know you're doing better and following up on the case," Dick said.

"Wait, I have more to tell you," I replied.

"What's up?" he asked.

I then told him about meeting up with Cormac in Metairie and finding the other body, which brought the current death count to three. I also filled him in about my suspicions with the other locations on the map.

"This just keeps getting weirder and weirder," he said in a low voice. "Why didn't you bring this up at the briefing?"

"Would you have?" I asked.

"No, probably not, but I'm curious about what your thoughts are. Why?" he asked.

"Probably the same as yours. Why were we having a meeting so soon with city leadership? We've never done it before this early in an investigation. Surely someone is trying to stay ahead of the power curve, either to cover something up, or maybe working parallel with us to stop whatever this means," I said. "Everything was status quo—weird, yes—but no weirder than usual until that lady jumped in my head and started talking."

"Go on," he said.

"So, I figured I'd sit on it until I understood the score," I said.

"Yes, I think you're correct with your thinking. I think the same thing," Dick said.

"That's why we get along, Dick," I said.

"Eh, I'm not sure about that, but it works for us," he replied. "All right. Well, back to what I said before...I'm going to let Lt. Martine know you stepped out to clear your head since you weren't feeling well. Just giving you a heads-up in case she asks."

"Gotcha. Much appreciated," I said.

"And Lou?" he asked.

"Yeah?"

"If something comes up, let me know and I'll be there. With the way things are heading, it'd be a good idea to pair up when going out to look for stuff."

"Yeah, sure, but I think I'll..."

"Lou, I'm serious. It's always the things we don't think about that get us, and besides, I don't want to be at this desk any more than you do," he said.

"Even in the middle of the day, out in the bright sun?" I asked.

"Most definitely then. You'll need someone to hold your leash," he replied.

"Ha, all right," I replied.

I hung up the phone and stopped off to pick up chicken pad thai from a nearby food truck that was known for its Thai food. The panel truck with a side window was in its usual spot and the orange and white color scheme was a welcome sight. My stomach growled in anticipation.

I went up to the window and ordered. They had quite an efficient system and before long, they called out the number they handed me when I ordered. I thanked the person behind the window, then found a quiet spot to enjoy my meal. My stomach thanked me as I threw the empty container in the trash.

I walked back to my car and sat behind the steering wheel, going over the day's events. I'd been all over the place and it still didn't seem like I had gone anywhere.

I looked at my watch and saw that it was close to 3 PM. My thoughts drifted toward Cormac and the body we found at Lafrienere Park that morning, but I knew he wouldn't have anything for me until tomorrow at the earliest. With nothing else to go on, I figured I would return to the office and talk to Captain Benoit to see what his thoughts were on Ms. Dufrene.

I put the car in drive when Harry from the bookstore called. "Hello?" I answered.

"Lou, can you come over?" he asked.

"Yeah, is everything okay?" I replied.

"Fine, but Hannah needs to see you," he said.

"Okay, I'll be right over," I replied and disconnected.

I think that was the first time they had ever contacted me out of the blue like that. And also, the fact that I had just been there that morning reinforced how important it probably was. Captain Benoit would have to wait.

The sign on the door to the bookstore read "Closed," which was highly unusual since the store hours reflected they should be open. I tried the door handle, and it was unlocked. The bell on the door dinged my presence. Strange—Harry wasn't at the front desk and there wasn't anyone in the store, at least at the ground level.

I heard a thump on the second floor and my heart leapt into my throat. I wouldn't be lying if I told you that I almost turned into my alter ego right then if it wasn't that it just hurt so darn much, causing me to hold back. I did take that energy and use it, though, as I moved forward quickly and took the stairs two at a time to get to the second floor.

Harry was there with a box on the floor in front of him, with its contents sprawled out. When he noticed me, he looked a little sheepish.

"Are you okay?" I asked. "You scared me."

"Yeah, I accidentally tipped the box. I was organizing. How'd you get in? You got here faster than I expected," he said.

"The front door was unlocked," I replied.

"Really? I thought I locked it," he said. "I was just stepping away to put some books up since we didn't have any customers. Anyway, Hannah is upstairs waiting for you."

I walked over and went to one knee to help Harry collect the books. That's when I realized that even though Harry looked old, he could move with the alacrity of a young man. He must have felt me watching because he quickly spoke up, "It's okay. I have this covered. Go up and see her. It's pretty important."

I shrugged, returned to my feet, and headed up the stairs to the next floor. Hannah was in plain sight, pacing back in forth. She made straight for me when she saw me. For a moment, I thought she was going to pounce.

"What took you so long?" she asked.

She spoke quickly and with a sense of urgency.

"What's wrong? I got here as quickly as I could," I replied.

"It's bad," she said.

"What's going on?" I tried again.

She stopped and looked straight into my eyes so the message she was about to give was crystal clear. "The case you are working and the spell that goes along with it?"

"Yeah," I replied.

"Well, you better find the ones who cast it by next Saturday morning," she said.

My spine felt a shiver even though I was quite warm.

"Why?" I asked.

"Because if you don't, the world as we know it will be over."

Chapter Eleven

"What do you mean?" I asked.

"I asked around, and I found out a little more about what you told me about the aroma and the ritual. At first, it didn't bother me, as I thought you were just investigating another one of those run-of-the-mill cases that involved unrest...which happens...but after researching..." she said quickly. Words tumbled from her mouth in rapid succession and I felt that if I didn't cut her off, she would keep going.

"So..." I interrupted.

"Oh right," she replied, looking sheepish...well, as sheepish as she could as a cat.

"The spell cast was a binding spell, and a summoning spell," she said.

"What would they be summoning?" I asked.

"I don't know, but it's huge. Unlike most summoning spells that summon rather quickly, this is like summoning the atom bomb. The life force it took to begin the summons...well...I am at a loss for words," she said.

She was never at a loss for words, but what she said scared me. I still didn't know who was behind this, but I now had an idea of what the ritual was for, so maybe that would help me narrow down what was going on.

"So, why do I have a week? Or heck, less than a week at this point," I said.

"Because everything I found pointed to rituals of this magnification take a week," she said. "It's on the magnitude of...of something like Tunguska. Remember that one?"

"I wasn't there but I know what you're talking about. That explosion that happened in Siberia back in 1908, but from what I heard, it was a spell gone wrong. Everything within like 500 square miles was destroyed, or so I heard," I said, "At any rate, it happened when I was just a child, so I don't know for sure."

"Well, that's just one event. Pompeii was another. I would even say the last two devastating tsunamis resulted from these kinds of summonings. Their objective is to upset the balance of things, if I'm correct," she said.

"Who would want to disrupt things that bad?" I asked aloud, more to myself than to Hannah, but then noticed she was watching me. I felt I had to say more. "I mean more than usual."

"I don't know. I'd go and ask all the factions and see if anyone has a bone to pick and a large one at that," she replied.

That made sense to me, and that was something I probably should have pieced together myself. Yes, you had the high councils that kept things in check, but that didn't mean there weren't factions in the area, each with their own hierarchy and leadership. Vampires were one, werewolves another, witches, wizards, Voodoo shamans, the Fae—yeah, they exist too. And I already mentioned the dryads, and now that I mentioned them, there's also the druids. Ugh, the list goes on...and some factions were more organized and dangerous than others. The best way I can describe it to you is like modern day mafia families or gangs. Each have their own territory and interest, and squabbles often arise between them. I know I mentioned this before but wanted to go a little more in depth.

I only had a few days and something bad—very bad—was waiting. My mind raced at the possibilities, but then I had an overwhelming sense of despair and hopelessness at the task before me. You know how that happens sometimes. I'm sure you've experienced it your-self at some point in your life...the kind of situation where there are so many avenues, and you don't know where to start, so you'd rather just curl up in a dark place somewhere and go to sleep. Unfortunately, I couldn't do that, though it was a very attractive thought as I'm sure you could agree.

"Okay, thanks Hannah. I appreciate the heads-up. I will let you know," I said.

She didn't respond, just paced back and forth, still agitated. I reached down and patted her on the shoulder. Surprisingly, she didn't react. Normally, she hated that sort of thing. It was "beneath her," but this time, she didn't protest or even respond. She was lost in thought, and I could smell her fear.

"It'll be okay. I will work on it," I said gently. She again didn't respond, but she nodded her furry little face, so at least I was sure she heard me. Which brings me to another point: just like a "normie" can shut down when they find out about all the "special" things in the world, it can also happen to those in the know. A being, no matter what side of the veil they stood on, could only take so much.

She'll be okay, I thought, but she needed to process it. I mean, heck, even I had a moment right there where I had to reel myself back in. Fear and panic are strange things that feed into one another. Sometimes you win the fight, sometimes you lose, but the most important thing I've learned in my experience is to do something—work, fight, whatever it takes—to keep your focus on the outcome. So, that's exactly what I did. I focused on the next steps.

I hurried down the stairs and almost ran over Harry. "Did she tell you what was going on?"

Harry didn't react but merely shrugged, meaning no, she hadn't. She had waited to tell me the news, which probably added to her state of mind at the moment.

"Well, you should probably go check on her. What she had to say was very off-putting," I told him. I then ran past him and out the front door. I fumbled for my phone and called Dick to tell him to meet me. After I disconnected, I called Cormac to clue him into the meeting as well. Somehow, I felt this was going to need all of us because this would certainly bleed over into other jurisdictions.

I gave them about an hour to meet me, so I drove home to pick up some goodies that I thought we might need. Never go into a bear's den unprepared. When I arrived at my home, I had so much on my mind that I didn't even notice the front door until I was right in front of it. Can you believe that? Anyway, the front door was slightly open, and that gave me concern, which stopped me from plowing in like I originally planned. I stopped and quickly asked myself, "Did I or didn't I shut and lock the door this morning?" Then my heart jumped in my chest. Morgane! I then continued to plow through the front door, regardless of what was on the other side. I didn't know what was there, but if I were in for a bad day, so was the other guy waiting for me...only there was no one waiting. My house was in disarray, and Morgane was nowhere to be found.

I sniffed the air, and I smelled new scents. Familiar in a sense that I knew what it came from, but not enough to identify individuals. I walked through the house cautiously because even though the smell told me that whoever had been there was long gone, one could never be too sure. They could have used spells or incantations to hide themselves from me. As I walked from room to room, I could see that everything had been trashed. I had originally come here to collect my "hunting" gear, which was comprised of silver bullets (that I handled with the utmost care), wooden stakes, holy water, charms, etc. But my eagerness to collect changed when I saw everything. My alarm turned from fear to anger and then jumped to worry. I called out for Morgane, but she didn't respond. She should have been there, but she wasn't. Her scent was as old as the other scent that had been there, which led me to believe that whoever was there took her with them.

I walked back to the kitchen, where I found a note waiting for me.

"Lou,

By now, you realize we mean business. If you want your bird back in one piece, then you should back off from the case you're working. You know which one we're talking about."

There was no signature, but they said "we" so that meant there were more than one. With the smells that wafted through my nostrils, coupled with the fact that most wolves run in packs, it pointed to them, and I had an idea of who it was. I felt myself become even angrier, if that was possible. With utter disregard for the pain I knew it would cause, I almost allowed myself to turn into my monster to go after them. Fortunately, a small voice in the dark recesses of my mind slowly fought for control and inch by inch, the voice of reason clawed its way through my mind for sanity.

If I turned and went after them in the light of day and showed the world what I was, I'd be a hunted wolf as soon as I left the front door. Once you break the accords, no matter your status, you must pay for transgressions.

I didn't know where Morgane was, but I knew what I smelled. It was other wolves, a pack of them to be exact. I think I even recognized the scent; it was a pack that I've long known about but kept away from. They were in for a rude awakening, but I couldn't go waltzing in there without being prepared. I would need Dick's and hopefully Cormac's help if they would be willing to help. Dick was a 99% surety. Cormac...well, who knew what a wizard would or wouldn't do, especially one that focused on justice and laws.

I went to the back room and checked the floor, where I kept my stash of supernatural weaponry. The room had been trashed, but thankfully, they didn't smell or sense the cache since I had it warded to remain hidden to magic spells and supernatural abilities. It had cost me dearly, but clearly, especially in light of the events right in front of me, was worth every penny. I took a knee and popped the wood slat that hid the compartment underneath. I reached in and pulled the trunk clear and set it before me. With hands that shook in rage, I unclasped the latches that held it closed and opened it.

I couldn't help but smile. A lot of work went into collecting these items over the years. I pulled out a box from within that held a Colt 45 revolver, already loaded with silver bullets. I then carefully removed a box that handled two speed loaders already filled with more silver bullets. All told, I had 18 rounds of pure silver hatred ready to go. They weren't cheap. I just hoped I had enough to meet the threat. I know I said earlier that we had magic and medicine that helped with our allergies and weaknesses, but just because we had these things didn't make us suddenly tolerant. These silver bullets would slow rapid healing to the point of making it useless and cause a wolf to react like any other individual would.

I also reached in to grab blessed wooden stakes, because since I had the trunk out, I may as well grab everything that I might need in the next few days. There were some other blessed trinkets and even an enchanted ring I slipped on after I took everything out. Some added protection, and the ring made me faster—well, faster in human form and only slightly faster in monster form.

Next, I called Dick and told him about the change of plans. Since I needed to move quickly, I asked him to meet me at the only place I knew where this particular pack lived. I also asked him to reach out to Cormac on my behalf because honestly, I just couldn't handle the rejection if he said no, and I didn't want to waste my anger and lose focus from what I needed it to be focused on. I tore out of the house like a bat out of Hell.

First, no one was going to tell me what I needed to do when it came to my job of keeping the peace and second (more importantly, so maybe it should have been first), no one was going to threaten a friend of mine to strong-arm me into doing anything. People had already died and whoever was behind it was going to pay. If I didn't do it, someone else would eventually follow up. There are consequences to every action. Some just took longer than others.

I sped over the Crescent City bridge down Interstate 10, headed to New Orleans East. Once there, I turned onto another highway and took a side road that led me to an abandoned amusement park. Back in the day, before the hurricane of the century hit, it was home to fun, games, rides, and plenty of tourists spending money that made it into the local economy. After it was heavily damaged during the hurricane and never repaired and reopened, the place had become a shell of itself. It was like a nightmare that stayed long after you woke up and wouldn't disappear. The skyline was familiar with the roller coaster, but it hadn't run in years, and to some, it was just a skeleton of a previously lively establishment.

Although no one was supposed to be there, rarely did anyone in an official capacity ever go out to the area to patrol it, so at times you had squatters, adventurers, photographers, etc. that went to check it out or take up residence. In the past couple of years, a new group of squatters had taken over the place. I'm not sure who they paid off or who they worked for, but they were left alone and were allowed to stay. It was a wolf pack that I knew, and although I didn't look forward to this confrontation, it was coming just the same.

The place still looked dead for the most part. The parking lot had huge cracks and potholes, many with rampant weeds growing out of them, which had developed from years of disuse. With no repairs planned in the foreseeable future, if ever, it would keep deteriorating. I got out of my car and walked to the locked gate that "kept" outsiders from going in through the front entrance, which is basically all it did. Outsiders could get in from all sorts of other entrances. It was quiet, which surprised me. I didn't think that the wolf den had moved, but maybe it was because I wasn't actually in the park yet. Or maybe they had paid for magical words that concealed the sound from escaping and alerting any random passersby.

I didn't have time, nor did I particularly care about decorum. I reached down and put my paw...just kidding...I hadn't turned quite yet...but I could feel the monster begging to get out. I put my hands around the padlock and chain. I gripped hard and pulled, willing my strength to tear it apart until I heard and felt the quick release of chain and lock being wrenched from one another. I then pushed open the gate and walked through.

I should have waited for backup, but with rush hour traffic, there was no telling when Dick and Cormac, if he came, would show up. I continued through the front gate and past the entrance turnstiles. There was a large lake in the middle of the park and sadness passed over me as I saw what this place had become. A night and day experience, since I had come to the park once or twice during its heyday. The park sprawled out around the lake and even had its own lakefront. I came to a fork in the pathway and took a right. It followed the curvature of the waterfront and led to the skeleton of a roller coaster.

I was halfway to the coaster when I felt a barrier as I walked through. It's hard to describe, but I felt the static roll over me as I went through it, which confirmed that there indeed had been some sort of ward or magic barrier placed. It felt like when you were a kid, and your older sibling dared you to touch your tongue to a nine-volt battery. It wouldn't kill you, but you definitely felt it. That's kind of what it felt like, but since it was dispersed throughout the whole body, you didn't feel the need to react to it like you did when you were a kid.

As soon as I passed, I heard sounds of the living. I even smelled them. It wasn't a foul smell, just the smells of a settlement—food, drinks, people's scents, etc. The sounds came from a building at the base of the roller coaster, and

I walked toward it. I saw motorcycles parked out front, indicating that this was the den.

When I got about a 100 feet away from the door, bodies—maybe 15 to 20 of them—poured out and created a semi-circle between me and the building. This wasn't the entire pack I knew. Some wolf packs operate like a biker gang—people come and go at all times of day and night, carrying out tasks. There's some organization and serious loyalty to family.

They didn't come any closer than halfway, then stopped. A pathway was created, and another man stepped out from the shadows of the building and walked through the wall of people, stopping halfway between them and me.

"Hello, Lou. How have you been?" the man asked.

"Hello, Frank," I replied.

Chapter Twelve

"You know I don't go by that name anymore, Denny," he said, using my former name like I had his. "I go by Luke these days. You'd know that had you stayed with us."

"Yeah, maybe, but you know how things ended. I couldn't stay after that, but looks like things worked out well for you, though," I said.

"Perhaps, but you really shouldn't have come back today," Luke said.

I've known Frank (or rather Luke) for a long time. In fact, we were in the military service together near the turn of the century—last century. We were both turned into what we currently are during the same engagement, but that, again, is another story for another time. We probably could have passed for brothers and maybe in some ways we were, with this supernatural bond we shared...but that ended long ago. Some lifelong friends and family change, or the circumstances change and so does the relationship.

"Well, what can I say?" I replied. "Your pack left their scent and a note. How could I not? I'm no omega."

"Neither are you the alpha," he said.

"No, I'm not that either. I guess I've grown beyond those stereotypes. I am...whatever I need to be," I replied.

"You never were a coward...I give you that...but you really should have heeded the message left in the note and stayed away," Luke said.

"You threaten me and then you take my companion. Of course I'm coming after you...but you knew that," I said.

"Yeah, I guess I sort of did," Luke replied, but then laughed and continued, "You also always had bad luck. Your bird escaped, so there was no need for you to come."

I felt the blood drain from my head and a certain iciness replace my soul as I thought to myself, "He could be lying to me." But that wasn't his style.

"She's not here?" I asked.

"Nope, and that's not just some regular crow, is she?" Luke asked.

I shrugged my shoulders. "I don't know," I replied.

"We've been watching you for some time Lou and we always thought the bird was just that—a bird—so when we received the opportunity to take it to get you to come, we jumped at the chance," he said.

"But why now? You've had ample time...60 years I think...to take me down," I asked.

"You know grudges die hard and while yes, it was a goal to come after you eventually for what you did, it never lined up until we were hired to intimidate you, which kind of got the ball rolling again. Which, by the way...whatever you got yourself involved in, you're in deep, but that doesn't really matter now," he replied.

"Fran...Luke, we've known each other a long time. Quit talking and let's get it on," I replied.

A smile formed on his thin lips, "Yes...let's."

I knew I was on troubled ground here. I should have waited. I didn't know if back up was here yet or even coming at all. If they did come, I hoped they wouldn't arrive too late. I can hold my own in a fight, but not against an entire pack of werewolves.

They all began the change. I knew I had to act quickly to take some out of the fight, otherwise I would be overwhelmed. I didn't worry about changing to my monster form yet, though I knew the moment would arrive shortly. I quickly unholstered the 45 revolver and aimed in at the mob around me, firing off all six rounds. My aim was true for more than half, but acting as quickly as I did, my aim wasn't perfect and missed a couple of times. The four I hit quit changing immediately and were on the ground. I didn't know the damage dealt, but silver bullets were nothing to sneeze at, and they hurt...a lot.

I began to reload, releasing the latch for the cylinder in order to dump the casings to the ground, but before

I could insert the speed loader to load the gun, Luke was fully into his monster form. He towered over me at a good seven feet and slammed into me, causing us both to tumble. The force of the impact caused me to lose hold of both my revolver and my speed loader, but in the blur of moment, I grabbed onto Luke and rolled as we both flew through the air. I pushed away from him so that I landed on my back, then used my momentum to back roll into a standing position, ready to fight.

At that point, I had already started the change, and I was kind of angry about it. Another suit ruined as my muscles morphed and I felt the material stretch, then snap, apart...but whatever...I certainly had bigger things to think about at that moment than some cheap suit. Every one of them that I faced were already in full form and had grown long in the tooth. I wish I meant that in terms of age, but it was literal. Their teeth were long and sharp, with drool falling off in long strands. The jagged teeth were bad enough, but their hands had also grown into massive hybrid paw-hands with fingers that grew into tapered points. The group was excited, and they thought I would be an easy kill. They were letting themselves go to the rage, but in the process of their eagerness, there was something they forgot and something they should have remembered from last time, some 60 years ago. I wasn't easy to kill. I could forgive the young bucks. Most of them hadn't enjoyed the newfound powers until after I was long gone, so had no memory of me other than what others had told them, if they had been told anything at all. I knew how it was. To them, I was just another obstacle for the pack.

Luke was five feet to my right and moving quickly. I judged his movement and coldcocked him with my right hand, which caused him to stumble past me to my left. This actually wasn't good for me, because now I was about to be the bull in the ring with him on one side and his crew behind me, fanning out into a circle.

So, I took advantage and charged Luke, barreling into him almost exactly like he had done to me just a moment prior, except he felt me coming or something because he braced himself and grabbed on to me. It then became a test of strength. If you've ever seen any evenly-matched arm wrestlers go at it, that was probably how this looked—no one really moving, barely trembling—but the amount of focus and strength that took place in that moment would have ripped some people apart. This was a dangerous position to be in, especially when fighting in a group. If you're tied up with one person for too long, be it a grapple situation or if they have you in a hold of some sort, you best be quick about it and move, otherwise the rest of the group will take advantage of your situation.

Since we were mere inches from each other's face and muscles bulging from effort, I knew I wouldn't be able to keep up, for various reasons. I leaned in closely and whispered, "Hey Luke?"

He didn't answer. He was straining as hard as I was, but he was listening. "What's the sound of a devil dog?"

He immediately lost focus at the absurdity of the question, which I took advantage of and at his momentary lapse of strength, I stepped forward and intertwined my right leg on the outside of his left and instead of pushing I grabbed, turned, and pulled with all my weight, using momentum and simple body mechanics to twirl him through the air. Sometimes, when someone asks or does something out of the blue in a fight, it takes a moment for the other to register. It can be as simple as a soft slap to change focus or an off-the-wall question or action that makes their mind focus on something else momentarily. Of course, that question had meaning to both him and me. Before we were werewolves and before we were part of any pack, I told you that we both served in the military—the U. S. Marine Corps—over a century ago. This was at a time before the Marines became known the world over for being "teufel hunden," the German word for "devil dog," for which we were partly to blame. If you stick around, I'll tell you that tale, as well.

Anyway, getting back to this story...he landed hard and then stood up in a fighting stance.

"You were always wily," he said.

"I'm hurt Luke; I've never been a coyote in my life," I replied.

Luke rolled his eyes and motioned for his pack to charge. I saw them coming, and it was going to hurt—a lot. Then the strangest thing happened. A ball of light whizzed past me from behind and landed in the line of charging monsters and erupted, sending them flying.

Oh geeze, the cavalry had just arrived. I felt a moment of huge and immediate relief at the thought. Another ball of light whizzed by and again disrupted the pack. I could see Luke's anger grow unchecked. Since he was closer to me, he charged by himself, and that was when Dick emerged from somewhere off to my side and stood in front of me. Normally, he wasn't an imposing picture of intimidation, but when he let his monster out, you would never have recognized him. The sunglasses he usually opted for were gone and his eyes were a brilliant violet color...and the fangs behind that ferocious hiss...well, even in my monster wolf form where thoughts and reactions can be dulled to some extent, he still scared the bejesus out of me.

"Glad you showed up," I said.

Dick spared a quick glance back. "We almost didn't. You know how traffic is during this time of day."

"Just what is going on here?" Cormac asked, coming up to stand by my side, throwing darts of flame to keep the horde back.

"Old grudges, I guess," I replied.

"Well next time, keep me out of it," Cormac replied gruffly, annoyed at what he assumed wasn't his problem—and it wasn't.

"Glad you're here, just the same," I said, which only got a snort in reply.

Wizarding powers were indeed formidable, but they weren't infinite, and every spell that Cormac threw required material and power. His hands moved swiftly, reaching into pockets deep within his jacket to retrieve what ingredients he needed, then coupled with weaving motions and word, he unleashed Hell on earth with each point or swing of his hand. All this sapped his energy.

Within our "special" community, there are some amulets and trinkets of power that negate magic, and it quickly became apparent that a couple of the mob members possessed these types of items. I knew that even with the arrival of Cormac and Dick, if we didn't get out soon, we would slowly lose our momentum and be overcome.

I tried to be optimistic, but then I heard more motorcycles and their rumbling pipes behind us. I looked behind us and saw that another horde had arrived that had not been there when this altercation kicked off. Apparently, there was a special entrance for motorcycles to come and go, that I hadn't seen coming in. My grand entrance had invariably kicked the proverbial hornets' nest.

One werewolf broke through the barrier of fire that Cormac had created and engaged with Dick. Dick grabbed the creature and lifted off the ground some 50 feet and launched him. I knew Dick was really into his "form." In all the times that I'd been around him, he rarely levitated or flew. Only when he was one with the ego within did he do it; like Cormac and his wizardry, it took energy and willpower to get so close to the flame, so to speak. When one succumbs to their monster or alter ego, it's easy to lose control. Werewolves weren't alone in this; vampires also had to struggle to maintain control. The feeding frenzy they felt, when held in check, made them merely superhuman, but when the frenzy became unchecked, they were unworldly.

Cormac looked behind us and saw the other group that had shown up. At least 10 more fully-turned werewolves came in behind us, shutting our escape and he yelled to me, "Lou, if you have anything up your sleeve, I'd like to see it. I'm almost out. The fireballs I cast earlier to disperse the group took a lot out of me."

I didn't want to say it, but I honestly had nothing left up my sleeve. My pistol and speed loader with ammo were still missing, but I had the extra speed loader attached to my belt in a pouch. When I turn into a wolf, yes, my shirt and pants are usually ruined, but my belts usually stay right where they are because there are few changes in that area. I reached down to the remaining speed loader on my belt, ripped it off and threw it to Cormac. He caught it and looked at me with an accompanying wild look. "What am I going to do with these?"

"They're silver!" I shouted back.

He looked back at his hand, then back at me, then his eyes widened as the dawning of understanding took place. Even though we didn't have a revolver to shoot the remaining rounds, wizards could cast spells that would mimic the force and speed of a bullet, and that's exactly what Cormac did next. He took the rounds from the speed loader and held them loosely in his hand. I'm not sure what he said, but he murmured something that built up to a crescendo, then yelled out, taking the momentum of air around him and the bullets with it. They arced toward the group of werewolves. As the bullets passed, Cormac said something else, causing the bullets to slow and hum loudly. They emanated a glow that grew brighter. I wish I could convey the beautiful destruction of it, but it happened so quickly, then I had to take cover because...well...I am a werewolf and exploding silver bullets would be no bueno for me, either. Silver could be harmful for vampires as well, so Dick, who noticed what Cormac was doing, grabbed another werewolf and used him as a shield...just in the nick of time. As he did so, the six bullets burst and became something akin to small grenades. They weren't large enough to kill anything, but the irritation from the slivers of silver would be enough to distract the enemy. In some ways, it was similar to what tear gas or pepper spray would do. Sure, people say it's less than lethal and maybe it is, but the pain it causes makes you wonder if it's really worth it to experience the pain it brought. At any rate, it will seriously slow you down.

Thankfully, I avoided the shrapnel and although the fallout from the blast hit about 15 of them, there was still a ton left, and they were closing in. I looked for Luke; he was the alpha here and if I could single him out and put him in a position that he couldn't escape, maybe he would call his dogs off. Of course, I doubted that because if he did anything that made him look weak, it wouldn't bode well for his leadership. A wolf pack leader had to have complete control, but that created its own problems. People were loyal, but only to a point. There would always be individuals vying for power. It was a moot point anyway, though, because in the confusion, I couldn't single him out.

Dick kicked the werewolf he had been using as a shield into the group and backed up. I backed up as well, and the wolves closed around us. Cormac, Dick, and I were in the center. This looked to be it. I had almost given up hope when I heard a caw in the distance. Amongst the yells and growls and straight-up howls, that small caw was barely audible. I wondered why or how I even heard it in the first place, and even then, I wondered if I had heard it at all.

The frenzy of the group intensified. I could feel it coming off them in waves, which, to be honest, only added to my own frenzy that I had to fight to control. I heard the caw again and this time, I was positive I heard something. In fact, some of our opponents must have heard it, as well, because they stopped dead in their tracks and turned to look toward the direction it came from.

Again, the caw came and this time, everyone heard it. It was surreal. The battle had essentially come to a complete standstill as everyone turned, mesmerized by the cawing sound of one bird. It was like we couldn't help it.

Even Cormac, the gruff wizard, stood there in slack-jawed fashion before shutting his mouth so quickly, I could have sworn I heard his teeth chomp together.

We all stood there silently, looking into the distance at this small, black speck in the sky of which there was no mistaking that it was the source of the sound. It was closing in fast—faster than what a normal black bird could fly and by now, it was apparent it was a crow. Its call became louder and steadier, like an opera singer who held onto the last note as long as they could, but in this case, it didn't stop...it just kept cawing.

As it got closer, its speed increased and the cawing became deafening. Without slowing, the black speck of a bird plowed into the front line of werewolves, knocking them to the ground. I believe we were all speechless at this unexpected maneuver. It moved so quickly that I had my suspicions when I first heard it, but now that the bird was here, there was no mistaking it was Morgane...and she was pissed. This was a new one for me because she had never interfered in any of my dealings before. Like I said, we had a "live and let live" policy in our household. It was a place of refuge, and it wasn't expected, but then again, we'd never been in the position where one of us was used as a bargaining chip against the other.

I looked at Morgane and apparently, she was not finished. She flew up quickly in an overhead circle while the force of her flying picked up even more speed. It was breathtaking. The cawing didn't stop until she took in one long breath of air. If I hadn't seen it, I would have never believed it. It felt as if she breathed in the world, pulling us all in, but when she exhaled, not only air, but also flames burst from her tiny mouth.

Chapter Thirteen

I'd seen a lot of things in my lifetime that were both beautiful and terrifying, as well as just plain unexpected and this...this image of this slightly larger-than-normal crow belching out fire ranked up there in that list. Every single one of us that still stood was paralyzed out of shock, at least until the flames hit the first of the victims. I almost felt sorry, but then I realized had the roles been reversed, there would have been no love lost.

In fact, I was so surprised by the turn of events, my anger and rage were gone. I turned back to human form, and I wasn't sure whether that was by unconscious choice or if someone or something compelled it. I began to think it was the latter when I noticed other werewolves were turning back to their alter egos, as well. That's when the horde broke. Between those that were on fire, dancing a jig and the others returning to human form, the tables had obviously turned. One started to run, then another, then all of them, with their proverbial tails tucked between their legs. I couldn't blame them. Honestly, I would have done the same thing. Sometimes it really is better to live to fight another day.

One remained, and that was Luke, who was still in monster form. The look he gave me was of pure hatred, then he turned his gaze to Morgane as she flew, still breathing fire way above her weight class. Luke untangled something from his belt and my blood went cold. It was a wand of some sort, and that scared me. He must have had it the whole time, just waiting to use it or maybe only use it as a last resort, but that time had clearly come. Wands were magical, but one didn't have to be a wizard, witch, warlock, necromancer, Voodoo priest, shaman...you get the idea...to use one. Anyone could use it. It was like a pistol. In the hands of someone who knew how to use it, it was dangerous to those around them. In the hands of someone who didn't know how to use it, it was dangerous for everyone.

He looked and aimed at Morgane and without thinking, I leapt into action, sprinting through the wall of flames, which had dissipated to some extent. The heat, though, was still very real. With Luke's attention focused on Morgane, he didn't see me, nor did he really expect me to cover the ground as quickly as I did. Even though I was in my normal human form, I was so pumped up on adrenaline that I moved swifter than I ever remember moving...and I had some help from that trinket I brought with me. I aimed for his snout, jumped, and swung with all my might.

Surprisingly, it landed squarely. I have to say, I was quite impressed with my actions because it lifted him off his feet, and he landed on the ground, knocked out cold.

I looked at my hand, then down at his unconscious state; he was shifting back to his normal Luke form. I couldn't believe it. I looked back at my hand and then a form brushed my side. It was Cormac.

I looked at him and he said, "You can thank me later."

And then I realized it hadn't just been my proficient fighting skills. Cormac must have cast a sleep spell and apparently, the combination of my fist coupled with the power of his spell worked together to take Luke down.

"Uh...Thanks," I said, feeling slightly deflated.

The area was clear except for us. The pack had backed off; they were still around and watching, but they kept their distance. This fight was over. All the wounded were pulled away and they would have done the same with Luke had he been closer to them than us, but they were unable to get any closer, with Morgane bringing down the depths of Hell on them. I looked up to see Morgane do a few more circling swoops, which I assume was to assure we were indeed safe before she flew down to land near me.

"Squawk!" she began before she continued, "Quite an excitement for the day."

She muttered something under her breath to herself, but I heard it because of my keen hearing ability. "I really hate doing that. My throat is so scratchy after."

"Are you okay, Morgane?" I asked.

"Caw...are you?" she replied.

"I'm so glad that you're okay! I was worried when I saw the note that they took you," I said.

"Yeah, I let them think they had the upper hand...caw...but really, I just wanted to see what was going on before I left to warn you. When I got home, I saw that...caw...that you had already come and gone. I figured you came here and so...here I am as well," she replied.

"I didn't know you could breathe fire, Morgane," I said.

She cocked her head, and her little yellow eye looked at me appraisingly. "There is much you don't know, Lou. Caw! But don't go making it a habit to start asking questions about it."

I held up my hands, palms out, to show that her secrets are hers for as long as she wants them to be.

She continued to look at me hard.

"Squawk! Good," she concluded before hopping around on the ground and looking at everyone else.

"What are we going to do with him?" Dick spoke up as he walked over, indicating to the unconscious form of Luke at our feet.

"I'm not sure," I replied.

"We could cut him up and leave him in the intracoastal waterway for the gators to get rid of," Cormac said.

"What? No!" I said incredulously. "We're supposed to stop people from breaking the laws of the land and the accords."

"Oh stop, you don't have to lecture me. Killing him wouldn't break the laws of the land. There isn't a law against killing werewolves and as for the accords, those accords were written to stop us from letting the real world know that the second shadow world exists," he replied.

He had a point. There was a grey area there, but then I wondered just how many times Cormac had taken advantage of that grey area before. He seemed so nonchalant about even suggesting it. I would have to keep an eye on him.

"No, I can't do that. At least not yet. We need to find out who hired him," I said.

"Whatever. You owe me a favor," Cormac replied.

"I know," I said, "But whatever we're facing, I believe it will affect all of us."

"Maybe so, but coming straight to this den wasn't a good idea and getting me...hell, even getting your partner involved was a dangerous proposition," he said.

"I can speak for myself," Dick said, "But yeah, Lou, he is right, you know."

"I know. I asked for a lot and you both delivered, but I had to come get Morgane here—or at least I thought I did," I said.

"Hmm. So...what is this 'bird' with you?" Cormac said as he turned his attention toward Morgane, who was now keeping her small yellow eyes on Luke.

"Squawk!? Is it a bird? Is it a plane?" she began mockingly, then changed her tone abruptly and peered up at me. "This conversation bores me. See you at the house."

And without another moment's thought, she hopped into the air and was gone as quickly as she came. Cormac watched her go. His face gave nothing away as far as his thoughts, but he opened his mouth after she had disappeared from sight. "That's no bird."

"I don't think so either, but whatever she is, I'm glad she's on my side," I replied.

"Agreed," he said quietly, then turned toward me. "Okay, let's get the information we need—and quickly—before the pack knows that the fire-breathing bird is gone."

"Good idea," I said and reached down to rouse Luke awake. Now that we didn't have a horde to fight off, Cormac had more time to concentrate and cast a barrier spell between us and where we saw the pack licking their wounds. On top of that, he also cast some sort of binding spell to keep Luke from fighting or escaping.

I shook Luke and he bolted awake, struggling at the unseen bonds that held him. He grappled until he was almost in a panic, but when he realized that there was no escape, he calmed down and looked at me. "Seems you have the upper hand today," he said.

"Just barely, but if you help me, we can make like today never happened," I said.

Cormac snorted behind me, obviously disagreeing with the way I wanted to handle things. I looked at Dick, but like Cormac a moment before, his face gave nothing away about his thoughts.

"Why would I help you?" he said.

"We weren't always enemies and, to be honest, we aren't really enemies now. You know it. I know it. You would have come collecting years ago if we were," I said.

"Don't you tell me what I am or am not. I will decide that for myself. This has always been your problem," he snarled. "You think you know everything."

"You done?" I asked impassively.

Luke looked at me. His face tightened in frustration, then smoothed out to a blank expression, fight gone, as if he realized that nothing he said was going to get a rise out of me. That was probably true and he wasn't going to waste any more effort on it. He laid his head back down to look toward the sky.

"Who hired you?" I asked.

"What does it matter?" he replied.

"Because if I don't find out, it's the end of the world as we know it here," I said.

"What?" Cormac asked, "Since when did murders..." He stopped abruptly as the realization hit. He was a wizard, after all. "Well, I'll be damned. I should have known the murders were the bind for the summoning. Were they?" he asked.

"That's what I heard and was going to tell you before this detour took place," I said.

"Damn, that's not good," Cormac said. "That's some Old World destruction stuff and definitely outlawed by the accords," he said as he turned his attention to Luke, who still lay on the ground. "Those who help or are accomplices in the act are hereby ordered to death," he told Luke.

"Wait, what?" Luke said. "I don't know anything about that. All I know was I was hired to stop Lou from interfering."

"And you didn't think to ask just what Lou was looking into?" Cormac asked.

"No, I didn't," Luke replied.

"Well, you know that ignorance has no wiggle room when it comes to the accords," Cormac said.

"Hold on...he'll tell us," I said to Cormac and then turned to Luke. "I know we have our problems, but we're both in something way over our heads. I need to know who hired you. We can have our issues later, but right now, we have bigger problems to attend to."

Luke looked at Cormac, then at Dick, then at me. "I don't know who it was," he said.

"What? Come on, man," I said.

"No, I'm serious. It was a phone call. The voice sounded like it had been disguised, and I didn't care to ask. I just knew they were paying quite a bit of money to get you to stop," he said.

"When were you supposed to collect?" I asked.

"When you stopped," he said.

"How much?" I asked.

"$100,000," he said.

"Seriously?" I asked. "That kind of money and you didn't even ask what it was regarding?"

"For that kind of money, one doesn't ask questions," Luke replied.

"I wonder why they didn't just try to bribe me," I pondered aloud.

Luke laughed.

"What's so funny?" I asked.

"Lou, you have a reputation, and everyone knows it here in good ol' New Orleans," Luke said.

"Really?" I asked.

"Lou, have you ever taken a bribe?" Luke asked.

"Well, no, but..." I began to reply but was cut off by Luke interjecting. "Exactly," he said.

"Hmm...maybe, but at least they could have asked," I said.

"I don't think they were going to pay you," Cormac interrupted after apparently giving something some thought. "What they're summoning...well...it's a high power. The equivalent of...if I'm correct...they're summoning the equivalent of Samael the Death Shroud, because everything that comes from that kind of summons brings only death in spades. Think of Pompeii...ultimate destruction."

"Listen, I told you everything I know. You gonna let me go now?" Luke asked.

"I didn't say that," I replied.

"Oh, come on Lou. I don't know anything else, but if I had known...really, the pack and I wouldn't bring the end of the world. You know as well as I do, we're just tools to be used and aren't usually included in the decisions," Luke said.

"The iron hand, huh?" Dick asked.

"Sometimes," Luke replied, shifting his gaze toward him.

"All right. Fine, let him go," I said.

"Really?" Cormac asked. "You know they're going to want payback for today. They have to save face for today's failure. Wolf packs always do."

"I think we can let this slide today, if what Luke says is true," I said. "Then we may need him and his pack when the time comes, and if what he says isn't true, then the end of the world comes, and it won't even matter."

Cormac gave a look that spoke volumes of, "Well don't say I didn't warn you, but I give up." He shrugged his shoulders and waved his hand while wiggling his fingers in a slow back-and-forth motion toward Luke. This apparently released the binds that held Luke because he immediately sat upright and rubbed where the invisible lashings that held him down had been.

I walked over and stuck my hand down. "Like I said, we can continue our issues later, but now is not the time."

Luke squinted back up at me with a hard look. A few moments went by as he obviously mulled something over in his mind. Whatever he was contemplating, he evidently came to a conclusion when he gave a small nod and took my hand to stand up.

"Now what?" Cormac asked.

I looked back over my left shoulder at him. "Now we leave this place and go find the other locations where the bodies are. I think the sooner we can find them and disrupt the sites where they are...well, hopefully we can lessen the power of whatever is coming."

"That's a good thought but I think it's too late for that," Cormac replied. "That's a school of magic I haven't studied but I'm sure it's similar to others, as in, once it's cast, it's done."

"Probably so, but still, we need to find those locations. Maybe evidence will point us in the right direction," I replied.

And that's how we left things, with Luke standing there as we trudged back to the parking lot and left the amusement park. To be honest, I almost suspected we'd hear the sound of motorcycles following to get one last shot in but down deep, I knew Luke wouldn't have allowed it. I really believed he was used and if roles were reversed, perhaps I would have done the same.

Before we made plans to meet in Westwego, Cormac said one last thing before we left. "Lou, that's some wild bird you keep company with."

"I know."

Chapter Fourteen

At that point of the day, the sun would soon be taking its nightly voyage, but we still had an hour or so before Dick could feel more comfortable. Traffic was crap. There was a car accident that shut down the Crescent City bridge over to the west bank where I lived. I usually know my way around, but sometimes when traffic is terrible, I pull out the GPS to see how long the wait will be or if it will reroute to make the trip faster. The GPS routed me to take the long way around via the Huey P. Long Bridge, where traffic looked to be backed up just as badly. Fortunately, since the town of Westwego (where I thought the next body would be) was basically a hop, skip, and a jump away from the foot of the bridge, it made sense to head that way. Personally, I always hated the Huey P, but it's now much better since it was renovated a few years back. Before, it was a rickety four-lane bridge with a train track running right down the center of it, with no breakdown lane or even enough space to pull to the side. It felt cramped and claustrophobic, with nowhere to go if you had an accident.

After the renovation, it was widened to six lanes and a breakdown lane for each direction. Years of avoiding it wouldn't go away overnight, so I still had issues with that bridge, even though the reasons for them were long gone.

Now, I wasn't sure where the body would be in Westwego. There were plenty of areas and to be honest, the fact that we found the one in Lafreniere park was a fluke, at least in my eyes. At the foot of the Huey P, I got off on Louisiana 18 that would take me to a road that followed the Mississippi River, appropriately named River Road. It ran between the river and the heart of Westwego, which had previously been a large area for industry, mostly oil related. There remained plenty of large, abandoned warehouses that had lain dormant for years. If I were going to perform secret rituals and wanted to be out of the way, that's where I would have conducted them. I had little to go on—only a hunch—but sometimes only a hunch is better than nothing at all.

I followed the curvature of the road and pulled off to the side where one of those side roads crossed the levee. Those roads were rarely used and... oh, I'm sorry...I forget myself and who I'm talking to sometimes. Not everyone knows how things are in Louisiana. If you aren't familiar with the levee system, they're high earth berms along the river that protect low-lying areas from flooding and, for the most part, they work pretty well. That is, of course, unless a hurricane comes through and weakens the levee, causing it to fail, in which case, it's a disaster. It's kinda weird at times too, because some roads are below sea level, and to see a large ship or barge float by above you is always a strange sensation. But anyway, getting back to my current story…every so often there are roads that traverse the levees that separate the river from civilization and since there isn't much traffic or they're for restricted traffic, they make good stopping points.

I got out of my car, texted both Dick and Cormac where I was and that I was waiting. The weather was pleasant, so I noticed some families were utilizing the concrete sidewalk referred to as the Mississippi River Trail, which was installed atop the levee for hiking, bicycling or whatever leisurely activity that brought them there.

I didn't have long to enjoy the view before the other two showed up; they parked behind me and walked over.

"You think the body could be in this area?" Dick asked.

"I don't know. All I have is a hunch," I replied.

"That's not very promising, Lou," Cormac said.

"I know, but it's all I got. You have anything you can cast that will help?" I asked.

Cormac's face tightened into a grimace, and I wasn't sure if it was from disgust, frustration, or something else but after a moment, he replied. "Well, if we didn't have that extracurricular activity at the amusement park, I would say that I did but I blew through more than half of the materials I need to cast that kind of spell. Not to mention that I'm worn out. I'm not even sure I would have the ability to cast such a thing in my state, even if I had the material."

My mind raced for ideas on possible locations and as I did so, I looked at Dick.

"Hey, don't look at me. I got nothing," he replied.

"Well, we could drive around, and you could just hang your head out the window like a dog and sniff. I'm sure eventually something would alert your senses," Cormac said.

One thing about Cormac—you were never really sure if he was serious or not and that always made things difficult to gauge.

"Have you ever smelled this area? I mean, really take a deep whiff?" I asked.

"Can't say that I have any more than anyone else," he replied.

"Well, it's downright awful, being so close to the river. There's the smell of dead fish and then add in the petroleum runoff from the passing boats and the chemicals from the factories in the area...well, it's a not a good idea. I may have a great sniffer, but if I were to spend more than my fair share doing that, I believe it would rot off and that wouldn't do anyone any good," I replied.

"Ah, well, it was just a suggestion," Cormac replied.

We sat in silence for a few moments more before Cormac excitedly spoke up. "I think I have an idea."

"Whatcha got?" I asked.

"Well, the spell that was cast was a binding spell, but to do so, the ritual had to be completed in different areas at the same time to link them. I may not have the energy to cast a spell that would locate the body, but I think I might have another option. I can cast something to see the thread," he replied.

My ears perked up. "Really? I don't think I've ever heard of such a thing."

"Me neither," Dick added.

"Nor should you. It's one of those things that's not used very often. It's a very specific spell and usually summoning spells are small in nature, and don't leave the room they're done in. I mean, you don't really need to see the thread for those, but for large rituals done in conjunction with one another...well, that's where this comes in. Give me a second, and I will see if it works," Cormac said.

I stood back and watched as he reached into his coat, searching for the material and ingredients he needed.

"How many pockets do you have in there?" I asked, trying not to appear nosy as I attempted to see where he was reaching and pulling items from.

"It's a secret..." he replied.

"Oh, okay..." I said.

"Nah, just kidding. I have four pockets, but inside those pockets, I have a spell that condenses spells' components. Most wizards have something similar, and they can organize it how they like. Mine is sort of like a file folder. I reach in and run my fingers across the page until I'm at the right slot, then I go in to retrieve whatever I need," he said.

"That's amazing," I said, and I truly meant that. I mean, can you imagine how cool that would be? I have trouble stuffing a wallet, cell phone, keys, pocketknife, and other items in my own pockets without it looking bulky and out of place. Then a question nagged at me.

"How do you know where something is? I mean, four pockets with...I can only guess at how many options," I said.

"Experience..." he replied. "Everyone is different and does what works for them, but for me, this is how I do it and it works."

He fumbled around and dropped what he needed on the ground in front of him. It didn't take long, but now that I knew what went into it, I was mesmerized watching him reach in and, a short time later, pull something out.

"Okay, done," he said and reached down and gathered all his items, which consisted of sand, fishing line, a lighter, and wood shavings. He looked at me and added, "I have to use the trunk of your car for a flat work surface."

"Be my guest," I replied.

We all gathered and looked around to make sure that there weren't too many eyes on us, and there weren't. There was the occasional car that traveled by, but at that time, it wasn't rush hour traffic and even it had been, most people don't pay attention, so we were okay...well, depending on how much of a ruckus his spell would cause. I took one more glance up at the levee to see if anyone was nearby and all the pedestrians I had seen earlier were either gone or too far to be able to clearly see what we were doing. If anyone saw us, they would probably say we were looking at a map or something, but most people forget what they see.

Cormac took the fishing line and laid it out carefully, then took the sand and sprinkled it.

"Different spells require different things," Cormac said when he noticed Dick and me watching intently.

So, to fill the silence and admittedly out of curiosity, I goaded him into explaining more. "What differences do you mean?"

"Things like this," he replied, gesturing toward the materials laid out in front on him. "Some spells are instantaneous—we take the material in hand, do some mental weaving along with incantations calling on the magic and boom, a spell is cast. But magic is a strange mistress and different kinds of magic call for different things. In some ways, it's similar to women...or men, for that matter. Some magic seems to prefer being manhandled...demanded even, but others require a coaxing and very slow, methodical treatment to make the spell or magic respond and come alive. Like the difference between throwing fireballs earlier at Jazzland, and now where I'm taking my time to organize and conduct time-honored rituals to cast the spell."

"Fascinating," I replied. "How long does it take to learn it?"

"Pfft..." he snorted. "Why? You want to learn?"

"Never thought about it," I replied.

"Well, it's kind of like the game of chess," Cormac replied. "It's easy to learn a move or two, but it's extremely hard to master and even then, you may know it all and still be bested. That's why wizards and the like live a long time. It takes just about that long to get any good at it. Okay, stand back."

He took his right hand and stuck his finger into the pile of sand. I hadn't noticed, but there was a little wind and surprisingly, at least to me, it didn't disturb the sand at all. It only moved when he touched it. He took his finger and traced a circle several times. Each time around, his finger picked up more sand until the pile was spread out in a circle. Once he finished that and seemed to be satisfied, he then took the lighter, flicked on the flame, and touched the wood shavings, which he had placed in the center of the circle. Before long, a flame formed on the wood, but he didn't allow it to stay lit very long. He blew it out, leaving it to smolder and create smoke which drifted up but never beyond the boundaries of the sand circle. The slight wind still didn't seem to disturb the circle or whatever was in the circle. The smoke rose lazily through the air. By this time, the sun was setting, but it wasn't yet completely dark. It was the in-between stage of day and night where the energy transfer was greatest. Cormac stuck the lighter back into his coat, then started speaking some language I had no understanding of.

I saw an ebb and flow of something; it was very faint and barely comprehensible. If I didn't know that Cormac was casting a spell, I probably wouldn't have seen it, but since I did, I was able to notice it. Of course, it could have been my imagination, but the longer he mumbled, the more I realized it couldn't have been my imagination. The wisps of smoke took on a purple hue, then red, then yellow, then back to purple. It changed direction from rising into the air only long enough to wrap tendrils around the fishing line and then as the smoke passed over, under and around the line, it lifted it into the air to eye level. I glanced again at our surroundings to make sure we weren't seen and again, the coast was clear, much to my relief. Last thing I needed was someone to call in to the sheriff's office to report strange men doing strange things. Granted, it was Cormac's jurisdiction, but that's just not kind of the attention you want. One weird thing to happen and it's a fluke, but if strange things happen more than a few times, you might come under suspicion. Well, a police department and a sheriff's office are no different in that respect. It's like high school—word gets around quickly, but I have to be honest with you, I could be totally talking out of my tail on that one. It's been many decades since I was in high school and it was a bit different 100 years ago, so what do I really know? Anyway, all that to say this—the more attention you bring to yourself, the more you have to deal with.

I looked back at Cormac and his mumbling chant grew in volume, but also deepened in tone. And when he finished, he blew into the wispy smoke, which caused the wood shavings to flair and pump out more smoke, but then it ceased. With the wood shavings no longer smoldering, the purple, hazy smoke disappeared into the night, but the fishing line glowed a neon orange. It reminded me of a blacksmith that heated metal to a soft orange. So strong was the resemblance, I unconsciously stepped back as if I could feel the heat emanating off it until I realized I couldn't. Then, as quickly as the glow came, it was gone.

Cormac looked at us and said, "Now, here comes the fun part."

He then turned back and broke the circle made of sand with his left hand. As he did, I felt a whooshing of air, like it had been released from a deep vacuum or the sensation of opening a window during a storm. The air rushed past us at such a speed that had it been any faster, it would have resembled a shock wave, however, there was no audible explosion in the release of energy.

Cormac smiled, "And there it is..."

Chapter Fifteen

And there it was, indeed. It was faint, but to my eyes, it was vibrant. The fishing line had disappeared. In fact, everything was gone, all material spent, but in its place was a small area pulsing with light.

"So, what do we do now?" Dick asked.

"Shh...one second," Cormac responded.

The light then expanded quickly and faded at a speed that was on par with the same sense of the rushing wind from a moment before, and then that, too, was gone, leaving nothing.

Cormac frowned and said nothing, but I could tell that something was wrong.

"Everything all right?" I ventured.

"Yeah, yeah...I guess we just aren't in the right...oh?!" he cried.

The frown on his face quickly shifted to a smile, and I turned my gaze to where he was looking and saw a thin red line off in the distance, about a half mile away. The red line had the appearance of a spider web that could only be seen when the sun reflected off of it, but the sun was below the horizon now.

"Can anyone see this?" I asked.

"No, only us," Cormac said.

"How does that work?" I couldn't help asking.

"Magic," he replied, and after a moment he continued, "It's all in the way you cast and the voice inflections of the words I said that makes the difference."

He said that as if I understood, but I didn't. However, since time was of the essence, I nodded my head and turned my attention back to the red line that came out of the northwest and continued toward the southeast.

"All right, time to go," Cormac said.

I couldn't have agreed more, so we were on the road again, trying to see where the red line led us. As we got closer to the line, it grew in brightness. Not enough to be annoying, but enough for it to be easily seen without strain.

It would have been much easier if Dick could have followed the line via the air because following something like that while driving can lead to its own kind of frustrations, especially when it crosses land where there are no roads and you have to figure out a route to go around. Unfortunately, even at this time of evening, with the sun below the horizon, there was still enough light that someone seeing a man floating along 20 feet in the air would bring about unwanted attention.

I drove along trying to gauge where it ended and I came to the conclusion that my original hunch was probably correct; the red line ended at a rather large, abandoned warehouse. I imagined that, in its glory day, it was a significant part of the industry along River Road, but now, the parking lot was overrun with weeds and there were large sheets of metal missing from its walls to the point that you could see straight into its interior. It still looked structurally sound enough, and I guessed that the damage was too significant to repair, yet too expensive to demolish the entire building.

The chain-link fence around the property wasn't paid enough to do its job anymore, and there were sections where the fencing sagged and had become detached from the framework. The front gate that led onto the property was closed with a rusty chain wrapped between each section of the gate to keep it secure, but surprisingly, the lock that should have been there was gone. The chain was tied in a knot as well as it could have been, then wrapped to appear secure. It's not like whoever came here before needed to worry about appearances, because this place certainly wasn't checked on a daily basis, unlike the location in Lafreniere Park.

I unwrapped the chain and swung open the gate. The red line led directly to the warehouse in front of us. After parking, we didn't have any problems getting inside. A heavy padlock secured the front doors, but like I said earli-

er, there were enough missing wall sections that those pad-
locks could have been used elsewhere and fulfilled more
purpose.

It was dark inside, but thanks to my vision, I could
see, and so could Dick. Cormac, on the other hand,
couldn't and that was confirmed when he swore loudly as
he tripped over some debris and almost careened to the
floor. Luckily, he was able to catch his balance at the last
moment.

"Screw this," Cormac said to anyone that would listen
but mostly to himself. He went on to utter a word that
sounded something like "Sherlock," but whatever he said,
it must have been magic because a globe of light appeared
over his left shoulder and hovered there, waiting for him
to move. When he did, it faithfully followed wherever he
went.

The ball of light wasn't blinding. In fact, it was quite
pleasant, almost offering a false sense of serenity.

"What is that?" I asked.

"It's a ball of light," Cormac replied.

I felt so dumb. Knowing the wizard like I do, I expected
him to say the most obvious things, probably because he
secretly enjoyed making others feel dumb. Almost immediately, he would always go on to explain further, and this
time was no different.

"It's a wisp. It's attached to me, kind of like a familiar,
but the only usefulness I've ever found for it was to give

me light to see by. I won it in a poker game and although I won, I'm not completely convinced it was worth what I had offered in the bet...but I won, so it doesn't matter," he said.

The wisp bounced along, following us as we went. The interior was one spacious room, with old, abandoned equipment scattered here and there. There were plenty of places to hide if you didn't want to be found, as well as plenty of places to stash a body.

The red line that pointed the way apparently didn't stop at the wall of the warehouse. It beamed right into the interior, but unlike the small wisp that gave off a friendly glow of light, the red beam didn't. It looked weird to me. Up close, it reminded me of what you might see if someone had taken a hypercolor marker and drawn through the air. Being this close in proximity to a vibrant stream of color that sliced through the air, the part of the mind that makes things whole couldn't comprehend something about it since it didn't give off any ambient light.

We followed it to the end, which ended up being right in the middle of the warehouse but hidden behind rusted equipment. As soon as the beam ended at the body of this victim, it shifted course and I could then see the same beam of light heading east out of the warehouse, presumably to the next victim.

Of course, by that time, I could smell death. In fact, I caught a whiff of death as soon as I entered the warehouse.

It hadn't been particularly strong and the magical line helped us to ultimately find the body, whereas my smell would have taken a bit longer to follow. Standing right there next to it, however, was a bit overwhelming.

The ball of light that had been bouncing on Cormac's shoulder bounded forward and above the crime scene, where it hovered in a place to provide adequate lighting for everyone. Pretty neat trick, I thought. Should have become a wizard, but I knew that was only a passing thought. I probably would have turned myself into a toad, which would have been a long couple of steps worse than having the ability to turn into a wolf.

"Well, here we are," Cormac said.

At our feet was the victim. Every crime scene that involves a dead body, or hell, anytime you come across a dead body, crime scene or not, there is always a surrealness that surrounds it. Everything looks fake, although you know it isn't, and there is always a sense of sadness that rips the normal thoughts of the day world in two.

This body had begun to decompose. From the looks of it, it looked to be that of a man, but it was hard to tell as the body had semi-long hair and bloat had already set in. We wouldn't know for sure until the body went to the morgue. The smell was strong, but the body still appeared intact. There were no obvious signs of trauma or clues as to how the victim was killed.

The dust in the room was thick and yet the only thing that looked to have disturbed it was Cormac, Dick and me walking into the area. I sniffed again, looking for the familiar scent of cinnamon, and it was there, but very weak. The smell of decomposition overpowered it almost to the point of choking it out of existence, but there was still a hint of it.

"No signs of struggle," Dick said.

"Nope, I don't think we'll find any. It will be similar to all the others," I replied.

"I don't like this one bit," Cormac said. "All this death for what?"

"Something big, I guess," I replied.

"Hmm..." Cormac replied, mulling it over.

The body had been placed on its back with arms crossed over the chest. If I remembered correctly, the placement of the other body in the park looked exactly the same.

"How many people does it take to complete a ritual like this? I mean, do all the ceremonial killings have to take place at the same time?" I asked.

"I'm not sure," Cormac replied. "It depends on the strength of the caster and the amount of energy it needs. One person could do it, if they were someone like Nostradamus, or maybe Rasputin, but I would know about them. Wizards with that much power aren't usually quiet and have a tendency to become known in the normie world. But for this, maybe one person per ritual site, so what does that give us?"

"At least four so far, five when we find the next site, but that scene in the park...that was gruesome. It seems to have been symbolic...or something...about where all the others would be found. Still not sure if they were killed there and moved."

"Could be. Like I said, I don't practice those dark arts. I'm vaguely aware of what can be done but also, when it comes to manipulating the world in ways that the magic casters can...well, there are many ways it can be done and still accomplish the same goal, albeit slightly different," Cormac said.

"Do you know if the body we found in Lafreniere was placed, or did the killing, in fact, happen there?" I asked.

"I'll have to talk to the crime scene bubbas tomorrow. I didn't stay very long when they came and collected. I had reports to write," he said.

"I'm wondering if we should report tonight's finding," I said.

"That's an odd thought," Dick replied. "Why would you think we shouldn't? You think it really matters?"

"Probably doesn't, but if they—whoever they are—have plants inside different city and parish departments, they know how close we are," I said.

"Yeah, but they already know you're onto them, so I don't think it really matters," Cormac said. "Besides, it's my jurisdiction out here and I'm going to call it in."

I chuckled. "Fair enough. What are you going to tell them?"

"I'm going to tell them the truth—that three kids snuck in here, didn't know what the hell was going on, and called me since they knew me," Cormac replied.

"I guess that's a version of truth," I replied.

"You know as well as I do, truth is whatever's written in the report," he replied. "Don't worry about it. I'll make sure it's believable."

He was right about that. Truth and reality are close most of the time, but sometimes, they aren't. But what's written down on paper? Well, that becomes the truth. And no, I don't mean some conspiratorial cover up. I just mean perception, memory, and what people see and think change from the time something happens to the time one writes a report.

"So does anyone see anything that stands out from the other crime scenes?" I asked, then I remembered they were at different ones. The only constant was me, save for the one in City Park but I had visited the site afterward. "Well...between the ones you saw and this one?"

Dick bent down to observe the body. "Besides the decomposition, not really. Whoever did this didn't leave much, if anything, behind."

After Dick finished his thought, I looked over to Cormac, who also appeared to be inspecting the crime scene, the body, the surroundings—everything. When he looked up and saw me staring, "Oh, my turn?" he said. "Okay, well, let's see. I saw the first murder victim this morning, and my second this evening, and the only difference that I can tell is location at this point."

"Unfortunately, that's the only thing I see the difference in, as well," I said glumly.

"Dick, your connection to the families?" I asked.

Dick stood up straight as if he had been slapped. Families, or rather vampire families, were similar in a lot of ways to that of a mafia-type of organization. Meaning they were akin in structure, organization, and were businesslike and very methodical in the way they dealt with things. Dick looked at me in the light of the wisp, which still bounced along happily over the body, and replied, "About as good as your connection to the packs."

Then it wasn't very good. I think you can gather that from what I just told you about our scuffle with the wolves out at Jazzland. "There's no one you talk to?" I asked.

"No, not really. Why?" Dick asked.

"I'm just wondering if they might know what's going on. The way they operate, they always seem to know things. At least that's been my experience in the past," I said.

"Well, I may know one or two, but they're low in the family and won't know anything about what's going on. They only act on what they're told to do," Dick said, then added, "Could talk to their representatives on the high council."

"Yeah, I've tried that before for other things and they are so political that there is never a straight answer. In fact, I leave more confused than when I began most of the time," I said.

"Who isn't political that's on that council?" Dick replied.

He wasn't wrong there. The way I said that made it sound like I went to the council all the time, but the reality of it is that it had only happened a couple of times, and those were extreme cases. I try to stay away from the high council as much as possible because, like Dick just said, who wasn't political on that council? The political games they play with each other are dangerous and the less you're involved, the less chance of getting wrapped up in political maneuvering. I call it the high council, but what I'm referring to is the regional high council. Each region has a representational council for the area that only has one goal—to keep the normal and "otherworldly" worlds separate. Of course, there are accords and rules, but beyond that, there's a lot of wiggle room with maneuvering for power and that's something that everyone wanted, no matter what side of the table they sat on. They wanted power that encompassed both the real and the shadow worlds.

"Well, I don't think the packs are involved, seeing how Luke seemed surprised," I said.

"But what about the other wolf packs in the area?" Dick asked.

"There aren't that many, generally. They like to stick to their own territory, and I think I've only seen one of my kind on the council before. They just don't really care," I replied.

"There are plenty of vampire families and their representatives on the regional council here, with big oil and shipping coming through New Orleans. I mean, every family wants a piece of the pie, so to speak," Dick said.

"I guess that's why I like being a wizard. We like to stick to ourselves and work alone. We see everyone as competition, even our friends," he said.

"But don't you have an association?" I asked.

"Well, yeah, but I can't tell you more than that," he replied. "It's like that one movie that came out years back...if you're in the club, the number one rule is that you don't talk about the club. I'm sure you understand.

I lifted my hands in defense, palms facing forward. "Not prying," I said.

"Good, I wouldn't have told you anyway," he said stone-faced, then after a few moments, gave a wicked half grin.

"I think I may have to report all this to Captain Benoit. Maybe he might have an idea or contact," I said to Dick.

"Well, we should probably keep him in the loop anyway, as he is the one that assigns us these cases," Dick said.

"Captain Benoit...I've heard about him," Cormac said.

"What have you heard?" I asked.

"Oh, you know...a little of this and a little of that," he replied.

"You aren't very straightforward, are you?" I said.

"Only when it matters," he stated matter-of-factly.

"All right, well, we found this body. It's getting late, but we're running out of time," I said.

"Right, but we could come back tomorrow morning and look for the final location," Cormac said. "I'll take care of this and call it in but it's been a long one and after that fight at the Okay Corral at Jazzland, I'm done, end of the world coming at the end of the week or not."

"I think you're right there," I said, and like a freight train, I felt the sap of energy all at once. It had been one hell of a day, and that fight was one for the books. I should have had an adrenaline dump in the drive over to Westwego, but I guess that fight gave me so much adrenaline that the dump didn't come until hours later. Sometimes, that happens—your body just goes into overdrive and as long as your mind is focused, you don't notice it.

Cormac made sense; we were stretched thin this evening. If another group or powerful adversary had been at the warehouse, we probably would not have fared well. Hell, if it wasn't for Morgane, we wouldn't have walked out of that altercation as well as we did. That reminded me that at some point, maybe I should pry and see what Morgane was up to before she came into my life.

We said our goodbyes with the intention of meeting the following day to track down the next murder victim. If Cormac cast the same spell he used at the warehouse, I knew there wouldn't be a problem. Just a matter of following the yellow brick road...or rather the spidery red beam of light.

I drove home and walked through the front door. Morgane squawked at me upon my entrance and flew over to greet me. The room was still a mess as I hadn't had time to clean it when I headed out earlier.

"Where've you been?" Morgane cawed. I may not have mentioned it before, but her voice is guttural and raw, much like you'd expect a bird of her size to sound like, if they could indeed talk.

"It's been quite a day," I said, but was interrupted before I could add anything else.

"Squawk! You don't have to tell me. I was bird napped," she said.

"I know. We went to get you, but you were long gone by the time we arrived," I said. "But thanks for coming back. I'm not sure we would have made it. By the way, when did you learn to breathe fire?"

"There you go asking questions again but...it's a little trick I picked up over the years. Squawk!" she replied. "Did you find what you were looking for?"

"Why do you ask?"

"Well, most people would go home after a fight like that," Morgane replied.

"Yeah, we found what we were looking for, but we aren't finished. A lot of bad juju going on around New Orleans lately," I said.

"There's always bad juju going on somewhere, but what's going on right now in particular?" she asked.

I told her about my day and what Hannah the cat told me.

"So, someone wants to destroy New Orleans? Squawk!"

"It looks that way—a powerful spell, victims murdered in rituals. It points to something big," I replied.

"Maybe I should fly over to Baton Rouge for a few days," Morgane said.

"And leave me here? I'm hurt," I said as I feigned concern, but then I said more seriously, "but if you do go, you may want to keep going, at least as far away as Lafayette."

She hopped on one leg, then calmed down and peered at me with those uncanny, yellow eyes. "I'm not going anywhere, Lou. There's nowhere for me to go."

"But you just said..."

"Squawk! I know what I said, but I also know what I'm going to do. I have nowhere else to go."

I don't know why, but the seriousness with which she said that made my blood chill.

Chapter Sixteen

The next morning came early, and I didn't sleep well, which is what often happens when you have something outside your normal routine planned the next day. Although going to talk to Captain Benoit about what I found so far wasn't that abnormal, I think what did it for me was the gravity of what was unfolding that got to me.

Captain Benoit worked for the department years before I started. I think he came from somewhere out west before settling here. As far as I knew, he was one of the few "normies" who knew about "our world." In all the time that I had known him, he never indicated or shown anything other than normal human reactions. It had been a year or two with me working patrol before the man ever approached me. He was a lieutenant at the time and when he did finally approach me...well, let's just say that when he told me that he knew what I was, I didn't know just how the meeting would end. There are some misguided folks out there that are monster hunters. They see us as abominations. Maybe we are—who's to say, but regardless, I wasn't sure if Benoit was one of them. But he was quick to mention that I was going to be reassigned from working patrol to the investigations unit. That was how I started keeping New Orleans from being a tipping point from the natural world.

I stood tall outside his office and rapped my knuckles across the jamb of the open door. "Come in," I heard his voice say. I entered and crossed the room to sit in one of the two overstuffed, blue leather seats he kept for visitors. He said nothing. The pen he had in hand, he put to the side and brought his fingers to his face in a steeple formation, gazing at me and waiting for me to speak.

"How'd the meeting go after I left?" I asked.

"About as well as you could expect with those types," he replied coolly. "What do you need? You got something?"

"Yes sir," I said. I then relayed all that I had found out up to that point. I told him about other murders and working with Cormac, and then about the fact that someone was trying to stop me from looking further into the case. When I was done, I looked at him and he remained still and silent. Nothing I said seemed to surprise or change his gaze one iota. He dropped his hands to the desk, gave a little sigh, and replied "Well, this isn't good. Why did you wait 'til this morning to tell me?"

"Just one of those things, sir. Still piecing and putting it together myself," I replied.

"I understand," he said. "It was definitely a good thing you didn't have this information at the meeting. That wouldn't have gone well."

"I suspected it wouldn't. Do we know anything about that lady, Mrs. Dufrene?" I asked.

"I do not. I'm not sure if anyone does," he replied.

"Did she...umm...delve into your mind?" I asked.

Captain Benoit looked at me curiously. "Excuse me?"

"Did she talk to you telepathically and try to open doors into your mind?" I asked again.

"No, but I assume she did to you?" Captain Benoit replied, with inflection that usually comes with a question.

I nodded, and he leaned back in his chair. "That's interesting...and a bit concerning. I'll see what I can find out about her using back channels. In the meantime, keep following up and disrupt whatever is coming. I understand how quickly things can happen, so inform me as you go, and do what it takes," he said, then after a pause, "...within reason."

"Yes sir, I'll get on it," I said and in the back of my mind, I could almost hear a bomb timer ticking away. You know the kind I'm talking about—the ones with a digital display and when the number strikes zero...Kablooey! But usually, in the movies and TV shows, the defuser ends up stopping it at one second to oblivion. I think this is one of those situations where I'd rather be dealing with a bomb instead of this unknown.

I got up from the firm yet comfortable seat and headed out into the hall, then right through the next hallway intersection, where I almost ran into Lieutenant Martine. Had I not caught myself, I probably would have bowled her right over, but her quick reflexes were right up there with my own. I quickly stepped to the side to avoid both of us tumbling to the ground.

"Excuse me, ma'am," I said.

"Oh Lou, how are you feeling today?" she asked.

"Much better than I was yesterday," I replied.

"That's good. While you're here, I need you to file your vehicle reports," she said.

Crap. You'd think that hunting bad guys was all sexiness and no mundaneness, but you'd be wrong. Every dollar spent had to be accounted for and for the police department, it was no different. Gas, mileage, and all other expenses had to be accounted for, and I just didn't have the time. Come this time next week, if something didn't change, this vehicle report and all the expenses would be worthless.

"Yes ma'am, I will get right on that, but I have to track down a lead," I replied.

Her body tensed. She had a job to do, and she was going to do it, even if it was just the admin side of the job.

"It'll get done…I promise…but this is a hot lead and I have to get on it right now, or we'll lose out," I told her.

"Working on something for Captain Benoit?" she asked as she looked down the hallway toward his office, then back at me to see my reaction.

"Yes, ma'am," I replied. "If you want, you can go ask him about it."

"No, no, that's okay. I've done that before and I was put in my place," she replied absentmindedly, then looked back at me and sighed. "Get me that report as soon as you can. I need to submit our section's and then let my bosses know it's complete."

"Yes, ma'am," I replied.

She looked at me one more time with an appraising look, then back toward the captain's office before disappearing down the hall toward her own office, without further word.

I, too, disappeared, but in the other direction toward the stairs, which I descended with a quickness. A moment later, I was in my ride and about to depart. I had the photos of the of the crime scene in City Park loaded onto my phone. I paused to look at them. The last site seemed to be downtown Gretna, which was on the west bank and almost due south from my position. There used to be a ferry terminal that connected Gretna to a section of New Orleans called the Irish Channel, but it hadn't been in service for years. The only working ferry at the time was the pedestrian ferry between Algiers, where I lived, and the French quarter. There were two vehicle ferries a bit further down the river, one leading into Chalmette and another in Belle Chasse that connected that part of the west bank to Scarsdale on the east bank. Sometimes, depending on where you were and where you needed to be, the ferry came in handy, depending on the time. It would save you a good 30 to 40 minutes to get to the same spot on the other side of the river. Thankfully, where it looked like I needed to go, highway 90 and the Crescent City Connection would do just fine.

I texted both Dick and Cormac and told them where to meet, if they did indeed decide to meet me. The weather was clear, sunny, and almost blindingly bright. I was pretty sure Dick wouldn't like it, but like I said, he could function, just not as well as he did in the dark.

About 20 minutes later, I pulled into the downtown area of Gretna, or what locals call "Old Gretna." It was a quaint area for the town that was home to about 5,000 souls. You would think it a small town but with the sprawl of New Orleans and other towns nearby that were familiar with Gretna, it had the appearance of being a much larger area and it was also the county seat for Jefferson Parish. Downtown had several restaurants, a covered parking area that was once part of a train depot and for years, has been used for festivals and farmer's markets. All this bordered the Mississippi, so after parking, a family could go enjoy the sights. Oh, I almost forgot—they had a sidewalk atop the levee that spanned the three miles between the Gretna and Algiers ferry stations, and a dirt trail that went even further beyond the paved areas. Quite a few people used it for hiking or cycling. A picturesque scene that could have been anywhere in America but just happened to be Gretna.

I got out of my ride and waited in the area along the main drag. Dick walked up from the south and wore his usual dark sunglasses that, if the same shade were on the tinted windows of a personal vehicle and tested for legality, would have failed miserably.

"Dick, I was always curious. When do you rest?" I asked.

The question caught him off guard. "What do you mean?"

"Well, I know you're sort of a night guy, but here you are, out in the middle of the day. Do you sleep at night?" I asked.

"Yeah, something like that. Back before the wonders of this day and age, obviously, I would not have been caught dead in daylight or that would have been exactly how it played out. Around the 50s, things changed and now, those that have turned to modern medicine are like anyone else for the most part—some are night owls and others aren't," he replied.

"Yeah, I think I remember that back in the 50s when I came across the first vam..." I almost completed the word before I realized where I was and stopped to make sure no one else was near before continuing. "Well, my first experience with seeing someone like you walking in the daylight really surprised me, though I do feel for the first son of a gun who tried that out. I mean, I don't think anyone would have jumped to be first to see if it worked," I finished.

"Well," Dick began, "From what I heard, I don't think they had much of a choice."

"How's that?" I asked.

"I don't know, but I heard that the first trials were done on people condemned to be punished," he said.

Now listen, I know I'm a police officer but some laws that I would enforce in the normie world on normie people, I wouldn't do so on the other kinds of folks that walk the land. Every magic, supernatural, other-worldly...whatever...had their own customs and rules. What they did to themselves or to each other didn't matter much to me, but what they did to another species in broad daylight or to a normie...well, that's another story. Just thought I would catch you up on that little tidbit, so you didn't get confused. Anyway, Dick continued, "It was usually reserved for those that deserved death but were given an alternative."

"I guess they really didn't have much of a choice," I said.

"No, they didn't," Dick replied, and then, seeing Cormac show up from the west, added, "And there's our wayward wizard."

"And good morning to you two, as well," he replied.

"Right. How'd last night end up?" I asked.

"About how you'd imagine. The paperwork was stupid because I had two to catch up on—the one in Lafreniere Park and the one last night, so I'm not too happy right now. Didn't sleep long, or well for that matter," he replied.

"Would you like some coffee? My treat," I offered.

"You owe me more than coffee, but that's a start," he said.

"Dick, I would ask you, but I know you don't stomach such things," I said.

"Oh, that must be dreadful," Cormac said.

Dick shrugged. "It's not as bad as you think. I hardly remember the stuff and, to be honest, when things make you sick, you never really desire them."

"I guess, but damn..." Cormac said.

I stopped by the Daily Grind; it was a café along the main drag which sat across from the covered parking area where the farmer's market was usually held Saturday mornings. The place was always packed at that time. I headed inside and went to the bar where I ordered two coffees to go, then stood near the entrance by the black and gold "Please wait to be seated" sign. Since it was midweek, the place was steady, but it wasn't crowded, and thankfully, it didn't take long for the two steamy coffees to make their way to the bar top.

I headed back outside and handed one to Cormac, who nodded his thanks.

"So, where do you think this one is?" Dick asked, referring to the reason we were in good ol' downtown Gretna.

"Beats me. It has to be somewhere around here. I mean, Cormac, can't you do your thing again?" I asked.

"You mean here in broad daylight?" he replied.

"You have any better ideas?" I asked.

"I could think of a few but right now at this time of day, no," he replied. "The only reason that worked so well last night was the dying light of the sun. In full daylight, it would be very difficult to see. The darker it is, the better it is to see a light. Get it?"

"Damn, can't seem to catch any breaks. I'm sure that the crime scene is around here close by. The last ones were very close in proximity to the locations on the map," I responded.

With no better ideas, we strolled across the street toward the covered parkway, this time bringing us close to the non-functioning train caboose that had been at its current location since 1986. Bright red with letters that read "Illinois Central." Not sure why a train labeled "Illinois Central" was basically a monument in a south Louisiana downtown, but hey...stranger things have happened, right? I mean, you're talking to a werewolf, so there's that. I mean, I do know that the Illinois Central Railroad had a terminal here in Gretna. In fact, I rode it a few times over the years before travel by car became easier and before the Canadian National Railway bought it out. As for the little red caboose (that actually wasn't so little in person), an individual at one time could do tours of it, but that was years ago and by this time...well, I wasn't sure what it was most recently used for. As our stroll took us near this caboose, I felt my hackles raise. If I were the monster instead, my hair would have stood on end.

"Wait a minute," Cormac said.

"Yeah, I feel it too," I replied.

"As do I," Dick added.

Sometimes, when there is a powerful spell of warding or barrier of some type, it gives off an electrical sensation—a sort of buzzing—and whatever it was, was close by. I looked around, but the only thing that was really close by was the red caboose from Illinois.

"I think this just might be it," I said.

"Could be," Cormac said. "Give me a second and I'll have that side door open in a moment."

With that, he hopped up onto the small landing area on one side of the car and tried the door. It was locked as we thought it would be, but knowing Cormac, I knew a locked door wasn't going to stop him. He looked around, which made him look super suspicious—enough to make me also look around to make sure no one noticed, which, in turn, probably made me look suspicious. But I just couldn't help myself. Dick, however, just nonchalantly stood there while Cormac did his thing.

Cormac's face became focused. He put his hand over the handle and locking mechanism and I assumed channeled magical energy. Nothing happened. Cormac glanced at me, then back to the door, where he then closed his eyes, took a deep breath, and again attempted whatever it was he had just done. His efforts were to no avail, it seemed, because after a moment, he looked disgusted and a bit frustrated. He turned toward me and hopped down.

"I'm not sure what's going on. My wizardly ways aren't working," he said. "Probably some sort of dispel magic or something...I don't know."

"I can give it a try," I said.

He chuckled. "If I can't get it open with my stuff, I don't think you will."

"I'm stronger than I look," I replied.

"I know that," Cormac said in a voice that had a serious inflection of sarcasm, "but what I meant was, you need to be careful. You rip a door off its hinges and not only will that be hard to explain, but I don't think you want to answer to the city of Gretna and its citizens on why you destroyed their monument."

I was about to say something snarky back, but he was absolutely right and that wasn't something I had considered. I probably would have ripped the door clean off if

I weren't careful. So, I kept my mouth shut and nodded back, then gripped the railing and hoisted myself up onto the platform. I stood in front of the door and gave it a slow, steady tug. It didn't budge. I put my left hand on the doorjamb and my other hand beside it on the door, creating a diamond wedge. It looked like the door opened inward and if I could create enough focused force, I thought maybe I could budge it without causing too much damage. These are the days where I wish the story about the wolf in the three little pigs' story was true and I could huff and puff, but as far as I know, that wolf was a magic-user like Cormac and didn't do any unaided huffing and puffing.

My inner monster always wanted to get out, and it was sometimes hard to gauge how much I could withstand before it took over. Over the years, I've gotten better at it and obviously with modern medicine, that's helped too, but it was still always a controlled chaos kind of thing. It's kind of like fire—if you weren't careful, you'd burn yourself, and others, while you were at it.

I let a little bit of it go and I could feel my muscles bulge, then I had the unfortunate thought about what would happen had it gotten away from me. Not only would another suit be ruined but I'd also be letting half of downtown Gretna know that there was more to the world than what they thought. I'd hate to have to explain that. In fact, I would have rather destroyed the little caboose and have to explain that. Thankfully, I reined in my concentration and honed in on that small area of the door between my palms. With the extra strength, I pushed, and I kept pushing. Five seconds went by, then 10, then 20. I kept adding force. I would have done better with a crowbar, but since I didn't have one, well, that was it. A minute went by. I could feel my face was flushed with exertion.

"Hey, Lou," Cormac said, "If you can't get it, that's okay. Don't stroke out."

I ignored the comment and kept going. Two minutes went by, and I could feel myself getting angry and frustrated. The good thing is that I don't turn green, but I have the perchance to turn brown and hairy with my condition. I approached that fine line between controlled chaos and uncontrolled chaos, and it was over a stupid door that wouldn't budge.

My body shifted, and I could feel the onset of the change. My muscles grew in size in response to the strain. I had to be really careful at this point because this was like dancing on the bladed edge of a knife—one mistake and you fall to either side, or straight down and cut yourself. It was a dance where failure had no options for a good outcome. The voice down deep within my mind asked, "Why are you doing this? There is no need to run the risk."

My body began to hurt, bones reconfiguring, and the material of my suit grew uncomfortably snug against my growing muscles. Any more change and the threads that held the cloth together would rip apart. I had to stop, but I was fixated on opening the door. I couldn't bring myself to stop, so I pushed harder. It must have worried Dick, because I sensed that he had jumped up on the landing with me. He put his hand on my shoulder, "Lou, stop. Let it go."

But I couldn't. Come Hell or high water, this door was going to open or the residents of Gretna, Louisiana were about to get their first glimpse of a full-blown monster. That thought caused me to chuckle because I could just imagine some old granny enjoying retirement getting the shock of her life, and for some reason, it made me laugh to myself. For the record, I would never intentionally harm an old grandma, but my gallows humor made me smile at the mental image. Well, I wasn't sure if it were a smile or a grimace at that point.

I could feel something shift, ever-so-slightly, with the door. I pressed and focused harder, then suddenly, the door burst open, and I tumbled inside to the floor. The exertion and sudden relief drained me, and I stayed on the floor of the interior to regain my composure and give me a little rest as I "came back." I looked at the door from my position and saw Dick standing at the entrance, but he wasn't looking at me. He was looking into the room and I gleaned from his expression and general look of horror, that it was something serious. I shifted my gaze toward the interior and my face, too, took on the same expression of terror.

There was a low table in the room, and on top of it, there was a body, but unlike the others that had a peaceful, almost mannequin-like display, this body looked far from peaceful. Someone had ripped it apart and left it in a bloody jumble on the table. Whoever put the barrier there must have done it to keep the odor from seeping out. Since I had opened the door, the smell had become overpowering, as if it had taken on a life of its own and assaulted the senses. If I hadn't had such a strong stomach, whatever I had eaten in the prior few hours would have immediately joined the scene from my position, but thankfully, I held on. It could have been because my sense of smell was so powerful, but I doubted it was that alone. I could see Dick's face twist in response to the putrid smell, and when Cormac stuck his face into the doorway, he had the same response. It wasn't a pretty sight at all.

Now that I was back to my normal self, Dick stepped in and stuck his hand out to pull me up.

"Thanks," I replied.

He said nothing as he walked in to inspect the scene. The interior of the caboose had become a storage area. There were boxes all along the walls and miscellaneous items displayed throughout. The boxes that lined the walls had overtaken the windows so no one would have been able to see the carnage, and with the scent masked, no one would have had any reason to look in.

I sniffed once again to see if I could smell the telltale scent of cinnamon that I had detected at the other locations. It took a moment, and I had to really work at it, but eventually, I made out the ever-so-faint spicy aroma. It was negligible, but it was there, all right.

"Well, we found it," I said.

"Wish we hadn't," Cormac replied.

Chapter Seventeen

I had to agree. This wasn't something that anyone should or would look forward to if they were in their right mind. Unfortunately, there are some things you have to be realistic about, especially when dealing with otherworldly creatures and events. Some don't think at all like you would expect them to. Some are so abstract that even get a glimpse would cause confusion due to being counter-intuitive to what normies know and believe, but to whatever that being was, it would be completely normal for them.

"Why do you think this one is different from the others?" Cormac asked.

"I don't know. Maybe it signifies the last point, the first point being the messy location at the hill in City Park. Maybe the victim struggled. I just don't know," I replied.

Looking at the carnage, I could see long hair. The fingernails had polish on them, but in this day and age, that didn't mean anything concrete. It could have been male or female. I also saw a high heel attached to one foot, but again, nothing is what it seems these days, especially in a place like New Orleans and surrounding areas.

"You know anyone on the Gretna Police Department?" I asked.

"No, not really. As far as I know, they don't have a special investigations unit," Cormac replied.

I caught his meaning. "Have you ever had to deal with something here?"

Most of my cases were in New Orleans proper. It was very rare for me to go beyond the city limits because, let's face it, New Orleans had enough to deal with on its own. But every once in a while, a case like this became multi-jurisdictional, which was fine for the most part until a case went into other states. Then it became a big hassle. If you thought dealing with feds was bad, just think about dealing with feds with special powers. It's a whole different ball game.

"Yeah, I've had to investigate this area a couple of times over the years. I know the process. I will contact my guys at JPSO and they'll come take care of it, letting the police department know it's ours," Cormac said. "It'll ruffle their feathers but they'll get over it. If they don't have to pay for it and things are still getting resolved, so much the better."

"So now what?" Dick asked. "Besides locating all the victims, what else is there to do?"

"Beats me," I said, but the clock in the back of my mind was ticking away. I could feel the countdown and an uneasiness about everything. What if we didn't find the solution in time? It's hard to maintain composure and get focused when you have a possible end of the world, or at least end of the world as most know it, that looms over everything.

"Who'd benefit from destroying the area?" I asked.

"Depends on how bad it's destroyed," Dick replied. "Remember after Katrina, a lot of property changed hands in the aftermath because half the people left and said good riddance?"

"Could just be a group that wants to watch the world burn?" Cormac interjected. "We can't rule out folks like those that committed 9/11 and just want to cause destruction over some perceived notion."

"Well, whatever it is, you know as well I do that time is ticking," I replied.

"You don't have to remind me," Cormac said.

Cormac did indeed call it in. Shortly thereafter, units from JPSO arrived and along with Gretna Police department, cordoned off the area and removed the body. Crime scene technicians went through with a fine-tooth comb, but from what I saw, it didn't look like there was much to collect other than the body. I noticed, however, that the blood spatter was unnaturally lacking, which seemed at odds with the state the body was found in. I wonder if the unfortunate victim was murdered and dismembered elsewhere.

"Cormac, do you know if your office has identified the other bodies yet?" I asked.

"Probably not," he replied, "But I will...ahem...get them to focus on this."

I wasn't surprised at his answer. I was hopeful, really, but I knew that with the backlog, along with the short staff that law enforcement agencies encountered these days, it might be a while before they made a determination.

About an hour later, I was in my ride and driving back to the office. I had no other angles to work. When I turned onto the Westbank Expressway, heading back toward New Orleans, I had a moment to think. The previous few days had been a blur and at some point in the journey, it occurred to me that I never followed up with detective Green or Allain about the meeting they had with the werepig. Granted, I couldn't tell them that he was a werepig, but it didn't detract from the fact that they talked to him and that I needed to see what they were working on. We were supposedly working on this together but it's kind of tough to work together when one half of the team has to be kept in the dark. I hoped they had found something or had other ideas or options I had either overlooked or wasn't even aware of. Sometimes, it's the good old mundane police work of reviewing records that lead to justice.

I arrived back at the office at the same time that Dick did, and we rode the elevator up together. We left Cormac back in Gretna and he assured us he'd catch up with us later that afternoon once he had more of a handle on his end.

"This case is one for the books, so far," Dick said conversationally.

"Agreed. Everything about this seems to lead to dead ends or nothing really to show for it, but at least we appear to have found all the victims, and that will bring closure to the families once we find out who they are," I replied.

"Yeah, either that or grief, if they hadn't known their loved one was missing," Dick said.

"That too," I replied. "Hopefully, once we identify them, we will piece together their last known whereabouts as of last Friday night."

I said that confidently, but down deep, I was shooting in the dark here, hoping to connect with anything that made sense. The elevator dinged its arrival to the detective bureau's floor, and the doors slid open to reveal Lieutenant Martine. It looked like she was waiting for the elevator to take her somewhere. Upon seeing us, she stepped back to allow us room to get off. "I heard you found a body in Gretna," she said.

"Yeah, we were meeting with a friend of mine on JPSO sharing information, and wouldn't you know it? We stumbled on that body," I said.

She cocked her eye at me, not believing one word of it, but she didn't say anything. "Well, jurisdiction or not, I want a report about what happened and...get me those damn vehicle reports. The deadline is close of business today. If you don't, you are going to get days on the beach, and I mean it." That's police-speak for a couple days of leave without pay.

"Yes, ma'am, I will get that for you right away," I replied, and knew that I would have to bite the bullet and just do it. The end of the world was coming, but the little stuff still had to be done.

Her face still gave off an "if looks could kill" expression as the door closed. "She was in rare form today," Dick said, then continued, "Not usually like that. I wonder what's up."

"These killings make for high-profile cases. She's 'in charge' and she doesn't know what's going on. That and she needs those vehicle reports," I replied mildly, but I could appreciate her position. I'm sure it's frustrating when you truly didn't know what was going on in an area that you had responsibility for. But such is life. It's like that sometimes.

I felt like I didn't have extra time, but it really is amazing all the time you have when you just focus. After encountering Lieutenant Martine, I went straight to my desk and knocked out my vehicle report. So, now I didn't have to worry about that for another month. It was always the small stuff that added up that made the job stressful. Shootings, homicides, grand theft—sure, those are bound to create tension. Paperwork, miscellaneous budget items, accountability—I could go on, but all of it all mixed together made for both good and bad days.

I looked over at Dick in his cubicle and could see that he was finishing up his report, as well. Good vamp...uh...man.

Now, if Detectives Green and Allain had been around, that report might not have gotten done right away like it did, but they weren't, so it did. It was around lunch time, so I figured they were out grabbing a bite to eat. That reminded me, but my stomach let me know I was hungry, as well. I asked Dick if he needed anything from the vending machine, but then stopped. No, of course he didn't. No matter how long I've worked with him, I've always felt the need to ask. It's the polite thing to do, but he's a vampire and old habits die hard.

Out in the hallway, I stood before the vending machine to make a selection. I don't know how much money I had put into that machine over the years, but I know whoever owned it had a pretty good chunk of change from me alone. But the good thing about it was that the inventory was usually pretty fresh and replenished frequently. The bad thing was that I was the reason that it needed to be replenished frequently. Hmm...D12 and B32 were always good selections—honey buns and a ding dong.

From behind me, I could smell the food from one of the local favorites that Greene and Allain liked to grab food from before heading back. It was a barbecue joint near the

Central Business District. It was a neat little place that had the entire block cordoned off, using shipping containers as walls around the perimeter. They had one way in and out, but in the center was parking, and the building was off to one side. The rest of the "yard" had elevated platforms for entertainment on weeknights and weekends. It was a nice setup and the food…well, it was much better than a honey bun and a ding dong. The smell alone caused my stomach to grumble a little louder at my poor choices.

"Ugh, how can you eat that stuff?" I heard Detective Green call from behind me.

I turned around to respond. "Very easily. I mean, someone has to keep this guy in business. Central City again?" I said, looking at the nondescript bags they had in hand.

"Very good. How did you know?" she responded.

"Because you are a victim of habit," I said and then to myself, "and I have a nose like you wouldn't believe." But seriously…she wouldn't.

"No, I'm not…am I?" she asked.

"No, just kidding. Just a good guess," I lied.

They walked past me, heading to the break room to eat. Some detectives ate out, some ate at their desks, and others ate in the break room. There wasn't a hard and fast rule, but people tended to go with what they felt comfortable with. Before they got too far down the hallway, I asked, "Hey, the interview the other day…did anything come of it with that manager from the gentleman's club?"

Allain turned. "No, not really. A lot of nothing, if you ask me. He reminded me of a pig, but I honestly think that's just the kind of person he is."

I almost broke out in laughter, but luckily caught myself. He couldn't have said a truer statement about that werepig manager.

He continued, "We heard you found more bodies. You think they're connected? I mean, you never really know, right?"

"I think so, but I'm waiting to hear back from my contact with JPSO. I'll let you know what I find," I replied.

They both nodded and headed on to fill their stomachs. I was left in the hallway with...well, with nothing. I needed to find out the other victims' identities, but I had to wait for that. I hated waiting, especially when the stakes were so high. My mind drifted for a moment, thinking about things and then my stomach rumbled loudly to remind me. "Hey, fathead! Eat!" So, I did what anyone in my position with hands full of snacks would do: I ate.

Chapter Eighteen

With the smell of barbecue lingering in the hallway, I headed back to my desk. "Dick, let's go talk to that club manager. Something just doesn't feel right."

"Didn't Green and Allain already talk to him?" he asked.

"Yeah, they did, but I don't think they broke him, and besides, I think you and I can provide a little extra leverage," I replied.

Dick looked straight ahead and didn't acknowledge what I had said for a moment. He must have been mulling it over in his mind because he shrugged his shoulders and said, "Makes sense. Let's go."

Before heading over to Bourbon Street, I hopped into Dick's ride and off we went. My phone buzzed, and I saw it was Cormac.

"Hello," I answered.

"Hey Lou, I got something back on the body from Lafreniere Park," he said.

"Yeah, whatcha got?" I asked.

"Samantha Reardon, age 22, exotic dancer. Records show that she worked at the Top Level Club on Bourbon Street," he said.

"Strangely enough, that's where we're heading now," I said.

I heard Cormac curse on the other end of the line. "You serious?" he asked.

"Yeah, something about that place and the manager don't set right with me," I replied.

"You want me to come?" Cormac asked.

"Nah, I think Dick and I will be all right. Besides, we're almost there," I said.

Cormac said nothing, but I could tell something weighed on his mind. "It'll be okay. I'll call you as soon as we're done," I added.

"Hmm...okay," he said, but he didn't sound convinced.

We disconnected, and I relayed to Dick what Cormac had said.

"Maybe he should come," Dick said when I finished.

"Eh...we'll be all right," I replied, but since Dick seemed nervous...well...that kind of crap has a way of being contagious, and I was no longer so sure. This whole thing was weird—multiple murder victims and two that worked at a place could have been a coincidence, but when three happen to work at the same place, it's more than a trend and connection. That location had something to do with this whole thing. If not the club itself, the people associated with it were. Oh well...it was just us at that point.

"If we get into trouble, I'm sure some of the foot patrol will be nearby. They always are on Bourbon Street," I said.

"Yeah, but there aren't as many of them as there used to be," Dick said, emphasizing the loss of manpower that NOPD had faced in recent years.

"Meh...we'll be all right," I said again.

And I really thought we would be, even with the shade of doubt that bloomed a small shadow in the corner of my thoughts. That was until we came around the last corner and parked on a side street down a block from the club. When Dick and I left the car to step up onto the sidewalk to head toward the club, that's when we heard gunfire.

Whenever you hear a gunshot, the immediate reaction is, "Did I really just hear that?" no matter how many times it happens. It could be fireworks, and this city is kind of known for its fireworks around the 4th of July and New Year's Eve celebrations. In fact, it sounds eerily similar to a heavy firefight during wartime, but that wasn't July nor was it New Year's Eve, and it was during the day, which also wasn't a prime time for fireworks. Dick immediately unholstered his weapon, and I followed suit.

The gunfire continued. It wasn't a "pop pop" sound; it was a sustained rate of fire with brief moments of rest in between. Someone was shooting up a place. We had an active shooter on Bourbon Street. I cursed to myself. Just what we needed today, of all days. Dick took off at a sprint and I loped behind him, keeping up. The mid-afternoon crowd ahead of us broke into a run to get away from the source of the gunfire. Since Dick and I parked on a side street, Bourbon street was in front of us as a cross street, so all we saw were people running from right to left in front of us, and we couldn't see the threat. Thank God this active shooter situation didn't happen at night. That would have been utter chaos with the number of people that frequent Bourbon street after the sun goes down.

We got to the corner and by the time we arrived, the street had cleared, for the most part, at least around us. People had either run into bars or other establishments for safety, or they continued to run until they found an alleyway to go down. On the street itself, we still couldn't see the threat, but continued to hear the gunfire. Both Dick and I homed in on where it originated, the Top Level Club. The gunfire then became more sporadic and less sustained. Dick and I bounded ahead, covering each other, moving from one restaurant door to the next. Yeah, we could have run blindly toward the source, but when something crazy happens, it's easy to get tunnel vision and lose all sight and comprehension of what's going on around you. More than one law enforcement officer has learned that lesson the hard way. Make it a point to know your surroundings as you engage a target. You don't want to run straight into an ambush inadvertently. Dick and I had worked together long enough that we knew each other, so we responded slowly and methodically. Well, maybe a bit faster than slowly, but we were very fluid and deliberate with our movements.

So far, no one had left the front entrance to the club and with no windows, there was no way to tell what was going on. We got about half a block away from the establishment and saw two individuals with long arms leaving the front entrance. They were dressed all in black, but from my distance, I couldn't tell if they were wearing black suits or jeans and long sleeve t-shirts. I could see that they were wearing full-faced helmets—the kind that bikers wear which conceal features.

They wasted no time moving to engage us. The back of my mind rang with alarm. These people knew what they were doing. They moved with confidence and didn't seem to be tweakers looking for a score or just some lunatics out on a bender of rage.

There wasn't much cover to fight from, but the gunmen didn't have any either, so instead of waiting for them to find cover and set up defensive positions, I started unloading my pistol. We were outgunned but if Dick and I could establish some sort of fire superiority, maybe we would get lucky and wing them first or at least cause them to break for hard cover. Dick followed my lead and started spraying with his pistol, one bullet at a time, in quick succession.

I don't think the two targets expected that, and they quickly reversed themselves and backed into the club, which gave me great relief. My little gamble worked out, but I wasn't sure how long I could play that game.

When they went back inside, the whole area was strangely quiet and surreal in the absence of gunfire, but I knew it was only a lull before lead would fly again. Dick and I moved closer. At least if we could contain them to the club, no one outside the club would be in danger, I hoped.

Dick and I ran forward and closed the distance between ourselves and the entrance. By then, I could hear sirens in the distance, but that didn't mean help was imminent. We got to the entrance, with Dick cautiously moving up to the side of the door. I quickly ran across the opening, which was probably a stupid move, but thankfully, no one shot at me as I passed the doorway. I took up the other side of the door. From my vantage point, I could see into the foyer of the club. I couldn't see the entire room, but in the part that I did see, there wasn't a threat. I looked over at Dick and he shook his head. Apparently, he saw nothing either. I did a quick peek to get a full view and whoever the gunmen were, they must have retreated further into the interior. Normally, in situations like this, we would set up a perimeter and wait for SWAT to arrive and do their thing, but knowing what I knew, we didn't have time for that. Dick and I shared a knowing glance and nodded. We launched into the room. I proceeded first and crossed the opening again, but this time I entered the room and moved along the wall, initially clearing the right corner to make sure no one was waiting there. Dick did the same on the other side. There was a science and art to room clearing. Like I mentioned earlier, it was easy to get into a tunnel vision mode, meaning that if something wasn't right in front of you, you wouldn't notice it. Many a person have made that mistake by not checking corners when entering a room where a threat might be located, and unfortunately, it was often the last mistake they made.

Further inside, we could hear movement and moans from what we could only assume was someone, or several someones, who had met their demise. An open doorway between the foyer and the rest of the club led to the carnage that awaited us. I knew there were at least two assailants, but who knew? There could have been a whole mess of them just waiting for us. I still couldn't get the idea of a trap out of my head, especially since I had been sent messages to stay away. Was this another message? Kind of extreme, but really, what was extreme when whoever was responsible for this was plotting the end of the world as we know it? No, this wasn't a warning. This was a last-minute cleanup order to keep things on schedule. And that pushed my mind to the next question—if they would do this in broad daylight, in front of everyone, just how far would they go to keep the train on the tracks and plowing ahead? I guess it wouldn't matter if all the witnesses were dead in a few days, depending on how bad the fallout from whatever was coming. Or, it could have been a complete coincidence, and perhaps this was just a "normie" incident involving an organized crime element knocking off competition. Even that felt far-fetched, but you never really knew. My mind raced through these thoughts and I had to fight to bring it back to the issue at hand—surviving this encounter—so I could be there to figure out the rest of it.

It seemed like they had finished shooting inside, but evidently they had not. I then heard more singular shots as if they were mopping up. Screams suddenly ceased as well as some of the moans. If Dick and I were going to get anything worth using, we had to forge ahead. The monster wanted to come out. I could feel it seething under the surface. I could be quick, but in my alter ego form, I was lightning fast and could move at speeds that were almost incomprehensible to normal humans, not to mention that my healing abilities would be on point. In close quarters battle, which is what this situation had become, violence of action more often than not won the day. Since my sidearm would only do so much against two or more people with long arms, I was about to become the most violent entity in the building. I holstered my weapon because, again, the things on my belt usually stayed with me for the transformation. I took off my suit jacket. No sense in ruining yet another secondhand special from Red, White, and Blue

Thrift Store. The shirt would be a total goner though, as I didn't have time to remove it carefully. The beast raged against the cage deep inside and I unlocked the door and swung it wide. Immediately, the familiar churning in my stomach began. Dick stepped back but continued to cover the entrance just in case some individual became brave and rushed us. My forearms tightened and grew in size. My face hurt as my jaw dislocated and readjusted. I know being a werewolf sounds cool and all, but it's no walk in the park.

If anyone had watched the transformation and could keep their sanity, it would appear that it happened almost instantaneously, but for me, the pain it involved caused time to slow down. It felt like an eternity in what would normally be a few seconds. Maybe that's why werewolves were always portrayed as scary and perpetually cranky. A bad mood was unavoidable when the pain caused one to go to the brink of insanity. However, when in dire situations, it was an ace up the sleeve only to be used in case of emergencies, which Dick and I realized we were definitely experiencing.

My vision was clear, and my already heightened sense of smell became more acute. I took a deep breath, and that gave me all that I needed to know. Yes, there were several victims inside, but I could detect distinct smells. Obviously, among those was blood, but I could also smell the weapons they used in the mix of used gunsmoke from spent rounds. In the hodgepodge of aromas, I could identify the telltale smell of gun oil and due to the various degradation of said gun oil, it told me that there were at least four rifles. Okay...so there should have been four individuals in the club unless someone was really gung ho and carrying more than one rifle, but I doubted it from what I saw of the two a moment prior. I took another moment and shifted focus from my nose to my ears. I could hear them moving inside.

From my previous trip here, I knew that the room opened up into a long platform from the other side of the room on which ladies of the profession would ply their trade. It was front and center as you entered the room. To the right and left, along the wall, were booths and tables. There were two other platforms at each side of the long walkway for more viewing pleasure. There was one long bar on the right where the bartender served their overpriced drinks. I couldn't remember, but I think the bathrooms were to the left, then there was another hallway in the back left corner where the manager's office was, then led to private rooms and, off from that, the dressing rooms for the dancers. So far, judging from the sounds, there were two behind the long bar to the right, and two in the booths on the left. If I were them, I would have been covering the door. In fact, it would be pretty stupid for me to go through that next opening because...well...it was a sort of death trap just waiting to get sprung. Unfortunately, I had to be the one to spring it. Well, I guess Dick could have, and had it been nighttime, I would have let him. As fast as I am, he is definitely faster after dark, but during the day, even with the meds that allowed him to walk in the sunlight...well, let's just say that he wasn't on his "A" game during the day.

I looked at Dick and touched him lightly on the shoulder. When he looked back, I leaned in and told him what I surmised from what I gathered from my senses. I also ripped off my magazine holder, which had one remaining magazine full of ammo. I wasn't going to use it and since we used the same model of pistol, he might be able to. He took it from me and nodded his thanks, then stood back to give me room.

I then stepped through the doorway.

Chapter Nineteen

Although I entered that doorway at a sprint, I didn't expect what confronted me. The gruesome nature of the room nearly caused me to pause at the horrific scene. That is, until I realized that at least four rifles were trained in on the door. I moved quickly as the report of bullets being fired rang in my ears. Since sound moves slowly, that meant that so far, the bullets had missed, and I only heard the sound after they passed me. The fire was so rapid and excessive that it produced a staccato of sound.

I went right, intending to take out the two behind the bar, using the bar as cover against the other two across the room. Being in beast mode with adrenaline pumping only added to my wicked strength. I didn't even have to run very far into the room before I leapt with all my might into the air. This move could have been dangerous, as it's impossible to change direction midway in the air. If the target in front of me had a good aim, I would have been shot multiple times as I flew to the end of my trajectory. So, instead of jumping straight to the target, I leapt toward the wall to the right, then as soon as I touched the wall, I used my momentum to kick off the wall directly into the bar area where two gunmen were spraying. This kind of jump did two things: it avoided my jumping straight into danger, as I mentioned, as well as made it more difficult for all four of the gunman to aim in on me. There are three rules to engagement that every police officer or military member should know in a firefight—shoot, move, communicate. Since I didn't have a gun, I couldn't shoot, and since I knew Dick would come in shortly, I didn't have to communicate. He knew what we were dealing with. The only thing I had at my disposal was movement. If you stopped out in the open with people shooting at you, you only made it easier for them.

I sailed over the bar and into the gunman closest to me. Unfortunately, since I was closest to him and there wasn't much wiggle room, he was able to bring his rifle in line with my movement and the rounds from his rifle grazed my shoulder. But fortunately, since I already had momentum, it didn't slow me down as I slammed through him, taking him to the floor behind the bar. I could hear the bullets from the two across the room slam into the bar at my side. If it had only been a wooden bar with shelves, I would have taken those rounds, but since there was a deep sink and ice-filled cooler where the bartenders retrieved bottles of beer, I didn't. They slammed through the wood, but the metal slowed the rounds enough to prevent them from posing a serious threat.

My shoulder was on fire, and that only added to my anger and adrenaline levels. The target on the floor had a helmet on. In fact, all of them had helmets, now that I noticed, so there was no way to identify who they might be. I grabbed the person underneath me, raising him up between me and the next gunman down the bar. I then ran forward, using the body as a shield. Professional or not, those gun nuts didn't seem to care or slow down, even though one of their own was in the way. It didn't faze them one bit. I could feel the vibration through the body as bullets from automatic fire perforated my human shield...or at least, I assumed it was human.

When I got close to the next gunman, I noticed long, flowing, jet-black hair streaming from the helmet and down the back. Gunwoman? The body seemed to be smaller, and I saw telltale signs in the chest area that would confirm a woman. I hated to hurt women...I mean, I absolutely hate it, but when they're trying to kill me...well, in that case, I didn't mind so much. I rammed right through her with the body I had in hand. She went down under the onslaught. Her rifle waved through the air, still in her hand below me, and I grabbed it by the barrel, stood up and hurled it, striking one assailant across the room. The lady rolled to the side and came up, blade flashing in hand. She was fast—supernaturally fast—but I was quicker. I slashed with my right hand, meeting her arm, which couldn't withstand the sharp nails at the ends of my fingers. It took her arm clean off and she dropped to the floor, motionless. I would have thought blood would have spurted, but it didn't. In a normal situation, I would have stopped to think about that, but there were two shooters left and I didn't have time to focus.

I don't know how many magazines they had, but they were burning through their ammo rather quickly. I think they realized it, too, because the tempo began to slow. They still had fire superiority...I mean, of course they did. I didn't have a gun handy to shoot back. The one on my hip didn't fit into my big ol' hands very well.

Dick joined the fray and entered through the doorway, gun blazing. The focus shifted from me to the new threat, which was the moment I needed. It gave me enough time to leap over the bar and lope to the side of the platform that split the room. It reminded me of another time when I learned a ditty to be used in situations like this while assaulting a position: "I'm up. They see me. I'm down." You only wanted to move within your opponent's visibility for a couple of seconds because as soon as you did so, they'd traverse their aim back, but by the time they had you in their sights again, you were behind cover of some sort and would hopefully avoid being hit. This time was no different because I heard a few shots splinter into the platform.

Dick dove for the booth closest to him and took time to reload his last magazine, or rather, my last magazine. Once he emptied that one, he was out of ammo and although the booth was technically cover, it wasn't the best. I knew I had to move quickly.

I waited for the moment I heard one of the shooters hit the magazine release to reload and when I did, I pushed myself into motion with all the might my legs had. This launched me into the air and as I flew, I saw the dancing pole and used it to my advantage. I grabbed a hold of the pole and the momentum from my launch, along with the natural centrifugal force of swinging on the pole, allowed me to release at the apex where my natural fall would end up right on the shooter closest to the hallway of private rooms.

I knew he saw me coming, but he was also so focused on reloading his rifle that the image of a huge beast charging would cause anyone to panic, leading him to drop the magazine to the floor. He should have gone to the sidearm but instead, he reached for the magazine, not gauging the time he had left. I landed on him as planned. He was stronger than I thought because when he stood up, it caused me to fall backwards where I landed on my back.

At that time, the shooter must have gotten his sense back because he abandoned his rifle and went to unholster his sidearm. I was at a disadvantage. He was standing over me while I was on my back, about to unload whatever he had in his pistol. I'd probably survive it, thanks to my healing, but it would hurt, and one couldn't rely on quick healing all the time. I knew some wolves in the past that did and misjudged. They are no longer with us.

Taking my feet, I did the only thing I could do—I slammed them against his knees. I could feel the bones snap beneath the pads of my feet. I heard a muffled cry, which would have been a wail that would hurt my ears if it weren't for that stupid helmet blocking the sound. After the carnage I saw upon entering, I couldn't help but feel a sense of glee at the pain I caused in this individual, but I didn't have time to gloat because there was still a threat. Although the guy I had just taken down was no longer much of an imminent threat, he could still be one. I hopped to my feet and took a side step to kick the downed shooter in the head. Unfortunately, I kicked too hard as I felt another bone crunch. Well, so much for having someone to question later. Hopefully, we'd be able to keep the last shooter alive.

Both Dick and I turned our attention to the last remaining figure. They raised their rifle and pulled the trigger. The round missed, but I heard the distinct sound of the bolt locking to the rear, indicating that the rifle had run empty. I stood up to full height, and Dick came out from behind the booth he had taken cover behind. Since they had quit shooting, there was no more perceived threat. Dick had his pistol trained on them, just in case. Something about this whole thing gave me warning bells in the back of my mind. These shooters were obviously not "normies." I mean, there I was, an almost seven-foot-tall, massive, hairy monster out of nightmare and they didn't react like any "normie" would have. Most would have run, cowered, cried with fright. Not these shooters—they maintained their cool like it was another day at the office, except now at least three wouldn't see another day.

I thought the situation was near resolution when the door to the back alley, which was at the end of the hallway of private rooms and dressing rooms, opened and two more assailants came in. Thankfully, Dick was not in line of sight. Unfortunately, I was and had to hurry to avoid the rain of lead that erupted from the hallway. As I moved out of their line of sight, my last glimpse of them indicated that they were advancing. So much for the situation being resolved.

Then a strange thing happened. I saw light emanating from the hallway that crackled with a sizzling sound. If I hadn't known better, I would have thought it was lightning. I felt the static raise the hair on my body, which was quite a bit at the moment. I also saw flames follow the lightning show in quick succession. All gunfire had ceased at that moment, and everything went quiet.

I questioned what force of nature we would have to deal with next. I crouched down slightly so I could spring into action once I saw the new threat enter through the door. Just as I was about to lunge, a familiar smell stopped me.

Cormac came walking out through the doorway. He had a field of blue around him, which I could only assume was his way of protecting himself from rifle fire. He looked around the room at the carnage and then at me.

"I thought you could use some help," he said.

"Yeah, maybe a little. Did you kill those shooters?" I asked, nodding toward the hallway behind him.

"Yeah," he replied. "I could have shot them, but you know how that goes...mountains of paperwork to account for one round discharged."

He stopped and smiled. "You okay?"

"Ask me later," I replied.

Now that the new threat had been neutralized, I turned toward the last remaining shooter, who now had the rifle hanging at their side. "Put it down and we can talk," I said.

The figure didn't move. They just stood there and, to be honest, it was kind of creepy, even to me. "Can you hear me?" I asked.

By that time, we could hear the sirens closing in outside. The cavalry had arrived, but as usual, too late. Always too late.

The remaining black-clad, helmeted individual looked toward the entrance and then all around. There was no escape, and I believe they knew it. I then truly believed that the situation would be resolved, and moments later, it was…sort of…but not in the way I had expected. I mean, how many times do you run into people carrying explosives?

The figure dropped the rifle with their right hand and reached into their coat pocket. I was in the midst of telling them to show us their hands when indeed they did, but their hand was not empty. It held a small, cylindrical tube, not much larger than a Magic Marker, except this was all black, with a button on top…and there was a thumb coming down on it. It's funny how time speeds up sometimes and slows down others. That was one of those times, as I initially saw the thumb move in slow motion and then speed up.

"Watch out!" I yelled and jumped back, scrambling to get to the other side of the raised platform. As I was moving, I saw Dick get to cover behind another booth and Cormac…well, he just stood there, but he put his hands up and his translucent blue force field turned red. That would have mesmerized me had it not been for everything going on.

The concussion from the explosion caught up to me and threw me in the direction I was heading anyway. My eardrums burst and excruciating pain entered my brain. It was a powerful piece of explosive, but there wasn't much as far as shrapnel. When I landed, the wind was knocked out of me. I stood up and all sounds were muffled and distorted.

"Amm yu alaghit," I heard Cormac say and I couldn't quite understand but as my mind reached and put it altogether, I realized he was asking if I was all right.

I shook my head and looked around to get my bearing. With my ears blown out, my balance was off pretty badly, too. Thankfully, I wasn't close enough to the explosion to breathe anything in. That's why some people die when a bomb goes off. It's not the always the piercing, disintegrating shrapnel but the concussion and inhalation of heated air that burns everything in your airways that sometimes kills. The explosion rocked the building, and the lights went out save for emergency lights and the smoke emitted from the bomb. The dim light and smoke cast eerie shadows throughout the room. I could see Dick moving, but barely. He seemed to be okay. I looked over to where the last shooter had been and there was nothing besides scorch marks and a blast area. I then looked for the other shooters' bodies, but I was in for a shock because they were gone, as well. The only remnants of them were the helmets and ash, and the ash was disintegrating at a rapid pace even as I watched it.

My healing ability kicked in and the ache in my head and my shoulder where I took a couple of rounds went away. I finally had a moment to check myself and was grateful that the rounds went clean through, so that was good. No surgery needed to remove any fragments. My hearing was clearing too, since my eardrums were healing at a rapid pace, as well.

I knew I had to change back quickly because the cavalry was now outside. I could smell them. Each time this sort of thing happened, I'd say it was a fight, but not really, as I caged the beast. Like an old dog you have to give medicine to, it sometimes fights back but you know you can control it. Every now and again, it might bite you.

I felt the beast retire within and my body molded back to my human form. When you move into beast mode as a werewolf, the pain is intense. However, when you transition back—and I'm not sure why—but it doesn't really hurt. Maybe it's because your body already went through Hell and nothing can compare to that in such a short amount of time. Who knows?

A moment later, I stood barefoot, with my shirt gone and my pants reduced to rags below the knees. I knew I looked a fright to anyone who didn't know better. I guess the explosion was a good thing, in that I no longer had to come up with some lame excuse to cover for why I looked the way I did. The explosion did it. Yeah, that's the ticket. Unfortunately, after the explosion and the work of the shooters beforehand, we had nothing. I could already tell that everyone that was here when the shooting started was dead. I knew that in his office, the werepig of a manager suffered the same fate. Back to square one.

Cormac's force field winked out, and he came over to check on me.

"I have got to stop hanging out with you," he said.

"I think I'd like to quit hanging out with myself, too…"

Chapter Twenty

As I had suspected, the werepig was in the manager's office. Looking around, it could have been much worse had this whole fiasco happened at night. During the day, there weren't that many in the club, save for a few employees and maybe one or two customers. For those that were here, however, it was deadly. Talk about being at the wrong place at the wrong time. As more blue uniforms showed up and secured the scene, I took a moment to look around, which brought me to the manager's office. I almost had to fight the first couple of officers to let me do my job before they had the chance to cart me away in an ambulance. Yes, it appeared as though a float had dragged me along Bourbon Street during Mardi Gras, but I had a job to do.

The manager's office wasn't large, but it wasn't small either. It had a decent-sized desk in the center and behind it was the rotund manager. His face was caved in from the two or three rounds it took to do the job. From where the manager sat, there was one of those two-way mirror deals where he could see out, but patrons couldn't see in. Made me wonder if anyone had been in there when I, or when detectives Green and Allain had been there. The manager saw it all before they got to him. There was nowhere for him to hide or to escape. I could see and smell that he had soiled himself, which probably happened when the gunman entered the room, and he knew there was no way out except for the way he left. The body acts in strange ways when overloaded with emotion, fear, or adrenaline. Can do things that one can only imagine but can also leave you in a state of no control. I almost felt bad for him. What a way to go.

Dick had entered behind me. After making sure we were okay, Cormac quickly left by opening a portal before the other cops arrived. Something about even more paperwork that he didn't want to be involved in. Who could blame him, really? Getting in a shootout in your own jurisdiction is bad enough, but to get into a firefight outside of your own area of responsibility? Well, it's a headache and one we generally tried to avoid.

"See anything?" I asked.

"Nothing out of the ordinary," Dick replied.

He walked over to the table along one side of the room that looked like it had a surveillance system. Both he and I could tell at a glance that someone had ransacked the system. The recording device, whether it was VHS or digital hard drive, had been completely destroyed.

"Well, that's unfortunate," I said.

More uniforms arrived, their presence adding to the growing crowd. Among them, the other detectives appeared, including Lieutenant Martine, who approached Dick and me.

"We came as soon as we heard on the radio that shots were fired. Are you okay? You look like hell, Lou," she said.

"Yes, Ma'am, we're good. A little worse for wear, but we'll be okay."

She gave me that skeptical look. Whenever she wasn't certain about a response, she would give that familiar "I think you're full of it" look.

"Good...good...well, now that you've both been involved in a shooting, we'll put you on administrative leave while LSP investigates," she said. If you don't already know, "LSP" is the Louisiana State Police, who typically examines the circumstances surrounding any local officer-involved shootings.

She continued, "Where are the shooters? I saw a lot of bullets out there and y'all are both still alive, but I don't see any bodies."

My mind was reeling at being put on administration leave. I had to give up my badge and my department-issued gun while they investigated...and who knew how long that would be. I had stuff to do.

"Lou!" Lt Martine shouted.

"Huh?" I replied.

"I think I lost you for a second," she said.

She was right—she had. My mind was racing with all the ramifications, but I remembered her question.

"Oh sorry, I'm not sure. We were exchanging fire and then that explosion went off. After that, the gunmen were gone," I replied.

Dick stepped in and added, "That's correct, Lieutenant. They just disappeared."

I exchanged a quick, knowing look with Dick and nodded my thanks. He knew the deal and since he would have to answer the same questions the same way to avoid further interrogation and suspicion, he went along with it. And what we said wasn't exactly a lie, as it was a sort of version of the truth...or at least a truth, anyway. They did disappear. We just didn't tell the rest of the story. It was good enough...good enough for government work, at least.

Unlike before, she didn't give me that skeptical look she's known for. Instead, she fully believed what I was saying. "Thank God," I thought to myself. I hoped the state investigators would believe us, as well. She had the crime scene techs take both Dick's and my pistol for processing, then told me to go check with the paramedics outside. I was about to protest, but she made it an order, which irritated me. Not only was I being told to go home, but I was also told to go home right then. I looked around the scene one more time to gather what I could, but knew I wouldn't see anything else that would stand out. I did it more out of habit than anything else.

What did I know? The shooters turned to dust and faded away. Who does that when they die? Vampires. The damage I did shouldn't have killed them. They had healing ability—not as good as mine—but definitely more efficient than your average human. I thought about this as I walked out of the manager's office and back through the club toward the entrance that led out to the street.

The club was buzzing with police officers and emergency personnel from various agencies, creating a chaotic atmosphere reminiscent of a disturbed anthill. So much activity and there'd be nothing to show for it. A crime scene technician stood behind the bar, carefully examining the surroundings.

"Hey, look at this helmet," I heard one of them say to the other.

I slowed my steps so I could hear the exchange on my way out.

The other technician bent and looked at what the previous one had pointed out.

"Woah, that's crazy. I don't think I've ever seen a helmet with lights on the inside," they said.

I couldn't contain myself. I changed direction and walked to the bar.

"What did you say?" I asked.

I think I surprised them, as they were talking low to begin with and didn't realize anyone else was listening, but they obliged.

"The helmet here. On the inside of the visor, the brow had lights embedded into it," the technician said. "I guess they got burned out and melted from the explosion, but you can tell they were tiny strips made for light."

"From the looks of it, it looks pretty expensive, but it's weird. Why would someone have lights on the inside of the helmet?" the other technician from the ground said.

They both looked at me questioningly, like I knew, which I didn't, but I had a pretty good idea. Even if I knew the answer 100 percent, I wasn't going to tell these "normies." With a shrug, I turned around and headed outside. But before leaving, I made a quick stop in the foyer to grab my suit jacket that I had left there before the party began.

All said and done, there were nine deaths inside the club that day. The pig manager, two dancers, a bouncer, a cashier, a bartender, and three customers. 15 deaths if you counted the six shooters that we took care of, though that would never make it into official reports. Again, wrong place at the wrong time and over what? A cover-up to keep things going, I guess. The werepig manager knew something, but that lead was long gone.

Walking outside into the sun, the smell of Bourbon Street drifted across my face; it was the unpleasant combination of mustiness, stale beer, garbage and...well...bodily fluids. My mind fell into a moment of deep thoughts. I didn't bother with the paramedics. I knew I was okay and besides, the lieutenant was inside; she wouldn't know the difference. Once we got a little distance away from others, Dick spoke up, "What do you think?"

"Nothing makes sense. You heard what those technicians said about the helmets?" I asked.

"Yeah, pretty strange. I don't think I've ever heard of anything like it," he said. "Any light shining directly into the eyes would kinda hurt and affect your vision."

"That dust they turned into. You know what that means, right?" I asked.

"I do, but it seems to be highly unusual. My kind aren't so brazen. I think it comes from centuries of working at night. We're more subtle. Unless, of course, we're backed into a corner," he replied.

"You think those lights were ultraviolet?" I asked.

"I shudder to think, but maybe," Dick said.

For eons, when vampires went out during the day, it wasn't necessarily the sun itself that killed them. It was the ultraviolet light. I don't know why. Something to do with undead tissue and the certain vibrations. With medicine that had been used in more recent years to block out whatever it was, a lot of that fear had gone by the wayside, but it got my brain jogging with the thought. If the vampires we encountered in the club were somehow kept from using medicine and threatened with death by ultraviolet light if they refused to do whatever was demanded of them...ugh, what a horrible thing.

"Do you think they might have been coerced into doing it?" I asked, the thought still swirling in my mind.

"Maybe...or maybe it was the setup, so there would be no one to talk if they were caught. That last one had a choice. They didn't have to detonate that explosive," he replied.

More and more questions kept appearing, but none came with solid answers, only speculation. A lot of times when it comes to detective work, you narrow the field of suspects by process of elimination. You gather a list of who would benefit, or some other factor, then you start whittling away at it. Do the alibis check out? Were they where they were supposed to be? And so on and so forth. It slowly narrows down until you have one solid person or organization backed by evidence. And so far, we were still out on pretty much everything with this case. I took a deep sigh as I thought about the mountain that still loomed over us. I felt like I was standing in front of Mount Everest, and it was about to collapse on me. When the mind begins thinking that way, it's easy to feed it and continue in that direction. It doesn't help one bit except to keep you from doing something about it. The mind is a funny thing, and you have to be quick to realize what's going on before you lose it. When I realized the thought of being overwhelmed was...well...overwhelming, I changed my focus to think of something else. The only solid lead we had was that yes, vampires were involved somehow. Which family and the reason behind it remained to be seen, but I guess that was something, and something is always better than nothing.

"Well, if I know department policy, we're going to be rubber gunning it for a while," Dick said.

"Rubber gunning" is what we call it when someone is being investigated and isn't allowed to carry a department-issued firearm. So, you're still a police officer but with no gun, which is sort of like a dog with no teeth, except that I have plenty of teeth and big ones at that.

"Yeah, that's what she said, but we don't have time for that," I replied.

"I know," he replied.

"We need to be careful. It's only a couple days 'til this all comes to a head and if they were willing to do this..." I said but didn't need to finish the thought. He understood. The whole situation felt like a pot full of water, slowly coming to a boil on the stove. If left on the stove, that water would bubble over and create a mess, and that's exactly how I felt about it.

We went to the vehicle and drove back to the station. Green and Allain had missed the action. They were working away at their desk as if they hadn't heard a thing. So, when Dick and I walked into the detective's bureau, they immediately asked what was wrong. I mean, judging by my disheveled look with just a jacket and tattered pants that bordered on the look of going to Hell and back, that was no surprise. We told them the gist of what happened.

"So, the manager of Top Level is…dead?" Green asked.

"That's correct," I replied.

She cussed and continued, "I knew that guy had to have known something. The way he was shifty and…I just couldn't nail him down. I wanted to go back there to follow up."

"Well, don't have to worry about that now," I said.

"Yeah, but now we don't have anything. You said the shooters weren't there after the explosion?" she asked.

"That's correct, but we know they killed the manager to keep quiet," I said.

"We don't know that for certain," Allain said.

"No, but we can guess. The people that attacked that club were professionals. They didn't seem like street thugs to me," I replied.

"I guess we have that, then," Allain replied. "Professional hitmen take out the manager to cover up what?"

"I don't know," I said, but in the back of my mind, I knew the reason. It was to cover up the connections and the trail that would lead to the perpetrators who killed the initial victims in order to complete the summoning ritual and drop the equivalent of a nuclear bomb…but like I said, I kept that to myself.

Since they put us on administrative leave immediately, there was no sense in sticking around the department. I ended the conversation with, "Well, with the day I had, I think I need a drink."

"With the day you had, you certainly deserve it," Green replied.

I nodded toward Dick, who understood that I would contact him later to continue working, but a drink did sound pretty good and so did food, for that matter. I left the station and headed across the river, planning to visit my favorite bar in Algiers after I went home to clean up and change clothes. I couldn't exactly expect to get service with no shoes and no shirt. The days of that were long gone, and rightfully so. Morgane wasn't home when I arrived and things were still in disarray from the day before. I hadn't had a chance to truly work on putting things back to where they belonged. It looked like Morgane had fixed some things, but there was still a lot to do before it would be back to normal.

After making myself presentable, I left the house and walked toward the bar. As soon as I saw the familiar blue phone booth that identified the entrance, a stretched black car pulled up along my side and the front window rolled down.

"Mr. Giroux?" I heard a voice.

I stopped my stroll and tried to peer in, but the inside of that car was blacker than night and I couldn't see anything in the interior. I sniffed the air, but there wasn't anything beyond what I would normally smell.

"Yes?" I replied.

The door to the back opened and the voice I couldn't see said, "Please come closer, Mr. Giroux."

"Nah, I think I'm good," I replied.

"Be that as it may be, Mr. Giroux, I request you come closer," the voice said.

The voice had a strange commanding presence, as if it expected to be obeyed, but I didn't care who it was. I can be stubborn, too.

"And like I said," pausing for effect, "I'm good."

"Fine, have it your way," the voice said.

The other back door opened and four very large figures in black suits stepped out of both sides of the car. If I hadn't known any better, I would have thought it was the same cut and style as the shooters I had dealt with earlier, but where those shooters were normal in size and lithe, these figures were massive. Even in my beast form, I believe that these would have only been a few inches shorter. I looked at them as they approached and wasn't sure if I would have to fight or run. Either way, I wasn't looking forward to it. My saving grace was that it was daytime in a usually heavily-traveled area, though I didn't see anyone else out and about at that time.

I looked at the black limousine and wondered how they all fit inside of it. They made it look like a toy. As they stepped up on the curb, I could tell right away they weren't human. Sure, they looked human, but magic was a great concealer. If you thought some of those makeup artists that can change people's looks were talented...well, you'd be shocked at what magic can do to disguise someone's looks. Their appearance didn't give them away—it was their scent, but to most people, even that wouldn't have given them away. Of course, I could tell the difference. They smelled faintly of animal fur. It was somewhat concealed by shampoo and conditioner, but it was there. I knew the smell—satyrs.

Satyrs are half goat-half man, almost like centaurs, but instead of four legs, they stand on two. They have the face, chest, and arms of a man and the eyes, horns, and hooves of a goat. From the waist down, they have fur. Since I had made the distinction, I noticed I could hear the clop of their hooves striking pavement instead of the sound one is accustomed to hearing when a regular shoe hits pavement. Satyrs are great with illusionary magic, and they're strong. Some say they are tricksters and maybe some are, but not all of them are. I know because some of them are bodyguards for the regional council.

I crouched slightly, ready to defend myself, and the voice from the car rang out, "Oh, there's no need for that, Mr. Giroux. It's not that kind of calling."

Maybe, maybe not. I was still on guard. Once the satyrs took positions near me, they then turned around and faced outward. After a few moments, the one closest to the vehicle walked over and waited patiently. They didn't wait long before I saw another figure emerge from the back. In the back of my mind, I knew that car couldn't hold that many people and with the satyrs being concealed by magic, there was no telling what that car really was. I couldn't think long on it as the figure before me took my full attention. He was an old man, bordering on ancient, in flowing red robes. I recognized him at once as a wizard, a powerful one at that, but also as the regional council's current high chancellor, Elis Sattorn. He walked over to me, and his bodyguard stepped in line right behind him and to his right so he could still keep an eye on me. The voice in my head whispered that the high chancellor didn't need bodyguards.

I know I've said it before, but I never enjoy being the focus of the regional council, and I wanted to protest, but I had to be very careful. This was the shot-caller. I towered over him, but somehow, I felt very small looking into his deep-set eyes. There was no amusement there.

"Really, Mr. Giroux, you could have just stepped over to the car. I usually reserve this kind of request for other people, but considering the events in the city the past few days, I wanted to make sure it was done right," he said.

"I don't think you have to worry about things being done right, even if you ordered others to do them," I stated.

"You are right, of course, Mr. Giroux, but I also wanted to see you in person to give you an idea of how honored you are and serious it is to receive a personal invitation from me," he said.

"I am honored," I said, showing deference. Sometimes, you had to play the game, and somewhere down deep, I did feel honored, but it was more of a fear-based honor than one of pride. Immediately my thoughts went to, "what did I do wrong?" but I was smart enough to keep my mouth shut on that.

He said nothing for a long while. He just continued to stare at me with his sharp and cold eyes. They gave nothing away. It became uncomfortable, to say the least.

"Invitation...uh...sir?" I asked.

A few more moments of silence went by, his gaze unshifting, while he weighed everything about me in those emotionless eyes. He then nodded slightly and reached into his robes and retrieved a black envelope with gold trim. Without saying a word, he extended his bony hand with the envelope held between his index finger and thumb. As soon as I had it in hand, he silently turned and walked back to the vehicle and disappeared into the darkness that was on the other side of the door. Once he was gone, his group of bodyguards collapsed together and left the same way, one at a time. The last one looked at me before stepping in. The door closed, and the car pulled forward down the street, turned onto a side street, and disappeared from view.

I let out a breath I hadn't realized I'd been holding and looked down at the envelope. The gold trim looked like the real deal. I opened it with care; I felt like I was a bomb squad technician handling explosives with the amount of care I took. Inside was an invitation written out on cream-colored paper with red ink.

"You, Lou Giroux, are invited to the emergency regional high council meeting tomorrow morning at 0700. A ride will await you at your residence at 0630 sharp."

High Chancellor Sattorn had signed it.

I was in trouble.

Chapter Twenty-One

I must confess that the recent events had made me feel like I was in a Bizarro World. It's probably how you're feeling now as I reveal things about your world that you didn't know. But believe me, all those things were strange and unusual, even for me. I don't think I had ever heard of the high chancellor personally inviting anyone and the more I thought about it, the more it creeped me out.

Right at that moment, I definitely needed a drink. I stuffed the invitation into my pocket and headed toward the pub and through the entrance that looked like a blue telephone booth. The dark, cool interior contrasted with the daylight outside and created its own welcoming familiarity that kept me going back to that spot. I walked to the bar and sat down. Being midday, the bar was deserted, with me as the only customer. I pulled out cash, maybe around a hundred dollars, and handed it to the cute, blonde bartender, Sam. I told her to keep pouring drinks until a third of the money was gone, and then keep the rest as a tip.

"Tough day, huh?" she asked.

I didn't really feel like talking about it, so gave the best non-excuse I could think of, "You wouldn't believe me even if I told you."

I know, it sucked as a reply because it begged for more questions or at least more attention and sure enough, she replied, "Oh yeah? Well, you'd be surprised at what I hear and what I believe. It sort of comes with the territory of piloting the bar."

"Was in some nasty business earlier and now I've been given days on the beach because of it," I replied.

"Oh…" she said. "My dad was a police officer back in Boston. I know what that means…I'm sorry. You doing okay?"

"Yeah, better than the other folks, but gun fights always come with their own issues, immediately and then afterwards."

Her blue eyes grew wide in understanding. "Oh, were you involved in that robbery in the quarter? I heard about it on the radio on my way to work."

"That's what they're calling it? A robbery?" I asked.

"It was, wasn't it?" she asked.

And I knew I had said too much already, so I backtracked. "Well, yeah, it was but unfortunately, they killed several people only to get nothing in the end." I was thinking to myself, "And they sure robbed me of any answers from that place."

"Well, the first drink is on the house. You deserve it," she said and gave me a smile. She poured me a draught and set it on the bar in front of me. I nodded my thanks, and she left me alone, going back to her work of cleaning and getting ready for more arrivals as the evening wore on. I pondered what she said about the news—that it was a robbery gone bad. Of course, it wouldn't be anything but that. Because if the news exposed what had truly happened, there would be more questions asked and answers that couldn't be provided. That would have only made things more suspicious and that, my friend, is how conspiracy theories begin.

I was on my third drink before the next customers showed up in the bar—a short guy and his short wife, carrying cameras. Must have been tourists. They only stayed for one drink before they left, and I was again by myself. Having a lot on my mind, the mood of the place suited me. I hadn't realized it, but time got away from me and before I knew it, it was evening. I should have been buzzing, but no matter how much I drank and how fast I slammed them down, they weren't having an effect. It cooled me down some, sure, but not enough after the day I had. My healing ability was a real pain at times. I could still get drunk but sometimes after a day like that day, I had to "work" at it. I suppose I really shouldn't complain, because most people would kill for that capability.

That thought sparked my next. Who would want to kill half of New Orleans? And for what reason? To change up the natural order of things? Maybe, and that seemed to be the most likely, but why now? "Why not?" was my only logical reply. Could have happened at any time; this time was as good as any.

Larry came into the bar, saw me, and came over to grab the stool next to me. "Man, you don't look so good," he said.

"Is that how you greet all your friends?" I asked.

"Who said we were friends?" he replied.

"Your girlfriend, last night." I said.

"But your mom, at the same time, said we weren't," he replied. He smiled at his comeback but the smile quickly faded away. "Seriously though, you okay?" he asked. "Was it that mugging the other night?"

"What?" I asked.

"You know, the last time you were here."

For the moment, I didn't follow, but then I vaguely remembered that night. Man, so much had happened that week that I had almost forgotten about that. "Oh that? No, that's not it. It's just been a busy week, you know?"

"Let me get you a beer," he said.

I raised my own. "It's okay, I'll get you another," he said.

I watched him walk toward the bar and order another round for us. When he returned, I swiftly guzzled what I had left in my glass and the one he brought. I then went and grabbed two more because hey, that's what you do when someone buys a round. You get the next one. We killed those just as quickly.

As I was sitting there in that welcoming den, sharing a moment of relief with good people, the alarm bells rang off in my head. "What are you doing?!" I thought to myself. I tried to quiet that inner voice that was small at first but kept building the longer I "hung out." And I succeeded for a little while, but it kept building and that curious thought of what was I doing wasting time transitioned to a feeling of guilt. Guilt because there had been a lot of deaths the past few days and there would be a metric crap ton of deaths within a few more days if I didn't do something. When that thought hit me, I became stone-cold sober, which wasn't hard because I wasn't that drunk. I needed to get back to it. It had been a rough day, but if I didn't do everything within my power and those people died...I'd feel so...well, I guess I wouldn't feel much because I'd probably be dead, as well. So maybe this thought was more of a self-preservation thing. A sort of "Lou, get your butt moving. Your life and the lives of everyone else depends on it." Why did it have to be me? I didn't ask for this, but that's life how life is sometimes. You do because you can and sometimes there's no one else that could or would. We all make choices that lead us down the roads we take, and my choices had brought me to that moment, and it was my choice that was going to lead me out again. For that to happen, I needed to quit wasting time and get back to it.

A few minutes later, I was out on the street corner. I heard the bell of the ferry down the street, indicating that they were about to take their cruise across the Mississippi. It was a pleasant time of day; the sun hadn't completely winked out and there were still the last vestiges of sunlight left. With everything on my mind, I felt the need to call Dick to compare notes when strangely enough, I reached for my phone and it vibrated. I looked at the screen and it was Dick calling me. How fortuitous.

"Hey man, how are you?" I answered.

"I'm doing okay. I became a day sleeper again since I...well...since we were sent home," he replied. "But that's not what I'm calling about. While I was sleeping, I had an envelope waiting for me when I awoke just now. It was inside my home and lying on the floor at the entrance to my resting place.

"Oh..." came my reply. That must have been something. Vampires didn't sleep in coffins or caskets. I mean, they might have way in the past but now, they didn't. Yes, they had to have rest and during that time, they were still vulnerable so most these days, or at least the one I knew...Dick...had a sleeping place similar to what "normie" folks would have called a panic room. It was a self-contained interior room with a door, but Dick's was made to blend in like a normal part of the house, concealed behind a bookshelf. If anyone had broken in, they wouldn't have noticed it. So, not only did they break into his house while he was sleeping, but they knew where he slept, and for Dick, I'm sure that had to have been a rude awakening.

"Are you okay?" I asked again.

"Yeah, yeah, I'm fine. I...uh...just wasn't expecting that. Did you get one, as well?" he asked.

"I did, from the high chancellor himself, along with his satyr goons," I replied.

"Really..." he said, drawing the word out in surprise. "He came to you personally?"

"That's right," I said.

"He doesn't normally do that from what I know," he said. "Where are you?"

"I'm in Algiers," I said. I didn't want to tell him I was drinking my blues away, even though I had probably killed half a keg in there.

"You at that bar?" he asked.

Well, crap. So much for that. "Yeah, I was just leaving and thinking of you when you called."

"Want to come over and we can compare notes?" he asked.

"I'm kind of hungry. Want to meet up at..." The line went dead.

I took the phone away from my ear and I had a full signal. When I tried calling him back, it went straight to voicemail. Strange, I thought. I tried a couple more times, and all had the same result. If anyone had been with me, they would have seen my face fall into a speculative frown. I decided I better head over to his place. He lived uptown, a nice area not too far from City Park. I didn't have my duty weapon any longer, so I stopped by my house to pick up the revolver I used earlier, but I only had regular bullets this time. I attached it to my belt before heading out into the night. When I stepped back out to the porch, I found out why the phone had disconnected. On the street in front, there was the same black car that I had seen earlier. Flanked on either side of the rear door, two figures that could have been the same satyrs from earlier, stood.

"Things have changed. We need you to come with us now," the one to the right of the door said.

I immediately had to fight down a snarky reply, but I had to ask, "What's up?"

They didn't answer. They opened the back door and motioned for me to get in. Well, so much for an explanation or even conversation, but somehow, I knew it would be this way. Guards aren't paid to talk.

I slowly walked forward, warily. I didn't know who was behind any of this and who knows, maybe the high chancellor was...and maybe this was an elaborate trap, but that didn't feel right. They could have attacked me earlier or even at that moment, for that matter, and they didn't.

In fact, the guards seemed bored and moved in a matter-of-fact manner.

I got into the back seat and there was nothing extraordinary about it. I still think it wasn't exactly a car, though I wasn't sure what it was.

The two guards got in behind me and moved to seats where they could observe both left and right of the vehicle as it moved and keep an eye on me. Their mannerisms were almost robotic. This was just another day to them, and though they glanced at me, it was nothing more than when you check your rear-view mirror periodically while driving. It was second nature, no more and no less.

"So, did you pick up Dick, as well?" I tried again, but the answer was the same: nothing. I threw up my hands in an "okay, fine" gesture and leaned back in the seat to gaze out the window. The rest of the ride was silent.

One thing about the high council meetings—they were always in the same location, but the entrance moved around. I know, it's kind of hard to explain, but for safety reasons, the way to the high council chambers changed sporadically and you had to be in the know to get there. Some kitchen door in the back-alley of a hole-in-the-wall restaurant would, for a minute or two, transform into a portal to the chambers. A minute later, that same portal would change to another door, such as the entrance to the New Orleans Museum of Art. It changed frequently and never in the same place in the same week, from what I understood. This cut down on disruptions and unknown threats from targeting and exploiting the meetings. Of course, the council had used secret, stationary doors for a time before the jumping door system, and I knew of a couple since I sort of worked for them, but they were so rarely used that they had almost been forgotten.

We headed toward the Central Business District of New Orleans and got off the exit that took us near the Superdome. We parked in an eight-story garage off Girod Street and parked on the fourth floor. Since it was evening time, there were plenty of open spots to park. When we parked, the satyrs opened the door and got out first to secure the surroundings before motioning for me to follow. They knew their job well and since I was their charge for the moment, they were going to do their job and make sure I got to the meeting safely.

We took the elevator down to the second floor and the hallway entrance to the hotel that was in the building. I had been there before working security for one of the many conventions—from comic book to professional conferences—that the hotel hosted from time to time. The hallway led us to a coffee shop, but it was closed, the large glass doors shut tightly and the lights off inside. In fact, there was no movement anywhere and it was quiet, but that was to be expected due to the time of day and the fact that there wasn't currently a convention in the building.

From the coffee shop, we veered left and walked to the back of the rather sizeable area that we had turned toward. There were glass elevators that rose to dizzying heights as well as to the floor below us. We walked past them and it was all so strange to me—like being in a library past closing time. You were in the wrong place and at the wrong time, but regardless, it was a place to remain quiet, even during normal hours. In the back of the area, the room collapsed into hallways with doors that broke off into ballrooms or exhibit rooms. We came to a "T" intersection and took a right toward a large door at the end. The satyr leading went up to the door and knocked twice. From the other side of the door, I heard an answering chime, like the sound of an elevator arriving, followed by the guard turning to look at his partner and at me. I didn't know what to do; I had never come to the council chambers in this fashion, so I just looked back at him and raised my eyebrows. He then turned back toward the door and opened it.

What was inside was not the actual room that was supposed to be there. Where colors of the hallway were cool and neutral, the interior had brick and dark stone. I had been to the council chambers before and every time, it was awe-inspiring. I'm not sure where the council chambers are in New Orleans or if they're even on this plane of existence. No one has ever told me.

I walked through and the doors shut behind me. I glanced behind me and realized that I was alone.

Chapter Twenty-Two

I didn't have time to dwell on this because, although I had come through the door alone, I wasn't alone in the chamber. The door had brought me to an alcove, which was an outcropping to a much larger and cylindrical room. There were alcoves like the one I stood in that went all the way around the room. In the center of the main room, a giant, heavy wooden table stood in the shape of a "U," with the council representatives having chairs along its perimeter. The table was designed so that whomever the council wanted to question would stand inside the "U," with all the members surrounding him or her, and everyone could examine them. Opposite the opening in the table was the raised platform where High Chancellor Sattorn sat. It was a full house that night.

Around the table, I saw representatives from two vampire houses, and one older werewolf that I recognized as Alce Fenric, though I hadn't spoken to him in decades. There was a Fae representative; I could only tell because they had folded their wings neatly behind them. I saw dwarves, sprites, elves of different kinds, and even a dryad. Like I said, the table was large enough to sit at least 30 people and there they all sat, watching me enter the room. I felt like I should have heard a record scratch.

I saw that Dick was already there and standing in the center. He was a cold one, so I couldn't glean any information from just looking at him. He looked bored and when he saw me, he looked neither relieved or angered. There was nothing, and I wasn't sure if this was his way of trying to convey something to me. Of course, I guessed I'd find out shortly.

The high chancellor sat on his chair and looked down at me.

"Mr. Giroux, please come and tell us what you have found," he asked.

I walked slowly to the center. I felt like I it was my last trek down the death row mile, just waiting for the headsman to drop the axe or someone to give the death squad permission to shoot.

I felt sweat bead on my forehead, though it was cool in the room, almost like being in a basement on a hot day—a place where you usually found comfort... but not for me, and certainly not on that day. I had to focus on putting one foot in front of the other and eventually, I ended up right beside Dick.

"I can see why you hung up," I said.

He glanced at me and in surprise and, for whatever reason, he began to laugh. Personally, I didn't think it was that funny, but sometimes stressful situations will do that to a person, and I'm no different. Seeing him laugh caused me to giggle and the more I tried to stop it, I laughed even more. It was such a stark contrast to the decorum in the room and the emotions and demeanor you'd expect when in one of these meetings. I couldn't stop and the more I thought about it, the harder it became to stop, which only egged Dick and me forward. We were stuck in the throes of the giggle loop.

"Please gentlemen, really," the high chancellor said. He then slammed his hand to the table in front of him, which made a thunderous sound. The force and volume of the gesture deflated the humor we had found in the situation and we stopped laughing. As I looked around the room, I could clearly see the obvious disdain for our laughter fit.

"I would have thought that you would have treated this meeting with a little more professionalism of your stature, detective," High Chancellor Sattorn said, but then continued, "We moved the emergency meeting up as the gravity of the situation has called for such action."

I couldn't help but think to myself that I'm glad they did, as I always hated to wait for meetings where I would be front and center. I would rather get it over with as soon as possible so I could turn my attention to other things and not have it weigh over me.

"Tell us what you know," the high chancellor finished.

"About what?" I asked. Of course, I knew the reason they had taken us there, but there was always that chance of being wrong. No need to prematurely show the cards in hand.

"You know very well about what," the high chancellor said coolly, though I could tell (or rather feel) the impatience rising in the speaker.

"I hate to disappoint you, but I really have nothing to explain," I replied.

The temperature dropped in the room, though I couldn't tell if it was really the temperature or just me. The silence was overwhelmingly deafening. In a room that large and with that many people, there were always murmurs, or at least the sound of pens or pencils scratching notes on paper, but none of that was happening.

"Perhaps you can tell us of your investigation so far into the murders that are plaguing the city," the high chancellor said. "Maybe that will help draw out something."

They probably knew more about what was going on more than I did. They seemed to already know everything and really, what position was I in to be reticent? In a way, I sort of worked for them already in order to keep the peace. They just wanted my testimony as confirmation of whatever they already thought.

"Well...sir," I began, "There have been several murders that you have heard about. I believe someone or something committed the murders in some sort of ritualistic manner to bring about something cataclysmic in nature. Today's shootout in the French Quarter was part of that. I believe the motive was to silence witnesses and throw water on the trail to keep me from finding who is behind it. The ritual makes me think a wizard is behind it, but I am not sure. A wolf pack threatened me to keep away, and I thought maybe they were behind it until I found out that an unknown source hired them. The shooters in the French Quarter were vampires of some sort, though I didn't get a good look at any of them, as they were all wearing helmets. They didn't want to get caught though, and they all died, so I thought maybe it was one of the vampire families. But those helmets...I think they had ultraviolet lights installed on them so maybe they had a failsafe or they were coerced to do it under distress. I have more questions than answers at this point, but we don't have much time left. Whatever is coming will be here in a couple of days, at most. Unless it was miscalculated, we are dealing with a very evil and ancient kind of magic."

I hadn't intended to say so much at one time, but you know how it goes. Once the dam breaks, it flows wildly. I would have thought that there would have been silence at the gravity of my words...but no. Immediately upon finishing my piece, the heads of each vampire family stood up and yelled that they were not part of it. At the same time, the wolf clans' representative stood up and said the same. A wizard who spoke for that faction did the same. No one wanted to be on the hook for this, and rightfully so. It's easy for suspicions to grow rapidly to dangerous proportions. The rest of the hall looked at the ones speaking, looking back and forth between them all. It was somewhat chaotic until the same sound came from the high chancellor that silenced our laughter earlier, hushed the chatter then. The quiet roar slowed until there was silence again.

"Your news is upsetting, Mr. Giroux. Most upsetting," he said. "What are your plans to find the people behind this?"

I looked around the room and all I saw looking back were somber stares, waiting for an answer. "I will…"

Before I could finish my answer, a strong knock came from one of the many alcoves that housed different entrances. Everyone turned to look and there was a moment's pause before one door exploded inward and in came two hulking demons. They were each about nine or 10-feet-tall and ugly. Now that was something. Demons did not like this plane of existence at all. If you were dealing with a demon, it was most likely pissed off because it was a pawn in something more significant. However, with that being said, killing them was extremely tough. Their bodies were interdimensional—so they were a challenge here, but also somewhere else. To truly kill one, you had to do so on its own plane of existence. Otherwise, it would only cause enough damage to temporarily banish it there, because its body would be so weak that any binds keeping it here essentially became null and void. I saw them enter through a door to a room that resembled a summoning circle, but that image vanished in an instant. The wall that should have been behind the door blinked back into existence, and the portal disappeared.

"Who dares disrupt this meeting?" the high chancellor shouted, highly annoyed at that point.

Everyone else in the room looked on in disbelief, as this had never been done before. Demons were tough, but they weren't tough enough to take on the combined power in a room full of kin. This thought went through my brain as the door in another alcove exploded in and two more demons joined. I quickly did a mental calculation in an attempt to determine how many demons would be necessary to overtake the lot of us, if it, in fact, came to that. Of course, in the back of my mind, a little voice made the connection to a child's poem. "How much wood would a woodchuck chuck if a woodchuck could chuck wood..." well, you get the idea. Judging by the number of kin in the room, I estimated 10 to 15 demons would be needed to balance the fight in their favor. Thankfully, there were only four...and wouldn't you know it...no sooner had I thought that, three other doors flung open and six more joined, making it a total of 10 demons. Once they had arrived, I thought maybe it might be a peaceful calling. Perhaps it was another faction that wanted to be included in the conversation. I guess I was just kidding myself because all hell broke loose. The demons attacked.

I cursed to myself. The room erupted once more into chaos with some rising to fight this new threat, but I evidently had not been only one that made the calculations because some of the lesser kin ran toward other alcoves to escape. I couldn't blame them; they were just fodder at this point and weren't particularly combat-effective from the start. With that being said, it was still a kick to the ol' morale crotch to see others running away, leaving you high and dry to fight it out.

It was pure pandemonium. The demons didn't speak or demand anything. They grabbed, punched, bit, and threw people to the side. I was pretty sure that Dick and I were in trouble because at least four of them looked to be heading our way, with the other six heading toward the high council. The vampires bared their fangs and the wolf clan representative, although an old longtooth, didn't waste any time releasing the monster within.

Dick went full blown vampire and me? Well, I hung out a bit to see what would happen. No sense in going through that excruciating pain if I didn't have to. Wands and staffs appeared in wizards' hands. The Voodoo priest, accompanied by a shaman, appeared to be making incantations and cutting themselves for blood magic. Wizards I knew about. Vampires I knew about. Werewolves...well, obviously I knew about them. But Voodoo and the like? Well, it was all Voodoo to me. You'd think that in all the years I had lived here I would have learned more but honestly, I had been so busy with other stuff...and the fact that most Voodoo practitioners keep to themselves, as it's a very sacred and secretive sect.

The demons marched forward, throwing people left and right. They were gruesome. Demons are always difficult to look at, because since they're from another plane of existence, our brains and senses from this existence can't fully make sense of what our eyes see, so they combine various elements of known knowledge and perception and compress them. That's why some look to have bull heads, others to have dragon heads, or dare I say, some may appear to have wolf-shaped heads.

The fight was in full swing. Spells with colors of red, yellow, blue, and amber flew back and forth across the room. The demons used their otherworldly powers of telekinesis, along with their brute strength. The spells cast by all of those who were present before the demons arrived didn't seem to do much harm. The demons had some sort of barrier that the fireballs and lightning couldn't impenetrate.

Dick poised himself, ready to strike, and I put my hand on his shoulder, nodding to the far side of the table, just beneath the platform of the high chancellor, who was casting his own spells into the fray. Dick looked at me, then back at the demons, who were, by that time, laying complete waste and inching ever closer. He then returned his gaze back to where I had indicated. He gave me a nod, and we both backed away. The fight was coming, but sometimes it was better to fight from a place of your own choosing rather than to rush in haphazardly.

The high chancellor's platform was raised about 10 feet. Normally, it was imposing, but not so much now. I looked at the pistol on my hip and my lip curled in momentary frustration. It wouldn't do me any good at the moment, as it didn't have the right kind of ammunition to hurt this kind of enemy.

They steadily kept coming and the more that those in the room saw the losing battle, the more of those who had the means to fight slipped away. Sure, it was a regional council to keep the peace in the area, but come on...mutual help would only go so far when you had yourself to think about...at least that's what I imagined most were thinking as they fled. There remained approximately 15 people fighting from different distances within the room. The rest were either dead, injured, or had escaped. Of the 10 demons, there were seven left, and it wasn't even a minute or two into the fight. It had been quick and devastating.

I knew I was delaying the inevitable because at any moment, the long-range battle fought with spells, spiritual missiles, and incantations would become a close-range fight with tooth, nail, and whatever else one had in their hand. I saw the vampires close rank to one side of the room. The wolf spokesperson was by himself and went to the high chancellor to provide aid. I bit the bullet and underwent my transformation, though it was different. I mean, it still hurt like hell—and maybe it was because I had already turned once earlier in the day—but when I let the monster out, there wasn't much of a fight for control. Maybe it was because I was scared. Don't get me wrong—I was scared earlier, too, but something about fighting a real demon...well that's enough for anyone to be scared straight or scared sober or whatever. It was as if my subconscious and that of the monster understood what was at stake and allowed me to be in total control without a fight because they both knew. Now, I know I talk about how the monster has a mind of its own and by my description, it sounds like it does, but in reality it's just me and my attempt to stay tethered to my own sanity as a result of my body reacting to instinct or whatever it is. But that time, none of the usual internal conflict was there.

After I stood there, towering over most of the other occupants of the room a few moments, I patted Dick's shoulder to let him know I was okay. I then indicated that we should hop up onto the platform behind us. He launched himself and sort of glided his way upward, coming down lightly beside the high chancellor; it was all so graceful...as if he had been a ballerina in another life. I, however, leapt and almost took everyone down off the platform as I lost my balance upon landing and almost went over the other side.

The high chancellor's face was beet red with fury. "How dare they assault the high council's chambers," he said, not speaking to anyone in particular, but more as a statement to himself. If we survived the attack, there would be hell to pay and it probably wouldn't be coming from me (though I would have liked to have been in on it). It would come from this ancient being with vast knowledge and mystical powers of which I could only scratch the surface of comprehension. Cormac, the only wizard I knew close at hand, was a baby compared to the red-robed mage that stood before me.

I looked back at the demonic attackers, and it looked like the tide was definitely shifting in their favor. The vampire families fled, finally realizing that whatever powers they held, it wasn't worth testing the limit. I glanced at ol' longtooth Fenric and even in his monster form, I could see eyes of intelligence and wisdom sparkle over the scene. His mind was working, and it was sharp. He wasn't going to run, though; I didn't even have to waste energy on such a thought. Yes, there were werewolf packs, but every werewolf was an alpha for sure. Betas didn't survive. It was as if the weakness drove them insane and either they committed suicide or turned (for lack of a better term) feral, with the beast taking over and either dying or being killed. Those of us that dealt with it and survived over the years had a grit to them. If they were presented with a fight, they wouldn't shy away from it. Some were more active than others about looking for them, though.

Five demons were left.

Fenric looked back at me. "I know you don't believe in or support the pack, but we are the only ones here. Fight with me, brother, and let's take these abominations down."

I swear, those words gave me goosebumps, but I had to act cool. I wanted to say something equally as profound, but as I was about let loose some long-winded response that would have been full of stuff like, "Tonight we dine in Valhalla" or some other trash like that, I said, "Okay..." I would have said more but at that moment, a demon unleashed a mighty fireball spell toward the platform, causing it to rock back and forth. The integrity and stability of the platform became suspect, and we knew we had to move off in order to keep it from collapsing with all of us. I couldn't help but think to myself, "Okay? Seriously...all I freaking said was 'okay'?" So much for making the history books of quotes.

The powerful spells that the red-robed wizard threw were powerful indeed, but didn't seem to slow the attackers down one bit. Someone had spent an awful lot of money on barrier magic or in obtaining ancient trinkets that had powerful anti-magic barrier attributes to them. Those things weren't cheap to buy and the ingredients to make them yourself weren't, either. Whoever was behind this was flush with resources.

Fenric loped to the attack and grabbed a hold of a demon that was closest to us. I followed immediately behind him and went for the other arm. Demons were strong—very strong—and massive. Like I mentioned earlier, they stood about nine or 10-feet-tall. Both Fenric and I, in our beast forms, were at seven feet so they had height and reach on us. Since there were two wolves on one demon…well there was enough between the two of us to slow it down. The stench of sulfur caused me to gag, and I wished beyond anything that I could go back to the discomfort of everyone staring at Dick and me for reacting immaturely during our giggle loop.

We were pummeling away at what we could, and the demon stood upright, taking the blows as they came, but we sensed we were weakening it. Dick came out of nowhere and flew directly into the beast's head, grappling at it. The speed at which he pounced, along with the fact that Fenric and I had the demon's legs tangled up, caused it to teeter backward momentarily. It tried to regain balance, but the angle was beyond recovery, causing it to crash to the floor. Fenric reached around its neck and as his muscles bulged, I could clearly hear the crack of bone. There was a moment of triumph because, until then, no one had truly been able to take the fight to the demons. Sure, the others were casting spells and shooting weapons, but hand to hand...well...they were just as vulnerable as anyone else. The magic barrier or magic trinkets they had didn't account for that. Unfortunately, that moment of victory was short-lived because it had taken three of us to contain one demon, which then dissolved back to its own plane of existence. I looked up and saw that there were four left, outnumbering us. Everyone else had fled. In the back of my mind, I was also concerned about future repercussions. Any demons we were able to take out that day...well...they have a way of keeping a grudge. Sure, they didn't want to be on this plane, but if they were banished from here without completing whatever they had been tasked to do...well I wasn't sure exactly what would happen to them in their own world, but I knew it wasn't good. Whatever it was, it was unpleasant enough for them to want to return for payback. You know demons...they're the vengeful type, but I had to worry about that if and when I crossed that bridge. I still had to survive this encounter in order to worry about the next one.

The whole battle had lasted maybe five minutes at that point. The demons spread out and there was only Dick, Fenric, High Chancellor Sattorn, and me. To be honest, the whole encounter was strange. The demons had not uttered a single word. They'd made no demands or said why they were here. Everything I'd ever read or heard made me think that they would have a mind of their own and be able to speak on their own accord. Each demon I'd ever encountered before (not that there were many) had its own personality. These didn't seem to have any of those attributes. They moved as if they were robots—mindless. They only had the mind for one task that seemed to have been "programmed" into them, and for nothing else.

I genuinely thought that our fate was sealed. The enemy hulked forward. The smell of sulfur became even more overpowering and I caught myself thinking, "Well, it's been a good life."

Suddenly, other doors in other alcoves opened and out of them came pouring the goatmen, only this time they weren't wearing the black suit getups they had worn earlier. They were there in full form—hooves clopping as they swiftly entered—and they were angry. Some had axes; some had arrows; one had a wand or two. There were at least 20 of them and well...I'll spare you the details, but an abundance of mad goatmen with axes make short work of pretty much anyone and anything.

Chapter Twenty-Three

The moments that followed were a blur. Though the demons were gone, the aftermath was far from over. Those who were wounded were scattered everywhere, requiring attention, and surprisingly, the death toll hadn't been as bad as I initially expected. I don't mean to sound flippant. Every death in that room was a tragedy, but I feared it was going to be far worse, so yes, there was relief. All told, only one or two who were in attendance before the attack (and who didn't flee), and maybe four or five of the goatmen in the final attack.

The high chancellor was no longer there. A few goatmen spirited him away while the rest launched their attack on the demons. Fenric, Dick, and I were all that remained, along with the rest of the cloven-hoofed, bandaging wounds, and doing what we could to comfort those that were alive but worse for wear. More workers and attendants arrived to help, and after about an hour, they saved those who could have been saved. There was a moment of respite for us. I was extremely tired. In fact, the entire week had been excruciatingly tiring. In the past, I would sometimes go months without changing form, but this week, I'd changed twice in one day. Extreme times for sure.

"There's going to be hell to pay for this, I'm telling you," Fenric said. By that time, he was the monster no longer. Since the threat was gone, we both melted back to normal form.

"But I'm still wondering who were gonna get to pay," I said.

"So much for the meeting," Dick said.

"Well, it's not like we had much to say anyway," I replied.

Fenric stretched his back and looked at me, then nodded, "Lou." I nodded back as he walked away toward one exit to escape the remnants of the horrific event that had just taken place. I glanced at Dick, who looked how I felt—drained, but that wasn't such a surprising look for a vampire.

"I think I've had enough for one day. I'm going back to my room and recuperate," Dick said.

"What? You don't want to go with our original idea? You know...get together and compare notes?" I asked.

His expression showed he wasn't amused by my "dad joke" and he simply responded with a firm "No."

He turned but then looked back. "I just don't get it. I'm with you...I thought it might be the wolf packs, but that doesn't seem to be the case. Then, I thought it might be my kind because they're the two strongest factions in the area, but now I don't think it was. The wizards? They would have only been the ones that were powerful enough for this kind of magic and summoning, but that doesn't seem right, either."

"I know what you mean. I've been dwelling on it, as well. Heck, I know there are some vampires and some from the wolf pack that practice magic, but…" I shrugged my shoulders. "I don't know. It's all over my head."

Speaking of which, I realized my head really hurt, and not just from physical pain. It came from working overtime, trying to figure out what this was all about. This was the straw that broke the proverbial camel's back. Whoever felt that it was okay to just launch an attack on the regional council obviously didn't care about repercussions. That was worrisome. It meant we were dealing with someone or something that felt they carried all the cards. They were playing a game of poker and were pretty confident with the hand they held. I wished I had an ace up my sleeve, but even if I did, it would be pretty hard to play when you didn't, in fact, even know what cards you held in your own hand. At that point, it felt like a trash hand.

Dick and I walked toward the exits.

"We'll figure it out," Dick said, sensing me brooding.

I looked up, surprised, because I didn't realize he was looking at me. "Huh? Oh yeah, sure," I replied.

Then we both left. He left through the alcove he had entered and I left through another, which took me back to the hotel conference door. That was the thing about these meetings. The entrance moved every few seconds, but whatever door you entered you would also have to exit through, which was another reason I wished we had caught at least one demon. We could have possibly gone back with it to wherever it had entered from, but it was pointless to think about that now.

The hotel hadn't changed since I left. If anything, it felt even more devoid of life and hollow. I didn't see any of the chauffeurs that brought me here. I cursed quietly to myself, "Just great, I'm gonna have to find my own way back home." But to be fair, they had probably been involved in the emergency response so I couldn't be too mad. If all the bodyguards hadn't shown up, then I probably wouldn't have survived the encounter and wouldn't be here cursing to myself that I didn't have a ride.

I meandered through the hotel until I got to the escalator that took me to the ground floor and to the front desk. There were one or two tourists dealing with the receptionist as I walked past them. One tourist turned around and gasped when they saw me. I had forgotten that my shirt was gone, and I looked like I had just been mugged.

"It's okay. I just finished filming a movie and I'm supposed to look like this," I lied quickly.

The look of shock changed to a look of enthusiasm. I picked up the pace before they had the chance to question me. I went out the door and into the pickup area before they did.

I looked at the time on my phone. It really wasn't that late and to be honest, I was tired, yet energized. The adrenaline hadn't worn off, and I doubted it would be a while before it did. I could always call a ride share if I suddenly felt like it, but I didn't, so I walked toward downtown to catch the ferry across the river and walk home.

The night's cool air felt comfortable, almost on the cusp of being too cold, but the temperature didn't really affect me unless it was extreme. I breathed in and the air that filled my lungs was refreshing. After the day I'd had, I could use a leisurely stroll in temperate weather. I padded along Poydras Street until I hit the cross street of St. Charles Avenue and connected to Canal Street. Canal was the entertainment hub, with four lanes of traffic split by two lanes of trolley car tracks and palm trees that lined the street. It was a picturesque view. More tourists were on this street. I rarely made it down that way. Most locals avoided it like the plague, but I didn't mind it so much because I like to people watch. Bourbon Street was just up ahead on the left and...dang, the shooting massacre happened not too far from where I was heading. I was avoiding crowds of people but I didn't have to work too hard at it, again, because I looked like shirtless death warmed over.

One couple handed me a few dollars, and I looked at it, dumbfounded, not knowing what it was for until I realized they thought I was one of the many homeless that call the streets of New Orleans home. As realization hit, I turned to give it back, but by that time they had disappeared into the next crowd. Besides, if I had chased them down, how odd would that encounter have been?

Cars went by with roaring, thumping music, with smells of exhaust accompanying them. That area is truly what gives New Orleans the reputation as a metropolis. A street preacher was at the next corner with a bullhorn, shouting about the end of the world. I wondered just how much he knew or how close it really was, but decided against engaging him, so kept walking. It took me maybe 20 to 30 minutes to walk to the ferry, which set sail every 30 minutes. Thankfully, when I arrived, I saw it was heading back from the other side of the river and would dock at the city side within a few minutes.

A few minutes later, I paid my fare and sat down in the boat's interior. I was utterly exhausted. Somewhere along the way, I felt the sapping of my strength and energy. The adrenaline dump had finally caught up. I was also hungry, but that would have to wait. First, I had to get home, get cleaned up, and figure out what to do next.

A couple sat in the seat across from me, totally oblivious to the world around them. I have to admit—the way they looked at each other made me jealous, but not in the way that you'd think. It was more along the lines that they maintained their innocence in that they weren't aware of just how crazy the world really was. But they were young, and unfortunately, I believe everyone has a rude awakening at some point. I saw another guy board, rolling his bicycle along, looking at his phone without looking at anyone else. That guy was really no different than the young couple, except they were enthralled with each other, whereas he gave all his attention to his phone.

I couldn't help but watch people. It comes with the job, but you can learn a lot about people by watching how they move and how they communicate with one another. I shifted and glanced out through the window into the night, giving the couple and the phone guy privacy. I was starving now. I should have taken a detour and bought one of those hot dogs from the vendor on Bourbon Street, but it didn't appeal to me. I figured I wouldn't be returning to that street of my own volition for a long time.

The current rocked the boat slightly—just enough to lull me, along with my exhaustion, to the cusp of nodding off when I was jolted awake by the ferry docking at the station. I stood up and stretched and when I looked around, I realized that this was the first time that the other three had seen me. Their wide-eyed stares, followed by avoidance when I noticed them, told me all I needed to know. "I'm not a bum, guys," I thought to myself, but whatever...I was so tired, I didn't even care. All I cared about was getting home and stuffing my face with whatever was left…or…maybe I'd order a pizza and take it home.

The ramp went down, and I let everyone get off before me, then once clear, I followed. The river below the ramp was black as night and lapped up against the pylons. Hard to believe that just a few nights before, the whole week had started on the wrong foot, not far from where I stood, on the other side of the river.

I wondered what the repercussions of the day's earlier events were going to be. Of course, the whole time I walked, it was in the back of my mind, whether I was actively thinking about it or not. It's funny how some thoughts seem to worm their way into your thinking regardless of whether you wanted them or not. The couple headed off into the darkness. The guy with his phone went in another direction on his bike. I walked alone toward my home.

A few moments later had me back at my shotgun house. I heard Morgane squawk as I entered. "Where have you been?"

"This day…won't end," I replied.

"Caw…it's not over yet…caw…" she replied.

"Dang it," I thought to myself. I hadn't ordered the pizza on the way home like I had thought about. I opened the fridge and only saw the remnants of a professional bachelor that seldomly stocked the fridge well. At least I had some sandwich makings, but I was so hungry, I couldn't wait. I haphazardly tore the ham package open and started wolfing it down. Pun not in...okay, fine, it's intended. Anyway, I must have startled Morgane by my (quite frankly) uncivilized act of just eating it straight out of the package...not just one or two slices, but the whole pack became its own sandwich. It was on par with drinking straight from the milk carton. Sure, you can do that, but even living by yourself, it's just not something you should do. Morgane hopped back and canted her eye at me.

"Caw..."

"What?" I asked.

She didn't say anything. Just shook her head and bounced away, done with the conversation. I felt like my mother had caught me doing something I shouldn't have. "After the week I've had, this is nothing."

I was beat. With my belly at least somewhat sated for the moment, I took a shower to wash the worries away, but they remained. At least I was clean as I began padding toward the couch, but made a quick detour near the fridge to grab some beer to assist in vegging out. I should have been able to go right to sleep, but I knew I was too geeked up and would need a little down time before I could finally drift off to that la la land of rest.

I popped the top off the beer and took a sip as I sat down and turned on the TV. I flipped through the channels and came across channel six; the news was on and what I saw made my blood go cold. The beer bottle slipped from my hand and shattered onto the floor. I was so focused on the news that I didn't even notice.

"Yes, it looks like there was some sort of explosion in the residential area of Metairie this evening. Windows were shattered for blocks and the blast could be felt miles away. Officials say that it was likely due to a large natural gas leak, but there is still an ongoing investigation," the female reporter said.

The video they kept showing went between shots of a street reporter and a helicopter view. It was clearly a neighborhood in old Metairie. I wouldn't have recognized it if it weren't for the distinctive gas station that I saw in the vicinity of the wreckage. When I was able to distinguish the location, I realized that the house I should have seen there was gone. In its place was a black crater, with only debris remaining. It reminded me of my time in World War One before I became the creature in front of you now—bombed out indentions of the earth. The house that should have been there was nondescript and looked like any other house in that neighborhood, except I knew that one. Hell, I'd even been to it once or twice over the years. It was Cormac's.

Chapter Twenty-Four

I felt the tiredness leave my body as I quickly dove into my bedroom to get dressed. It took me longer than usual since everything was still strewn all over the place from the previous home invasion. I really needed to get things back in order, but that could wait. At the moment, I knew I needed to focus on going to find out what had happened.

I reached for my badge and...Crap. I had forgotten that I had to turn in my credentials and gun. There'd be no way they would let me near the scene without those. Even with my credentials, since it was a different jurisdiction, they probably wouldn't anyway, but I still had to try. I ran out of my room and Morgane was there.

"I'll come with you... squawk!" she said.

I stopped momentarily to think about how it would look with me being accompanied by a large crow, but then shook my head. It didn't matter. I nodded, and we both hurried to the car. Well, I hurried. She sort of just glided along with me, keeping up with every footstep I took.

The drive was a blur; I was on autopilot. My mind raced with worry about what I would find when I got there. Would Cormac be there? Was he home or was he gone when it happened? Why did this happen? All these questions and more were whirling through my head like a merry-go-round, the same questions popping up, one after another, in order with every turn of the wheel. Even Morgane could tell, as she said nothing to break the mood. Sometimes it was better to let people deal with things their own way, and Morgane always seemed to know when and where to interrupt or stay quiet. I loved her for that.

I don't even know how long it took me to get there. The traffic was light and my foot was to the floor. If I were the monster that dwelled within me, I would have probably rammed the pedal through the floorboard. When I arrived at the neighborhood, I slowed down. There were flashing lights everywhere. The incident happened a couple hours before, but since it happened to one of their own, everyone who worked for the Sheriff's Office and their brother flocked to the scene like moths to a flame.

I found a parking space a block away and Morgane took to the sky. I didn't even notice, as my attention was completely fixed on the flashing emergency lights in front of me. It was mesmerizing and with my mind abuzz with thought, it was a surreal moment. It felt like I was in a dance club, drunk out of my mind, numb, with a disco ball of flashing lights, but unfortunately I wasn't. I was there on the street corner looking at 10 to 15 police cars, along with multiples of every other imaginable type of emergency vehicle, lights going full bore.

They had the street to Cormac's house blocked off and there was yellow police tape that roped off the perimeter to keep lookie-loos, like me, away. There was a deputy near the barrier that kept neighbors and reporters away. I homed in on him.

"Deputy?" I asked.

I wouldn't say the guy was bored, but I could tell he would have rather been anywhere else than pulling this ungrateful duty of telling people to stand back.

"Yeah? What do you need?" he asked.

"I know that house was Detective Monroe's house. Is he okay?" I replied.

"Who are you?" he asked.

"I'm Detective Lou Giroux, NOPD. I was working a case with him, and we're friends." I said.

"Got your badge or creds?" he asked.

Damn. Of course, I didn't.

"No, I forgot them at home in my rush to hurry over here to find out what happened." I lied...well, it wasn't a total lie. I was only evading part of the truth.

"I can't let you in, then," the young deputy said. His face showed concern in such a way that he wished he could help me out but couldn't. His hands were tied. I understood where he was coming from. If I were in his position, I wouldn't have either. There were many people out there that would claim something that wasn't true in order to get access to a crime scene, either to gather information or destroy evidence if they could.

"I understand deputy. I'm just wondering, is Cormac all right?" I asked.

The deputy's lip went tight, and his look became a grimace. He looked at me and replied, "I...uh...I don't know, but I don't think it looks good."

"Is he at the hospital, then?" I asked.

"No..." the deputy replied, but I could tell he didn't want to tell what was on his mind.

"Then what?" I prodded. "We were working a case together and I need to know."

"He's..." the deputy sighed, "gone."

"What?"

"Listen, I don't know but if he was in that house, there's nothing of him remaining," the deputy said. "I really can't say anything more. I'm sure if you work for NOPD, you understand."

And I did. As a law enforcement officer, you didn't want to say much to the public because, in this day and age, you never knew how it would be taken and used. You wanted to keep your cards close at hand at the beginning of an investigation.

I nodded my understanding and tried to peer down the street toward the bombed-out home, but I couldn't see anything. It was dark and all the flashing lights were almost blinding, so I walked back to my vehicle. Lost in my thoughts, I almost forgot about Morgane being there with me. She glided down and landed on the roof of the car.

"Did you see anything?" I asked.

She didn't say anything outright. She cocked her head and looked around, peering in different directions to include straight up and down. As she hopped closer to me, she balanced on the very edge of the roof nearest to me.

"I did," she whispered. "Everything around the house is gone…"

"Cormac?" I asked.

"I flew down and looked. I saw his coat, and it was… .it was scraps. Burnt through and through, leaving only patches of it," she said and bowed her head. She then turned toward the scene of the attack. I wasn't absolutely certain that it was an attack but it was all too coincidental not to be. She spread her wings as wide as an angel would, to offer comfort as her way to show respect. After a few moments of holding her wings out, she folded them and waited for me.

I was stunned. I didn't think that day could get worse, but it had. Cormac never went anywhere without that coat of his and if that was destroyed, I could only assume that the wizard wearing it was destroyed, as well. We weren't the closest of friends, but we were friends and we had each other's back. The fact that I wasn't there for him made me angry and hurt. I knew I couldn't possibly have known about it and been there, but still...the mind does what it wants to—casts blame and doubt wherever it can.

I opened the car door and sat in the driver's seat. Morgane hopped in after me and into the passenger seat. "Caw...where to?" she asked.

I had no idea. This whole week had been one long, strange trip that didn't seem to end. I knew I should call Dick to let him know, but I also knew that he would have his phone on silent as he lay resting in his safe room. I thought it might still be a good idea to drive by and make sure everything was okay over there. Additionally, it crossed my mind that it might not be prudent to return to my home. I needed to find another place to lie low while I figured things out, but I really had nowhere else at the moment. No one owed me any favors, and I was pretty sure I owed plenty.

I didn't have an answer, so I put the car into drive and started rolling. 20 minutes later, I arrived in front of Dick's house. It looked undisturbed. Outside lights were on and everything looked like it should. I drove on.

On the ride over, Morgane remained quiet. I finally broke the silence. "Who do you think is behind all of this?"

"Some pretty pissed off people," she replied. "All of this is more than just an agenda. It's a grudge."

I thought about what she said, and she was right. There had been far more carnage than what it would take to act out a scheme. It was someone or something that was so angry that the ends justified the means, and they didn't care. Bomb the whole city and rule the graveyard was just fine with a person like this, I supposed.

"Who'd be this upset?" I wondered aloud.

"I'm not sure, but they'd be powerful, either by themselves...caw...or together," she replied.

I had no leads, except for maybe the lady at City Hall, but somehow that didn't feel quite right. She didn't strike me as one to use such brute force. I couldn't totally rule her out, though, but it wasn't a strong lead by any stretch. The wolf pack, like I said before, didn't care that much. They liked the way things were and wanted to be left alone. That left the vampires with their multiple families, and the lesser beings...I say lesser beings, but I wouldn't call them that to their faces. I mean, I refer to them as lesser beings because they lack organization for political maneuvering. Like the dryads I met at City Park or the golem that protects certain areas. They are supernatural and of the kin, but their focus or role wasn't usually to "get ahead," so to speak. They were what they were, and that's it. The Fae? Could have been, but they didn't come through the fabric very often, as they were elusive and dealing with them was...well, it was always a nerve-racking experience. That left just the humans and their archetypes—the wizards, witches, Voodoo shamans and people of their ilk. I mean, I was one...or still am...or rather, I'm a shade of one. Humans were always vying for opportunity and political maneuvering for power and resources.

I guessed it was time to go to work. And by work, I didn't mean my day job at the NOPD as a detective. Since I was on administrative leave, I was a free agent, and that meant I didn't have the protections of the day job, but it also meant that I had options available to me that I normally wouldn't have.

The next morning, I decided the only place I could go next was back to the French Quarter and the good ol' Voodoo Emporium. Back in the day (roughly 80 years ago), shops that sold Voodoo items weren't so numerous or conspicuous as they are today. It was back-alley kind of stuff that respectable New Orleanians wouldn't have dared to dabble in...well...not in the open anyway. But...we all have secrets those that dabbled kept it close at hand. Nowadays, you couldn't throw a rock in the city without hitting something that claimed to be Voodoo. Most of the shops were for tourists, making money hand over fist by selling trinkets and other items that had no actual power, other than being a conversation piece for the tourist when they returned home. But there was one in the French Quarter that seemed different. It had a touristy area in the front for the sake of appearances, but something about the place...hardly anyone ever went in. For some reason, when tourists—or heck, even people like me—got near it, some sort of weird feeling came over us, keeping us at bay. Oh, you'd never be able to put your finger on it, but it was there. There were brave souls who would fight through it and still go into the shop, but those were few and far between and even the few that did, didn't stay very long. I had no desire to peruse the shop because it creeped me out, but I had work to do, and this was a business call. I had planned to be at the shop first light, but after the night I had, I slept in and was dead to the world until mid-morning. As it was, I got there shortly after 11 AM. It was sunny out but surprisingly, the street around the shop was relatively empty for a Thursday late morning. Again, it probably had a lot to do with that feeling I described earlier. After parking and heading toward the shop, I felt it too, but again, I had things to do—friends to avenge, a city to save. I walked through the open door and through the hanging beads that separated the front room from the outside.

A heavy scent of burning incense caused my nostrils to flare. There was no one in the store's front, which I kind of expected. Like I said, the front was for tourists, but the back...well, that was for those that were in the fold. I knew the proprietor by name only. Even though I had never met her in person, I had heard she was a beautiful lady. I walked to the back of the shop and saw all the same powerless trinkets that I would have seen elsewhere, along with Bourbon Street T-shirts, some of course with crude humor or Louisiana-related pictures like alligators and fleurs-de-lis. Near the door, I saw a sign that said, "Smile. You're on camera." to dissuade shoplifters but I knew that this shop didn't have to worry about shoplifters for some reason. Maybe it was the feeling of being watched as soon as you entered the threshold...and maybe it was true...maybe I really was on camera.

I knocked on the door to the back. I knew that behind that door lay another room and in that room was the real stuff—shrunken heads, ceremonial daggers, and other tools of the trade for Voodoo incantations. At least, that was what I had heard in the past. No one answered when I knocked. I only wanted to ask a few questions, but this setback was making me angry. In all honesty, I stepped back and was about to kick that door down. I think they knew it too, because as soon as I coiled up to kick, the door opened and out stepped Madame Lavant. My breath caught. The stories I heard were true. She was absolutely beautiful. Her dark skin shimmered and her raven-colored hair flowed in waves down her shoulders. Her full lips looked soft but firm and her eyes were hazel. I couldn't tell how old she was. One moment she looked like she could have been middle-aged, and the next, she looked to be in her 20s. She had never been to the regional council meetings while I was there. I would have remembered. She looked at me coolly. Her expression was firm, neither afraid nor welcoming, as if she was thinking "what are you doing in my store and why are you looking at me like that."

"Madame Lavant?" I asked.

"What do you need?" she replied. Her voice was low, sultry, and the tone came across like rich, smooth caramel.

"I need help," I replied, and that was the truth. I hoped she could give me something...anything. Tales traveled, and in different circles, they traveled at different paces and sometimes had conflicting information. I was clutching at straws though, as this could be a dead end.

She looked around the empty shop, stepped back, and nodded for me to enter the back room. What I had heard indeed turned out to be true. This was a shop for real practitioners of Voodoo and other arcane arts. I couldn't tell you for sure, but I could swear that the reason people felt the way they did about coming into this shop and the reason that most passed by was because of this second room. It emitted a peculiar aura that I could only tell because of being in its presence. I could see shelves filled with items that would give "normies" the heebie-jeebies, such as chicken bones, bat wings, and other unconventional items that would repulse you if you didn't know their purpose. The single bulb in the room cast long shadows, although I saw florescent lights above. They were not turned on. I wasn't sure if that was just on my account or if she kept them off for some other reason. Madame Lavant shut the door behind me as I walked in. I could tell that we weren't alone, and shortly after, my strong suspicion was confirmed.

"Ah…Mr. Giroux. I knew you'd be here," said a voice that came from the shadows on the other side of the room.

That worried me.

Chapter Twenty-Five

"Don't be alarmed," the voice said.

"Easier said than done, pal," I thought to myself. Out of the shadows, a man whose age I couldn't place stepped into the light. His dark skin blended into the darkness but in the light, it had the same shimmer as that of Madame Lavant. Upon closer inspection, I could tell that even if the fluorescent lights had been on or if the room had been pitch black would have made no difference to this man. Around his head and across his eyes, he wore a dark-colored wrap. He carried no cane but moved around the room with ease, avoiding tables at knee height and shelves that were chest high.

"Yes, yes, come in. Make yourself at home," he continued. Madame Lavant passed me and joined the man in the center of the room where there were chairs. They both sat down, and they both looked at me...well, Madame Lavant looked, but the man was different, in that he only appeared to shift his gaze toward me. In fact, I could have sworn that he looked right at me, even though his eyes were covered.

He gestured to the open seat in front of them. I proceeded cautiously and lowered into the seat, gently maintaining my balance in the event I had to react quickly. The feeling of the room was tranquil, yet there was a hint of danger, lurking at the sides of the room...that I couldn't quite put my finger on.

"Please, Mr. Giroux, relax. My name is Houngan Hain," he said, apparently noticing my lack of understanding of the title. I may have lived in New Orleans for a long time, but my experience with Voodoo was surprisingly lacking. Practitioners generally kept to themselves and very rarely did they cause trouble that would bring my kind, a keeper of the peace that had one foot in both worlds, to them. He continued, "Priest Hain, and as you know this is Manbo, or Priestess Lavant, but I know you call her Madame."

I nodded. I had nothing to add, so I remained quiet to see what they had to say. Sometimes in those kinds of situations, that was the best course of action because you never knew what someone would say to fill the silence, especially if silence brought feelings of discomfort. Somehow, I didn't think the two in front of me would. Even though Hain was pleasant, both were cool as cucumbers. I thought nothing would shake them and whatever they said would be calculated.

"I know why you are here. The bones told me, but why don't you tell me so I don't miss anything," he said.

"I need answers and you crossed my mind, so I'm here," I said.

"Yes, we heard about that unfortunate business at the regional council meeting last evening, and the bones speak to me of something else coming soon, but what it is eludes me," Hain said.

Madame Lavant hadn't said one word since I entered the room and as I looked at her, she seemed to have slipped into a trance, which obviously alarmed me. I tensed because even though I felt nothing electric in the air, it didn't mean that something wasn't being done. Before I could move, Hain quickly moved and shouted, "No!" as he swept his hand in an arc toward me. I was thrown back into my chair, unable to move. I mean, I could move my fingers and my toes, but the rest of my body felt stuck, as if I were paralyzed. There was an incredible weight holding me in place. I could breathe, but volitional movement was out of the question. My mind reeled and all I could think to myself was that I was caught! I unleashed my rage and let the depths of my soul respond to the threat. My body started the change, and Hain again shouted "No!" while making another sweep, this time with his other hand. Although my body was at the initial stage of accepting the gift of change, it was suddenly as if clutching at open air—there was nothing there. It was like a sneeze that you couldn't quite release and was just beyond your reach. It didn't feel like a barrier, but more like...well...like a severance. I was cut off from my alter ego, the wolf. I was really worried at that point...and of course, angry. I was also scared, but which was the more powerful emotion I couldn't tell.

"Mr. Giroux, calm down. Madame Lavant is assisting us in our conversation. A sort of concentration to keep out prying eyes who may want to peer into our conversation," Hain said.

I couldn't move, but I had the liberty to use my mouth, so I could speak. "Then why am I being...held down and cut off?"

"You know as well as I do that you were about to do something drastic, so I stopped you. Are you ready to have a civil conversation now?" Hain asked.

I looked from his face back to the figure of Madame Lavant, who was still not with us, and back to Hain. I nodded my agreement ever so slightly.

"Okay then," he waved his hands again, but this time in reverse to what he had done before. The weight on my chest lifted and my ability to move returned. I also felt the monster in my subconscious return, and angrier than ever. I would have changed right on the spot if it wasn't for the years of discipline behind me that taught me to maintain control.

"What did you do?" I asked.

"You are in my domain. My power here is most potent," he simply replied.

He stated that without a hint of bragging. He meant what he said. I moved forward in my chair just to make sure I could, and after confirmation, I leaned back in my chair and forced myself to look relaxed, though my thoughts were far from it. I wondered just how powerful those two were and if they were behind everything that had been taking place. But as soon as I thought that, it didn't make sense. If they wished me ill will, they would have just done something to me a few seconds before, when I was truly vulnerable.

"That's right, Mr. Giroux...we could have, but we didn't, so we aren't," he said.

"So, you can read minds, too?" I asked.

"No, your face betrays you and I'm a good guesser," Hain replied.

Clarity returned to Madame Lavant's eyes, and she rejoined the conversation. It surprised me because I thought she was going to be down for the count for the entire conversation, so when she spoke up, it startled me.

"Mr. Giroux, what brings you here? You never answered Mr. Hain's question," she said. Her voice was remained low and sultry.

"There are bad things going on. A shifting of power and summoning. I don't know who is behind it, but they're striking out against those in the city. Not only do "normies" seem to be fair game but they've also attacked the high council, which you heard about, and they openly attacked and killed a peacekeeper, a wizard by the name of Cormac," I said.

They didn't flinch. Golem, the statue I had spoken to a couple of days before, could have taken lessons from these two. They gave nothing away. Silence followed and wouldn't you know it—they used the same technique on me. I was uncomfortable enough to continue talking in order to fill the void. It just goes to show...it gets the best of us.

"And..." I continued, "I hoped you might know something."

"This is very perplexing," Hain said as he leaned back in his chair and looked over his steepled hands. "I will throw the bones," Madame Lavant said.

She leaned forward, showing ample cleavage, retrieved a bowl and placed it on a small table in front of us. She then took a bag from the same place and upended the contents to the side. They looked like chicken bones...or bones of something similar. I wasn't going to ask. She then brought forth a bottle, from where I didn't see, and placed that to the side. It was filled with a dark liquid. She took the bottle and poured its contents into the bowl. My nose told me that the dark liquid was blood of some sort. She took the bowl and swirled it around, ensuring the blood coated its interior while she muttered words I could neither hear nor comprehend. She then set the bowl back down, grabbed the bones, and threw them. From my vantage point, I couldn't see how or where they landed, but they both leaned forward and for the first time, their facial expressions changed. I wasn't sure if it was a look of frustration or worry, but as quickly as it came, it was gone again. It happened so quickly that I even questioned whether or not it had even happened.

Madame Lavant performed the same ritual again, this time omitting the blood since the bowl was still coated with it. She threw the bones in again and again. Whatever they saw disappointed them.

"Is everythin..." I began.

"Be quiet!" Madame Lavant said hotly, clearly upset about something.

The temperature in the room seemed to become hot, and it had nothing to do with an actual thermometer. I could feel it. I kept my mouth shut and waited. I still wasn't too far from fight or flight.

She finally broke the sternness of the moment and looked at Hain. "I don't understand. It's not showing anything."

"I don't understand either, but whatever it is, the omen does not look good," Hain replied.

He then looked at me. "We can't help you, and to be honest, Mr. Giroux, whatever is going on, I'm not sure we want to be a part of it. I'm really sorry."

"If you were really sorry, you would help me," I said. When that seemed to have no effect on them, I added, "This Sunday, you all are going to die...me too, probably."

He cocked his head to the side and looked toward me with a level of scrutiny that I thought I had already seen, but was nowhere near this level.

They exchanged a glance at this, but the cool, serene looks they had didn't break. I grew tired of their game, like I was in a cage and couldn't break free, as if I was some circus freak, pacing back and forth with unfettered energy...and I wanted to pounce. I stood up and walked to the exit without saying a word. If they didn't want to help, that was on them. I knew who I wasn't going to send Christmas cards to. When I got to the door, Madame Lavant spoke up and I turned to face her. "There is one thing we can do...the bones didn't reveal anything, but..." she paused to look at Hain before turning back to me and continued, "You could do a dream walk."

Well, of course that meant nothing to me and my face obviously showed it. Madame Lavant went on to explain, "It's utilizes a potion and a ritual that will grant sight in vision. Whatever the powers that be want to tell us or show us, this opens the connections for that to happen. I must warn you, though—this is dangerous. It's a melding of your spirit with spirits from beyond that grants the sight. If one is not careful, they lose themselves to the stronger spirit and then possession takes place. Understand?"

I understood quite well. I've been fighting another spirit most of my life. Even though I knew the wolf is me, it's also not me. I control it for the most part, but it took a long time to get to that point. Even when I was first turned into what I am, about a century ago, I wasn't always in control, but thankfully (as far as I know) I never hurt anyone while in that state who didn't deserve it. So, I knew exactly what she meant when she said that there was a fight for control.

I really had nothing to lose. If I failed, which I seriously doubted, whatever took my place wouldn't be around very long. If I succeeded...well...I would come out okay and hopefully with knowledge that would help me find whoever was behind everything.

"Okay, what do we need to do?" I asked.

I would be lying if I told you I said that bravely. Although I might have seemed confident, I must admit that I was apprehensive about it. Madame Lavant gestured for me to return to my seat, and I did. She got up and lit incense that had been in holders around the room. This apparently wasn't your normal incense because the smoke that bellowed from it quickly filled the room. Despite the amount of smoke that filled the room, I was surprised that I could still breathe with no troubles. The smoke only dimmed the room and did not have that acrid smell that incense usually had. She went to a table on the other side of the room and lit candles at the four corners of the table.

I couldn't see what she was doing from where I was seated, but it was evident that she was working on something. Hain said nothing. He continued to sit there politely but quietly. I'm not sure how long it took, but whatever Madame Lavant was making required extreme concentration. She was obviously very skilled because her movements were fluid in a way that only came from years of experience.

She stopped moving around to collect items, then became stock-still, as if in prayer. Maybe it was a prayer for all I knew, but whatever gods or spirits she prayed to, I had no knowledge of. I heard her murmurs become louder and louder and when it hit the crescendo, she threw something down and a puff of smoke plumed in front of her. She then went silent. She picked up what was in front of her and when she turned around to return to where we were seated, I saw it was another bowl.

She gently set it in front of me. I looked down at it. It was again a dark liquid, but this didn't smell or look like blood. "What is this?" I asked.

"It's the potion to help you see what you need to see," she said.

"What's in it?" I asked.

She just smiled and cocked her head to the side. I knew then that she had no intention of answering that question. Hain leaned forward. "My piece of advice to you is to relax and let your mind go. Let your mind go on a walkabout.

Let it expand. That's imperative to start the process...but the thing is, once it starts, you must scramble for your identity within the dream. Otherwise you'll lose yourself forever."

Well, that just gave me all sorts of warm and fuzzies. Of course, I'm lying through my teeth, but I got what he meant. The stakes were high and if I messed up...well, it would be the last mistake I would ever make.

Madame Lavant picked up a small glass I hadn't seen before, scooped up the liquid and handed it to me. "It's best to drink it fast. Once you start, it can cause you harm not to finish."

I took the glass from her hand and looked at the liquid swirling inside. I felt all of five years old, about to experience some grand thing and wasn't sure if I should be afraid or excited. With the stakes at play though, I had little time, and I rolled the dice. "Bottoms up," I said as I half toasted-half saluted them with raised arm and glass in hand, then upended the contents into my mouth.

The taste was...well...the taste was God-awful. It reminded me of an acrid, not-so-fresh seafood dish that was heavy on the fish and decay. It tasted like the Bonnet Carré Spillway smells when thousands of fish get caught inside after the spillway closes. It was overpowering and I could understand why some people would quit drinking right off the bat after that first drop touched their lips, but I kept going. I had an iron stomach, but this was pushing even me to my own limits. Whatever the outcome, I knew I would have to go buy gum after this adventure. I was reminded of the TV and radio jingle, "Dirty Mouth? Clean it up!" I thought I'd have to stick the entire pack in my mouth to clean that up.

At last, I was done, and I felt my stomach clench. If I were a weaker man or wolf, I would have spewed it all over the place, but I was able to hold it down. I wondered if I had been poisoned and maybe I had. Maybe you had to be poisoned in order to experience the kind of spirit visions they spoke about. I don't know, but it wasn't a pleasurable experience.

My limbs felt heavy. I could feel and hear my heart beating as the blood pumped through my veins and near my ears. I quickly thought, "I hope I haven't made a mistake," but sadly, I'm quite accustomed to making them. I just wanted to make it out of this one in the end. I could feel myself become sluggish. This was faster acting than any Roofie or Mickey I've ever heard of but then again, those were usually undetectable. This was all detectable. The room began to spin, while Madame Lavant and Hain remained in place, which was weird. It was almost like some sort of green-screen effect taking place in front of me. That led to more feelings of nausea, but even in that moment, I had a little self-pride, so I was able to keep everything down.

The figures of Madame Lavant and Hain smiled, but something was wrong. Their smiles were way too wide. It looked almost clownish. "Yes," I heard them say, but their voices sounded like they came from another room instead of right in front of me. The image of their lips moving was also off sync with their voices, like some 80s Kung Fu movie. My mind felt sluggish, along with the rest of my body. They continued, "Yes, this worked out better than we thought it would."

Everything went dark.

Chapter Twenty-Six

I awoke with a start, unsure as to how long I'd been out or if I was even really awake. As I looked around, I couldn't help but notice the peculiar sheen or fog that cast an otherworldly vibe over everything, creating a sense of familiarity mixed with a touch of the unknown. Both Hain and Madame Lavant were gone. I was by myself and my entire body felt like I had been shot up with Novocain. I could control it, but it felt numb. Standing up, I could faintly feel the hardness of the floor through the soles of my shoes as I walked toward the exit. My nose was filled with the unmistakable aroma of incense, a fragrance that clung to me even outside the room. The sounds that touched my ears were also different. It seemed like everything I heard was on a record playing at a slow speed, with the sound unnaturally stretched, forcing you to pay very close attention to figure out what you were hearing. I walked from the back room and into the shop, and from there I stepped outside. It was bright out and definitely not anywhere close to the time that I had arrived. I guessed it was approximately noon. There was no one else on the street. It was deserted—no cars, no tourists, no birds, no nothing. Just a street in the middle of the French Quarter with nothing that pointed to life.

Stepping off the sidewalk, I looked up and down the street. I really had no idea what was going on. I looked up at the sky and saw a clear, blue expanse, but the haze around me cast everything in light that resembled old Polaroid photographs—yellowed with age. Upon hearing music in the distance, I realized I was not alone as a second line came around the corner. A second line in New Orleans is a funeral march led by a jazz band. At one time, a coffin was carried but in modern times, it was an epitaph or photo and sometimes, people in costume marched behind the band. If someone didn't know what it was, they would think of it as a parade of some sort, and who could blame them with lively music and dancers following the band?

This second line had a coffin being carried at the lead, along with the jazz band, and everyone was wearing a very elaborate costume...so much so that they may not have, in fact, actually been costumes. There were werewolves, vampires, wizards, dryads, golems, and other creatures dressed in suits, playing different musical instruments. The crowd that followed was just as varied in appearance. The fleeting thought of "One of these things is not like the others," ran through my head, reminding me of a catchy song on a popular children's show.

When the second line got closer, the music ceased, but its appearance remained the same. The band members looked as if they were still playing. As they passed, those directly in front of me turned their gaze toward me, almost like you would see in a military parade when all the troops turned to look toward their commanding officer. I was no commanding officer and the whole process creeped me out. Once the march went by, I had the distinct impression that I was to follow, so I did. If I sped up, they did, as well. If I slowed down, they also slowed down. They turned a corner, and I followed. In fact, I followed for what seemed like forever, going down this road and then down that road. The sun overhead did not move.

We eventually ended up at a small cemetery, St. Louis Cemetery No. 1. It's in the heart of New Orleans, on the edge of the French quarter. It had the familiar image of above-ground tombs that Louisiana is famous for, as the ground is below sea level, so anywhere you dig, it's not long before you strike water. This fact, along with a tendency to flood during storms, if graves were placed under the surface, you might see coffins and caskets rising from the ground along with the water level. The cemetery was known for being one of the oldest in the area, being established back in...I'd say 1789.

The procession entered the hallowed grounds and serpentined up and down and around the rows until they came to the center of the yard. It was only at that point that I was able to catch up to them. Even though my limbs still felt numb, I moved with ease and for the amount of the time it took for us to get there, I surprisingly wasn't breaking a sweat or breathing heavily. They set the coffin down, then began to form a circle around it. I wasn't sure, but the crowd appeared to grow in number as the circle formed with the jazz band in the center, still playing. The rest of the crowd then took up spots as the circle spiraled outward. It was tight quarters, as the cemetery was packed tightly with tombs and people. In order for me to get to the center, I had to push past bodies. As I pushed past them, I brushed against some and what should have felt like real skin, felt more like rubber. Ironically, as I got a closer look, they all looked like genuine vampires, werewolves and the such...as real as if I had been looking in the mirror...yet they felt like they were wearing rubber suits. It was a bit disconcerting. As I approached the center, I saw faces I recognized—Dick, Lieutenant Martine, the captain, the lady from City Hall, Ms. Dufrene. I also saw Fenric the werewolf, and even Cormac. This pained me a little because I knew he shouldn't be there, as he had likely just passed. Then I encountered others I vaguely knew, and their presence surprised me. There was the dryad from City Park. I also saw the decayed vampire I had tussled with a few nights ago. At least I thought it was him. It was hard to tell features in the dark when I had met him, but something told me it was him. The golem in the shape of

Satchmo was there. Even the werepig manager was there. On the other side was Larry from the bar I liked to go to. It was the who's who of the past week of my life. I stepped closer. In the band, I also saw several goatmen playing horns, along with High Chancellor Sattorn.

They didn't look at me. All eyes remained on the coffin. It looked small compared to the tombs next to it. As I walked past the most inner circle, an irresistible force pulled me toward the coffin, its dark mahogany color reminiscent of blood that had been meticulously wiped away. I walked closer to stand over it and looked down. I didn't know what to do at that point. It all seemed so bizarre and my mind was still attempting to process exactly what was going on. I reached down to touch the lid, but it exploded. The force of it knocked me back and off my feet. I landed on my butt, but I recovered quickly. I couldn't see inside the coffin, but when I moved to get to my feet, a figure rose from inside of it, which stopped me cold. It was me in wolf form, and it scared the bejesus out of me. I'd seen myself in the reflection of mirror glass before, but I never realized just how intimidating I looked until I saw myself peering back at me.

"It's time to die," the other me said and leapt out of the box.

I tried to think of a comeback but hey, I already told you my mind was acting a little sluggish. With the threat coming at me, I abandoned the idea of saying anything and rolled out of the way as the wolfman landed where I just had been. I came up in a crouch, but the figure who looked like me was already on me and knocked me back against a mausoleum. The force of the blow threw me through the outer wall and into the vault. My lungs lost all air, and I struggled to breathe. Inside the vault, I saw Morgane. My crow friend was in the top corner of the vault on some unseen perch. She cocked her eye at me. "You shouldn't be here."

"I know that now…" I whispered because that was all the air I could summon up on short notice.

I moved to get up, but Morgane swooped down, landed on my chest, and pecked me in the face. The move shocked me and it hurt like hell. Until that point, I could feel things, but they were suppressed, like I'd imagine you'd feel if you're doped. This felt real. I could feel it completely and intimately. Behind her, I saw my alter ego appear at the hole in the wall, looking in. Morgane turned her head to look at the newcomer, then back at me, and pecked me once again. The pain was just as sharp as it was the first time. "You must fight like you've never fought before, Lou Giroux," she said.

And before my very eyes, she melted into smoke and drifted away. This would have mesmerized me, but a big, beefy werewolf hand reached through the smoke and grabbed me. It lifted me up and threw me out of the hole I had made going in, to the ground outside. The coffin was gone, but the mob of people—musicians and followers included—was still there. They were motionless, like they had been frozen in time, and reminded me of mannequins. From the ground, I saw my assailant rise up.

As I regained my ability to breathe, I knew I better start fighting this fire with fire. It was at that moment that I made the choice to change. Strangely enough, the dullness in my body and limbs did not fully relay the pain like it usually did. It was one positive instant in that not-so-positive, not-so-normal moment in time. In fact, I didn't really have to undergo the "change." It was as if I was in my human form one moment, and the next, I had seamlessly become my werewolf form. If only it could always be that easy. The werewolf looking at me laughed as it watched.

Up to that point, it had said nothing to me except "It's time to die," and I was glad it hadn't. I mean, just how many conversations can you have with yourself? Other than those inside your own head, that is...and those are bad enough. I would be afraid of what I'd say if I actually talked to myself and there was something else that answered.

The mannequins lurched forward. That was new. I was on one strange trip. I should have listened to the advice that you usually get from your parents about not taking stuff from strangers, but it was too late. I was there, and I needed to survive. The mannequins walked forward at a slow but steady pace with intention, and that intention was me. The werewolf that threw me into the vault hadn't moved. It was as if my alter ego in form had become a master tactician who could have shamed the likes of Napoleon, while he appeared to be moving pieces on the board as the mannequins inched toward me.

I had never been into hallucinogens before and after that experience, I definitely never would be. I prayed that this bad trip would soon come to an end. The mannequinesque figures of all the different beings kept coming. My panic rose, but then I became angry and frustrated with myself for being in this position. I felt strength pump through my fur-covered arms and legs. I reached out and grabbed the closest figure, which crumpled in my hands. The same thing happened with the next figure and the next. As soon as I touched them, they lost all pretense of solid, tangible beings and fell, crumpled on the ground, like balloons that had been full of air that was no longer there to keep them upright. I made for the other me and he didn't move. It was as if he was waiting for me. The figures kept getting in my way and even though they all deflated, more and more moved between me and myself. I know it sounds confusing, and believe me, it was just as confusing to me, if not more so. Eventually, the crowd was gone and at my feet were mounds of plastic-looking remains of what once was, but were no longer. Even as I waded forward through the mess, they dissolved.

I didn't run; I slowly advanced and the other me stayed put, leaning against the mausoleum, showing no signs of concern. I walked up and stood right in front of him. We gave hard looks to each other, then the figure posing as me sucker punched me in the stomach. I doubled over, but I didn't go down. I used the moment to barrel into the imposter, taking him to the ground. With my lower center of gravity, I was able to effortlessly sweep his feet as I moved forward. I should have paid attention because the figure used the momentum to jab his knee into my gut. As we tumbled, he threw me over and rolled to his feet. I sailed through the air and, like a gymnast, I landed on my own feet. Then the battle really began. Fists flew...some connected, others did not. There were grabs, throws, kicks...you name it. It was a real knock-down-drag-out, as we went at each other full force but neither of us could get the upper hand to finish it. We were both strong and fast, and we were both extremely resilient, not to mention our quick-healing capabilities. We broke apart at last and we stood, looking at each other momentarily.

Surprisingly, through it all, I was not breathing heavily though by that point (and after the energy I had exerted), I would have normally been out of breath, despite my supernatural abilities. In the back of my mind, I still didn't understand what I was supposed to gain from this vision. I didn't know if Lavant and Hain had, in fact, double-crossed me or not, but then again, they could have hurt me when they had the upper hand in the storeroom.

They could have just let me leave, so that didn't seem the case.

Everything was so confusing, but I was in the middle of a fight and couldn't spend anymore more time thinking about it while dodging the next lunge that came from my doppelgänger. After that, the figure reversed and swung his arm forward with claws outstretched, in an effort to rake me. I narrowly missed that attack as well, but could feel the wind generated from the speed with which it came. I took the moment to step forward because in his effort to slash me with both hands, it left a side open to me for attack. Stepping in also allowed me to grab and hold his outstretched arms as I went for the side. The figure couldn't swing back. Since I had an opening and held my opponent's arms at bay with my left hand, I stepped even closer and struck, palm facing up, and dug in with my claws. Once I connected, I swiped upward, leaving nasty lacerations behind. Doing the only thing he could do, the figure rolled forward and out of my line of attack. I turned left to face the werewolf and noticed the lacerations were gone. No one's healing ability is that fast. For the first time in this whole altercation, I felt a moment of fatigue with the realization that no matter what I did to this "other me," it wouldn't slow it down.

The werewolf smiled wickedly as if it knew what I was thinking and finally spoke again. "Now you die."

I smiled right back. "No, I don't think so."

Then I did the only thing I could think of. If I couldn't win that fight, there was only one other thing I could do in that situation. I ran.

Chapter Twenty-Seven

Screw all that nonsense about being a coward. Sometimes, a retreat is the only appropriate action, as it might be the only chance you have. It provides you with the option to choose a time and place for when and where you're prepared. I also truly didn't want to know what would happen if I lost the battle in the dream state I found myself in. Maybe that was the spirit guide or whatever just trying to challenge me for control. I didn't know, but I knew I didn't want to play anymore. Racing away from the cemetery, I headed back toward the French Quarter, my feet pounding on the ground, their sound reverberating off the buildings and into my ears. I also heard feet slapping the ground behind me, but didn't waste time to turn and look. It would have only slowed me down. All I needed to know was that I was ahead and at that moment, that was all that mattered.

The streets were empty, so that hadn't changed. It was so eerily opposite of reality, which only heightened the bizarreness of the situation. But again, I couldn't dwell on that. I had places to go and creatures to escape to hopefully solve the mystery of who was behind the recent events. Thankfully, I could still breathe and felt as fresh as I had been when I first started the vision, or dream, or whatever it was.

Eventually, I found myself back where I started—the Voodoo shop disguised as a regular store. I still heard the footsteps follow, but when I stopped at the shop and turned around, the sound of footsteps ceased and there was no one behind me. That caused even greater concern. I knew the other figure was right behind me. Where did it go?

The sun remained overhead, and the streets were still empty. The only thing I could hear was the beating of my own heart in my ears. At that point, I desperately wanted to get out of that God-forsaken vision, and I didn't even care if it would give me an answer to what I was looking for. I could deal with all that in the real world. There, in that other realm, in a time and place that I didn't understand how the rules worked, I was truly vulnerable. And don't think for one second that dreams or visions aren't real and don't have lasting consequences. I mean, sure, bad dreams after watching a scary movie while having a pizza and beer are one thing, but there are dreams that teeter on reality. Thankfully, I've only had maybe one or two encounters of this type over the years. It's definitely not a glorious experience. It's real, and the rules work differently.

And depending on the dream or plane of existence you're transported to, the set of rules from one plane can be quite different from the next. Needless to say, during that Voodoo dream, vision...whatever it was...I was starting to feel claustrophobic and wanted to return to my body.

"Leaving so soon? You just arrived." I heard a voice behind me.

I whipped around and saw a familiar face.

"Cormac?"

"Maybe."

"I thought you were dead." His face looked gaunt. He was skinny to begin with, but what I saw in front of me was a caricature of what he actually looked like.

"I might be. After all, this is all a figment of your imagination," he said as he gestured to the street and buildings around us. "None of this is real. I'm not; this place isn't. And you? Well, you might be a little, but only barely."

"What am I supposed to see here?" I asked.

"Everything. Maybe nothing. You survived yourself, so that's one thing that's positive. You don't have to worry about the dream spirits conquering you."

"So, this was pointless, then?"

"No, I wouldn't say pointless. You got to see me one more time," he said, which is exactly what he would have said. Whether or not it was really him, it was real enough to be him, and again, I felt the pain of loss in the center of my chest. If he really was dead, that would be the last time I would see him.

"I know we weren't close, but I'm going to miss you," I said.

"Solve the case," he said.

"Got any clues?"

"Nope, only what you see here."

"So, everyone and everything?" I asked.

"Correct."

"Everything is so confusing."

"It's meant to be. Did you really think that it would be handed to you on a silver platter?"

I looked away from the figure of Cormac and down the street while I thought it over. "No...but I at least thought I would..." I returned my gaze only to find that he was gone. A sudden rush of sadness and longing washed over me. I know we weren't the best of friends, but in my world, any connection that doesn't send you running for cover is a valued commodity. I don't have packs, sects or families backing me up. Just favors, friendships, and experience. Well, I guess you could say I have the police department, the thin blue line, but that's only for the day-to-day stuff. The nighttime, otherworldly aspects of my life...well...I had a thin blue thread as I was on my own, except for Dick and Captain Benoit. And for that matter, I was still out to lunch on the captain because we had never been in a fight where it mattered.

I had my friends down at the Crown and Anchor and a wishy-washy relationship with Hannah, the cat down at the bookstore, but beyond that, not much. Then my mind went to the suspects we had thus far and to a ditty from an old movie. I couldn't help but murmur the words in the same singsong way—Werewolves, and wizards, and vampires! Oh my!

I was still in my dream walk state, but the edges of my vision began to waver. I didn't know what it meant, since I had never done one of those before. I could only assume that the effects of the potion were waning...at least, I hoped so. I was ready to return to reality. That state was a prison in some ways, as I was stuck, and I couldn't leave on my own. Thankfully, I survived and I felt pretty good about that until I heard heavy breathing behind me.

"It's not over yet," I heard my own voice say from behind. The other me had returned. The touch of his hands on my back was swift, followed by a powerful shove that sent me soaring through the air. I had a moment to re-orient myself, and thankfully, I regained my balance and started to turn around. I couldn't see behind me, but I figured he would still be close by. When I stopped, I closed my left hand and formed a tight fist, then executed a spinning back jab. It connected squarely into the side of the jaw of the werewolf who looked just like me in beast form. I swear it was like looking in the mirror, but instead of an image that mimicked your movements, this image did anything but. I couldn't imagine my luck because the force of the blow and the surprise of it all sent Mr. Opposite Werewolf into the wall. Using the momentum of my now-completed spin, I took my right fist and drove it into the same spot against the side of my opponent's face, driving it against the wall again. I don't know what came over me after that because I just kept pummeling, using the wall as weapon, bouncing his head off my fist over and over again. This went on for a very short while before my alter persona fell to his knees, causing me to miss and ram my fist into the wall. If I thought it hurt to punch his head repeatedly, ramming my fist into a brick wall (which had no give) probably hurt three times as much. I immediately pulled back, wincing, shaking it, hoping to relieve the pain, but it didn't.

From a kneeling position, the monster drove straight up at a 45-degree angle with all its might, connecting with me. The surprise attack knocked me to my back and he pounced on top of me, doing the exact thing I had just done to him. Instead of bouncing my head off the wall, he repeatedly bounced my head off the concrete sidewalk.

"Victory!" it growled and opened its mouth for one big ol' bite. I thought for sure I was going to be jambalaya. I should have been more wary of Lavant and Hain. In fact, I should never have taken the option to complete a dream walk. I was going to die and would be stuck in this nightmare forever.

From my position, I couldn't gain purchase because my arms were pinned to the ground. I was trapped and the monster above me moved in to produce a fatal bite to my neck, I assumed, but it didn't connect. I saw a quick shadow behind the beast and a moment later, instead of the expected bite, I saw his eyes go wide. The shift in his body weight allowed me to reposition myself and wiggle out from underneath his mass. Something had motivated him to focus his attention elsewhere. When I finally freed myself, I looked up and saw Morgane!

She was busy pecking the back of the monster's head and drawing blood. Her beak was sharper than I had ever imagined, or at least there in the dream, it was as sharp as any knife I'd ever seen. When she saw that I was free, she hopped up and dove one last time, with all her might, into the back of the beast, taking him to the ground. The beast rolled over and Morgane was able to manage another hop to ensure she wasn't trapped beneath him. Unfortunately, that placed her within reach of his arms and claws. The beast moved swiftly—almost too fast to see—and connected his claws with her breast, directly under her wing. The blow caused her to go sailing through the air without the aid of her wings.

I was livid and was about to go tearing into the bloody monster before me, but Morgane shouted out, "No! Your time here is over. Get clear!"

I was momentarily stunned with disorientation, as I wasn't sure what my next course of action would be. Instead of launching forward, I took a step back and watched the black bird grow. I could clearly see the wound under her wing, but that didn't seem to slow her down.

"I'll take care of this," the much larger image of Morgane said.

I wasn't sure what she planned to do but I was dumbfounded by what I was seeing. I realized that it was all likely an apparition since it was, after all, a dream. My vision wavered, but the battle continued before me. Morgane mumbled strange, unintelligible words while bright, colorful streaks of light flashed from her and toward the werewolf.

I didn't see if the streaks connected or what happened after that because the next thing I knew, I awoke with a start. I almost felt as if I had been held underwater for a time and was coming up for fresh air.

Lavant and Hain were standing over me, looking down with concern. "Mr. Giroux," Hain said, "Welcome back. We were getting a little worried."

Once the immediate shock wore off and my heartbeat recovered from being on the brink of an explosion, I took a few more breaths before I spoke.

"What do you mean? Why were you worried? I was only gone a few moments, wasn't I?" I asked.

"No Mr. Giroux, you weren't gone just a few minutes. You were gone for hours. It is now evening. I have never seen a dream walk take so long," Hain said.

As I regained my composure, I was flabbergasted. Thursday evening and I still wasn't sure who was behind any of it, and I was fairly certain that I had just over two days left to stop some cataclysmic event from happening to the city I loved.

"I saw..." I said.

"No," Lavant said, interrupting. "Dream visions are not to be spoken of. The vision is for you and you alone. To speak of it to others only brings bad luck."

"Lady, bad luck is all I seem to have lately."

Chapter Twenty-Eight

I stumbled out of the Voodoo shop. I didn't want to be there anymore. My mind was reeling and I needed to get to a place where I felt safe in order to allow my mental state to come together again. Madam Lavant and Hougan Hain didn't stop me, though they made sure I would survive before I left. Out on the street, I was more perplexed than ever. I didn't feel like that vision had helped me at all. I was quickly running out of leads, and that was not a good thing.

I looked at my watch and the time gave me anxiety. Just one more reminder that the clock was ticking. When I checked my phone, I noticed multiple missed calls and texts from Dick. I quickly dialed him back, as I didn't want him to call in to report that I was missing. That was the last thing I needed. I don't think I would have been able to come up with a good story to explain my absence.

"Yes, officer 'so and so taking my report', I'm okay. I was just out of my mind...or rather I was stuck deep inside my mind talking to and fighting figments of my imagination,"

I thought to myself. Yeah, they'd kick me off the police department real quick following that discussion.

I dialed Dick's number, and he answered on the second ring. "Jesus, Lou! Where have you been?"

"It's...complicated. I'll tell you when I see you. What have I missed?"

"Nothing, but I assumed we would compare notes and continue working the case," Dick said.

"Sure, that sounds good. Where do you want to meet? I don't think it's safe to meet up where we live...you heard about Cormac, right?" I asked.

"Cormac? No, I haven't heard. What's up?"

I quickly filled him in on the night before. It was a few moments before he responded. "I hadn't heard, and I didn't watch the news today. Man, I hate to hear that," he said. "I think you're right. Let's meet somewhere in public."

"Yeah, let's meet at that sandwich shop on Poydras and Baronne Street. I'm starving. 30 minutes?"

"You and your food."

"Hey, I can't help it. I'm starving. I haven't eaten anything all day."

"All right. See you there in 30...oh and Lou?"

"Yeah?"

"Be careful."

We disconnected, and I headed toward the location. It took me about 20 minutes, and I was there before Dick arrived. The place was known for its quick service, so I was in the middle of my sandwich when Dick walked in. He saw me and joined me at my table.

"I would have waited but..." I gestured toward the food since he didn't have a need or desire to eat real food.

He only nodded in acknowledgement and sat down. "So, what do you have?"

"I went on a dream walk."

"What?"

I then explained what happened to me and why I had been out of pocket for most of the day. Just as I was about to tell him about the dream, I was reminded of Madame Lavant's warning to not share what I saw during the walk.

"I'd tell you what I saw, but it made little sense to me and I'm not sure it would be safe for you or me if I told you, judging by what the Priestess said about sharing," I said.

Dick lifted his hands up and out as he shook his head, "No need to share, then. We have enough problems to deal with. Don't want to add a Voodoo curse on top of it."

I had to agree.

I was about to start the conversation in earnest about what we had—facts, rumors, thoughts—anything that would give us an edge or shed some light, but before I could, I heard the rumble of motorcycles heading up the street. With the tall buildings and the fact that most of the storefront consisted of windows, it made the motorcycles sound louder, as their roar echoed off the surface of each building. I did mental calculations and I could hear eight distinct engines. I don't normally do such things, but the revving of the engines in this area was purposeful and especially obnoxious. It reminded me of...and my suspicions were correct as I saw through the window. Soon after, Luke and his wolf pack pulled up outside and parked on the sidewalk. Totally against the law, but I didn't think they really cared.

"Looks like we have company," I growled under my breath.

Dick turned and looked outside while I glanced around the sandwich shop. There was a full shift of workers making sandwiches behind the counter and customers were coming and going. Some took notice of the new arrivals, but they didn't appear worried. If they only knew just who they were looking at, they might have been. I knew the wolf pack was reckless and dangerous, but they weren't stupid enough to openly attack me there. It would have broken the accords, so I wasn't sweating just yet. However, if the world was going to come to a close for New Orleans in two days, who knew what they would do, especially if they were behind it. I looked back outside, and Luke and I locked eyes. He and his goons, some of whom I recognized from our encounter earlier in the week, looked better than when I left them last time.

The look on his face didn't tell me anything, so I braced myself for whatever this visit would turn into. There was no one else near where we sat in the back of the shop. Dick was sitting with his back to the door. He got up and moved to another table beside me, so he could watch the entrance, as well. I was already making escape plans. There was an emergency door to my right and those large windows that I saw Luke through. I supposed I could always bound through those. I was sure Dick was making the same mental plans I was. One thing I'd always heard throughout my long life was "proper prior planning prevents piss poor performance." Even if the plans ended up not being useful, at least I'd have a start if things went south. Sometimes just having some idea about what you want to do is better than a split second decision with hesitation. Hesitation is what kills people. Making a plan and moving right away has saved more people than those who'd have to come up with something right on the spot. Just ask any squirrel crossing the street.

Luke and his crew walked in the door on the corner. The atmosphere within the shop became tense. I could feel it and, by the looks of it, so did everyone else. The few customers standing in line decided that they weren't hungry after all. They all left through the second entrance on the side of the room opposite me. Those that had already ordered food moved to the side of the room and the workers? Some of them noticed but went back to sandwich-making.

Luke walked toward where Dick and I were sitting, but his pack remained near the entrance. I waited with my whole being, on the verge of pressing the emergency button and changing into my alter ego but if I had done that...well...that would also break the accords. That was a choice of last resort, meaning that only if I had no other options would I choose that one.

I sat and tried to act nonchalantly, like his visit was nothing or that it was one that I had expected, but I'm telling you now...I was totally bluffing. As the adrenaline surged within me, I started to feel uncomfortable. I didn't want anyone in the shop who wasn't involved to get hurt. Just as I was about to speak, Luke interrupted me and took me by surprise.

"No need to go and get all riled up, Lou. This is a social call," he said.

I said nothing. I just looked at him coolly and hoped that he would get to the point shortly.

"Fenric told me to come tell you personally...I was against it but he insisted." He said that in a way that meant Fenric hadn't just insisted, but he'd commanded. He continued, "So, I'm here to tell you that you have our support."

I couldn't help but frown, as that didn't provide me with any more closure and possibly another loose end. Maybe they were a part of what was coming and what he said was just a ploy. Or, maybe they really wanted to help. I had no way of knowing, and so I would continue to hold them at arm's length.

"Don't flatter yourself, Lou. This doesn't change any-thing. This is only temporary. Consider this as "an enemy of my enemy is my friend." After that attack on the high council where Fenric was attending, you just became the pack's friend for the time being."

I stood up from my table and met him in the middle of the room, surrounded by empty tables and chairs. By that time, the sandwich shop had been deserted, other than the employees and us. Most of the employees must have felt something was going on because they all disappeared to the back. They wanted no part of it. Who could blame them? It's funny how that little voice inside your head tends to work. To the ones that listen, it'll help more than a few stay safe, but those that don't...well, they often end up being on the wrong end of a surprise altercation. If they had just listened to that little voice, gut feeling, or whatever you want to call it, they could have avoided an unpleasant situation.

I stood to full height and looked him straight in the eyes. "Noted," was all I said.

"That's it?" he asked.

"Yup," I said.

"We come all this way to tell you and that's it?" he said.

"How did you know I was here?" I asked.

"Everyone knows where you are these days," Luke replied.

"Meaning?" I asked.

"Meaning that someone doesn't like you...even more than we don't like you. Contracts are out, but so far no one is taking them because they heard what happened at the council meeting and want no part in...whatever this is. Faction renegotiation, civil war..."

"Do you know where the contracts are coming from?" I asked.

"No, that's just the word on the street."

"Why are you not taking them up on their offer?"

"Lou, we were already used once as a tool but something about everything that's happened this week doesn't add up. Fenric doesn't want any part of it. If what you said when we last met and at the council meeting is true, then we better be on the side where we have a chance at surviving whatever's coming."

"All right. Well, I appreciate the personal calling, and if I need anything, I'll be sure to reach out."

My words were cordial, but the tone of my voice didn't match. Luke looked at me for a bit, not giving anything away visually, then said, "I guess my work here is done."

"Guess so."

As quickly as they came, they left. The rumbling of their pipes took a long time to fade away after disappearing from sight. Only until a few seconds after the sound of their engines disappeared did I let out a sigh. In fact, I believe the whole sandwich shop let out a collective sigh.

"That was unexpected," Dick said as he returned to the seat in front of me.

"Totally. But that whole business has me concerned. They knew where I was," I said.

"Perhaps people are casting location spells on you so they can avoid you?" Dick offered.

"Makes sense. I never really had to worry about that before. But now that I think about it, that's probably how High Chancellor Sattorn found me. I guess I will have to go get a talisman made to hide myself from prying eyes."

The things that we, on this side of the spectrum, have to worry about that "normies" don't is just mind-boggling. But then again, with everyone having cell phones with active GPS, maybe it's not really that different. That made me think about my phone and that maybe they were able to track me that way, too. Technology and magic—they aren't always the "friend" that you want to have.

I took my phone out and laid it on the table. "I think I'm going to go dark and shut the phone off for a while."

"Good thinking. How are we going to connect if we need one another?" Dick asked.

"I guess the best way is to turn on our phones in a safe space every hour or so and check for messages. Do you need a cloak talisman? I'm going to go see about one after we leave here."

"I have one," Dick responded. "They aren't cheap."

I didn't know how much they were, but nothing magic was ever cheap. It always came with a price, and it wasn't always monetary.

"What do you think you'll do next?" I asked.

"I think it's time that I make a calling to the 'families'," he said, meaning that he planned to talk to the vampire factions.

"Is that safe?" I asked.

"Probably not, but not as unsafe as you are with your kin."

"Do you want me to come with you?"

"Lou, I don't know what happened with your wolf packs, but I know that you and they have had a feud of some kind. My kind...well...I know they don't care for me, but they aren't out to get me, so my meeting with them will be cold and most likely professional. I saw some of them in the chambers when we were all attacked, so I think they will be willing to at least answer my questions or be open to pointing me in the right direction. Something tells me they don't want any part of this, either, so I think I'll be safe for the most part," he said.

"Be careful. We still don't know who's behind all this. Could be anyone," I said. Dick gave me a look as if to say, "Thanks, Captain Obvious," which only made me feel dumb and rightfully so. Anyway, it was as good a plan as any.

"Okay, that works. I will turn on and check my phone hourly until you give me an update."

As I watched Dick get up and leave, my stomach again began to talk, so before I left, I ordered a sandwich to go.

Chapter Twenty-Nine

The sun was low in the sky, and the shadows of the buildings in downtown New Orleans lengthened. The bustle of the day transformed to the bustle of the evening and there was a moment's pause of liveliness with switching between daytime and nighttime activities. Where I was in the CBD, the foot traffic slowed down considerably, but wasn't nonexistent. I don't think there is ever a time when the activity on the street is truly nonexistent except for maybe the witching hour, before dawn breaks.

I felt the need to stretch my legs, so I walked to Hannah's bookstore. I failed to mention it before, but books and records weren't the only items they sold. When I first started telling you the story, I wasn't sure how much I should tell you, but we've gone too far and I've said too much already to hold anything back now. I mean, I still don't think it would be a good idea for you to tell anyone but that's up to you. Along with the books and records, they also had a room that isn't normally open to the public—or rather, not open to the normal public. Most businesses that catered to both worlds had separate rooms for the non-normal transactions, but you, as a "normie" would never suspect it. Usually, there are spells that prevent a normal person from taking notice of the doorway or room and sometimes, the rooms are hidden...so there you go.

With the way the week had been going, I wanted to check on Hannah and Harry anyway. I needed to know they were okay. Sometimes no news wasn't necessarily good news, especially in my line of work. About half an hour later, I arrived at the front door. By that time, the sun had set, and the shadows lengthened until they were no more. The overtaking of nighttime fully enveloped the cityscape. The evening was transformed by the glowing store lights, neon signs, and car headlights, lending a serene ambiance to the sometimes chaotic city.

The lights in the bookstore were still on and the sign at the front was still illuminated to indicate they were open. I swung open the wooden door with a glass pane and heard the familiar overhead bell announce my presence. Harry was behind the desk, perusing papers and looked up when I came in. His expression didn't change at all. He only nodded and went back to whatever he was focused on. He never was a warm welcome. I walked past and padded up the stairs, headed to the third floor, where Hannah usually hung out. Besides Harry and myself, I counted only two other people in the store. One was an older fellow, browsing the historical section and the other was a middle-aged, mousy-looking lady in the romance section. I know—stereotypical, but those stereotypes do come from somewhere. Anyway, I didn't waste much time and went up the last stairwell to the third and final floor. The lighting was dismal without the sunlight coming in through the windows. At that hour, the windows looked more like gaping holes of darkness, and if I looked just the right way, I could almost see the reflection of the room in that darkness bouncing off the glass.

From my left, I heard Hannah's voice. "Lou! I didn't think I would see you anytime soon with what I heard. Are you okay?"

Her voice was intense, which was strange to me because our typical conversation consisted of mere banter. To hear her actually sounding concerned for me made me feel good, but I had to maintain the balance. "Oh, come on, get a grip," I said.

"Well, then buy something or get the hell out," she replied, her voice right back to the usual tone and tenor that, in a way, brought me even more comfort.

"I'm okay, Hannah, but you're right. It's been quite the week."

"I also heard about Cormac. I know you worked together from time to time."

"Yeah, that one's going to be tough to come back from," I said.

"Have you heard anything?" she asked.

"Hannah, you probably know more than I do. That being said, do you know anything else about what's going on?" I asked.

"No more than what I already told you, but from what I'm gathering, there is no middle ground to remain neutral in," she said.

"No, I don't think there will be."

"If I hear anything, though, I'll let you know before I do anything else," she said. "But what can I help you with? You are here for something?"

"I need to peruse your other room," I said as I nodded toward the dusty wooden door that sat in the brick wall to the west. If you weren't looking directly at it, you wouldn't have noticed it. And if, for some reason, you did, you would forget about seeing it a moment later.

"Oh, I see," she said. "Unfortunately, end of the world or not, I can't give anything out for free."

"I know. Whatever I get, I'll pay for," I said.

Like I said before, magic items come at a cost and depending on what it was, the cost could be very weighty. Since her special shop wasn't utilized very much, it meant her prices weren't for the pedestrian.

She looked at me lazily, then turned her back to me as she sauntered over to the door. There she paused and sat on her rear as she raised her tiny paws and performed some type of intricate maneuver, casting a spell. When she was finished, the door took on a bluish hue and opened, revealing a well-lit room beyond. If someone were to see the door open in passing, it would have looked like the room was full of neon lights, but the light was emanating off of the unique items in the room, both on the counter and below the glass countertops. In truth, it looked like a shining jewelry store with display cases that ran the perimeter of the room. The difference between the room full of vinyl records we had just left and the room we entered couldn't have been more night and day. The dusty, old, dark room with dingy lights versus the secret, well-lit, well-equipped room would take your breath away, not just because it held magical items, but because of the stark contrast if you weren't aware of its existence.

She hopped onto the glass counter and turned to me. "What would you like?"

"It's been forever since I've been here, Hannah. Anything special going on?" I asked.

"Well, we could spend hours on that, but if you give me a hint of what you're looking for, we can take care of that first."

"I'm being tracked. I don't have hard evidence other than a wolf pack that showed up out of the blue, but I'm almost 100% on it."

"I got just the thing. Follow me," she said and hopped off the counter to cross the room to the other side, where she hopped up onto another glass counter.

Her tail twitched precariously over the side, but her focus on me remained fixed as I looked down into the display case. On the bed of soft, pastel velvet, there were rows of trinkets of various shapes and sizes. It certainly wasn't a jumbled or disorganized display. Each piece had its own dedicated space.

"See the one right there...the one that looks like a small shield no bigger than a silver dollar pendant?" Hannah asked.

It was hard to miss once she described it. It was crystal blue and gave off waves of soft blue light, but not to the point that it was overpowering or that I had to shield my eyes. The ebb and flow of light was mesmerizing.

"Yeah, I see it."

"That's the one you need. It will not only protect you from prying eyes but also from anyone using any kind of ability unique to their kind—like your wolf pack would not be able to sniff or hear you. Vampires wouldn't be able to locate you by blood. Spells with you in mind will fizzle out—and that's just on our side. On the other, "normie" side, technology created to track you such as GPS devices or software, again, just won't be able to locate you."

I was already racking up the worth of such a trinket and the value of such was worth more than I had. This wasn't a regular cloaking trinket like what Dick had. His charm had some ability to stop people from casting a location spell, but to have a trinket that would do that plus all the stuff that Hannah just told me? Well, that was priceless. I wasn't poor by any stretch of the imagination. I mean, I've lived a long time and I've come to learn the 8th wonder of the world was compounding interest and investments. Regardless of that, I was still just a regular working Joe...or Lou, for that matter. And even with all that money in investments, I had to be very careful about accessing it for bringing unwanted attention from the "normie" world. Both sides had an adage that was true to both—two things are certain: death and people wanting to screw you out of what they think you owe. Okay, maybe not that exact wording, but you get the gist.

At any rate, the value of what I was looking at would have taken a huge chunk of my net worth. I knew by what she told me about it and by its appearance, I couldn't afford it.

"It's beautiful...how much?" I asked.

She told me the price, and it was much more than I had even imagined. In fact, it was so much more that I involuntarily staggered back, like I was slapped in the face.

"What?" the stern little cat face staring up at me demanded. "It's worth every penny."

"Oh, I'm sure, but I don't think what I make at the police department, or what I have in my bank account will cover that."

"Come on, we both know you don't work at the police department for the money. I know you have the funds to cover it, but maybe we can make a deal," she said.

The hair on the back of my neck stood up. Making deals was serious business. It was sometimes downright dangerous business. Many a soul have made deals with the equivalent of a devil and didn't survive long with the consequences of their choice. Making a deal or a promise wasn't the same as it was in the normal world, though it should be the same. A promise is binding and failure to fulfill it can have serious ramifications up to and including excruciating pain and death. I didn't care how long or how chummy I was with the cat who wasn't a cat. Deals were dangerous.

"I'm not sure. What do you have in mind?" I asked.

"I want a favor," she said.

"Okay..." I said slowly.

"And a single strand of your hair," she said a little more quickly, as if she were trying to get that last bit in before she lost the chance.

"What? My hair?" I asked.

"Yes, only one strand," she purred back, nonchalantly.

That was a very dangerous area to swim in, indeed. To give another entity something of yourself, even as small as a strand of hair, was an invitation of sorts and that invitation couldn't be taken back. Once I gave her that, I would not only be beholden to her for whatever favor she chose, but if I gave her a strand of my hair willingly, that was next level stuff. She could outright curse me. In New Orleans, living near the U.S. epicenter of Voodoo, someone could do powerful things to another person using a doll...and Voodoo was just one aspect to deal with in the area.

"What are you going to do with my strand of hair?" I asked.

"This talisman is very powerful, but I want assurances to know where you are if something were to happen to you," she said. "And even though this trinket will hide you from pretty much anything, giving me that strand of hair will give me the power to find you if I need you...or if you disappear."

"And your favor?" I asked.

"I can only tell you after you accept," she replied.

I hesitated and she must have sensed my apprehension because she quickly added, "Lou, I promise it won't go against your nature."

I had to think about it because again, that was serious...I could come up with the money but the time it would take to move assets around and liquidate them would take time and I didn't really have time to waste. The way I figured it, if I gave her the hair and our world ended in two days, I guessed it wouldn't really matter. It was the lesser of two evils.

"Okay, fine. Deal," I said a moment later, after making sure my reasoning was sound.

"Shake on it," she said.

Feeling foolish, I lifted my hand and took her little paw into my palm and enclosed it with my fingers, but not tightly. I shook once, then let go, sealing the deal. I felt an energy shift around me as the bond between me and the cat became tangible; it engulfed me and shrunk until it settled all around my chest. I could feel the weight of it momentarily before it dissipated. It was still there. It was like donning soft body armor. After a while you get used to the weight and just like that, you couldn't feel it any longer, but knew it was there. The only way that feeling would go away was when little miss kitty asked me to fulfill her favor, whatever that may be.

It was hard to tell, as I don't hang around cats often, but it seemed the little kitty's face beamed with excitement. As buyer's remorse set in, I realized I had no choice but to accept that the deal was done. I plunged ahead and plucked one hair from my head and laid it on the counter.

"Go ahead. Reach in and grab it," Hannah said, indicating for me to retrieve the trinket.

I did as she said and went around to the back side of the display case where it was open and reached in. It looked like it would be so delicate that it might break the moment I touched it, but when I picked it up, it didn't feel like the crystal blue trinket that I saw before me. I laid it in my palm where I could get a better look. As I brought it closer to eye level, the blue light winked out, and I saw that the crystal look had been replaced with a rather ordinary appearance of wood. Whatever magical properties it outwardly displayed a moment before were gone. It looked like a trinket that anyone could have possessed.

I shouldn't have been surprised, as I've lived a long time and that wasn't my first time around magical items, but every time I came in contact with one, my sense of wonder always spiked, even after all those years. It made sense, though, as you couldn't exactly walk around with something that gave itself away as a magical item to anyone that happened to be walking by. Therefore, every magical trinket had a similar quality to camouflage it. Those that didn't only brought attention and calamity because if they broke the accords in some way, even if not intentional, you were still susceptible to the consequences and those punishments were harsh. Whereas the normal world has changed over the years regarding punishment and rehabilitation, our world—the world that no "normie" is supposed to know about—is still in the 19th century model for crime and punishment.

I looked back at Hannah. "So, what's your favor?"

"Wouldn't you like to know?" she said.

"Uh, kind of," I said.

"Well, I like to keep you on your toes, so I think I'll keep it to myself for now," she replied.

Well, that wasn't what I wanted to hear. The unknown can be so taxing because the mind tends to always go to the worst possible scenario and, with everything else going on, it was just one more thing to worry about. The favor could possibly have been a simple task—a "rescue a kitten out of a tree" kind of favor, but I guessed I would have to wait until she came to collect. Until then, my mind was going to run wild with it.

"Well, at any rate, I appreciate you working with me," I said.

"You may just want to hold on to that because if we survive the week, you may not be so thankful when I come calling," she said coyly.

Perfect...

CHAPTER THIRTY

An hour later found me back at home. I wanted to check with Morgane to see how she was doing. On the way there, I quickly turned on my phone to check for messages. Seeing none, I turned it back off. Sure, I was going back home and anyone who was out to get me more than likely knew where I lived, but I didn't have to make it easy for them.

Morgane had cleaned up the place. Everything was back to where it was supposed to be. And she was there, waiting for me. "Lou, where have you been?"

"You cleaned up the place?" I asked.

"Someone had to. With your life falling apart, I guessed I would...squawk!" she said and hopped in excitement from one leg to the next. "Don't change the subject. Where have you been?"

"Keeping tabs on me?"

"Yes," she said, her voice conveying that it shouldn't have come as a surprise. She cocked her head to the side and stared at me with one yellow eye, the pinpoint pupil piercing me with focus. "Of course, I have been. You winked out from my sight about an hour ago. I was about to come look for you."

"Really?"

This surprised me because...well, I don't know why this surprised me, but I felt like it should have, so it did. But at the same time, the pragmatist in me knew it shouldn't. It would totally be like Morgane to keep tabs on me.

"Quit stalling with dumb questions," she said, interrupting my thoughts.

"I..."

She hopped and flew to my shoulder, where she nipped my ear. It almost hurt. "Spit it out, caw!"

"Geeze, Morgane, what's gotten into you?"

"I thought something happened to you. Are you going to tell me?"

"Yeah, yeah...just give me a moment. I just got home and now I'm being attacked by a blackbird."

She nipped my ear again and said, "Har de har har. You deserve that." Then she flew back to the counter and sat watching me. I told her about my trip to the Voodoo store and my encounter at the sandwich shop that led me to getting the talisman. She remained still throughout the whole tale, which was rare because she was always so fidgety.

"You went on a spirit walk? Squawk!" she said, breaking the silence when I finished. "Those can be very dangerous. Don't you know people sometimes don't come back from those and if they do, they could be possessed or something catches a ride back with them?"

"They said something in passin..."

"Caw...and you gave someone a favor?! Squawk! Lou, you can be so dumb sometimes. You need a chaperone!"

"Oh, trust me...I know," I thought to myself. "Well, here in a short while, I didn't think it would matter. One of those, 'I'll cross that bridge when I get to it', if I ever get there at all," I replied.

She ruffled her feathers, then began preening herself, stopping to look at me with that piercing eye every so often. She was clearly agitated. It reminded me of long-forgotten memories of my mother giving me a disapproving look when I was a young boy a hundred or so years ago.

"Oh, we'll get there all right," she mumbled to herself before squawking once more, rather loudly. That seemed to conclude her preening, and when she was back to herself, I didn't get the feeling of anymore tension in the room.

"So now, what are your plans?" she asked. "Since I won't be able to tell where you are, I need to know so I can keep an eye out."

So strange, I thought to myself—twice in one night, others seemed to care about me.

"I'm going to keep checking for Dick hourly and hopefully I'll hear something soon. Maybe he'll dig something up with the families. Until then, I'm kind of stuck. I don't have to go to work, and I don't currently have any leads to pursue on my own...so, I don't know."

I looked at my watch and it was only 9 PM on a Thursday night. "And since I have nothing going on, I think I'll head on down to the bar."

"Pffft..." she said. I found that almost amusing and considerably hard for her to do since she didn't have lips, but it sure sounded like she did.

"You want to come?" I asked.

"No, but be careful. Just because you think you are more safe because people can't track you doesn't mean anything," she said.

She was absolutely right. I have to admit, I was feeling a little agitated and felt that heading to the bar to get some suds would help. I mean, I knew it wouldn't get me blasted but sometimes, activity in a pub setting was just the key to help a person focus on things at hand. Okay, not really, but in the passing of time, it helps.

About 10 minutes later, I walked through the blue telephone booth and was inside the pub. The mugs hanging from overhead hooks welcomed me, as did Boz behind the bar. He more or less nodded in my direction, which for him was a cheery "Hey buddy. How're you doing and what do you need?" He wasn't unfriendly at all, but like I said, I think he might have a little ogre in his bloodline and that kind of went with the territory. I looked around the room. It wasn't crowded, as only a few people were hanging about, so I bellied up to the bar and ordered a Black and Tan. It felt good going down, so I ordered another.

I felt a hand on my shoulder and looked back to see a pale, young lady that looked out of place in the pub. She was well-dressed in professional attire—black pencil skirt, white blouse and blazer. She looked as if she could have come straight from a board meeting...heck she probably had. I knew immediately that she was a vampire. She had that same cold but efficient quality that Dick had.

"Mr. Giroux," she said with a clipped accent.

Most people would have mistaken her for being from New Jersey, but I knew she was from Metairie. Oh, that's another thing about New Orleans...I've been all over the world, but New Orleans is the only place where they have so many different dialects in such a small region. You had the Cajun, the Creole, the southern drawl, the N'orleans, the Metairie accents...they were similar but distinct. All that melting pot of French, Spanish, Italian, African, and other cultures over the centuries settled in different spots of the sprawl throughout southeast Louisiana.

I glanced around the room for others, but it was only her. I looked at Boz behind the counter again and he only watched with mild...curiosity? Irritation? I swear, I still couldn't read that guy.

"Can I help you Ms...?" I let the question linger in the air as I looked back to her.

Her face gave no indication that she heard or even cared what I had to say. Her almost clear, crystal blue eyes continued to bore into me until the point that it almost became uncomfortable. I knew I was safe in the bar for the most part, but who was ever really safe anywhere? Call me crazy, but I suspected this vampire didn't want to be here and the fact that she was put her in a foul, temperamental mood.

"Mr. Lumin requests your presence at once," she finally said.

The Lumin family? That was big stuff.

"Dick is already visiting them. Why do they want to talk to me?"

"You are the one I was sent to summon, and we think you're the only one who couldn't possibly be involved in these dark endeavors."

That statement begged questioning. I mean, I know I'm not involved, but why did they think Dick could possibly be involved? Before I could ask, a crowd of folks came through the front door and since I was at the end of the bar closest to the door, they jostled me as they entered.

"Hey Lou!" I heard the familiar voice of my friend Larry. I moved to get out of the way and momentarily turned to greet him. When I turned back, I saw the back of the lady vampire as she headed toward the hallway where the back door of the Crown and Anchor was, which led to a courtyard with picnic tables and umbrellas. It was clear that she was there to deliver the message and now that the task was complete, she was leaving.

I quickly said "hello" back to Larry and excused myself quickly, telling him I would be right back. I followed the lady to the small hallway. Once there, I turned the corner, only to see the back door close at the end of the hallway. With a quickened stride, I went through the back door and continued to the courtyard, which had a perimeter of fences—a wood privacy fence on one side and a wrought-iron fence on the other. There was really only one way to that area, which was the door that I had just exited. I wasn't really surprised. In fact, I kind of expected it. No one was in the courtyard, not even the vampire who had just walked back there. She was gone. Vampires, like I have alluded to before, have special powers, but not all of them have the same ones. Some can turn into a mist or fog-like form, some can straight up fly, and others are extremely and blindingly fast. The older the vampire, the more powerful they become because they've been able to collect more skills over the years. Whatever powers this lady vampire had, she had used them and disappeared into the night. Suddenly, I didn't feel like drinking anymore and felt like disappearing myself.

I was hoping to elicit more information, but I guessed that was it. The Families requested my presence. I was feeling like a pinball bouncing from location to location, being summoned here and being summoned there. For being incognito and difficult to find, I could be found pretty easily, it seemed, even with the talisman. It was honestly my own fault; I'm a creature of habit and visit the same haunts. I thought that If I survived this, maybe it would be a good time to change my name and move on to somewhere else, like I had many times in the past.

I turned on my phone quickly to see if I had any messages from Dick, but nothing had changed. No messages, no phone calls...nothing. I had a little tickle of eeriness crawl up my neck and a spike of fear tear through the pit of my stomach. I had already lost one friend...well, an acquaintance I would have called friend if I were in a war, hanging out in some foxhole. Strange how that happens—extremes and shared misery meld people together more than any sunny day experiences ever do. Anyway, I had lost one "friend" already that week and I refused to lose another, and if I did...well, there'd be hell to pay and it would come back tenfold...literally. I've already done it once with the wolf pack, but that's another story for another time.

I decided to head back into the city, but first I had to slink out of the pub with no one noticing. I didn't want to bring attention or beg questions. Walking back through the back door, I took my time. The crowd had grown, but I didn't see Larry. He must've been out front. Halfway through the room, I felt a presence at my knee. I looked down to see a black and white dog looking up at me, the dog's owners in tow. I had seen them before; they were the couple with cameras I had seen just a couple days ago.

"Priscilla, come here," the man said, then apologized. "It's our first time bringing her. She thinks everyone is her friend."

The dog just kept looking at me with moon eyes, wanting to be petted. I thought to myself, "if only everyone could be her friend" but I knew the world and I knew there were things in the world that would never be her or anyone else's friend. But even with the end of the world as we knew it on the horizon, this dog (and most dogs) help remind us of what's important, and that it's hopefully going to be okay.

"No, it's all right. I'll be her friend," I said as I knelt down and gave her a good scratching behind the ears before raising up. I wished I could have kept scratching her ears, but I had things to do. As I got up, the lady with Priscilla said, "Now she'll be your friend forever."

I couldn't help but think, "Lady, I need all the friends I can get."

Chapter Thirty-One

Back into the city I went. 20 minutes after leaving the pub, I arrived at the entrance to the Lumin family's known place of business. I would tell you where it is, but I don't want you to go traipsing where you don't belong. Suffice it to say, it's in one of the high rises near the French quarter. It struck me as odd that a group of vampires (who the sun would disintegrate if it weren't for the wonders of magic and modern medicine) chose to live in places as close to the sun as possible—penthouses, top floors, anything with a view of the place they wanted to rule. Self-proclaimed kings and queens on their terraces, overlooking the land they thought they could control. Maybe they did for some areas, and certainly for all things pertaining to vampires. But there were also tenuous situations with other vampire families in the area. The Lumins were the most sophisticated, with many of their members being old...and I mean really old, on the cusp of primordial. They're led by ancient vampires whose looks of immortality could be compared to a wizened, old raisin. And when a vampire looks old...well, they really have to be old, as in a "land before time" type of old. The other families in the area included a family named Caldra, street vampires that hung out in the French Quarter. To the Lumins, this branch of little more than juveniles were nothing but opportunists that survived on quick wit and tourists. Then you had the Orleya family, who were in some ways just as powerful as the Lumins. They were "old money" vampires who lived in extravagant homes. They weren't as ancient as the Lumins, but much older than the Caldras. They could be described as middle-aged as far as vampires go. The families operated, much like normal society, in a class system—with high, low, and middle classes. However, they all had ample amounts of money and resources to survive, and they each had their own goals and way of doing things. Thankfully, they weren't much for turf wars and the lines between them stayed distinct. Perhaps there was some signed contract or unspoken agreement that kept them from going after each other. I don't know, but whatever the case was, I've always been glad they don't really cause problems.

These weren't the only vampire families in southern Louisiana. You had offshoots and small congregations elsewhere, to include the lone vampires who didn't associate with anyone, either because of class or personal preference. But the three I mentioned were the top three in the area and ones that you don't want to run afoul of.

Hence my reason for not telling you where to go look for them.

Anyway, I ended up at the front door, and rode the elevator inside to the top floor. The doors opened to a small hallway. At the other end of the hallway was a massive wooden door with intricate wood carvings. It made me wonder how they even got it up there to install it. It would have taken all my strength, supernatural or otherwise, to lift it if I had to. When the door opened, there was no hint of its weight as it moved effortlessly and without sound. The young lady—or rather, young vampire...she would be an old young lady to you...I mean...oh heck, you know what I mean. The vampire lady from the bar stood before me.

The look on her face made me wonder if I had wings and six legs because she looked at me as if I were a bug that was annoying her. She almost seemed surprised to see me.

"Uh...you told me I should come. I didn't have time to ask any question because you left in a hurr..."

"So, I did," she interrupted.

She turned and walked back into the penthouse, where she stopped midway down the hall, realizing that I hadn't followed. "Come in and follow me," she said, then turned around and continued. It wasn't quite a command, but it sure felt like one. At least she invited me in. Vampires and certain creatures of the lore were really big on decorum, and being invited into one's space is a huge deal. For vampires, they couldn't use their full powers in a protected living space unless invited in across the threshold. I'm not sure why—just one of those things as everything has a balance. If they weren't invited, they could still be a terror but not to their full extent. Now, if they tore down an exterior wall to your home to the point that it wasn't livable, whatever force was inhibiting their full power would disappear. Normally, it wouldn't come to that, though, unless whoever they were after was really worth it. Most of the time, they would just break down the door, come in, and drag you outside so they didn't have anything to hold them back if need be. All that to say this: they invited me in. And that was kind of a big deal.

I followed her in. The hall was vast, with what appeared to be golden teakwood walls and gold-flecked, white marble floors. The colors complimented each other, and I could just feel the wealth assaulting me from all angles. It wasn't gaudy by any stretch, but it was a show of money, and that couldn't be mistaken. The penthouse took up the entire floor and probably the top two floors of the building. It wasn't really used for a living area; it was dedicated to the inner workings of the Lumin family. And although the penthouse took up the top two massive floors, everything below it consisted of an office building. I'm not sure how many of the other offices were dedicated to the Lumin family or to other businesses.

The hallway opened into a large living area, which was very modern, yet there were artifacts and art pieces that likely cost more than my annual salary with the police department...which wasn't saying much. Each piece I saw appeared to be authentic. As I glanced around, I imagined that some countries' antiquities departments would have salivated at the chance to view them. There were other vampires in the room. There was no sense of chaos there. Every figure had a role and a reason for being in the room, as each moved with fluidity and purpose.

I had never been there before, though I knew of it and I had a strange sensation that it was very peculiar that I was even there. I got the impression that I was probably the first non-family member to be entertained there in a long time. The voice in my head warned me that I should have told someone where I was going to be, as I suddenly wondered if I would be accosted from behind, blindfolded, and taken to a back alley to have unspeakable things done to me. But they could have done that anywhere. There was no need to invite me there if that was the case. So, for a moment, the anxiety subsided, but I still needed to stay on my toes.

Past the living area, a door opened into a conference room complete with a probably 30-foot-long, ornate wooden table and chairs, which I assumed were worth more than the rental I lived in. At one end of the table sat a man who looked ancient—deep crevices marked his pale skin that looked to be the shade and thickness of old parchment. Vampires could indeed look young forever, but it took effort to maintain. At a certain point, it didn't matter, such as with the patriarch of an ancient family. I found myself looking into the wickedly intelligent eyes of the Lumin family patriarch. Don't let looks fool you, though...the monster that this being could become...well, this big bad wolf didn't want any part of it. I imagined that he was many centuries old, perhaps having been born before such empires as the Scythians or the Cimmerians were just a whisper on the wind.

As far as experience, I may have lived a long time, but while in the presence of the being before me, I felt like a newborn wiener dog that had barely learned how to walk. One thing I can assure you, I wasn't about to start yapping. I knew enough to keep my mouth shut. On that front, I was definitely house trained and could read the room.

The lady that led me there stopped and gestured me to an open chair. Once I sat, she left the room and closed the double door behind her, leaving me alone with the leader of the family. The silence loomed over me to the point that it felt as if another, invisible person was silently watching me. I felt the eyes of the ancient individual at the end of the table weigh me on some invisible scale. I had not seen him at the altercation at the high council meeting, but that said little. Most patriarchs/matriarchs of families didn't go to those types of meetings, as it was "beneath" them.

When the weighing was complete...well...I could only assume that was what he was doing. Perhaps he grew tired of waiting for me to speak, so he broke the silence. "Lou Giroux," he said simply. Though the sound of his voice was weak, the power behind it was not and I could hear the words very distinctly.

"Yes," I replied, then remained silent, waiting for him to speak.

"You know who I am, but since this is the first time we have met face to face, I will introduce myself. I am Hedrick Lumin, the head of the Lumin household."

Of course I knew who he was, and he was right—I had never met him in person. A fact that I was acutely aware of as soon as I came into the room. I felt compelled to return the introduction. "I'm Lou Giroux, NOPD detective," though thinking to myself, "I'm not sure for how much longer." With being on admin leave and something devastating on the horizon, who knew how long I'd keep that title.

"Pleased to meet you," he said with formality...and I can assure you that it was all a formality. With entities that old, that's all they had left. "Likewise," I replied. "What can I help you with?"

"I want to know who is behind the nightclub shootout," he replied softly.

"Don't we all," I absentmindedly said, but quickly realizing where I was and who I was speaking to. I had to rethink my response very quickly, so as not to seem rude. "I mean, if I knew, I'd be close to finding who's behind all of this. The attack on the high council, the summoning, the death of a Jefferson Parish Detective. I have roughly two days to figure it all out, but if I don't, then it won't matter."

"I don't care about all that," he said. "I care about those of my family that died in that club."

"So, your family was involved?" I asked.

"Not like you think. My family was involved, certainly, but not willingly. I don't know how they got them, but they picked the wrong family to kidnap and involve them in that chaos," he replied. "I know they were held captive and that medicine and magic were withheld from them, forcing them to comply. When things didn't turn out as planned, they were exposed to UV light and unfortunately, disintegrated."

"How did you know all that?" I asked.

He waited a few moments before replying. My question must have set him on edge because he leaned forward and through a voice that was tinged with frustration, replied, "Do you think I'm a fool?"

"No, I'm just trying to get the lay of the land here," I replied coolly, though my blood pressure picked up a bit. I had to will myself to stay calm. This was an unusual situation, but I didn't want to give myself and how I felt away to a creature that can hear and smell blood.

If he knew how I felt, he didn't show it. He leaned back in his chair to give it some thought, then looked at me and replied, "I have contacts everywhere. I know what happened there."

"When did you first notice they were missing?" I asked.

"It's a large family, as you know, but we believe we noticed them missing about four days ago."

"I don't mean to pry, but it's something I have never had to ask before. How long does the medicine that keeps you safe from UV light last?" I asked.

He cocked his head and looked at me. I felt like he was weighing me up again, but I must have passed because he answered, "Normally, it would take a few days to dissipate but there are antagonist medicines that have an almost immediate effect, meaning they will immediately counteract the effects of the drug that keeps us safe from UV rays."

Four days, I thought to myself. Enough time to be administered the antagonist to make those that were kidnapped vulnerable and put into play where I became involved.

"The next logical question I would normally ask in cases like this would be, do you have any enemies? But I know you do. However, are there any you can think of that are at the top of your list?" I asked.

"If I knew or had an idea of who was behind it, then I would have solved this situation myself."

He didn't say that with any bravado. It was a fact. And I knew that this family was perfectly capable of it. I was sure that I had even investigated some cases I couldn't close at the time in which the Lumin family was suspect number one.

"Do you have answers for me?" he asked.

"Not at the moment, but I am working on it. My partner Dick was supposed to come talk to you and ask some questions."

"He hasn't come here."

"Do you know where he is?" I asked, suddenly alarmed, but I kept my voice steady. Just because Lumin said that he hadn't come didn't mean that he wasn't stopped on the way and spirited elsewhere.

"No, Mr. Giroux, I do not. Why would I care where a wayward child went?"

I assumed Dick had gone there, but I began to kick myself mentally. If only I had been a little more thoughtful, precise, and avoided assumptions. I should have asked him exactly where he was going because if he wasn't going to see the Lumins, then where had he planned on going? There are the other families, of course, but it would have made sense to come to the Lumin family first.

"Is everything all right, Mr. Giroux?" Lumin asked.

"Ah yes, I was just thinking. If my partner hadn't come here, then I was wondering if I should be concerned."

"While he isn't a favorite of ours, I can assure you that my family has done nothing with him. Our concern is to identify who is behind what lead to the death of my associates. The means by which they were killed with those helmets and UV light…what a twisted sense of torture and manipulation. There will be consequences."

"Do you know anything about a Ms. Dufrene at the Mayor's office?" I asked. She was still in the back of my mind and I still didn't have a clue who she was.

"Who?"

"She's a blonde that works…" I began but realized that he had no idea who I was talking about. "Um…never mind."

"Do I need to know about her? Is she behind this?" he asked, leaning forward, his voice stronger. His eyes lit up with focus, or excitement, or…I don't know, but he was definitely interested in what I had to say on the topic.

"Oh no, I don't think so. She's just a new player in New Orleans, and I don't know anything about her."

The excitement of his eyes faded away to deep thought as he leaned back. His voice returned to a near whisper. "Our time is done here, Mr. Giroux. Please leave."

I stood up, relieved to leave, but I had one question. "Do you know where I should look next?" I asked.

"This is the same question you asked before but just worded differently," he replied.

"I know, but anything helps," I said.

"Perhaps the other families in New Orleans, or maybe the wizards, or even the pack of werewolves. I don't know. That's your job to figure it out."

"Thanks, that really helps," I said sarcastically and should have kept that thought to myself, but the absurdity of his reply begged a response and sometimes, I just couldn't help myself. Like a dog that knows it shouldn't rummage in the trash can but can't help themselves.

He looked at me shrewdly, raised his hand dismissively and, at once, the young lady that led me to the room came to lead me out. I breathed a sigh of relief when I was on the elevator and heading to the first floor. As the chime for each floor rang in my ear, I was already thinking about my next task. Where was Dick?

Chapter Thirty-Two

On the street, I turned on my phone again. Still no messages or word from Dick. I was beginning to regret the decision to keep my phone off. I tried calling him, but it went to voicemail immediately, which meant it was either turned off or not functioning.

I decided I'd have to track him down the old-fashioned way...the way I did things long before the advent of the internet and the era of instant communication. That meant I was heading to St. Charles Avenue to the Orleya family to ask questions on the whereabouts of my partner. St. Charles Avenue had the kind of houses that made you question your choices in life. In other words, I've made pretty good choices, but apparently I haven't made choices as lucrative as those who lived in the monstrous, beautiful homes that lined the street. It was a very picturesque area, complete with a green trolley that rumbled down the neutral ground and giant, ancient oaks that overlooked the street, standing guard with their Spanish moss draping down like tapestries and framing the entire area. Some of those oaks did indeed stand guard and were known as earth elementals. They differ from the dryads I told you about earlier. They're more akin to to Smudge the golem, but made of earth and wood.

Where the Lumin family was sophisticated and businesslike, the Orleya family was decadent and snobbish; they acted as if everything and everyone was beneath them somehow. They rarely fought their own battles but they had no qualms about paying other people to fight for them or to sabotage their opponents. That was another thing about the Lumin family. Sure, they were a formidable house to deal with and yeah, they would no doubt make devious plans of attack, but they would always do it themselves, so you knew exactly who the attack was coming from.

It was getting on in the night so it was dark out, but all the houses on the street blazed in the glory of artificial light, including many with gas-burning lanterns to preserve the early N'awlins charm. The Orleya house was no different. Of course, not all the vampires of the house lived there, but it was their main base for operations. I've heard, but can't affirm, that they had quite a large basement under the house that was three or four levels. How they were able to create it, I haven't a clue. New Orleans is below sea level, so they had to have hit water when it was built. I assume they probably used magic or some other phenomenon to make it so. Or, it could all just be hearsay and not exist at all.

Anyway, when I left the Lumin house, I walked to the trolley station and rode it over, making a couple of exchanges along the way. The St. Charles line ran 24 hours, so I knew I wouldn't get stranded if I felt like riding back to the French Quarter.

When I arrived at the Orleya house...no matter how many times I've seen it throughout my time here, it's always given me pause. Almost a gobsmack that left me contemplative, but most houses on St. Charles Avenue had the same effect. It was a beautiful house and a disgusting display of wealth. The ample, beautifully landscaped yard and semi-spiral stairs with hand-carved railings led to a large landing and from there, to a wraparound front porch. A wrought-iron fence kept passersby at bay, and there was an intercom at the small gate where a cobblestone walk led to the steps.

I clicked the button to notify them they had a guest. I didn't have to wait as long as I thought I would. Almost immediately, a clipped accent spoke through the intercom. "Yes? How may I help you?"

"Yes, I am Dete...ahem, I'm Lou Giroux. I'm here to see if Dick Dubois is here," I said.

Whenever I was "investigating," it was like clockwork for me to identify myself as a detective. Since I was suspended with pay while LSP investigated the shootout, I wasn't there on official city business, not that it mattered with those kinds of people. I mean, I was still sort of an enforcer for the local council.

After introducing myself, I felt kind of dumb. I had asked that question in a sort of "Can Dick come out and play?" manner. At least that's how I felt in the silence immediately following my question.

The silence lingered, and I thought maybe that the intercom was broken, and they hadn't heard me, then the voice crackled over the speaker, "One moment."

"Thanks," I muttered.

A moment came and went and again I was beginning to wonder if they were going to leave me out there until I caught the hint and went along my merry way. That wouldn't have worked, though. I had a feeling that Dick was here, and I would find out, one way or another.

When I thought I was going to have to force my way in, the very large, ornate front door opened and Dick was sort of pushed out of it. He didn't tumble to the ground or anything. But it seemed like, "Here's the door and out you go." I could tell, even from that distance, he wasn't happy about it. When he looked at me, I got the distinct feeling that it was my fault. He marched toward me, keeping his glare. Let me tell you something—if you've never been glared at by a vampire, I wouldn't recommend it. It has you questioning your life expectancy.

When he stepped up to the gate, he opened it, stepped through, then slammed it shut after him. He slowly turned toward to me and said, "What are you doing here, Lou?"

He didn't yell at me, but his voice had a force that I was not accustomed to. Before I could answer, he continued.

"Of all the times for you to show up somewhere, this wasn't the place," he said.

"What happened?" I asked.

"What do you think happened?" he replied. "I went in there and things were fine...even cordial. I was about to get answers but then there was a buzz at the gate your arrival set them off. Something to the effect of they didn't want a mongrel dog on the premises...their words...and it reminded them I kept with such company, so they told me to leave. Appearances you know. And it wasn't a suggestion; they about threw me out. So, I learned nothing and we are no closer. So, tell me, what was so damn important for you to show up?"

"You were," I said.

"What?" he said.

"I said you were," I replied.

"Did something happen?" he asked.

"No, I went to visit the Lumin family upon their request. I assumed that's where you were going. I got worried about you because you weren't there and I didn't have a voicemail or text from you. Since things seem to be pretty serious and your phone kept going to voicemail, I wanted to make sure you were okay," I spit out.

There was still heat in those cold eyes, but the temperature seemed to cool slightly.

I shrugged and continued, "I got worried."

Dick sighed and looked back in disgust at the house. "Well, we're done here. Didn't get much info, but I don't think they're involved."

"Why do you say that?" I asked.

"Because...well...I don't have anything other than gut feeling, but they aren't it," Dick replied.

"Let's get with Captain Benoit. We gotta figure this all out," I said.

"That's as good a place as any," he replied.

We walked toward the trolley stop, but I couldn't help myself and turned back toward the Orleya house. Since I knew they were watching and probably even listening, I held up one of my fingers in a crude gesture just for them and said, "I'm not a mongrel!"

Then turned around and mumbled under my breath, "Well...maybe I am."

Dick spoke up beside me, "No, you aren't."

We continued to walk in silence for a while until I finally broke it. "I feel like we're going in circles here and going nowhere," I said. "We haven't narrowed the list of potential suspects. In fact, it just keeps growing. I'm still at a loss."

"Pretty soon, it won't matter," Dick replied briskly. "It's Friday early morning now. We probably have around 24 to 48 hours left before whatever comes, comes."

The time clock in my head was deafening, and I knew it would only get louder as the day progressed and the time shortened.

"Unfortunately, we need to wait until the precinct is open for business before we can meet with Captain Benoit," he said. I made the mental calculation of 6 or 7 hours from that time...and we didn't have the luxury of just waiting.

"Or we could just go to his house," I said.

"We could do that," he replied.

And that's how we found ourselves in a pretty prestigious, gated neighborhood not terribly far from City Park about an hour later. We didn't bother going through the front gate and having to deal with a guard that was just doing their job. No need to bother them. When you have extra powers like ours, it's kind of easy to slip past the eyes and awareness of a human who's more than likely barely staying awake, anyway.

"Do you know if he's married or has a family?" Dick asked.

"I don't know. I never bothered to ask, but living in a place like this, more than likely. I mean, why spend so much to live here unless you have to? Makes me wonder what his significant other does. I'm sure he doesn't make enough to live in this neighborhood on a captain's salary," I said.

"True, but if he (like us) works for a bit more than just regular NOPD pay, I expect he's doing all right," Dick replied.

"Well, yeah, but still, it raises questions," I replied.

Dick shrugged his shoulders because he had nothing else to say on the subject. He was right, of course...working for NOPD and handling concerns of the regional council from time to time, along with our long life span, we weren't hurting financially. However, I didn't think Captain Benoit shared our long life span. It wasn't a smoking gun, but it did make you think since it was right in front of you.

The large, brick, two-story home did not disappoint the neighborhood in the least. With the extensive exterior lights on, I wondered if my own salary could afford the light bill that the display warranted. It shone on the house and, quite frankly, it was beautiful with the maroon brick and white shutters that flanked each window. It was the kind of massive home that would look classic in any Christmas movie.

"You know, this is the first time I've ever been to his home," I said.

"Mine too," Dick replied, then added, "It's 2 AM. Are you sure we should just wake him up?"

"No, we shouldn't, but we have to. We're already here and what's he going to do? Suspend us from the police department? Been there, done that, pal," I said, then shrugged, "If this isn't important enough to wake him up, then nothing is."

Waiting no longer, I stepped forward and rapped my knuckles on the door. I waited politely—well, as politely as anyone who wakes someone up at 2 AM can—a few seconds before I knocked again. We didn't wait long as the door opened and Captain Benoit stood there, looking at us. If our presence surprised or perturbed him, I couldn't tell. If fact, it didn't look like he had been asleep at all; he was still fully dressed in slacks and a button-up shirt. He moved as if he expected us. Who knows...maybe he did. He welcomed us inside as he stepped to the side to let us in.

While standing at the front door, I could see that interior of the home reflected the exterior's appearance—neat, clean, classic.

"We're sorry to disturb you sir, but..." I began.

"Don't worry about it. I don't sleep," he replied before I could finish. "What do you have?"

"Not much. We were kind of hoping you would have more," I said.

The look on his face told me that he didn't have anything to help, but his words confirmed it. "No, I don't. I can start some coffee for you both...well, at least for Lou and me. Sorry Dick, I don't have anything for you."

Dick shrugged, palms up in a "no worries" gesture and we both walked in through the front door. At the entrance, there was a foyer of sorts, with stairs on the right leading to the second floor. Two doors flanked the foyer, going off into other rooms, and a hallway that went straight back to the kitchen, which is where we ended. Since I was looking forward to coffee, I could smell it sitting in the canister in the sizeable pantry. I could also smell cookies, and with that, my stomach rumbled.

"Uh, Captain?" I asked.

"Yes?" he replied.

"May I?" as I indicated toward the source of the sugary aroma.

"Sure."

I wish my stomach wouldn't rumble so loudly and I didn't constantly feel hungry, but I can't deny my love for food. In the end, it's a win for me, especially when people are accommodating. I grabbed a handful and made sure not to grab the whole box. Although I knew I could have, I didn't want to eat all of them. I still have manners, you know...at least sometimes.

Captain Benoit put on a pot of coffee and we took our seats around the kitchen table.

"The word on the street is that energy is collecting and when it consolidates...well...the explosion and aftermath from it will be nothing short of disastrous," the captain said. "That's what I was briefed on from the high council this afternoon. They still don't know who's behind the plan, but they have everyone looking at it—not just you two. So far, unfortunately, they're no further than we are."

When Captain Benoit mentioned energy collecting, I couldn't help but feel the hair on the back of my neck stiffen. I'm not sure if it was because I could actually feel the energy in the air or whether it was just a sympathetic response to thinking I should feel it. Either way, I had a shiver, but luckily, it wasn't quite as intense as a wet dog shaking after a bath.

We told him of our adventures, but it provided nothing that would actually help except for possibly marking the two vampire families out of the equation...so maybe it was helpful, after all. We talked over coffee for about an hour before I looked at the clock. The sun would be up in a couple hours and I try to be a polite guest. Whether Captain Benoit could or couldn't sleep, I didn't want to be around when his wife woke up to unexpected guests. And with that in mind, I stood up and stretched.

"Well, Captain, I appreciate the hospitality, but I need to get some rest. If today is going to be the last day of our lives, I want to be well-rested for it." I said this without thought, but immediately knew it was the wrong thing to say the moment it left my mouth. I saw the captain's gaze focus on a photo of his family that hung on the wall.

"Dammit, Lou," I thought to myself, "Some people have higher stakes involved than you."

"Sorry Captain, I didn't mean that."

"I know."

"We'll figure it out, sir," I replied and headed toward the front door. Dick stood up and followed.

At the door, the captain said one more thing before shutting the door, "Good luck and whatever gods that are out there, may they have mercy on us."

His words made me regret my quip even more, but I couldn't take it back. And that little bit about figuring it all out—I was bald-faced lying there, but sometimes, a little bravado was needed, if only to give false confidence to see you through something tough.

"Good job, Lou," Dick said.

"Come on, you know me. I always say the wrong things at the wrong time, and we're still here."

"Yeah, let's hope we're still here in 24 hours," he replied.

"Yeah, I hope so too," I thought, but I kept that to myself.

Chapter Thirty-Three

I went home and slept for a couple of hours. It was a fitful sleep, and I was grateful when I saw daylight brighten the blinds in my room. I was still tired, but we had little time and with that weighing on my mind, I knew I would not get quality sleep. I moved into the kitchen, hoping to find Morgane, but she was nowhere to be seen. If life ceased as I knew it, which was quite possible within the next day, I hoped I would see her beforehand. She was the only close friend I had, even if she was just a bird. I know, I know...she was definitely not just a bird, but that's all I've ever known her as.

I felt like I was missing something...and it nagged at me. Well, I knew I was missing something, but this was more specific, like I had overlooked something and it gnawed at me. Like having a word on the tip of your tongue, but being unable to identify it.

I was restless, so I turned on my phone to check my messages and found one text waiting for me. It was Lieutenant Martine, asking me to meet her at 0630 at LaBorde Mountain in City Park, the same place where all the murders had begun. Good thing I checked my phone, or I would have missed her message. Weird, I thought. She was usually one for the rules and contacting me while I was on administrative leave wasn't something she would normally do, and it was earlier than she would normally do so while I was on duty. It must have been something very important. I tried calling her back, but it went straight to voicemail. Since I had so little else to go on to solve the case, I figured it couldn't hurt to meet her at the scene of the initial crime. I texted her to let her know I was on my way. Who knew? Maybe it would jog something loose in my thoughts to help figure out who was behind everything. That's how I ended up back at City Park about 30 minutes later. Thankfully, there isn't that much traffic to deal with at that time of the morning. If people had only known what was coming, they would have been leaving in a heartbeat...like it was a category five hurricane on the horizon.

No one was in the parking area. I thought Lieutenant Martine would have beaten me there, but I didn't see her car. If fact, no one besides me, nor any vehicles, were in sight. "Good," I thought to myself. It would give me a chance to walk along and retrace my steps from a week prior. Geeze, it felt like it had been a year. I got out and checked that my pistol was in place. Even though I had turned in my duty weapon, I still had that revolver, and

I've been alive too long to realize that I shouldn't go out in public without the ability to protect myself. I mean, sure, I could literally rip someone's head off but there are still rules to follow. Dealing with a normie requires dealing with them in normie ways. With the advent of cell phone and security cameras darn near everywhere...well, it's just gotten harder, so it's best to just pretend to be a normie as often as possible, except in extreme cases.

I walked down the path and over the bridge, heading toward the mountain. I wondered if I would see the wood folks today. They surprised me last time, but I was preoccupied. I wouldn't let that happen again and I shouldn't have let them surprise me last time. I didn't really have anything to worry about but it still perturbed me that they got the "drop" on me, so to speak. So far, though, I had noticed nothing out of the ordinary. At least not until I got to the bottom of the hill. From there, I heard voices but couldn't quite make out the words that were spoken. I treaded lightly because this new development was unexpected. I wouldn't have thought there would be anyone out there, so I remained quiet. I didn't want to give myself away and I certainly didn't want to scare someone. I then caught the scent of some-one I knew very well...but she couldn't have already been there, could she? Her car wasn't in the parking area and there was nowhere else for her to park. I hadn't heard her voice yet, either.

"There's no way it could be her," I thought to myself, but it sure smelled like her. The primary voice I could hear was that of a male. As I sniffed the air to hone in on the other's scent, the wind suddenly shifted and started blowing in the opposite direction, preventing me from identifying him by smell. I crept up and I could feel my skin crawl for no apparent reason, which only worsened my feeling of unease. Had my subconscious picked up on something that I consciously couldn't? I wasn't sure, but that had happened to me before, so I was on red alert.

"Yes, we must finish the ritual," I heard the other voice say, then an overpowering aroma of cinnamon filled my nostrils and that's when I knew. Whatever was going on, I needed to stop it. I hurried forward with my feet eating the ground between where I had been and where I needed to be at the top of the hill. The path curved upward around the hill and I only had a short way to go. As I went around and the top of the hill came into view, I saw four people. Three of them I couldn't identify, as they were in long, dark cloaks. The fourth I recognized at once, and my heart immediately jumped up to my throat in fear. I could feel my pulse pounding throughout my entire body. It was Lieutenant Martine, and she was lying in the middle of the map. She wasn't moving.

One figure, the one who looked to be in charge, had a knife in hand. Upon seeing me, the figure yelled to the other two, "He arrived too soon! Delay him. We must finish the ritual to complete the circle and bring change!"

The voice sounded familiar, but it was somehow off, and I couldn't quite place it. Immediately, the other two rushed me with a speed that spoke of supernatural assistance. I had adrenaline rushing through me, but the pace of their advance caught me off guard. They say that action is faster than reaction and whoever "they" are, they're not wrong. In the few moments it took for the imminent onslaught to register, they were on me and grabbing at my arms. I was behind the power curve, but since I can be pretty quick myself, I quickly closed the reaction gap. I grabbed one and threw them to the side, but as they flew, they slowed down and stopped completely in midair to readjust their position before barreling back. "Oh great," I thought to myself, "these things can fly." The other had successfully grabbed onto my left arm and the one in the air crashed into me, knocking us all to go to the ground, tumbling. At that time, I caught a whiff of what I was fighting and it nearly caused me to gag. I came to the realization of who these attackers were, as it tickled my brain while rolling with them. They were the undead, decaying vampires I had gotten into a brawl with near the Crown and Anchor just days before...the exact same ones.

My mind reeled, trying to make connections and how they were involved in this, but I didn't have time because I was fighting for my life. One took a swipe at me and I felt my shirt, as well as my skin, rip. Funny...I know how to play that game too, but before I could concentrate on turning into the big bad wolf, I felt myself flying through the air. Man, this fight sucked already, and I could only concentrate on not hurting myself in the landing. Thankfully, I reoriented myself and landed in a crouch. Breathing heavily, I dug my feet into the ground to launch myself back at them, but then shook my head to get out of the tunnel vision that was coming on. Lieutenant Martine was there, and she was vulnerable. I needed to grab her and get her out of there. "Screw this fight," I thought to myself. I had nothing to prove. I just needed to help Martine.

I shifted my stance to pounce in that direction. The figure in black stood directly over Martine. The figure was busy chanting words and to this day, I regret what happened next.

I reversed my momentum to move toward the cloaked figure and leapt. Whatever they were doing, I sensed they were almost done. I could only speculate about what they would do with the knife once the chanting was over, especially given the line of bodies we had followed over the week to get to this moment. Despite my quick attempt to close the distance, I failed to consider the vampires' swiftness, and damn it, I should have known better. However, I was abruptly reminded of that fact as it felt like a Mack truck crashed into me from behind, causing us to fall to the ground once again. I could feel violent slashing across my back as nails as sharp as knives raked repeatedly. I could feel the blood flowing from my wounds.

My vision had tunneled and only focused on the figure. I had to stop them. I stood up, which took considerable strength, as I was still in human form and had two vampires over me, trying to hold me down.

The chanting ceased. Whatever they had cast, the spell was complete, except for one thing...and that quickly followed. There was nothing I could do as I saw the knife descend into the chest of Lieutenant Martine, who lay peacefully before the figure. She could have been sleeping, but once the blade sank to the hilt, she shot up to a sitting position and let out a blood-curdling scream. I will never forget the sound as it pierced through my ears. I felt myself lose control. Usually, I try to maintain control of the beast within because it if gets out of control, there's no telling how long it will run until I can tie it back down into my subconscious. But seeing the vicious murder of Lieutenant Martine...well...there was no cage that was going to hold the monster in, no matter how strong or how well-designed it was.

What happened next...I was not in total control and can only speak of things as if I were watching a movie. I was there, yet I wasn't, so to speak. The vampires felt it. They moved to secure me, but they didn't stand a chance. My goal was to kill the figure. I heard my throat open into an ear-shattering roar that ended in a howl. If any normies had been near, the inhuman sound would have sent them running.

I felt my teeth lengthen; the beast was arriving and would soon be fully present, but in my rage, I was already there. The nails on my fingertips grew and were as sharp as razors. Witnessing my seething fury, the vampires released me and attempted to stumble back, retreat, and flee. Oh no...that wouldn't do. I extended my arms and slashed into the nearest vampire. As my claw tore into the flesh of its back, my finger sunk in enough to grab muscle and rip into it. The other vampire was in front of the one I had just injured, but was swiftly moving away. I picked up the one and threw it into the retreating vampire, which caused them to tumble in a heap.

Somewhere in my clouded thoughts, I knew the vampires would have to be stopped before they flew out of my reach. My dark persona knew this as well, and I pounced. I hadn't fully turned, but by the time I landed on them, I was every bit the monster I had ever been...and then some. I was no longer in control and these "things" would be nothing but a memory in short order.

A werewolf is always a potentially dangerous thing, like a grenade or a bomb when in a controlled environment. Sure, the possibility of causing widespread damage is there, but if controlled...no harm, no foul. An unhinged werewolf is something different. It's like a nuke and there's no hiding from it, and the collateral damage from such a thing is like a rabid dog in close quarters. There's no telling how much damage could take place.

The vampire closest to me was the one I landed on. I was vaguely aware of screams coming from the heap. It's my belief that they were screaming for help, but no one would come in time for these two...or three when I was finally able to reach the other black-cloaked figure. I bent down and grabbed the head of the vampire struggling to get up from the ground. It goes without saying that in full form, I'm inhumanly strong but geeked up on fury and anger? That's another level all together. As I latched onto its head, I felt all 10 of my fingers sink deeply into its neck.

I could feel my own elongated face quiver with rage as the excruciating pain from the change mixed with the fury. I twisted and wrenched the head and neck of the vampire I had within my hold. It didn't budge...at first. But I kept pulling and twisting with all my might. Panic was building in the creature below me. I could feel it. I had to work quickly or the other vampire would get to its feet, forcing me to divide my attention. My attention was still dimly aware of the cloaked figure, who had then turned their complete focus on me.

"Help me," the vampire in my hands croaked.

The black-clad figure pulled out a wand and moved it in a quick, swishing motion. I knew what would come next. I may have said before that werewolves are resistant to magic, but that's not completely true. We can still feel it and depending on how strong it is, it can kill us in some instances. I saw a bright light erupt from the end of the wand and blast my way, but once it reached me, it petered out into nothing. The only thing I felt was the talisman on my neck, the one that Hannah had given me, grow cold. I had heard of such trinkets, but the value of such was to be marveled. In my state, I was faintly aware of the great favor I owed that cat. Not only did it cloak me from magical prying eyes, but it was also a dampener that dissipated whatever magical energy was directed toward the wearer. The cloaked assailant's surprise was clear as they released two more bolts of energy, which had no effect other than cooling the item on my neck.

Of course, this all happened in the matter of a couple seconds. I was still in the midst of wrenching, twisting, and pulling. The screams from the vampire in my grip were piercing and suddenly, as loud as they had been, they ceased. I could feel the bones and muscles in the creature's neck snap and rip apart as I tore its head from its shoulders. I quickly used the momentum of the pull to hurl the head toward the cloaked figure who, by that time, was in the midst of casting another spell. The head sailed through the air but as it did, it disintegrated into a fine dust, as did the body it had been torn from. One vamp down, one more to go...then on to the black-cloaked wizard, witch, or whatever it was.

The last vampire, seeing the fate of its compadre, raised its hands in defense. "I will tell you everything!" it screamed in a plea for its life.

No matter how long an entity has lived—and although death isn't always final—almost every creature, no matter the type, has a strong sense of self-preservation, so the pleas came as no surprise. Since I was in my other form, the monster was mostly in control and I was merely along for the ride. No matter what that vampire had offered, it would have died a horrible death if I had had my way.

However, what happened next not only shocked the vamp into the next life but I have to say, it also stunned me. I heard a grunt of disgust from the black-cloaked figure. I glanced up and saw that it had opened a portal rimmed in light blue. What was beyond, I couldn't see from my vantage point, but before it stepped through and disappeared, it flicked the wand, causing an enormous fireball to erupt toward me. Well, at least I thought it was toward me. If I had realized who the intended target was, I might have stepped forward in hopes that it would dissolve into the magical amulet around my neck, so I would be able to interrogate the vampire. I'm sure you can figure out by now that I wasn't the target. The vampire watched in horror as the flaming ball of energy struck it square in the chest and engulfed it in flames. I quickly jumped back because, even though the fireball had been magic, the fire it had created was not, as I could feel it singe the fur on my arms. There was no longer the chance of eliciting any information from the moving bonfire.

With that source of information gone, I turned toward the figure and leapt. I could feel the power in my legs release as I sailed through the air like a coiled spring. The figure stepped through the closing portal but not before I managed to reach in and rake my claws across its back. My blow connected but there was no time for anything else because I had to withdraw quickly or risk losing my arm. As the portal shut, it was so close that it snipped some hair off the end of my paw. Dammit! I was so close, but had been too slow and they were gone. The entire encounter happened in less than a minute, and although it seemed like an eternity, my mind returned to Lieutenant Martine and I rushed toward her. At that point, my monster was sated and for whatever reason (and I'm certainly not looking a gift horse in the mouth...or in this case, a gift monster) it momentarily retreated, allowing me to take more control of my thoughts and actions. I dropped to my knees and applied pressure to Martine's wound. Her head was facing away from me and there was...blood...everywhere. In all my years, I've patched up many a person who were on the brink of death's door. Unfortunately, with all that experience, I've become relatively skilled in recognizing, at a glance, if a person would make it or not. I knew that Lieutenant Martine wasn't going to make it. I fought back tears. Her skin took on a greyish hue and she turned her head toward me. Her eyes danced in and out of focus in her attention to the point she had become blind to the world, which was a gift at that moment. I didn't want her last vision in this life to be that of a monster that she was unaware of and therefore, pass on in fear.

She struggled to speak. I picked her up and wrapped her into my arms, close to my chest and rocked.

"It's me, Lou. Shh...don't talk," I said. I wanted to say more, but just couldn't. In times like that, there's not really anything good to say, anyway.

Lieutenant Martine barely managed to gurgle out, "I didn't know," and I felt her soul leave as she passed away in my arms. I was covered in her blood, as was the map at the top of LaBorde Mountain.

Chapter Thirty-Four

I looked down at her face and thankfully, though the rage had been white hot a moment before, it burned itself out along with the monster within. My mind was numb and I couldn't quite think clearly, but a question that began stirring way down deep grew until I could no longer ignore it. "What the heck was going on out here?"

I felt a day late and a dollar short. My body was drained of its strength and my body had melted back to normal as I slowly laid her down. Blood was all over me. I gently reached up to her face and closed her eyes. Wherever her spirit was, I hoped she was experiencing something better than what this world had to offer. I don't know much about the afterlife, or what happens after we pass, but I hoped for her sake, she went to whatever afterlife she believed in.

My senses were starting to return, and my brain picked up on the situation. I didn't know what to do. I was shirtless, had a deceased police officer in front of me, and was covered in her blood. The same police officer that had put me on administration leave, no less. It most definitely didn't look good, however, I did have her text inviting me out there, so I figured that should shield me from suspicion. I looked over her body and she was armed. The pistol never left its holster, so she was caught by surprise. I noticed something in her pocket, and upon further inspection, saw that it was her phone. There was something nagging at me in the back of my mind, and I wanted to confirm something. Everything about the whole situation was very strange and murky to me. I retrieved her phone from her pocket and opened it. Thankfully, it was unlocked, and I quickly went to her texts to find what I sought to confirm. Once I found it, I rocked back and sat down hard on the ground, which happened to be the stone map of New Orleans. It made sense, in a sadistic and cold-blooded way. The text I found showed that it had come from my number and appeared to be me asking her to meet me at LaBorde Mountain. It was the exact text I had received from her, except it was from me to her. My world was rocked. They had warned me to stay away, but I just couldn't...or rather, I refused to...and now two of my friends were gone. I again looked at my phone and the message from Martine was still there but it would require an extensive explanation. With the world as we knew it coming to an end, there was no way I could spend all day down at the station while they figured it out. I knew that's what they would do, because that's what I would do. This must have all been an elaborate plan to keep me out of the way, I was sure of it. It only cost the life of my supervisor, Lieutenant Martine.

I made a call with her phone, and a moment later, a voice answered on the other end. "911, what's your emergency?"

"There's been a murder and we have an officer down at City Park."

"And who am I speaking with?"

I took the phone away from my ear, wiped my prints off of it with some of my remaining tattered clothing, and as I placed the phone on Lieutenant Martine's chest, I could hear the voice asking, "Sir? Sir? Are you still there?"

Upon standing up, I took one final look at her before resorting to the only course of action I could fathom—I ran.

I swiftly ran back toward my car. I had to leave that place, and I had to do it quickly. I knew it would only be a couple of minutes before they would arrive and once they did, they would triangulate the call to pinpoint the location. I already heard sirens in the distance. That was too fast of a response. That only reinforced my suspicion that I had been set up. I guessed they (whoever "they" were) would stop at nothing to keep me preoccupied. I ran even faster and at the rate my feet ate up the ground, I found myself in my vehicle a very short time later. The sirens were loud and with my hearing, I gauged they would arrive in less than a minute. They were coming from the west side of the park, which meant if I didn't want to get caught and bogged down in the mess, I had to leave going east…and quickly. I fired up the vehicle and tore out of the parking area, throwing up dirt and oyster shells in twin streams behind me as I catapulted forward and out onto the road. Once on the road, I stepped on the gas and ol' faithful responded, but after a few hundred feet, I slowed down. Heck, I wasn't guilty. So I didn't want to look like I was by hightailing it out of there. I just wanted to get far enough away initially so I wouldn't get caught in the cone of attention. On the other hand, if I had kept up the high rate of speed, I would have only drawn attention to myself, which would have piqued their interest.

The first responders were quite close and I wouldn't have been surprised if they had seen my taillights in the distance. After a moment, I gleaned I was safe because they didn't follow and instead, they turned into the parking area I had just left.

Everything that morning was incredibly bizarre and had happened so quickly. My body was numb, but my mind was blazing. First things first—I needed to call Captain Benoit and tell him what had happened to Martine. Since I usually have issues with clothes, I learned a long time ago to always keep spare clothes in the trunk of my car, so when I got far enough away from ground zero, I parked and quickly grabbed a shirt. I was still covered in Lieutenant Martine's blood. The smell was overpowering, so I wiped off what I could. I needed to make the call, but not with my cell phone. I didn't want to turn it on and leave a trail of evidence that I had called anyone. Although I was still carrying the magic trinket that would hide me, I couldn't have it on record that I called Captain Benoit. I would have to use another phone because once investigators found that message on Lieutenant Martine's phone, they would undoubtedly look at other activity associated with my phone. If Benoit's name popped up immediately after the time of death...well...that would just muddy the waters.

People don't realize it, but the stakes in life are real. We sort of get blinded by all the trivial and not-so-trivial tasks we need to, or are supposed to do for a job, family, or whatever, that we don't realize how quickly it can all end. I momentarily lamented about the loss of Lieutenant Martine. Everyone that worked with her liked her and had immense respect for her. She was a damn hard worker and was as competent as anyone I'd ever worked with. It was going to be a huge blow to the department. That fact, as well as the anger that her death was certain to cause, was going to be like kicking a hornet's nest. A hornet's nest full of pissed off police officers wanting revenge. And the fact that I'm a police officer wasn't going to save me if anyone suspected that I was responsible for it. My mind raced with all sorts of "what ifs" but I had to quench that down. I still had things I needed to do. What came next? I'd just have to deal with it as it came, the best I could.

Pay phones were becoming a rare thing in this town, but I knew of a couple of locations where they still stood. One wasn't very far from City Park, so I headed there. It was right outside a gas station on the side of the street, close to the corner. It's funny how society progresses...and I've seen it progress a very long time. Pay phones used to be everywhere and in more recent times, they'd become a cute antiquity of times past that have refused to die, but surely would in the next 10 or so years. Even now, it's surprising to see one, but people can't seem to break the old habit of checking the coin slots for loose change. The one I ended up at didn't have any forgotten change in the slot. Thankfully, though the booth was nasty and had plenty of names and other messages carved into the plastic, the phone had a dial tone and still worked. I dialed Captain Benoit's number. I still had a little black book of numbers that I kept near me. Another old habit of mine that hadn't died with the advent of mobile phones and their storage capability. I still liked using an analog address/phone number book. Usually, I kept it at home or in the car and I was thankful that it was in the car that day.

The phone rang, and Benoit's voice answered, "This is Benoit."

"Sir, this is Lou. Lieutenant Martine..." I about choked and had a to take a moment to collect myself. "Lieutenant Martine is dead."

"What?"

"She's dead," I repeated and then quickly, I followed up with what had happened. I explained about the weird texts, seeing Martine lying there motionless, the apparent ritual that was being performed, the fight that ensued, and the hooded figure that escaped. When I finished, the silence on the other end was deafening. I'm not sure how long it lasted, but it was long enough to cause me to wonder if the line had somehow been cut or disconnected. Eventually, Captain Benoit responded, "Lou, I can't help you right now with this. I mean, I'll pass on what you told me to those that be, but I don't think it will help now. Anything done now will raise so much suspicion that it will upset the balance."

"Who is that exactly?" I snapped. "I've worked with you for a number of years, and I never really cared about the chain of command beyond you. I was only interested in being left alone and doing my job. And now you're telling me I'm being hung out to dry? I want to know who's making these decisions," I yelled into the phone.

"You know I can't tell you that," he said. "It's done this way so things aren't corruptible. As you know...and really, all you need to know...is that we serve at the will of the regional council to uphold the peace and keep the balance between the normal world and our world. That's what you signed up for, remember? And now it's your duty to continue to maintain that balance. So, do your duty...and don't get caught."

I heard the audible click as the line went dead and I was left holding the phone and the proverbial bag that went with this whole situation. It was true that I signed up to do this job, which felt like more of a calling at the time, but at that moment, I was pretty sure I'd been set up and no one was going to go out of their way to help me. To be honest, it hurt. But that whole week, the hurts kept coming like a boxer on the receiving end of a flurry of strikes by their opponent. Losing one friend would have been bad enough but after losing two people I kind of cared about, having my home ransacked, being put on administrative leave...oh, and being on the brink of wide-spread disaster, along with possibly being framed for the murder of one of those people that I cared about, I felt used and abused. Well, after a while, it all gets jumbled together and in some ways, these traumatic events kind of cancel each other, meaning I couldn't dwell on the sadness of one too long before the next one came in to replace it. Kind of messed up, but it helped me to not get bogged down and waste time. It's kind of like hitting rock bottom. There was nowhere else to go but up and if something else bad came along...well, get in line. Not only did it hurt, but I was also angry...angry as Hell. I felt like the system had let me down, which again fell into the line of circulatory thought of losses and emotions.

At a certain point, though, a cold fury or whatever, kind of acts like cement in the process of curing...it brings everything together in a dull heaviness that weighs in the pit of your spirit. It does wonders for focus at times...and that was one of those times. I needed to focus on staying one paw ahead of my coworkers and still try to put a stop to whatever was coming in the following few hours. I had little time left. The exact time, I didn't know, but I knew it would be less than 24 hours for sure. I needed to gather what resources I could and (as much as I hate to be cliché about it) get to the bottom of it. I started walking back to my ride on the other side of the parking lot, but to get there, I had to pass some bushes and when I did, it momentarily obstructed my view of the station. As I passed the bushes, something started to tickle my brain about what Captain Benoit had said, but I had too many immediate tasks to tend to at that time to delve into it. You know how that goes, right? Those immediate tasks, you ask? Well, the most immediate one began when I saw a police cruiser, with lights flashing and siren wailing, pull into the gas station.

The day was not going well at all.

CHAPTER THIRTY-FIVE

The cruiser came barreling in, screeching to a halt as the brakes were slammed. Two officers hastily exited the vehicle, one from the driver's side and the other from the front passenger's side. They both ran toward the gas station and disappeared inside. It was pure luck, but they hadn't seen me because of the bushes that I had just passed. I jumped back. This was all wrong. I've been investigating murders and otherworldly things for a long time and the response time on this was the fastest I'd ever seen, unless there was a robbery taking place inside, but I didn't believe that for a second. I quickly retreated behind the dense bushes, blending in with the surrounding foliage to avoid standing out.

The two officers were not inside long before they rushed out. I was at a slight distance, but I could hear them speak as plain as day.

"He wasn't in there. Where do you think he is?" one of them said.

"I'm not sure. He isn't in his car either," the other replied.

"They said he had just used the pay phone, so he couldn't have gotten far," the first one said.

I felt a chill work through my body. They were after me and knew immediately where I was. First things first—before they became mobile again, I needed to skedaddle, so I used the bush to my advantage and backed away as the officers walked to their ride. I took that moment of their distraction to run down the street and away from the gas station, all the while angling myself in such a way that I knew they wouldn't be able to see me. It wouldn't be long before they would pull out from the gas station and start looking down the side streets, so I quickly turned south and hopped a small fence between two houses to get out of sight. I didn't want to leave my ride behind, but it looked like I didn't have a choice. Out of options, I was then on foot. I could have used my cell phone to call someone but I was afraid more than ever that, even though I still carried the trinket that Hannah had given me, a workaround was being used to track me. If so, they would target people I would obviously call like Dick or....well...like Dick. The list of people I would have called had gotten exponentially shorter that week.

There were more sirens coming my way. They were closing in and I needed to make distance before they surrounded the area. Where I was located, I had two choices, the first being to head north into the cemetery and hide out amongst the above-ground tombs. It would have worked if I hadn't been on a time crunch. With the impending disaster bearing down, I didn't have time to sit and wait. So, I decided I had to move south and cross Bayou St. John and get to the trolley line to take me back downtown. But first things first—I needed to get further down the block before I turned south. I allowed myself to use my current state of mind and near panic to shift slightly to my other self, then took off. It was still morning, so there wasn't much movement in the homes and the back yards I ran through, hopping over the fences between them to keep me off the street. Before long, I made it to the schoolyard of Cabrini High school, a Catholic school for girls. Thankfully, again, no one was out and after passing through there, I eventually ended up on the church grounds. From there, I turned toward Bayou St. John. There was a quaint footbridge that crossed the water nearby, and when I got to the road in front of the church, I realized I had gone too far. With those sirens blaring, getting closer and closer, I decided to just go for it and instead of taking the bridge, I dove into the water to cross the bayou in hopes of disappearing into the neighborhood on the other side once I made it. Was it ideal? Heck no. But at least it would wash the rest of the blood off my hands and arms. When that crossed my mind, it made me think of Lieutenant Martine, but I had to stow it away for now. I would mourn later when I had more time.

When I jumped into the water, the cold took my breath away. It wasn't the coldest time of the year but it certainly wasn't the warmest, so the water was cooler than normal at that time of morning. I was on a mission and kept going. I can actually swim pretty well and with the extra help my strength provided, I made it across in no time. Once out of the water, I didn't even take time to shake off. Trust me, you don't know how much I wanted to but...more important things, like I said. I quickly crossed the road and made it into the sprawl of housing about the time the rest of the police showed up across the waterway. Thankfully, I didn't think they saw me. They were driving slowly, peering around in search of me, though.

One thing about New Orleans: the houses are packed tight like sardines. Most cities grow out, but New Orleans can't really do that, since it's surrounded by water of some type on all sides. So, the houses are damn near on top of one another and have small yards, but it has its charm. I quickly moved from one yard to the next, making my way toward the trolley line.

10 minutes later found me in my normal state on North Carrollton Avenue, where I caught the first trolley I found going southwest. The green line, otherwise known as the 48 Canal Streetcar-City Park/Museum (there is another green line, but it's darker and runs down St. Charles Av-

enue) would take me from where I was all the way down to the French Quarter, which is where I wanted to be. From there, I would take the ferry back to the west bank and, though I was sure my home would be watched, I had to see Morgane. The trolley operator didn't even bat an eye. Sure, I had wet clothes but at least they weren't sopping...and I'm pretty sure it wasn't anywhere close to what one would consider strange working that job. Not many on the trolley that morning except for just a few people, but everyone minded their own business.

I would have stopped to say "hello" to Hannah, but I just couldn't bear the wet dog jokes that I was sure to follow. I was in no mood for jokes. Though, I knew she would have immediately felt bad after hearing why I was in the condition I was in. It would have been too late, though, and I just didn't have the extra energy to deal with it. So, I settled down for the ride. It wasn't bad. There was a reminiscence of a simpler time as the car jostled down the tracks, making stops intermittently.

People got on and people got off, but it never seemed to have more than two or three other riders. At one of the stops, a day-walking vampire stepped on. No normie would have spotted them, but I'm no normie and after a while, you just kind of knew who was and who wasn't a normie at a glance. I'm sure they knew I was a werewolf but in a town with this many inhabitants and so compact, you're bound to run into something when you least expect it. For the most part, though (just like normies), you just nodded, said "hello" or didn't, and went about your way. However, with everything that was going on, I still couldn't help but feel the proverbial hackles go up, which I made all the efforts I could to try and hide. Apparently, it hadn't worked, because at the next stop, I noticed the vampire kind of side-eyed me and got off. As the car pulled away, I saw that he hadn't left the stop; he stayed, apparently waiting for the next trolley.

"Oh well," I thought to myself. So much for me maintaining a low profile. Hopefully, they wouldn't think anything of it and talk about it to anyone soon. But I wasn't so sure. Vampires were smart, and they didn't stay alive for the amount of time that they did by being dumb...well, some not-so-smart vampires did but they were definitely the exception and not the norm. Actually, the more I thought about it, whether or not that particular vampire did run and tell someone, I figured I should probably get off at the next stop although I hadn't arrived at my final destination. I was still a lot closer to it than City Park was.

The next stop was just northwest of Interstate 10, on the corner of S. Claiborne Avenue and Canal Street. It was near a couple of large hospitals, one of which contained the only level I trauma center in southern Louisiana. I wished that what had happened to Lieutenant Martine could have happened at that location instead of City Park...she might have had a fighting chance. Seconds matter in some situations and unfortunately, being at City Park...well...there were just no feasible options for immediate life-saving treatment.

I quickly crossed Claiborne and went under I-10. There was ample shade, and the temperature dropped noticeably. Sometimes there are homeless camps in the area, but this morning, I didn't see too much movement. It was close to mid-morning and I could hear the traffic on the I-10 overpass speed by. I kept going and took a right to get off Canal Street. Though that street would take me where I wanted to go, it was also where the trolley ran. If that vampire had notified anyone, well, it would have been pretty stupid to stay on the same street, so I decided to go two blocks over and parallel it, which brought me to Tulane Avenue, right in front of the old Charity Hospital. The hospital had a commanding presence and even though it was shut down in 2005 because of the extensive damage it sustained during Hurricane Katrina and sat abandoned and in disrepair, there was just something about the place. The building had been constructed in 1939 and it was once one of the largest hospitals in the United States. Before its closure, there had been times I would drop people off there. It was nice, though dated as far as layout, but still...a lot of living and dying went on there and that kind of thing leaves energy, the kind that Charity Hospital certainly had. In my line of work, or rather, in my world, it had a lot of ghosts and by ghosts, I mean the kind I don't want to mess with unless I absolutely had to and was well-prepared for.

I resumed my southeasterly direction and thankfully, by that time, my clothes were semi-dry. Or at least, they didn't give the impression that I had jumped into the drink fully clothed. I patted myself to be sure, and that's when I felt my cell phone in my pocket. You have to understand, even though cell phones are pretty normal to have nowadays, they are still relatively new in the grand scheme of things. For someone that's lived as long as I have, even after a few years of use, it's not something that I always think about, which is why I then found myself without a functioning cell phone. I didn't even think of it when I jumped into Bayou St. John and obviously it wasn't waterproof. Of course, I had other, more pressing concerns at the time. "Oh well," I thought to myself. I guessed I no longer had a way to contact anyone in the event of an emergency unless I could find another pay phone, which I wasn't so sure about. I only knew of the pay phone by City Park because I had used it before.

I had walked a couple of blocks when I felt a raindrop. It hit lightly, then a couple seconds later, I felt another and then came a downpour out of nowhere. I looked up to see dark clouds swirling overhead. That surprised me as it had been blue skies that morning and the radio weatherman had reported a clear forecast all day (which, in and of itself is kind of a rarity in New Orleans). Apparently, the weather wasn't cooperating with the forecast because the wind picked up. When storms arrive, especially heavy thunderstorms, there is usually a palpable energy in the air. I'm sure there's some scientific reasoning for it, with the positive and negative ions moving violently, but this had a much different feeling. There was energy all right, but it was so strong that I could have probably counted on one hand the number of times I had felt something similar in the past...one being when Hurricane Katrina approached.

Well, I no longer had to worry about my wet clothes giving it away that I had taken a swim because I was drenched again. I picked up the pace and kept going at a hustle speed. At first, I tried to dodge the rain by using building overhangs, but with the intensity of the wind and falling drops, it didn't really work. The storm intensified, and I needed to get off the street, I thought to myself. My stomach started growling with hunger, and that's when I realized I had eaten nothing since I had returned home the night before. Again, I'd had a lot going on. I decided to stop at a café a few blocks away. I needed the warmth of a cup of coffee and some food. I also needed time to process everything with the threat of being chased. The place I had in mind had good food and was a regional chain. It had a bar in the center of the room that would put most nightclubs to shame. The location was close to the touristy part of town and most of the time, it had a wait list. When I arrived, since the weather had turned nasty, it was surprising there weren't more people who had taken shelter inside. It had an inviting feel, and I took advantage of it. I took a seat at the back, ensuring I stayed away from the windows. I settled down to think about things, which was harder than it sounds. It felt like the entire world, or at least my entire world, was against me. I was utterly exhausted. The week seemed to have lasted a year, coupled with a level of extremes that I wasn't used to. I ordered a hot coffee and a three-egg ham and cheese omelet, then waited. My hunger had grown exponentially and I couldn't think straight. When the food arrived, I quickly went to work but savoring each bite. Sometimes, when you're down and out, just the sense of something good, like the taste of a well-cooked meal or a cup of coffee, can go a long way. Once my hunger died down a little, my brain turned back on and a thought struck in my mind. Someone was scared and they wanted me silenced. Obviously.

I mean, it wasn't that surprising of a thought, really, but it was pretty self-evident that whoever was behind all this had some pull. I would have called Dick to discuss it with him (and boy did I have to fight back the habit of reaching for it), but since my phone was waterlogged, that still wasn't an option.

From where I was sitting, I could feel the building shift ever-so-slightly as the wind picked up outside. The storm was raging. I looked out the window across the room, then glanced at the TV over the bar. That's when the emergency broadcast system message appeared on the screen.

Chapter Thirty-Six

The blaring sound of the alert was so deafening that it caused my ears to hurt. However, the seemingly harmless message that followed, cautioning about flash floods and gale force winds, sent shivers down my spine. Although my experience in magic was lacking, I knew you couldn't cast the kind of summoning spell I suspected had been cast without a massive energy release, which can mess up the natural order of things. Heck, the storm outside could possibly even be part of the summoning.

I saw a blinding flash of light that was immediately followed by a clap of thunder. I would even venture to say that it was lightning quick! But jokes aside, it was getting dangerous. Suddenly, a powerful gust of wind shattered one of the windows, showering the patrons with shards of glass. Thankfully, I didn't see any injuries, but the smell of fear permeated the air, initially subtle but as the storm raged and caused rain and wind to start pelting those inside through the broken window, the scent became something that couldn't be ignored. One thing was for sure, I needed to get out of that café, but where would I go? I was sure the water on the Mississippi had become turbulent and the ferry to Algiers would be temporarily shut down due to dangerous conditions.

With this thing that was coming, I knew there was going to be a lot of death and dismay. I couldn't help but to think that the regional council or someone would have a back-up plan, surely. There had to be contingency plans. And that's when I decided I needed to pay a visit to the high council. Maybe I could help them implement whatever they were planning and with the police department searching for me, it would get me off the street, not that my coworkers would be able to find me in this storm. They would hunker down wherever they were and only respond to emergencies. I stood up from my table; the place had become crowded with more and more tourists seeking shelter. Fear hung in the air, its unmistakable odor lingering and likely affecting people's emotions on a subconscious level. I could tell by the way the eyes of various people darted around the room from each other to outside to their phones or whatever else they held in their hand. I made my way toward the exit and the power went out. Now, on most days, even in storms with dark grey skies, it would still be bright enough outside that you could see inside from light entering a window; it may be dimly lit, but you'd still be able to see. It was extremely dark out, almost with the feeling of night, coupled with heavy sheets of rain. And being inside, it was even darker. Me, being who I am, could see better than most of the others in the room because of my dark gift, but it still threw me off. Nothing about what was going on was natural.

I left immediately and the rain that hit me was freezing and, to be honest, it pelted so hard that it hurt a little. It felt like I was going 100 miles an hour on a motorcycle with no helmet; rain hitting you at that speed doesn't exactly feel good. It's manageable but not something a person wants to endure for long. The streets of downtown New Orleans didn't exactly help things either. In cities with long streets lined with tall buildings on both sides, it often creates mini wind tunnels that seem to cause the wind to whip a bit stronger than it does in an open field or in the woods somewhere.

Even though I left the shelter of the restaurant, I knew I needed to get out of the storm and get to where I was going quickly. I know I mentioned before that the regional council met in a place on another plane that could only be accessed by temporary magical portals. However, since I did work for the regional council, I knew of a way to get there. In all honesty, I had never used it before and it had been so long since I was told about it that I had almost forgotten its existence.

I went into a nearby alley between two buildings, in an attempt to buffer the wind and stinging rain a bit, but I wasn't out of danger. The lightning was quite active and werewolf or not, I could still sizzle with the best of them if I was struck. Out of eyeshot from passersby, I stood facing a blank, bare wall of brick. I felt kinda dumb and didn't know if it would even work, but I did what I had been told to do in case of an emergency all those moons ago. I bent down and with my forefinger, beginning at the bottom of the wall, I traced an unseen door as I stood up and then bent down again to complete it. After that was complete, I stood up and knocked three times at three second intervals and at three different locations within the imaginary door frame I had drawn. I'm not going to tell you the exact locations or the other parts of the process, because, well, that's still protected knowledge. Could you just imagine if a normie showed up unannounced in the chambers of the regional council? Crazy!

Anyway, once finished, I waited. Like I said, I had never done it before and wasn't even sure if I had done it correctly. The longer I waited, I felt as though I probably hadn't gotten it right and sighed in frustration. A ripple of air began ever so slightly. At first, I thought it was my imagination coupled with the wind from the storm, but then there was no mistaking it. The ripple effect intensified and spread throughout the confines of the imaginary doorway, then the wall dissolved completely, leaving a rather ordinary-looking door in its place. I didn't know how long it would stay, so I quickly opened it and stepped through. Relieved, I shut the door and leaned back up against it, glad to be out of the freezing rain. Inside, it was warm and quite pleasant in contrast to the conditions I had just left.

My eyes took a moment to adjust to the change in lighting, but my ears could hear just fine. There was a lot of commotion and as my vision quickly came to, the sounds found the confirmation. There were figures quickly moving all over the open room I found myself in. From where and to where, I didn't know, but they were moving with purpose. As I looked more closely, they were a healthy mix of goatmen, fae and all sorts of other creatures moving in haste, wearing robes that identified them as workers there. Some had boxes, others had books. It was honestly quite overwhelming as I tried to figure out what I had just stepped into.

One figure noticed me and stopped. "Are you here to help or hinder?"

The language was fast-paced, and I almost missed the message entirely. "Um...neither?"

The figure, a small being with wings, "tsked," at me and pulled away to move on but I quickly followed up. "I was looking for the council. It's been a long time since I have arrived here unannounced and don't know my way."

The figure stopped and turned back, and motioned to one end of the room toward a door, before hurrying off. "Through there, but be quick, there isn't much time."

My heart skipped a beat. Nothing about being here exuded confidence in a solution. It felt more like an abandoned ship than a bastion of safety. I moved toward the door, which led into a hallway, then opened up into the council chambers where I had come before. There were still marks all over the room that displayed evidence of the brutal battle with the demons. It must have been a hectic time for them because, with all the magic and expertise at their fingertips, it should have already been cleaned or repaired. The council tended to be snobbish in the way politicians usually were and wouldn't have typically stood for it.

I stepped in quickly and moved closer to the center of the room. Around the table sat representatives in chairs, though not as many as the last time I had been there. A hearty conversation was taking place.

"But high chancellor, surely there are steps to resolve this," one representative said. I believe it was one of the lesser representatives from one faction that didn't hold a lot of power.

"Don't you think we have tried finding a solution!?" the man that sat on the high platform shot back. "There is still time and all the ones under my charge here are actively researching and looking."

The tension in the air was high, and you didn't need any special abilities to feel it. There was also the unmistakable aroma of fear. It wasn't nearly as strong as it had been in the café earlier in the day, but it was there, though it smelled different considering the source of beings in that room weren't human.

I walked further into the room and was going to take a seat at one of the open chairs at the back but the moment I stepped forward, there was a lull in the debate. You could have heard a pin drop, except for "slop...slop...slop." I stopped immediately because I didn't want to bring attention to myself, but the damage was already done. The soppy slap of my wet shoes on the marble floor sounded much louder than it should have and all eyes were on me, with most of the representatives turning in their seats to look back at me.

"Lou!" High Chancellor Sattorn cried. "What are you doing here?"

I didn't have an answer, but I thought I had better come up with one quick. I was about to open my mouth to respond, but the chancellor didn't give me time. Instead, he ordered me to approach and stand in front of him. Weird request, I thought, but who am I to bicker with the high chancellor? I strode closer and the looks of curiosity from everyone didn't falter. In fact, they only grew more noticeable. Some in suspicion and others in irritation. Don't ask me how I knew that. It was just the general impression that I got as I looked around at those who were there. I saw Fenric, and I even saw representatives from the vampire families. Of course, Mr. Lumin was not there. I was sure he and the immediate family had left the area in order to survive whatever was coming, but his fanged representatives that were there were no doubt just as dangerous.

I slapped my soggy feet forward and came to a stop in front of the high chancellor. Once I was closer, I could clearly tell that he was angry, though I wasn't sure what he was angry about. Surely, with the devastation that was on the horizon, I wouldn't have expected him to be angry. It seemed...out of place, given the circumstances. Like he should have been...I don't know...more morose, I guess. I mean, if I were in charge and I didn't have answers, I might be afraid about not knowing how to stop this imminent event, or maybe a bit irritated at dealing with the people who weren't helping, but expressing outright, unadulterated anger? It threw me off a little.

"Why are you here, Lou Giroux?" the high chancellor asked again. I guess he wanted me front and center so he could get an eyeful. I was about to answer but he interrupted me again, "Shouldn't you be tracking down the person behind this? Surely, they are not here, are they?"

He battered me with questions, none of which I had an answer for. I felt like I was being made a spectacle—for what, I wasn't sure—and it was beginning to anger me, not to mention embarrass me. However, the berating continued and then he said something that was not only out of place but also utterly out of line. I had worked for the council, doing their bidding, for a number of years and never had my integrity been questioned. I had dealt with and brought to justice true monsters many times over the years and the council had always, without fail, sanctioned my actions. The next words that left his mouth were wrong on many levels. "Lou, didn't I hear that you just killed your supervisor from the Police Department out in City Park? Have you lost your mind? Are you going to kill someone here, as well?"

Time stopped for me, or at least it seemed to. My attention snapped to. My senses were sharp and alert. My body, fatigued from the combination of witnessing the death of my friend and sleep deprivation, the thrill of evading the police, and enduring the pelting rain and gusts of wind, felt like it might collapse at any moment. But when he said that, it was as if by a snap of fingers, my senses were on the point of humming on the edge of a knife blade. While the high chancellor captured my attention, I could hear the rustling of cloth and bodies moving away from me in the ensuing silence, following that question. Involuntarily, my muscles tightened, as if the sleeping beast within me had been stirred to life, ready and alert. My nose, which was pretty good to begin with, sniffed the air.

The goatmen, the de facto guards of the council, sensing a change in the air, moved closer. My nose picked up the scent of their hide, the sweat and fear from those that emitted such things in the room and, curiously, picked up another smell I had not expected but was undeniable.

I detected the hint of blood and the ever-faint smell of cinnamon.

444

Chapter Thirty-Seven

My mind was abuzz with thoughts. A lot of loose connections fell into place, and I just looked at the high chancellor. After the last accusation he threw at me, he waited for a response. So much happened in that short span of time, however, I then knew with a clarity that spoke volumes. It all made sense, though I couldn't quite form words as to why. I just knew. The words would come later, as the chilling sensation enveloped a part of me, causing the rest to grow numb. It was a perilous blend, sending shivers down my spine. In that state of mind, caution often dissipates like leaves in the wind. So, it was no shock to me how I responded to the chancellor's inquiry.

"That was not my intention, High Chancellor Sattorn, when I had arrived, but you have made a grave mistake. You shouldn't have brought me so close. You know I have an unusually sensitive nose."

Everyone froze. Despite my eyes being focused on the high chancellor, I could sense it. Out of my peripheral, I noticed Fenric lean in with interest. Perhaps it could've been my imagination, but the chancellor appeared even angrier at my response. However, did I detect a hint of doubt in those eyes? I wasn't quite sure, so I pressed forward and continued, "Yes, you have cuts on your back. I can smell them and it was I who put them there."

Those sitting near where I stood now felt the palpable tension and perceived danger of the moment, as some not only leaned away but also skulked in an attempt to not be seen or get involved in the altercation taking place in front of them.

"What are you talking about?!" the chancellor demanded.

"Really?" I asked. "You're going to continue this charade?"

"I don't know what you're talking about, but you're a danger to this council. Guards!"

With my palm out, I quickly raised my hand toward the guards closest to me, momentarily stopping them. I continued. "You killed Lieutenant Martine, and you did it to frame me and keep me preoccupied."

Churning emotions boiled beneath the cold fury and numbness I felt. The monster stirred and that cold fury deep within began to ignite a fire. A fire that, once unleashed, would be damn near impossible to extinguish. I weighed my options quickly as I didn't have much time. My certainty about the chancellor murdering Martine was absolute, so it was as simple as that. I'd lived a long time and if I died right then and there…well, that wasn't what I wanted, but so be it. He had set the ball rolling down that path and I was in the way, which brought the argument to the front of my mind. He wanted me out of the way. He was behind all of it. He had some sort of pact with those vampires who had no power and were shunned by society, both in the normie world, as well as "our" world. He had killed all those innocent people and cast the spell, which summoned whatever was coming. Because of that, I then knew I had to kill him. It was the only way to put a stop to the progression of the spell. Again, as I told you before, I'm no spell-caster but even I knew that 95% of the time, the power of a spell rested within its caster as a conduit until full completion. If whomever was responsible for the spell was taken out and that conduit were to be broken, the spell would dissipate. I just hoped and prayed that in this case, it wasn't the other five percent.

As I looked beyond his eyes, I saw him for what he was. Gone was the wizened chancellor doing his best to protect and take care of those in his charge. All that remained was his gluttony for power, and it all made sense. With the power struggle and a possible change of leadership, what better time to create a disastrous event that would either destroy most of his adversaries or make him appear to be a savior by swooping in and rescuing everyone at the last minute? I didn't know which tactic was at play, but it didn't matter to me.

"All those people," I said. "And you killed them all."

The room was as quiet as a crypt and the tension was as tight as a rope that had a two-ton weight dangling from it. Fenric stood up and spoke. "What are you talking about, Lou?"

"Can't you see it?" I asked. "He was behind it all."

"Lies! He killed his lieutenant. Probably killed that wizard he hangs out with, too," the chancellor cut in, but the damage was done. There was uncertainty, not only in the chancellor's eyes, but also in every other eye in the room. This certainly wouldn't have been the first time a supposed leader had become corrupt to maintain control. Even ol' Fenric had a look of uncertainty.

"Enough of this!" the chancellor shouted as he rose to his feet and pulled out his wand. "We've had enough distraction for today. We have more important and time-sensitive matters to attend to."

Fenric spoke up and said, "Are you so quick to break the accords? Here? Do you think you can act with impunity?"

As the accords laid out certain locations that are considered safe havens, or sacred, if you will...I know I spoke of it before. City Park was one of those places. The council chambers and surrounding offices were another. This was a place for debate without concern for harm...or at least it was until three seconds ago.

The chancellor seemed to realize his mistake, but instead of backing off, his eyebrows furrowed to match the snarl of his mouth. "Fine, it's of no matter. Most of everyone here will be dead soon, anyway. Guards have at them all."

The goatmen moved, and I was afraid it would have been the end of ol' Lou Giroux if Fenric hadn't spoken. "Guards, remember your oaths. The entire council and everyone entrusted to its care were sworn to the accords—not just the chancellor. Something serious has gone awry, but we will get to the bottom of it. Stand down."

I almost felt sorry for them as the look of confusion—no, not exactly confusion—came over them. It was an expression of uncertainty that they displayed with the command followed by the countercommand. It was sort of comical and almost laughable, but because of the gravity of the situation, I held back.

From behind, I heard movement and stole a glance. A figure stood up; it looked to be a representative of another sect or family, but I'd never seen them before. That, in and of itself, isn't all that surprising, given the number of people and other beings that come and go through the chamber. The figure came up from behind and stood to my right. After a moment of silence, they spoke. "Lou, I'm glad you came. It will make this next part easier." Facing the chancellor, they continued, "High Chancellor, you are a murderer and I invoke the right of accusation."

I was flabbergasted. I had no idea who this person was, but before I could ask, the figure reached into their jacket and pulled out a wand to quickly encircle their head. The image that was before me was of a person—a tall, slender person—but I couldn't tell if it was male or female as the features were somewhat androgynous. However, when the figure finished circling the wand overhead, its image began to waver, almost as if it was composed of water or melted wax, making it difficult to distinguish any features at all.

I bladed myself toward this thing. There was no telling what was about to occur, so I prepared myself to defensively step, jump, or roll back if need be. The transformation only took a few moments and when complete, I was speechless, yet the idea of any defensive maneuvers were whisked from my mind.

"Hey Lou," the figure told me. "Close your mouth."

"Cormac...I thought you were dead," I replied.

"I came pretty close...pretty close indeed. It took some quick wizardry and pure luck, but I survived."

Of course, there was no time to have a reunion or for an explanation of what had happened to him since we were still dealing with the high chancellor and still in his house, so to speak. The chancellor, seeing Cormac alive and well, didn't say another word to us, but directed a command to his entourage of goatmen. "It's over. Kill them all. Leave no one alive."

Apparently, some of his guards were still loyal to him because at least half of the protection in the room, probably five of the 10, quickly attacked the others. The tenacity and sheer surprise of their actions threw everyone into shock. The chancellor, his eyes narrowed and focused on Cormac and me, raised his wand and flicked his wrist, hurling a brilliant ball of light toward us. I gritted my teeth, bracing for whatever he had cast to hit. But instead, Cormac casted some magic of his own and the fireball stopped short at a barrier before disappearing. About 10 more goatmen guards entered the room, joining the original five. Their suits were drenched with blood, which told me they must have taken out the other goatmen who were more loyal to the council as opposed to the chancellor.

Two times I had been in the council chambers that week and both times, a knock-down drag-out fight had transpired and could've killed me. Well, it remained to be seen if I would survive the second one, but I planned to give it all I could, so I made up my mind to go on a full-out rampage. One, because I really had no other option, and two, because the remaining goatmen started to cut in on the other occupants of the room. The vampires who were present bared their fangs and began to fight back with a vengeance. So did Fenric. He, like I, changed in the midst of combat.

Being responsible for the spell that was intended to bring damnation by summoning something wicked, the chancellor had overstepped his authority by breaking the very accords that kept balance in our world. In doing so, he forfeited his life and therefore had to die.

I dove into a knot of guards near me, taking three to the ground. They were very well-trained and possessed the strength of two men, but up against an angry werewolf on a rampage...well...let's just say they didn't stand a chance. My hands grew and my fingernails sharpened into knives that would cut to the bone depending on the force behind the blow. Of course, a good punch to the face here and there and the satisfying crunch of bones breaking under the impact was very much called for, as well.

I dispatched the three into the afterlife and rose up, covered in blood. Of course, being in full monster form at that point, anyone else wouldn't have been able to discern just how blood-soaked I was due to the clumps of fur. But I knew. I could smell the volume of liquid that permeated my coat. I must have been a heinous sight because the two remaining guards backed away, but before they could charge, run, or attack someone else, a blue ball of flame engulfed them. Despite being half-crazed thanks to the monster within, I nearly attacked them anyway, but the rational part of me knew it would be pointless. Besides, I had to get to the chancellor and make him pay for everything he had done, especially for killing Lieutenant Martine.

I changed direction and moved toward my target. He was dueling with Cormac in the room's chaos. Cormac was strong, but the chancellor was stronger. He showed no signs of fatigue, whereas Cormac looked to be somewhat strained. Flashes of blue, green, red—all colors of the rainbow—danced back and forth. It was curious to me that, amid the intensity of a large battle, it was the outcome of the small-scale conflicts fought by single individuals that truly mattered. Even in this battle playing out in front of me. Sure, there were two sides fighting for superiority but that depended on the fight that Fenric was engaged in with the clump of corrupted guards he laid into, as well as the other individual altercations taking place between others for their survival. The ultimate victory depended upon the independent conflict between Cormac and the chancellor. In moments like that, it really came down to the actions of an individual and how that corresponded with the bigger picture.

I leapt and landed near the chancellor. He didn't even bat an eye before he conjured an earth elemental. If you've never seen a figure literally rise from the ground, breaking through the marble floor, that comprised earthen materials like mud, soil, and sand...well, I don't recommend it. It's hard to fight something that is extremely strong and doesn't bleed. The one advantage, though, is that earth elementals are a little slow. However, that doesn't detract from their danger. I was fully aware that if it got its hands on me, I'd be in for a bad day. I figured I'd be all right if I stayed outside its range. At least, I thought that would be the case until it bent down to effortlessly scoop up marble stone and toss it toward me. I scurried to the side, almost on all fours, to avoid the massive chunks being thrown my way.

I circled around until I was close to the chancellor again. The problem with fighting multiple beings is keeping a tab on all of them in a chaotic environment. I'm not sure he knew I was there, but he certainly didn't account for the earth elemental aiming at my location. Before I clamped down on the wizard, a chunk of marble landed at our feet, exploding and knocking both of us into the air. I know it sounds wild but if you throw any type of rock with enough force and it makes contact with another hard surface, it will explode. Needless to say, the elemental was very strong.

At any rate, every spell needs focus and concentration for it to be effective and remain powerful. The chancellor and I were both taken aback when we found ourselves flying through the air, leading to the dissipation of the focus needed to hold the earth elemental in our plane. As a result, the elemental was released and essentially crumbled into a large pile of earth. The chancellor and I both landed hard, no more than a couple of feet from each other. We both lay there, breathing heavily, attempting to regain some strength. Wizards are powerful and dangerous, attributes that increase the longer they live, but they can still be vulnerable at close range if caught by surprise and are unprepared. I did the only thing I could do at that moment. My massive fist connected with the side of his head.

455

Chapter Thirty-Eight

H e must have cast some sort of protection spell, or had a protective amulet on him because when my fist landed, it felt like I'd slammed my hand into an unyielding rock face. His head movement reacted from the force of the blow, but probably would have been much worse had he not been shielded in some way. I'm fairly sure I would have knocked his head from his body, but as it was, he reacted as if someone with no particular abilities had punched him. It must have been a reflective type of spell based on the volume of pain that radiated from my knuckles. To be honest, I questioned whether I had broken my hand, which would have been something because that had never happened while I was in monster form. But even if I had, I was confident it would heal shortly.

High Chancellor Sattorn and I both jumped up at the same time. He leveled his wand at me, but Cormac's wand hit him with a blast. Whatever spells were protecting the chancellor seemed to weaken because that time, his robe looked singed. When he turned his attention toward Cormac, I lunged forward and picked him up in a bear...ha ha...or rather, a wolf hug. And with my massive arms locked around his torso, I squeezed the breath out of him and since I was close, I took the opportunity to open my jaws wide and clamp down on whatever was in front of me. The barrier's sting felt familiar, similar to the one caused by my punch, albeit weaker, likely due to the discrepancy in force between a punch and a bite. It made sense if it was a reflective force spell, but regardless, I persevered through the pain and gritted my teeth. I tasted his blood as he let out a horrifying scream. People are rarely ready for the consequences of their actions.

When spells backfire, depending on their intricacies and power, the larger the energy release is when they fail. Since the high chancellor was behind the summons of the doom spell, the energy that it had absorbed that released in that moment was exponential. I'm not sure whether the chancellor had perished from my bite or what we call a self-destruct totem, but the next thing I knew, there was a deafening, blinding blast and I was violently flung through the air, settling into darkness.

***

When I regained consciousness, I was in a hospital. University Medical Center, from the looks of it. I was a bit groggy when I came to but someone was in the room with me and I tensed up, ready for a fight.

"Relax, Lou," the voice said.

"Captain Benoit," I replied. "What are you doing here? What's going on? How long have I been here?"

I had so many questions and was about to ask them all, but Captain Benoit calmly raised his hand to stop me.

"Lou, you've been here two days. The fact that you survived at all is impressive. Many of those present didn't, but Cormac did, and I knew you'd be happy to hear that. He's in a room down the hall," he said.

"Why did the high chancellor do it? Why summon disaster?"

Captain Benoit pursed his lips as he thought about it. "Well, we'll never know the complete answer or his motivations, but with his elected tenure coming to an end and his perceived problems of getting re-elected, I can only surmise that he tried to put things in motion to secure his position. We believe he linked up with the factions that didn't have representation...like the undead vampires...and that's where he found most of those that helped him try to carry out his mission."

"So, that's it, huh?"

"We believe so, but with him gone, we can't really confirm everything or identify all those that helped him. Even the guards that decided that they were more loyal to him than to the council knew little and they were put to the question. He kept everything highly compartmentalized. I doubt anyone knew much. With his death, we'll never really know, but he needed to be killed in order to stop the desolation of New Orleans. You did an extraordinary thing, Lou. I'm sure there will be awards coming down from the newly formed council."

"I didn't kill Lieutenant Martine."

"I know. I believe that was a killing of happenstance. She was in the wrong place at the wrong time and was used against you. And you don't have to worry about NOPD looking for you anymore. I mean, you are one of us and due to the revelation of the high chancellor being behind everything...well...let's just say that's been taken care of. When you heal up, we look forward to having you back."

I turned my head and looked out the window. It was a sunny day. The kind that had puffy white cotton ball clouds surrounded by deep blue. It looked peaceful and calming. I looked back at Captain Benoit. "I don't think I'm coming back to NOPD or to the council."

Captain Benoit's lips turned down, and he looked away. "I'm sorry to hear that, Lou, but I guess I can't blame you after all that's happened. Just know that, whether in an official capacity or not, there may be opportunities for you, maybe even as a consultant. I'd love to have you back to support our cause. If you change your mind, you know how to reach me. Take your time, heal, and give it some thought."

I had no idea what I was going to do, but like he said, after everything that had happened, I just didn't have the same trust in those that were supposed be backing me that I'd had a week ago. After an awkward silence, he made his goodbyes and left the room.

That evening, Dick stopped by, and we talked about everything. He didn't like the news either, but he accepted it. He did tell me he found out that the lady from the mayor's office, Ms. Dufrene had actually been sent by the national council because there were murmurings about the goings-on in New Orleans. So, essentially, she was just like me, doing the bidding of the council on a higher scale. I wish I could have known that prior. Maybe Lieutenant Martine would still be alive.

The next morning, they discharged me, but not before I received another guest, and this one surprised me. It was Ms. Celeste Dufrene herself. "Ah, Mr. Giroux, I'm glad I caught you before you left."

She was the last person I expected to show up, which must have been pretty evident by my expression. She went on without missing a beat, "Don't act so surprised. Surely you know that your efforts here saved countless lives and caught the attention of the national council."

I was too tired to deal with courtesy, but I had to ask. "Lady, I found out just last night that you were from the national council. How did you not know about Chancel-lor Sattorn?"

Either she ignored my manners or didn't care. She replied, "Because at the time, all evidence pointed elsewhere, and he wasn't on the list. But you found him."

"Too late," I said.

"But still early enough to stop the worst from happening."

"Captain Benoit was here yesterday and said that as of now, there's nothing concrete about the motive behind his actions or who else was involved. In your investigation, did you find out anything?"

Her lips tightened in slight frustration. "Mr. Giroux, unfortunately no. Like I said, he wasn't on my radar and by the time he was, he was dead."

I nodded my head and turned toward the window. Unlike yesterday, which was sunny with blue skies and cotton ball clouds, today was grey and drizzly.

Mr. Dufrene spoke again, "I hear that you will no longer be working for the local police department, nor the regional council."

I sighed and turned to look at her again. "That's correct."

"Well, Mr. Giroux, like I said, your efforts here caught the attention of the national council and as such, they would like for you to work for them as an agent of the First Circle."

The First Circle was big league type of stuff.

"Why would I want to do that?"

"Because it will be similar to what you were doing for the NOPD and regional council, but as an agent, you will work directly for the national council. Your authority will be outside the regional council and over every other local jurisdiction. In that position, you'd be on call to conduct investigations to answer queries by the national council. Any time that you aren't working directly for the national council, your efforts would continue much like they have been—keeping the peace and maintaining balance in the world," she replied.

"I'll have to think about it," I said. But in the back of my mind, the way I felt at that moment, I was pretty sure that wasn't something I wanted to get involved with. It sounded political...and as you can clearly see, politics get people killed.

"Of course," she replied. "Take your time."

She handed me her card and left.

On leaving the hospital, I made sure to stop by and see Cormac, who was still sedated in order to facilitate his healing. When the chancellor exploded like he did...at least what I can remember about the blast...well, it really was amazing I survived. If it wasn't for my rapid healing abilities, I don't think I'd be standing here today.

I showed up to my little shotgun home and although Morgane was happy to see me, she nearly pecked my eyes out for not letting her know I was going to confront the high chancellor. When she discovered that it wasn't in the plan until I got to the council and that it just sort of happened, she settled down. She had to learn about everything secondhand and I'm still not quite sure how she found out about my final encounter with the chancellor.

Later that day, I returned to the police department to formally resign and surrender my badge and gun. I was going to turn in my Crown Vic but surprisingly, it was going to be deadlined anyway, so I was able to purchase it. I really loved that car. And that was it. I went home, popped open a beer, and sat on the couch, with the intent to stay there for quite a while. I wasn't a cop anymore and with the loss of so much, I had a lot to unpack. For the first time since Dick had called me to investigate that body under the bridge, I felt like I could relax, at least for the foreseeable future...

Lou Giroux continues...

If you enjoyed this story, sign up for my newsletter to get the tentative beginning of the second book in the Lou Giroux series. Either go to this link https://geni.us/Lou Girouxteaser or go to my website www.jejack.com to sign up.

And if you enjoyed the story, I'd like to invite you to leave a review on the website or bookstore you purchased this book from. It would greatly appreciated! Thank you!

About the Author

J.E. Jack is an author known for blending supernatural elements with real-world settings, creating intriguing and suspenseful stories. Jack's works, such as *Them Bones* and *Grave Disturbance*, often explore themes of mystery, supernatural phenomena, and emotional depth. His novels are known for their page-turning qualities and atmospheric settings, which add a haunting, eerie quality to the narratives.

J.E. Jack draws inspiration from his diverse experiences, including almost two decades in military and law enforcement roles. This background influences his storytelling by giving his characters and plotlines an authentic sense of tension and danger. His stories often feature ordinary people encountering extraordinary, often paranormal, circumstances.

Jack's writing style appeals to fans of young adult mysteries and supernatural thrillers, and he is celebrated for his ability to craft suspenseful tales that leave readers on edge.

He currently lives near the coast of Louisiana with his family.

Nothing ever happens in the little village of Pittsburg, that is, until it does. For fourteen-year-old Joe Anderson, that was the case during the summer of 1992. The events that unfolded following a childhood game of hide and go seek in the woods changed the face of a small town and left a mark that was forever etched into the recesses of a boy's heart and mind. It was a summer of adventure, friendship, murder, first love, and pain. Them Bones is a coming-of-age, murder mystery novel set in a small, rural village with secrets of its own.

It's the last day of the school year in 1994 and for fifteen-year-old Chris, it's going to be another boring summer of staying at his aunt's farm in southern Illinois. At least, that's what he thought until he, along with his brother Brian and cousin Sam, meets the hermit. What follows is a summer of intrigue, suspicion, and fear that has lasting consequences. One thing is for certain though–things aren't always what they seem.

Detective Robinson is only trying to help his fellow detective by taking her duty weekend, something he had done many times before, and for the most part, had always been routine. That is, until this weekend. What starts off as a normal call for vandalism in a cemetery quickly turns into something much darker and deadly. As Robinson uncovers secrets from the past, will he be able to stop the threat before something more sinister happens? One thing is for certain, these secrets were better left buried. "Grave Disturbance," is J.E. Jack's third novel and is a supernatural thriller set in the small coastal city of Pensacola, Florida.

Bill Donovan is a man with a problem. As the frontman of Donovan's Delights Entertainment traveling carnival, the season started off pretty much like every other traveling season. That was, until the cancellations started. What began as a normal season of bringing excitement to communities along the route ends up being a summer short on locations and long on bills to pay. With the concern of taking care of his responsibilities, namely his employees, as well as his own family, he feels the pressure. Everything looks bleak until the mayor of a town that no one has heard of calls him out of the blue, with an offer Bill can't refuse. What follows is a tale of uncertainty and fear, where the stakes are high and the consequences everlasting. Something Wicked Waits is a novel set in southern Illinois during the summer of 1995.